DAVID Y

PRODIGAL time, 1969

outskirtspress
DENVER, COLORADO

This is a work of fiction. The events and characters described herein are imaginary and are not intended to refer to specific places or living persons. The opinions expressed in this manuscript are solely the opinions of the author and do not represent the opinions or thoughts of the publisher. The author has represented and warranted full ownership and/or legal right to publish all the materials in this book.

Prodigal Time, 1969
All Rights Reserved.
Copyright © 2014 David Morpheys
v3.0

Cover Photo © 2014 thinkstockphotos.com. All rights reserved - used with permission.

This book may not be reproduced, transmitted, or stored in whole or in part by any means, including graphic, electronic, or mechanical without the express written consent of the publisher except in the case of brief quotations embodied in critical articles and reviews.

Outskirts Press, Inc.
http://www.outskirtspress.com

ISBN: 978-1-4787-3414-7

Outskirts Press and the "OP" logo are trademarks belonging to Outskirts Press, Inc.

PRINTED IN THE UNITED STATES OF AMERICA

1
A Fatherless Time

Blizzard snows whited out hilltops to the lakeside road, Route 90. Kurt Kallini and Lionel, the black dude, retreated from Cornell to Wells College, where Lionel took the Cornell van and Barb Kelly to Berkley on the Coast. Kallini saw the Sixties end. Quinn the Eskimo voted for violence, bombs, and bringing the Vietnam War home. Bring the war home. One, too many Columbias. One, too many Chicagos. Bring the war home. Dark was the night in Quinn's apartment and blizzard snows whited out the January day. Kallini didn't sleep for his crippled leg, mattresses scattered about the floor, and when he did his dream of St. Genieve hung like bloody lightning across the sky.

A fatherless time. A time of Depression, worlds at war, and him selling news on the streets of Poughkeepsie. His mom worked for Deeves the Jeweler and Nana Morpheys kept the books. A Main Street of two, three story apartments hung over the walks and pavement down to Lucky Platt, Kresges, and FO Schwartz. Then Lower Main slid past Jewish shops of City fashion, ascots and flash, for the Blacks, Poles, Mics, and Guineas who hung out in the alleys downhill to the Hudson River and the train to New York City. Cripple on a skidboard with legs lost in an industrial accident handed him Journals to deliver upstairs. Old cripple with no legs and a guinea kid with one leg stunted from a bout of polio.

Police tapped on the glass pane of Deeves Jewelry, where Kallini's mom worked and Nana Morpheys kept the books. Deeves the Jew listened to the Irish cop tell how the boys gangbanged a Polish girl and she pointed out Kurt, recalling the kid's coal black eyes glaring at her. Kallini sold papers down Lower Main. Deeves and Kurt's sickly mom begged him to name names and the Irish cop jotted them down: Rick Reilly, Ted Dobrynski, and Nikki Cerniglia.

His sickly mom soon dead from cancer told him to pray to the virgin.

"Every morning you walk up-a steps to the church on the hill, St. Genieve, you pray the virgin she help you."

St. Genieve's cathedral stone masoned an outcropping of granite, uprising back to College Hill Park and looming over the downgrade of Main Street to the train station and the river. Both Kallini's walk to deliver papers down Lower Main and his ascent to St. Genieve took persistence. Nothing easy with his short leg and gnarled back. Granite steps terraced right and left and right again uphill to the cathedral. Kallini ascended to the heights and descended to the streets, mornings before school and afternoons to work. Kurt was a good Catholic boy for his mom. From St. Genieve he peered over to Haight Avenue where Nana Morpheys babysat him as a kid, street over from Vassar College, and his sight ranged over to Eastman Park and the eight stories of Vassar Hospital where he had his spinal operation.

There the bully mic bastard Rick Reilly caught him coming out the heavy wooden doors. Ted Dobrynski hid behind the door and jumped Kallini. Three buttons ripped from his scrubbed white shirt for school. Reilly grabbed his head and jammed a fist into his face. Kallini fell on the stone steps. Big mic sat on his chest smashing his face, breaking his nose, cutting his lips and mouth wide open.

Ted Dobrynski grinned to see Kallini take his bloody beating.

"Kid, keep your mouth shut or you're dead."

Kallini lost consciousness. Blood streamed into his eyes and choked his mouth, as he spit out teeth and globs of red spittle. In the sun he saw the virgin carving of St. Genieve soar above him on the ramparts, taking pity on his pain. He no longer hurt. Smell of spring air. The sky turned golden blue as cobalt. One of the Marist brothers who heard confessions helped Kallini to his feet. Looking into the sun above him he asked the brother if the carved woman was the virgin or St. Genieve.

"What carved woman?" the Marist brother asked.

There was none. The cathedral rampart soared above the stone steps with its lacquered panels, but no carving. Kallini had his first fit.

A month later Nikki Cerniglia stuck a gun to Kallini's ear.

"You're leaving the Jew's door unlocked or I blow your head off."

Kallini was nearly fifteen. Burglary set off an alarm. Nikki, Dobrynski, and Reilly got questioned by a special investigator, not a cop on the take. A list of robberies tagged them. They told the investigator how Kallini pawned a jeweled watch and wedding ring two days ago. The ring his mom wore, never married, now dying of cancer. Pawn ticket had Kallini's name and $75.00. No one took care of the scrawny Italian kid with bushy eyebrows, fits, crippled back, and coal dark eyes. He got sent across the river to the Highland Reformatory.

A fatherless time for Kurt Kallini in Poughkeepsie, New York.

2
Let the Physics Go

"You can't quit college. It's ridiculous.'"

George Morpheys stared at his son, David. Baseball mits for hands gripped the Ford Galaxy as if car and rider spun out of control.

"The whole thing's ridiculous," David replied to his dad.

Let loose the dogs of war and he better run. World spun out of control and he rode in a car on snowy routes over high hills and plunging valleys. Road to Wells College and Cornell too. He swerved off his rocker. Karmic roadkill.

"Quit college you do what?"

"Do anything that's not the army."

That fall David quit football and lost his scholarship. Smash went his head. Lights hazed out. No sound track till he checked back in showering. Blind side hit at defensive end. His ankle crumbled. He came as quarterback and quit as cannonfodder. His dad's word. Common folks who don't count, wasted in war, like linemen on a football team. His words.

George Morpheys let off the gas for a valley route drifting snow on the way to Wells College. His son graduated from "little Harvard" as the recruiter offering David a scholarship for football called Hamilton. Best college in New York. Best chance his son do more than dig ditches, work on a farm, and tool machinery at the Poughkeepsie IBM.

David had a hundred page thesis to complete. Then graduate from college. Then the draft and next stop Vietnam. Driving snow like electron bombardment dared him dream ways to smash up.

"Quit football and now quit college?"

"I see no reason to graduate."

"Quitting lost your scholarship from football. Quit and worse happens."

"Like you quit Bontecott?"

"That was different, damn't."

"You were my age."

"I had a family to support. Foreman hired his son and Bontecott backed him. It was my job."

"You punched him out."

"I had a temper and I was out of work."

"Well same as me."

"I had a family to support and you had a scholarship."

"You got a better job at IBM."

David knew he shouldn't argue with his dad. His dad had heart problems. But it was the same. His dad quit Bontecott's and David quit football after one concussion and one busted ankle too many. Three years and the fourth he dropped out. For the sake of school work. He quit football, lost his scholarship, then worked selling sandwiches to pay tuition. He wrote papers on Whitman's poetry and Dostoyevsky's madness and improved his French to a point of exhaustion before Christmas vacation. He was played out.

Western New York was all a blizzard. Between Binghamton and the girls college he saw Cayuga farms shrouded in snow. Oil furnaces fired under another layer of insulation. No one shoveled. No one checked mail. No one bought groceries. Lamps shone like campfires in the warm parlors, and the sun palled into pale grey morning.

Let the Ford Galaxy skid toward fatality. What mattered a wrong turn sideways? Why not flip over a culvert? Let hard truth smash the sheetmetal roof flat to seat and chassis. Let the glass shatter like starry dust. No matter if impact emulsified brainmeal, limbs, and organs to a funereal concoction painted red. Nothing mattered. Like another concussion. To lose consciousness. To cease and desist. The crash a godsend devoutly to be wished.

Turn off for Route 90 came too quick. A VW van lay still in swirls of snow. Someone walked the road. His dad swerved to miss the black coat, nearly clipped him, and turned in the direction of the skid. Galaxy lunged into the oncoming lane, spun backwards 360, and slammed into a snowbank.

David let the physics go. They slid out of control and veered sideways and the slide caught the surging wave like skis, surfboard, and hydroplane, like a pyrotechnic defeat of gravity on the 4th of July. Sideways on air suction, deflation, smash of snowbank and tire blowout. Let slip the tense expectation. If something bad happens, nothing bad did. David let go. Nothing bad happened. Some chance spirit set him free on a snowy highway. Question of physics. Matter of faith.

Front tire blew out. Other wheel spun gratefully. Guy in the black coat and black kid in the van helped push them off the embankment, and dad changed the tire. VW van left with one guy walking on.

Single pedestrian in black overcoat, shitkicker sharp boots, cowboy black hat walked the lake road into Aurora. Dude skulked along ignoring an icy wind. Sullen in his wiry beard, he was neither student or working stiff. Walking into Aurora like he didn't mean to stay long.

Dad slowed the Ford Galaxy and David slid down his window. Icy gale blew like jet engines and David made himself heard.

"Thanks for your help back there. You need a ride?"

Black-hatted walker glanced up, the engine running, his thick brows intensified as he saw father and son. His dark eyes bored into a person.

"No thanks."

Dad shouted over.

"You must be freezing in this blizzard. What do you say?"

"Thanks again, but I'm close enough to the Inn to pass on your offer. A walk works up an appetite."

His eyes like icesickles needled into a person.

"And you. Do you need directions?"

"To the French House, where my son stays."

"Quarter mile past the Inn on the lakeside. Brown gothic house with room for every Wells girl who can parley francais. Can't miss it."

"Appreciate your help," dad said.

David rolled up the window and the black coat faded to white. Dad chatted about the accident. David drifted into the Wells winter study. Angry words were to no avail between father and son. They parted in the storm. Fathers and sons. Father from a Depression whose social pain resolved in a world war too horrible to catalogue. Son spurred on by boundless optimism toward a dark journey lit by burning monks, burning ghettoes, and napalm burning off the jungles.

"Accident was his fault. With him standing in the road I swerved aside."

David nodded into his own world. One aloof from IBM and its THINK slogan.

"Still, he had a pleasant manner about him."

David tagged him as one of those Movement guys who travel campus to campus working resistance to the draft and the war. Dudes with cars and credentials, and a darling chick or two. Someday the war will end, nobody knew when. So the song goes. This dude had an odd gait, drifting along the lake road. As if walking took great patience or great pain, not to limp.

There was Aurora. College town with a string of houses along the lake. The French House on the far side of Aurora looked over Lake Cayuga. An odd manor house with two wings, a carved wooden door, cupolas, gothic arches and all. Over the lake hung billowed clouds, swirling above the icy waters. The storm moved eastward. In its exhaust came the quiet of a cold snap. An aurora borealis streaked the neon sky with arctic splendor. Heavens contended in meteor shots: black and blue and emulsified brainmeal painted red. A bad accident colored the sky, as the storm swept onto New England.

It was a college town. For girls, no less. David's brain brought with him a blizzard of busy thought. The sky lit up. Aurora was rosy-fingered dawn. Dawn to days brighter, flower warm, days so summer long that night meant no more than shadows, cast to call back day. Stay, stand still, and marvel in the setting sun. Aurora was the dawn.

A string of houses along the lake. Aurora was prodigal time in days dark beyond belief. So much darker with nightfall over the waters. Time simply ran out. What was undone was left undone. David returned home. For David Morpheys Aurora was the dawn and afterward the music of memory.

3
Let Lionel Go

Ford Galaxy nearly hit him. Leaping aside Kurt Kallini pulled muscles in his lower back. His back twisted wrong to a short leg from childhood polio. Morpheys didn't recognize him. Better for Kallini he owed nothing to the son. Kallini had a run-in with the Ithaca RYM where Quinn made briefcase bombs instead of sheets of LSD. Send Lionel to the coast with money, briefcases, and good will to the Oakland Panthers. They needed Lionel and Kallini sent him with Barb Kelly west. RYM blamed him. Kurt Kallini had longer range plans with the breakdown of SDS. Only a GI Resistance Movement put an end to the war. Panthers and the white RYM-rockers merely brought war and repression home.

Leaving the van. "Better I don't give you the combination. Let me call."

"How much bread in the briefcase?"

"All Quinn the Eskimo put aside. For the vanguard. For the Black colony in Amerika."

"Rich contributors?"

"All them in this Revolutionary Youth Movement got rich parents. They play at life and now they play at death."

"Kallini, you think I'm black enough for these Panthers."

"Lose you Rye way of jiving. Wear shades. Talk black. You the man, who set up the Black studies program at Cornell."

"But Julian Bonds. Can I match him?"

"Hey Lionel. Both coasts got their own politics. Color counts. Rage counts. Violence ranks up there too."

"You got the goods. I'll be your courier of cases."

"The coast gets down to cases and you're carrying."

"Last favor and we're flat."

Kallini nodded. Then nearly got ripped by the Ford Galaxy. For

Christ's sake, crippled for life, smacked on a stormy Route 90. He walked on to see how badly his back wrenched. To figure how bad Quinn the Eskimo came after him. His Cornell RYM blacklisted him and Joshua Steen for singing no songs of Mao, for refusing the cadre initiation, for voting against violence. Quinn quit voting.

Kurt Kallini connected to the Sixties movement resisting the war in Vietnam. Other business connected him with his Uncle Carlo, who lost respect in the City, and Evander Bontecott who gained. One group played into another, wheels within wheels, as Kallini played his role. Only the machinery wore out. Like the war and this phase of fate's wheel.

Kallini had Lionel rap through the Oakland move with Barb Kelly. He gave Lionel the Cornell van to take west to his black brothers in Oakland.

"Take Barb with you," he told Lionel. "Brothers at the Black Panther capital of the whole pig-watching world will like her. What better than a knocked-up, big boobed, blond chick at headquarters? Better than a sawed-off shotgun for protection. You tell them. And lose that crusty Rye accent. Talk like a brother. Be a brother. And take a stash of money, not dope, across the country. Hell of a lot safer."

The right move. For Lionel and Kurt Kallini. But one to end his role with more radical turns in the Movement. A move to bring down some heavy condemnation. Lionel got the Black Union at Cornell. Now the Blacks separated from SDS. Quinn and his RYM worshipped the Black Vanguard. So sending Lionel to the coast called down some heavy shit on Kallini. RYM wanted black and white together to bring the revolution home.

Let Lionel go. Kallini owed him. Lionel's references included Kallini's van, a good deal of dope money, and Barb Kelly. Barb was Kallini's bonus card to the Black Panther organization. A card he already played.

Kallini organized connections between east and west coasts of what he called The Brotherhood. It connected him to the 68' Freres of the Sorbonne revolution. SDS played itself out. From moratoriums and marches to cadres and solidarity cells. It was an end to the Sixties.

Kallini saw RYM at war with Progressive Labor and becoming more radical by far. Maoism, the NLA, and support for the black colony inside Amerika. The Brotherhood could fund GI Resistance if Kurt Kallini connected with outliers in France and Italy.

There was his work with Uncle Carlo. His uncle left Naples to avoid a first world war and Kallini left for France to avoid this one. Kallini was a go between, a connector. He connected the lawless codes of his uncle's generation with these GI resisters of his own. SDS split up by RYM no longer served his purposes.

Age 33 he wasn't too old and settled, nor young and rootless. He saw the time unhinged without losing himself in the abyss. It was time to salvage what he could. For Lionel to the coast, for Kallini into the chaos and out, and for his Uncle Carlo, anything for the only father he ever had.

Kallini came uphill from the Inn to the Townhouse. He saw the van parked and Barb beside it with her painting, Boobs at a Banquet. Herself nude on a guinea red and white tablecloth. Why weren't they gone?

"I got to say goodbye to my best friend, Kady Bontecott."

A whine in Barb's voice died in the swirling snowstorm.

Lionel in a half Afro waved his hands in apology. Lionel should be the Black dude and say, "Are you on the bus, bitch, or off?" Those green eyes of his and tan color didn't fit the half Afro, nor did his Rye accent.

Instead he pleaded. "Barb, come on babe, we'll be all day waiting in this weather."

He checked oil and transmission fluid. He went upstairs for Barb's four Samsonites. St. Louis plane stubs hung from Christmas with her preacher folks at the Episcopalian mission. Lionel had second thoughts too. Meet these Black Panther guns with a white chick. Only Kallini funded his politics. And helped him make a name. Here's the black dude who planned the Afro-American program and their own house at Cornell. He wasn't radical like the Panthers. Kallini said he needed connections on both coasts for a political career and that's what Lionel wanted. The one favor Kallini asked. Van all packed with Barb in a fur collared coat open in the wind. And she whined about losing her friend.

"Get in the van before you freeze to death," Kallini told her.

"I don't want to leave Kady without a goodbye hug."

"Hey, Lionel told you. In this blizzard Kady's not coming. You don't want her traveling in a snowstorm."

"You called her?"

"Her dad won't let her in the VW bug."

"Really?"

"Go west with Lionel. I'll give Kady your big hug. And your beautiful painting."

"You knew. It's for her."

"You got talent, Barb."

"But I have to leave, really, you sure?"

"Love, baby. In San Francisco they'll dig your talent. Here they're too hung up to love your flesh tones. Baby, you're a female Reubens."

Kallini's stared into Barb's vacant blues like shattering glass after a champagne toast. Female Reubens, she had the body of a plains madonna. She had to go. Her and Kady Bontecott got too close, like sisters sharing secrets. Before he knew Kady'd be with Barb in St. Louis or with relatives in Dalhart, Texas. Kady's dad had plans for her. Take care of her sick mom.

Kallini met Evander Bontecott when he was a Marist brother. When he helped the dying at Vassar Hospital. Kallini was good with death and dying as a seminarian. The Movement turned to death and dying. Suited his personality. He'd been crippled from a touch of polio. With Kady's mom dying of colon cancer, Kallini and Evander hit it off. Gradually he did work for Bontecott Stones. And Kady's mom survived the cancer so far. Kallini convinced him Kady's semester in Paris prepared her to tutor French at the Bennet School in Millbrook. But Kady and Barb got too close as roommates and Lionel owed him a favor. Done. Evander held up Kady, and Lionel got on the road.

"Okay Barb, I'll see Kady. Hit the road, Lionel. And get a pair of shades and a scowl for your face. You look like Rye Country Day."

Lionel grunted a "We be cool, brother." But it wasn't him. Kallini was the last white mother he'd be beholden to. The Panthers set his mind straight.

And Kallini saw white and black go separate ways. Down dark alleys of violent demise. Holding-hand days were a long time gone. Cornell SDS planted bombs in buildings. Quinn the Eskimo promised him a white-out Christmas. Get his protégé Lionel away. Wait for Quinn to come for him. Then return to business with his Uncle Carlo.

"Let me know which way the wind blows."

"I be shucking and jiving with the brothers. Get a weatherman."

"You don't need one."

Barb stuck her splashed hair out the window frame.

"Give Kady my hug. Wish I went to Paris with her."

"Sacrifice for the sake of your art, okay honey."

VW van let out the emergency, taxied downhill toward the Aurora Inn, and they too were long gone.

4
Promises to Keep

David Morpheys unfurled his sleeping bag on a top bunk. He stared into a desert of snow funnels playing spin the bottle. Mr. Clean came to the rescue over a frozen Lake Cayuga. Lunar surface. Like father, like son. Dad quit the Bontecott farm for IBM. Dad's dream to live on a farm, and he worked World War II as a farmer, until Bontecott treated them like peasant boarders. Never servant to no one. Off to IBM and Suburbia with a square of garden in the backyard for after work and weekends. David quit football and wanted to quit school. He planned to cross over to Quebec with his French before the draft called him up. Why he worked on his French this Wells winter study.

It was a bad deal. Like all deals with corporations like IBM, THINK. His friends in Hudson Park had worse. Not rich, they lived on the margin. Short term jobs like filling gas tanks, the bottomless A&P bag, or the bottomless stomachs at Dairy Queen. No, those were high school jobs. His buds moved onto unions, drugs, and the army. Kind of jobs they waited for weekends, careening in cars, crossing bridges to towns where bars stayed open, and waiting for sunrise in an alcoholic stupor, sleeping out the sun. Friday night, Saturday parties, and Sunday anxiety as the workweek came round again. No, that was high school life too. But his friends did pretty much the same. Some community college, to defer the war.

Swirls of snow cut patterns over Lake Cayuga. His room door rattled as if the blizzard broke in. The call came at his door. He spun surprised. A straw-haired girl bent double over an immense canvas bag. A backpack and a stray suitcase too. Tall girl peered in, her nose and chapped cheekbones glazed with freckles, her eyes cut grass green.

"Merde. Qui etes vous, Monsieur?"

She swallowed a breath and let it go like blown smoke from a Dunhill cigarette.

"You're in my room. Least I think so. That French bitch below told me, speak only French. I asked her where's my room and she blabs Non-Non-Non about ten in a row and shakes her finger and face like some damn epileptic. Who are you? Qui etes vous?"

"One of the guys."

"I mean why are you in my room?"

"Sorry, this room's mine."

"No kidding."

Kady looked at her mimeo. Check.

"Sorry I banged the shit out of your door, you in here sacked out and peaceful. One hell of a snowstorm! So thought I'd be solo here, except for the damn epileptic at the desk."

David stared. It took him time to find words. He knew this girl, this debutant type with a glacial reserve, the kind of girl he steered clear because she wanted no part of him. He knew girls from Hudson Park off to schools like himself, and with their affairs of the heart they hurt each other. They were like him, hometown, first generation off to college with opportunity to do their parents one better. One chance. Don't blow it.

He knew this kind of girl, yet he was mesmerized by her green eyes. Straw-blond hair the color of cornfields fell from her skicap, gold ringlets, like a bead curtain over her eyes. Her look cut David adrift. Sunny blond hair the color of straw in the field. Least he managed to speak.

"Hope I didn't scarf up your room with a view. With my French I make mistakes."

"Hey, Non-Non-Non. You got it right. Mamselle's clear as a bell about room numbers. I ignored her. She pointed her bony finger upstairs, sputtering in francais a mile a minute, schedule of classes, lab times, dinners."

David leaped from the top bunk with a lunge to the floor. Kady blew strands of hair from her eyes and kept talking. As she glimpsed this tall, gangly, bespeckled guy with Racine mustache and sleepy eyes, someone she might be interested in, had she the time, with her VW running, barely, dropping off stuff to pick up more stuff, with Barb

Kelly at the Townhouse, Barb waiting for her, as Kallini promised.

"How do you say politely in francais, shut the hell up?"

"Got me," David shrugged.

"Housekeeper downstairs, not you."

David understood.

"So off I grabbed the paper because I'm meeting my friend Barb Kelly at the Townhouse and my damn VW stops cold unless I leave it running. Give it gas it goes. Doesn't idle well and doesn't start once it stops. Friend at the Fargo talked about a tune-up before Christmas and now it needs major surgery. Jesus, I'm talking your ear off and you stand there polite as pie, just listening."

He knew this girl, debutant type, and she knew him. It didn't matter. He had plans to quit school and slip across the border to Quebec. It didn't mean he had no manners.

"Let me help with that bag."

"I can handle it. Really, don't bother. And parley francais, so Mamselle doesn't bebop upstairs and start lab exercises on us."

The jazzy inconsequence shut him up. He reached for the filled to bust carpetbag and lugged it with her vinyl suitcase. Freckles fluttered on her chapped face. Fall leaves frozen on a gaunt winter tree. Chill wind flooded upstairs like a door open to the cold. He'd recognize that look next time. She was pissed off at his presumption to carry her bag for her. Kady glared at this tall boy who kept her from Barb Kelly.

"Hey, don't touch the bag. Really, I got it."

David didn't dare glance up. Bead curtain hair like snakes and cut green glass for eyes. He lugged the bag to her door. What he should do and leave.

She saw this long hair with the drooping shoulders and Racine mustache. Another guy like Kallini who'd come by and listen to music. Open a door and it stays open.

"Then help me quick, okay. Once my VW stalls I'm stuck and I got to see my friend, Barb Kelly. Next room here. Set it down."

Kady unzipped the stereo from her huge bag. There it was, okay. All kinds of banned stuff.

"Hey, no tunes and no car, that'd be tough for a month. I know

Mamselle said no stereo. Merde alors, how does one live without the finer things? I can't picture Paris without a stack of records, can you?"

Kady mumbled, damn, no dice. She had to call her mom, say she was fine. Else get the guilt trip for not caring. Tall guy with wire-rims gawked at the stereo, like he'd ask to play it.

"No, I can't picture Paris at all," he said.

David prepared to explain he wasn't going with the French group, that he was here for winter study, that he intended to find a factory job until his head cleared or the draft called, when he figured to cross into French Quebec.

Kady hustled him from her room. With a Non-Non-Non she flicked her index finger like a 4th of July sparkler.

"Monsieur, toujours francais."

Her workboot slid in the stereo, suitcase, and backpack, and with a quick key turn she locked her room shut. Then she fastened green eyes on him and said as she bolted downstairs into the blizzard wind, "Hey sleepy eyes, don't you ask a person's name? Why not learn some manners?"

5
Kady and Kurt Kallini

Kallini greeted her. He had black hair and brows that made his eyes scowl. A book of Nietzsche he gave her to read had this scowl. Only he was Italian. Barb's painting was his idea. He told her of his uncle's Neapolitan place in Poughkeepsie. Barb had been with him. Now she was with Lionel. Kady didn't care who Barb bedded. Only her roommate was gone, and they planned a trip to Paris to break loose from their parents. Barb broke off to the coast. Kady had her mom to care for.

"Hey Kady, sorry I couldn't delay Barb a few minutes longer. Snow fell pretty bad. Lionel wanted to make Route 80 west before it got dark. You can't blame him."

Kady blamed every goddamned guy, all of them, Kallini, Lionel, specially the tall, gawky guy at the French House.

"You mean I missed Barb by ten minutes."

"Hey Kady, I held them up for an hour. Best I could do."

"Best you can do, it's not good enough. Do better for Barb Kelly? Care more, why don't you? Give her to Lionel and say split for the coast. Care for somebody other than yourself. You put San Francisco in Barb's mind, and off she goes, carefree as the wind."

Kallini's eyes bore into hers, his Nietzsche scowl, his brows knit together, like he meant her harm.

"The hell with all of you guys. One month and I'm out of here for good."

Kady threw up her hands at Kallini. She rushed into Walcourt with her huge bag emptied of the stereo and filled its cornucopia with all their records and things. She was out of the Townhouse. God she hoped Mamselle didn't stick a Wells debutant with her. Who could replace Barb Kelly? Nobody at all. She better have her own room. With a padlock to keep out guys like Kallini and the sleepy eyed boy with a Racine mustache.

6
Her Heavy Bag of Sorrows

David listened for her. He'd rue the time he missed her. He was quit of football and school. He was a heavy-winged raven like the black-hatted dude. He inured to icy wind and winter storm like the drifter dad swerved to miss. Learn francais and leave for Canada. He met girls like Kady but never knew them. Kady returned, lugging the heavy bag upstairs.

She saw him coming. His droopy mustache, gangling arms, and can-I-help-you brown eyes. She decided to unpack and head to campus. See her other friend, Jesse.

"Alors Monsieur. Sorry I split so fast. Had to say goodbye to my roommate and she was gone."

"Barb Kelly."

Mad her roommate was gone, this guy told her so. She dropped her heavy bag of sorrows.

"Let me help."

"I should've stayed at the Townhouse. All this stuff's a drag."

"Let me carry it. That's why they hired help for winter study. Do the odd job nobody wants."

"You're not in the French program?"

He gave her a devious grin.

"Then pick it up before the bag breaks my shoulder."

Kady had Barb's painting turned over. Morpheys threw her bag on the bare mattress and she lay Barb's art, face down. She unzipped the bag with a shared record collection, everything. He stared at covers.

"Rules against music, they're made to be broken, right? Hey, nothing more for the help to do. Let me tidy up, you go about your business."

"I was kidding, you know?"

"Really."

Kady rifled through the huge canvas bag until it lay empty on the bare wood floor. David watched her, speechless. Like a cornucopia of all the good things in life: music, love, friends, time to make a life together, or least imagine one. Fill it up again. He wished to importune her. Please replenish this huge canvas bag, this cornucopia of all good things. Sure she knew him and he knew her. Time here at the French House wasn't time wasted. No time need be. Look beneath the bead curtain of her eyes, like looking on the sunrise of Long Beach Island where he went one summer, where the sun and the sky surprised him. The look beyond school, where la mer melee au soleil. C'est retrouve, quoi, l'eternite. Rimbaud, why he wanted to parlez francais. Like songs he memorized whole poems of the symbolists, Baudelaire, Verlaine, and Mallarme.

Speak to her. Tell her about his plans. No, not the escape across the border to Quebec. Tell her about French poetry and how it made college come alive, more than football and classes, how it made Hudson Park less than memories of high school. It was the journey. It was the prodigal time. It was not what he was, but what he wanted to be.

And Kady Bontecott. Last part of her last college year she intended months at the Sorbonne. Put the finishing touch on her French. Have some good times even if Barb Kelly left for the Coast. Then return to her sick mom, her dad's horsefarm, to tutor, then teach French at the Bennet School. No glamorous life, but what she planned to do. Kady listened to him. Who else were there, but the two of them?

"Some blizzard we came through today," David said.

"Kind of storm stirs up the storeposts, my Gram would say. Dust in Dalhart, Texas not all that different from these cold New York snows. West Texas survived the Depression and pounded the posts back down. What my Gram said. Why my mom left. Who'd think she left Gram's farm in West Texas to end up stuck on my dad's horsefarm in New York?"

This Wells girl didn't talk like a debutant. Not like Dana Dupont. Still she knew him and she had a month to be off to Paris. Too bad for him. She kicked the deflated canvas bag under the bare mattress.

"Sorry, got to run to campus."

"See ya."
"You don't ask a person's name?"
He stared at her.
"No manners?"
"David Morpheys, at your service, waiting on your return."
"Kady Bontecott."
"My dad worked for a Bontecott before he quit for IBM."
"Bien sur, Monsieur. Mais pas d'Anglais ici."

Kady Bontecott scooted downstairs to her buzzing VW, barely running, on up to campus. David on second floor landing, looked downstairs to see if his vision of prodigal time remained, once the parlor doors swung closed.

7
Meet Your Mates

Kady left, and the parlor filled with girls and a guy with short hair and parka. Mamselle reviewed the rules in francais too fluent for the untuned ear. Intros in ragged francais. He met his roommate Doug Bryant, from Philadelphia and Hamilton too. The girl Deb spoke of basketball if David played afternoons. She and Trixsie roomed from freshman year. All hail to hoops, he told Deb walking the stairwell.

"Hey Doug, any of the beds they're yours. Bunkbed or single, take your pick."

"I'll have the single."

He set two leather suitcases on the mattress. He wore tweed jacket and tie beneath his parka. He looked the AD type like Steve Hancock, the coach's pick at quarterback. Only not. With his heavy glasses and jerky manner AD dangled his type from the third floor. Doug was the fool.

"You belong to a fraternity, David?"

"Did with DKE. No, not now. Too complicated, with these are the brothers and those are the jerks. You?"

"ELS. I tried them out. We dress for dinners. Why I wore the suit, in case it's part of the program."

"Damn I hope not. Mine got left at high school graduation. Used a friend's for the frat picture. Too much dress up at DKE."

"What if dinner here requires coat and tie?"

Doug's question suggested his shock. As if someone without pants ventured into the public eye. A punctilious code of rules his defense. Top of his suitcase his accountant dad tucked in a Playboy pack of come-ons to curry favor with girls. There was his shiteating grin.

"I'm going to use it or lose it. The book I mean. You're welcome to thumb through it when I'm finished."

David turned to see a third roommate appareled in gray wool coat, suit, and silk tie.

"Hey a hand my good man, my kingdom for a hand."

Walter stepped on springy feet with ready smile, and his hefty weight kept in motion with the gift of gab. Walter was the clown.

"Walter Rink at your service."

David helped him with a number of bags taken from a taxi, which Walter paid. Two bags David trundled upstairs to their room.

Walter saw Doug's book of one-liners.

"Aha, the Bryant by-the-book approach. I've tried everything. You're Morpheys?"

"The bagman, at your service. Why the taxi?"

"Unbelievable, what happened. You guys won't belieeeve what happened to me. Driving down Route 7 almost to Skaneateles, doing well on slippery roads, my GTO cruising near 60, listening to Fabulous Finds of the Fifties, you know, WOOH BABY! Great load of fire. And I'm sha-bob-bobbing along to the beat when this deer with a rack like tree branches busts my car. Jesus H. Christ! My car took a bounce before he took his last flying___ at the moon."

"No kidding," David said taking a chair for Walter's narrative. Doug stuck a pipe in his gaping mouth.

"My deer took his lover's leap into the wild blue yonder. And my GTO with a busted radiator, bent carbumper, stood there, bleeding to death. Steam hissed into the cold and headlights gave up the ghost. Hey, I'm in big ass trouble. Night coming on. I'm betting three to one here I freeze my balls on fire twenty miles from the most girls I'll ever meet in my life. Die in the prime of life, hell no. I'll walk, hitch, or crawl if I have to. You would too."

"How'd the taxi come by?"

"Half the town of Skaneateles came by. First hee-haw hick sees my car and sees the deer and says real nonchalant, hey, looks like the deer killed your car. I'll go down to the ESSO and see what they can do. Next comes the trooper with the same deer killed your car line. Then finally the ESSO wreaker, same line, only this hayseed asks if he can keep the deer."

"How'd the taxi save your sorry ass?" David asked again.

"I told the wrecker guy I was a good shot. Why not ride me to Wells College where the girls are? I see, he says. You're going deer hunting, hardee-har-har. You bet, I say. If I can tell the bucks from the does I'm doing my share of dosee-doeing. Wrecker guy's king of the comics. Says deerhunting going to cost me, lots of bucks and plenty of dough. Hardee-har-har. He called the town taxi and here I am."

Doug's shiteating grin needed his pewter pipe again.

"Hey Walter, you're a real card. Too bad you need a ride to dinner."

"You're driving what, Doug?"

"The Thunderbird my dad got me on my twenty-first birthday."

"Well it ain't no GTO."

"Neither is yours after the deer killed your car."

"Hardee-har-har. Let's go to dinner. And don't use the deer killed my car routine. Give me a week to bleed that sucker dry."

They took Doug's Thunderbird to dinner. Walter sat at the table-end like a liege lord; Doug, his straight-arrow retainer. The French group shared a room off the main mess supposedly to speak francais. Walter had the girls for his audience.

"Why are we quarantined to break bread by ourselves?"

Deb McGuire, among the beautiful, looked ordinary. Her dirty blond tinged with red and tied in a pony tail. David told her he played ball.

"We're quarantined because of your company. You skip dinner and we can sit in the main mess."

"Skip dinner, are you kidding? I'd rather skip breathing."

Walter's brylcreamed hair hung over his eyes. He belonged to the AD frat at Colgate. Jester among the aristocrats of Choate, Groton, and Rye Country Day.

"You girls cut me, personally, and my brethren. We men come to share your female company and we're greeted with disgrace. We come bearing gifts…"

"What gifts?" Trixsie asked.

"Nothing less than male companionship."

"Nothing more?" Deb asked.

"But nothing less, mind you. In this time of civil unrest we are the minority at Wells asking for fair treatment."

None of the girls knew him enough to test his seriousness.

"We'll give you a week and see if it works," Trixsie smiled to Debra, her roommate all through college.

"Then a week turns into a month here and months in Paris. Your humble servants. We accept your gift of gracious hospitality."

Walter flicked his eyebrows like Groucho. He had presence and poured coffee round the table. He had their bemused attention for his Deer killed his car rendition.

"You see me here for dinner by the grace of God and Doug Bryant come to the rescue. There I was in my GTO on the road from Colgate to Skaneateles, and what prances before my car? No, not Rudolph, but his second cousin. I was listening to Fabulous Finds of the Fifties…"

Douglas stuck his pewter pipe in his mouth. Trixsie and Deb, roommates till death, as Kady and Barb expected to be, nodded to one another. They would know better next time. Walter had Doug play the three hicks with a hardee-har-har. He had a part for Morpheys, had he not slipped away before this second helping of Walter's humor.

If Kady Bontecott dined in the hall, he wanted a word about Walter with her. Warn her. She was nowhere in sight so he took the mile walk back to the house. Raven dark with slivered moon he clutched his worn suede coat in the steely wind.

8
Les Jeux sont Faits

The French House lost its hollow sound. A few girls talked in the parlor. Mamselle played Debussy on the house stereo. An occasional board creaked in the hall and a flush upstairs blew its windy water organ. David's mind worked overtime. He wrote pages of poetry. Like Baudelaire, poems en prose. Like daydreaming. Take off for the coast like Kady's roommate, a sure-fire solution. On the road in a cross country van. Four years of college cooped up in classes, sports, and grades had gone on too long. It was an unreal time beyond recognition.

Either/or. Sometime near winter David decided he knew. Not a hell no, I won't go, but a check of alternatives, one's own body count, and a pull like a thin air day in September signaled fall and football frenzy. For birds the instinctual rudder turned south. He dropped football and lost his scholarship. Now he had loans. Drop out of school, worse happens. Plan his next move better. Worse wasn't necessarily bad. Least it's not the same.

David stared at the moon dusting the rippled black Cayuga with snowy incandescence. Blues in the next room. Offbeat acoustical blues complaining of trains taking him from his woman. Black smoking spirit of night like iron destiny between hearts already broken, and another town where whiskey and women bring an untimely end. "All my love's in vain."

Not the Stones and their British gloss on this primordial sadness. This blues blacker than Melville's chapel on Ishmael's cold, cold trek seeking shelter in a strange town. Seeking employment with body and soul already enslaved to a fate whose finish was in the beginning, the coming to America. High seas heist for one, and high seas voyage out with doom inked on the wage contract. Black blues and Melville's epic, dark side to the American dream.

Acoustical blues along the pipes connecting Kady's room to David.

Music meshed with thick incense on a Budapest express. Girl with green eyes and spring freckling her face slipped into her room and played blues, illicit as hashish, sad and low, so only she and David heard. Knock on the door and compliment her music.

He was too rash. Kady played blues to bewail Barb Kelly's departure, her sad escapade to the west coast when Kady traveled east to Paris. She sulked in private and resented his intrusion. Catching her on the fly like this afternoon, carrying her bags, collected her contempt. What was welcome and what wasn't? He wasn't. How to handle with care this male/female thing?

Lure of blues and David Morpheys tap-tapped on his neighbor's door, soft so Kady wouldn't think it was Mamselle. Tap-tapping in pentatonic time, his call went unheard. No response as the room suffered no human presence. No more than the dead bluesman misleading David's reverie. He knocked full blast, so much louder than normal he shocked himself. The landing echoed. He was the house arrest, waking the dead, stash the smoke and muffle the music, I'm coming in.

A male voice answered David's knock.

"Hey, whoever the hell's there, come on in. I ain't stopping you."

Kurt Kallini, who trekked to town from Cornell that afternoon, sat on Kady's bare mattress, lotus position, black cowboy hat, beard and thick brows, and piercing stare. Above Kady's bed the picture of a blond nude flirted with the viewer.

"Sorry to disturb your meditation. I wanted to ask Kady about the blues."

Kallini unwound from the lotus, tipped his bead-banded hat, and sat long black coat open on the single armchair. David stood. Indian band reminded David of a belt his dad gave him from a Quebec fishing trip with Grandpa. Where David went when drafted.

"Robert Johnson," Kallini said. He crossed his sharp-toed, leather boots straight up to his knee, staring, dark eyes and heavy brows beaded on David.

"My name's David Morpheys. We met this afternoon."

Then the blank stare back, like he said, Hey, my name Jose Jimenez. Dude's eyebrows shut down like window shades on a tomb.

"Delta bluesman is Robert Johnson. Black Orpheus who made the devil's deal to slide guitar whines at twenty one like Son House at forty. Immaculate conception of talent, flush with the gift and flashy with women. No cash. Just local notoriety, whiskey and women, and a waking doom ticking daylight in another Mississippi town, one day closer to the end. Jealous man poisoned his liquor and Robert Johnson spewed his insides in an empty room dead at daylight."

"The music's so cool. Type I like to play on harmonica."

"It's his soul ascending, sliding off like sparks and back like ash into the fire of endless silence. Acoustic guitar alive like an ashen coal with only one night to play."

"What's your name anyway? Kady complained of manners when I didn't ask hers."

"Name's Kallini, Kurt Kallini."

Morpheys knew how to name him. Kallini was the guru and he was the novice come to learn the groovy route to truth. David didn't want the connection. It was simply there. Like so much else.

"The blues calls you, then?"

"Yes, like the truth. Like a car spun out of control whose accident waits for snowbank or the flip into a culvert of flame."

"Father and son then. The Ford Galaxy that almost hit me."

"Two views of the blues, like everything."

"The blues is feeling, one step below sadness. Devil's deal its birthmark. All its joys are sparks in the darkness, the whiskey and the women, like the music itself. In the morning one's all strung out with only the bitter wind blowing you to the next honky-tonk town."

"I like Chicago blues."

"Who, Buddy Guy and Herbert Sumlin?"

"Don't know them. I like Mike Bloomfield."

"Kady likes Taj Mahal. College copy of twang and cornpone. Johnson is clean and pure. The deal is done. Les jeux sont faits."

"Bloomfield plays guitar like a sudden shower of notes, a burst of rain gone before one senses a cool wet in a summer heat wave."

David liked his words. Improvisation to match how Kallini talked.

"I saw Bloomfield at Silvio's with Muddy Waters. His fun

complimenting the master with high flying licks. Father and son, you know? Yet Muddy knows so much more about the feeling. The cotton fields, the slavery, and the Klan's maiming of the black man."

"Bloomfield's learning."

"Yea he's learning, like Clapton. Same night at Silvio's a black dude arrives between sets. Short barrel-chested dude held this Afro'd head by the hair, blood-soaked and dripping. Horrible sight, the hacked head of a human being. The Medusa. Sucker says to the barman cool as can be. Teach that jive talkin' mother to fug around with my woman. Terror takes his stool in the black man's bar. White guys cry to Muddy for a guitar father. But the blues cries its tears for a mother dead and no father at all."

David mesmerized by Kallini's heavy-browed eyes and his tale told. Kallini buttoned up his coat.

"Now Chicago is the city where cops beat kids and kids beat back until Democrats find nothing but chaos, Kennedys dead, Martin Luther king dead, Wallace taking up votes, and Nixon elected. Now the RYM can't wait to return to Chicago and bring the war home. They don't know war and you don't know the blues."

"I'd make a my own deal to play like Robert Johnson."

"Always more to the deal than simply the dotted line."

"It's all a bad deal. Whether I sign up or take off."

"You know it Morpheys."

David liked he had something to say back. Kallini gave him a nod.

"Kady's out and so am I. Take the record and when you see Kady, play it. Tell her Kallini came by."

David moved aside from the door. Mold of Kallini's face, jutting forehead and wide cheekbones, reminded him of Kady. Of course Kady had green eyes and cheeks splashed with freckles. Kallini was gone and the door hung open. What a fool he was, to play the novice to Kallini's mentor. But he couldn't help himself. The blues were too cool.

9
Kallini on Bass

Kallini returned to the Aurora Inn where he'd eaten dinner that evening and took a room. He hooked up with the band, a group of town kids, his cousin Joey Gallo's age. It was Don on drums, pimply Lloyd West on guitar, and Tim Burt singing. Eddie, their bass player, got an Auburn factory job. He was out but his amp stayed. Kallini said he played bass. He keyed into the drumbeat and played runs beside the guitar chords. Guitar and drums were adequate, but Tim Burt swaggering like Mic Jagger didn't cut it.

After a couple Stones songs Tim Burt left to see his girlfriend in Auburn. Kallini's arrival timed his departure. He saw Kady too. Usually the band did without a singer. Now they were pissed because Tim Burt cut out, and they lost Eddie on bass. Then they asked Kallini why he didn't sing too. He did.

Kallini thought he'd ask for Kady's voice along side him. A nice gesture, but her white bird voice didn't fit. Show her he could sing and get her involved. Payback for sending Barb out west. He sang House of the Rising Sun, Honky Tonk Woman, Thrill is Gone, and then Sympathy for the Devil. So happened the hotel manager came down cellar and liked what he heard. He talked with Kallini, but Kurt pointed to Don on drums. When the balding owner suggested a weekend gig, Don said sure, asking Lloyd for confirmation, who said, "I guess so."

The manager asked, "This weekend okay?"

Don sweated from the set. He realized the gig was for real, and asked Kallini if it was okay with him.

The hotel owner saw Kallini wasn't with the band, and insisted the bass and singer went with the gig. He turned with Don and Lloyd to see what Kallini would do.

Kallini said, "Sure, I'm with the band, if we can use the cellar for practice during the week."

The owner agreed, because he saw girls came to hear the band and drink a few beers. Sunday was an off night.

"I'm sure you can. Anytime we don't have a luncheon upstairs. Even when we do, they're finished by three, so you'll have a couple hours."

Don was all smiles. A gig weekends, and they didn't have to chip in to rent the practice room. He hugged Deb for luck. Maybe he should call Tim Burt back, but didn't. Kallini sat down by Kady.

"Those cassis sneak up on a person."

She liked the grape wine liqueur and her Dunhill cigarettes. Kallini impressed her too.

"I didn't know you played music. Barb was telling the truth, you have talents few people know."

"I miss Barb too. Especially her paintings of campus life."

Kady was put off by his reference to Barb's self-portrait. She didn't know if Kallini was hitting on her. She told him he sang pretty well.

"Thanks. Why don't you sing harmony on a couple tunes. Barb said you had a wonderful voice. One of those choral voices. Like to try?"

Kady shook her head no.

"I'd be too shy to stand before a crowd and sing. A choral voice doesn't fit your Stones set. I'm more Marianne Faithful."

"Exactly. What about White Bird and David LaFlamme stuff?"

"My favorite, how'd you know? You probably play violin too."

"No, but there are girls in the string band. We could train a violinist."

"Good gracious no. I'm far too shy."

Kallini looked up to see Joshua Steen from Cornell. So Quinn the Eskimo knew. Lionel cut out for the coast. Josh had a full brown beard which muffled the merry gleam he leered at Kady Bontecott. She stared back.

"Kady, a friend from Ithaca. His folks work the jewelry business off West 46th Street. Same line as Bontecott Stone."

"You know my dad?"

Same merry gleam as Josh shook his head. Josh had word how Quinn and RYM took Kallini's decision to send off Lionel, their black brother in the Union.

"Do you know my dad, Kurt?"

"No Kady. Barb mentioned him. Like she mentioned her Episcopalian father and how her and Deb's dad worked the St. Louis Mission. You're Catholic, I'm Catholic, even Joshua's religious in his red diaper way. Aren't you Josh?"

"Really Kallini. Quinn's coming for you."

"I'm in, then I'm out."

"Who knows what out means anymore? Quinn talks of white-out of whatever holds back the vanguard."

"The center will not hold."

"We worked too long for guns, bombs, and cadre squads to take over."

"It's the end of the Sixties."

"The end of participatory democracy?"

"Who wanted an endless meeting?"

Kady said she had to split.

"Whitebird, Kady, what do you think?"

"With this blizzard, certainly no Hot Summer Breeze."

"Marrying Maiden," Kallini said to Kady and Joshua Steen.

"Really, you got to come to Ithaca to calm Quinn the Eskimo down. Or else, all hell's going to explode."

Kallini left to ask Don about practice times, and then took the Movement dude with leering eyes to the bar. Kady settled back with Deb and Don, and Don was ecstatic about this first gig Kallini got them. Their joy spilled over, so Deb took him back to the Townhouse. Kady got another cassis and saw Kallini cornered by this guy Joshua Steen, raving his arms. Too bad Kallini let Lionel take Barb Kelly west. Good, Kallini caught some grief too.

10
Illuminations

Not much later Kady drove her VW home. It surprised the hell out of her to find a Robert Johnson record on the unmade bed. Then the note read: "I met this guy Kallini and he said to tell you about this blues guitarist from 1940. I heard him play and knocked hoping to rap about music. Kallini sat there in the chair and said he'd gone to the crossroads and made his deal. Robert Johnson, I guess, and maybe this Kurt Kallini too. I recognized the Cream Crossroads. What's sorrowful with Johnson explodes with Clapton. What I thought. I didn't mean to intrude. Don't mind the note. I write to think and I knocked to compliment the music. See you at our Sunrise Semester."

Kady saw weird people double stacked. Kallini had been there and hung Barb's painting. Then Morpheys came along. They set up my record player and leave me the record and the review. Too weird by far. She should move back to the Townhouse. Use this room as a blind, to avoid them both. Just pick up mail and take classes here. Her elbow arthritis acted up again and she couldn't sleep. She read Apollinaire, then Anais Nin till 3-4:00 in the morning. Nights at least belonged to her. No Barb Kelly returned to tell about sleeping with somebody new. Routines made her life easier. She played her stereo low as she moved to the bathroom to brush her teeth and undress.

David tried sleeping Sunday night, but couldn't. He tried yoga and stared at the moon. Storm clouds raced like furrowed flags across the lunar surface. Spooky, the moon rising over Lake Cayuga cascaded light like a bridge arched over the water.

After midnight David slept, but he woke in a sweat some hour between darkness and the dawn. In a dream he took a joyride with 18 year old Chink Anderson, same age as his older brother. David was twelve. His father was furious he rode in someone else's car. He warned David of teen accidents and harped on Bob Newman's death driving hellbent and drunk to the gills down Toller Hill. Kid was in Robby's graduating class and firemen scraped the stupid idiot off his windshield.

In the dream there was dark rain shading the night. The windshield filmed with torrents and down the approaching hill washed streams of water. The car spun sideways, and what shocked David they tumbled off the Mid-Hudson Bridge, up and open, like a drawbridge. Chink beamed hysterically as the car plummeted, slapped the water surface, and sank below. David struggled with the window and door and held his breath, closed in a coffin of black, and at last burst above the surface. He swam against the choppy waves and reached the far bank, exhausted. Chink Anderson never surfaced. As David recalled Chink's beaming eyes like Genghis Kahn, he saw those of Kurt Kallini, the dude in Kady's room.

He awoke, too shook up, to go back to sleep. He climbed from the top bunk and lighted the bathroom to read his thin copy of Rimbaud's Illuminations. The bathroom pipes connected with Kady's room because he heard her stereo playing the song White Bird, Kady singing, clear and resonant. Her voice spiraled like a mountain railway hitting notes without effort and far outreaching the record. "Whitebird ...."

It touched David with a peace-of-God holiness. Without thinking he tapped on the connecting pipe and said, "Very nice." No response but the silent night. Off went the stereo. David slept until morning, despite the swirl of faces, first crazy Chink and his burning eyes becoming the bearded face of Kurt Kallini and him in turn molding into the sweet face of Kady Bontecott. Heaven and hell do battle between darkness and the dawn. How David arranged matters in his mind.

II
Aurora was the Dawn

11
Le Pont Mirabeau

Early morning Kady was up for breakfast. Floppy eggs and greasy sausage turned her stomach. She ate a slice of toast and coffee with mostly milk. Cigarette had a metallic taste. Her mom's cancer needed extra supplements of iron. Taste her mom's cancer. Talk about paranoid. No friendly face like Barb's to share complaints. Class began at 9 AM. Wanting one of the armchairs she hurried back to the French House.

New cup of coffee and her Dunhills helped her settle into a corner with Alcools by Apollinaire. Madame Rochelle dressed perky with her styled hair curled neatly behind her darling ears. She was on a Boris Vian kick this year, as if he were beat poet of the French novel. Eels slithered from bath faucets to be fricasseed with brioche for a jazz dejeuner. Way her stomach turned this morning.

She had the armchair against a wall so she could curl sideways and maybe close her eyes, the better to listen, okay. She read this French lit in twenty classes, all a third time through. She prepared to teach prep school and knew what she needed. Of course she needed the French semester, but not Boris Vian.

She noticed David Morpheys propped against the portico to the livingroom, his feet tucked under him to let people by. Long legs and arms intertwined. Droopy mustache and slumped shoulders. Sleepy eyes too, since he banged her pipes at 4 AM. Let Deb deal with him. She read her book. Madame Rochelle lectured on Boris for an hour. Then Madame asked her to read a favorite poem because Kady wasn't swept away by Boris. So what? All this ecstasy about Boris and syncopated lit. Boris needed a good flush.

"Yes Kady, read us a poem. Something you think good as Boris Vian."

She saw Morpheys squirrel up his eyes from his thick brown hair.

He dozed too. Eyes with curtains pulled halfway down. Touch the curtain and TWANG! They sprung and spun around. Hectic eyes spirited with a visionary gleam.

"Kady, read Sur le Pont Mirabeau, would you?"

Morpheys didn't shout across the room. His request transferred from Deb to the professor over to Kady. Odd way of picking on her. Like he was in league with the teacher. So what?

The poem was a melancholy one. Two lovers stare like a bridge of their eyes connect them. Waters flow by like time. Church bells sound. Lovers and love flow by too and they never return. So alone, if joy did not always follow the pain. Sappy in its own way as Boris. Then Morpheys filled the pause with a "Very nice" and flicked a hand like some hotshot conductor. Christ, the guy knew how to piss a girl off.

Madame Rochelle called her hour quits. Like she taught them a quirky beat and topped it off with love hurts. Bet she got off on Morpheys' remark. On with Mamselle to do exercises. She had a dumb 50's bouffant and little jet black eyes. Mamselle was too scared to look the three boys in the face. And Morpheys hid out since it was talk time. Deb protected his view of the teacher and Trixsie answered the form question. They'd done the exercises since freshmen, and Kady since seventh grade.

What is the best way to spend time in France, le moyen le plus bon, etc? Like anyone knew what to do in Paris. Certainly not sit in classes all day. Trixsie bought her Europass and saw the country chateaus and stayed in youth hostels. Mamselle looked close to Morpheys as she dared. But Deb said, contrary to the country tour, she stayed in Paris to enjoy the sidewalk cafes, walks in the park, and tours of the museum. Right, her and Don, Townie drummer for the band, drinking in the culture.

Morpheys smirked to Deb, "You two are in cahoots."

Of course they were. Mamselle said, "tres bon", and so he got to imitating her. He had his nerve and Mamselle asked him. Halfway through the form he got tongue-tied. He had a few French words to say work, life of workers, do what they do. He meant to say, to know the folks and be like them. To work each day, commuting, dinner, tired out, then do it all over again. Like people do here.

Made sense, but Morpheys made the error to switch to English. Mamselle knew none. Both were fish out of water between languages. He got cut off. Too bad, it served him right. Kady kept her curious eye on him with his dreamy glances here and there and inside himself. She'd shout across the room, "Quit daydreaming, Morpheys!"

12

Sorry, No Manners

At lunch Kady heard Walter Rink entertaining the troops. He redid his deer killed my car story she heard about. Only this time he used, le moyen le plus bon to kill a deer or kill a car or kill a town full of hicks from Skaneateles. "And that's why I'm riding the wild west highways with Doug and his undercharged Thunderbird, baby."

Doug gave a oddball grin like he was cool with Walter yakking away, and put the pipe back in his mouth. Weird the way guys get around girls. Then Morpheys came in with Kady's friend, Jesse, and a thin book sticking from his pocket. The book looked familiar.

Funny how Kady agreed to do yoga with Jesse that afternoon and there was Morpheys with her. Kady told her Morpheys had ideas but few French words for them. And Jesse knew him from dating a roommate of hers freshman year. Morpheys came back with a stacked full tray of food. Kady was about to leave.

She saw Morpheys come sit beside her. She got up, lighted cigarette in hand, and turned away to put on her Navy coat. He did an about face and sat near Walter. He didn't listen to Walter's hullaballoo, but took out the thin Larousse and read while he ate fries with sticky fingers. Wasn't that her copy of Alcools? She'd put it in her room and Morpheys took it, and had the gall to read it at the lunch table. What was this guy: a klepto, a burglar, a midnight whisperer on the bathroom pipe? Kady had about enough.

She glared at him. Sure thing, he looked up, TWANG went the curtain! He smiled at her.

"Hey Morpheys," she said, shaking her half smoked Dunhill, "Did you steal my book? Did you piquer mon Apollinaire?"

He looked perplexed about two seconds and said, "No, I bought my own. Already I got that Pont Mirabeau about memorized. Want to recite it for us again?"

"No. And I didn't like your asking for it in class."

"Tres bon, Kady Bontecott, compris."

Walter with his brylcreamed hair and gleam in his eye stopped his merrymaking. Douglas the pipe smoker too.

"You mean all this time you've been in the bookstore picking out poetry to sit with a tray full of food, and read with all of us here?"

"Sorry, no manners."

Kady glared at him until she discovered everyone else stared at her. Especially Walter and Doug. Girls took their trays back to go to lab.

"I just like to eat with a book in hand. Thanks for turning us on to Apollinaire. Come over here and sit, and let me piquer one of your special smokes."

"You don't have time. We got lab class."

"Let Mamselle wait."

"Finish those greasy fries, Morpheys, wipe your fingers on a page of Pont Mirabeau, and get moving."

"Ja whol, Herr Kolonel!"

"Next building over."

"Okay Kady. Ainsi soit-il. Eat and read on the run. When my stomach quakes, I'll remember, la joie viens toujours apres la peine."

Kady sat close enough to Morpheys in lab to hear how poor he repeated the phrases. He tried his best. When Mamselle corrected his response, he thanked her, merci, and repeated a line of Pont Mirabeau. Kady saw Mamselle react with this odd look like a bug crawled up her brassiere. Then the creases of her thin lips quivered with humor. Morpheys gave a little finger flip to Mamselle as he left lab, like a duck shadow cast on a wall.

13
Fools Rush In

Jesse met her in the dance room where they practiced yoga. The prima ballerinas of the dance seminar took up the room, so they carted the mat out on stage. Just Deb, a teacher's son, and three other girls played. Kady was relieved Morpheys didn't show up. Returned to the bookstore for Rimbaud or surrealism. Should she apologize for saying he stole her copy? She'd rather not.

"Yes I did. I saw Morpheys in the bookstore. He slipped a whole set of french poets in his coat."

Jesse lied to catch Kady's attention. She had that nippy Goldie Hahn look, cute little nose and candy blond hair. Short girl who took math courses and languages because, as she said, she liked logical structures.

"I don't doubt he'd do it."

"Really."

"You should have seen him charm Mamselle with the Mirabeau poem he memorized."

"Saw him freshman year with Dana Dupont of the Friends School. A brother-sister thing. We met him on a frat roll. What ugly things we endured as freshman."

"Where was I?"

"Home to take care of your mom. Morpheys wrote her every week and came to visit when Dana gave in. She let him sleep with us and he coughed an hour keeping us up. She got in bed with him and they got going at it. It made me uncomfortable, so I left and Dana left, and I guess that's as far as it got."

"I missed a lot that first year."

"You missed a lot every year."

"My mom's sick you know."

"I know she is and you're a good daughter to help her out. Theirs was a talking relationship, her and Morpheys. He was a bit déclassé for Dana Dupont. He aimed to please, he was smart, and he wrote long labors of love without being love letters. He wants to write. She transferred to Hamilton and I guess they stayed friends, nothing more. Morpheys was too rough around the edges for her. We liked his friend Peter Bergman who came with him to Wells. Nice guy."

The preliminary stretching made Kady ache in the elbows. Blood flowing she felt better. Run again like prep school for better, or worse.

"Hey look, Morpheys did show up," Jesse said.

Down the other end he tapped the ball off the backboard, shot close, further back, and then dashed toward the basket, leaped, and tried to throw it through the net. But the ball ricocheted off the backrim about 50 feet up in the air. Kady saw he played ball enough to show off. He couldn't see her back of the stage.

In the game with Deb he passed without looking, hooked, made unusually long shots, and whooped out loud when anyone got involved. He looked awkward in class; here he moved with a kinetic ease weaving through the game. Kady didn't know basketball, but the heightened awareness of sport she recognized from her high hurdles at track meets. Morpheys enjoyed it all. Kady stared at his smooth athletic grace. Jesse saw he could play too, and made comments about his physique.

Kady turned talking to Jesse, when Morpheys out of nowhere, sat beside her, grinning, breathing deep breaths, and sweating profusely.

"I tried yoga a few times and damnitall if I didn't have the worst nightmares of my life. I'd be riding after midnight, rain pelting, skidding across lanes on a bridge, crashing through guardrails down into the muddy Hudson, struggling to hold out till the surface and barely making it. Let me wake up, please."

Kady stared at his perspiring face afraid Morpheys never did make it to the surface. Too much enthusiasm this time. He held her with his sparkling eye. Then she felt embarrassed, which Jesse noticed, if Morpheys didn't.

"Somebody's got to teach you yoga," Jesse said. "How to control your breathing and enlighten you along each of the steps."

Kady wasn't offering.

"Of course I rush in to give it a try. Fools do, you know."

"How's Dana doing?" Jesse asked.

"Dana's finally got a guy who suits her. He's a good looking, sophisticated guy in her brother's frat. But not the frat type. He's sensitive to her. I chatted with them, drinking a beer. Nice of Dana to say come sit down. He's not like the jerk who wanted to curate a museum."

"Dana's doing okay without you?"

"No sweat. She always did okay without me. When she came to Hamilton we shared a history of philosophy class. She let me escort her to the frat parties where she'd introduce herself as David Dupont's little sister, when some asshole who hated the Chi Psi crowd asked coldly, who the hell is David Dupont. She'd hang her head and whisper, mon dieu, another faux pas, what would my well-mannered mom say?"

"She never realized her brother was a jerk."

"No, she didn't. But the new guy with sweater knotted over his shoulder likes Dana and her little sisterly way. Read a Raymond Chandler Little Sister, but that's a different story. They're eager for ballgame number two. Sorry to interrupt your yoga soiree."

Kady watched him flex to his feet, leap off the stage, into the fray of another game. He dripped sweat, yelled to Deb to "shoot you fool", and trying to tap the ball through the strings fell sprawling to the hardwood floor. He shot back to his feet unhurt and unfazed.

"Jesse, what's with Morphey's enthusiasm?"

"His vulgar display of energy? He'll never be cool and collected. Social graces don't come natural to him. Like the townies in the band, he gets his kicks in music, sports, whatever brings moments of intoxication."

"He bothers me. Way he intrudes on my space."

"He likes you."

"He likes Dana Dupont."

"He didn't say a thing about her when I met him in the bookstore. I asked. He said, she's okay. He was obsessed to find that poetry book of yours. In fact I've never heard Morpheys talk for more than two minutes before."

"What was their relationship then?"

"He listened to her Friend's School talk when no one else would. He was sympathetic. He shared philosophy with her since that was her brother's major. He listened to her mom problems and told her manners were her own affair, not knowing the social class of the Duponts."

"I never had a brother."

"Well my older brother graduated Yale, worked for Chase, and then took his poli-sci courses to a government job in DC. Nixon elected and he's in. We aren't close, anymore. Guys like the professor's kid and Kallini, it's like having friends who aren't close friends, just guys. An infatuation's different. Like a real relationship. You know what's important."

"You think Morpheys likes me. He's not just hitting on me?"

"See the infra-red glare in his eyes like he's burning up, that's different. From him and Dana for sure. Of course, what's he know about you?"

"Nothing at all. Why should he?"

"And you about him?"

"Nothing. Only he's fascinated with what I read, with what I think, with who I am."

"Go ask him why."

"You're kidding?"

"They're finished playing. See Tom, the professor's son, toweling off and telling why he missed his shots."

Before Morpheys returned, Kady creaked her knees upright and said enough yoga for an afternoon. Jesse intended to do her 120 breathings and half hour retreat stage, then use the sauna. Kady wanted to get back to her room, eat something, and … well, call her mom. What she did every afternoon.

Out to her VW wind swirled yesterday's snow into subzero cold. Her car started after the Fargo guy fixed it that morning. Kady discovered she was starving. She had little but coffee and toast all day. In her room she had her chamomile tea and stone crackers. She listened for Morpheys to hear him over her Joni Mitchell Blue. She planned to meet for the Monday string recital. Later in the week a Bergman festival.

She used the downstairs booth to call her mom. Without a room phone like the Townhouse her mom said call collect. And mom waited between 4:30 and 5:00 for the phone to ring. She put off medication and dinner. She tried embroidery to pass the time. Kady called punctually at 4:30 when Morpheys interrupted her dialing by opening the double doors. His ski cap covered his wet hair frozen in the return mile. His drooping mustache frosted brown with ice and snow. Just gloves and a suede coat to keep warm.

His teeth chattering he said, "Hey, don't hog the phone."

"Go away, me and my mom talk for a half hour. You must be freezing."

"It is a bit nippy."

"Go shower before you catch your death of cold."

"Ah, concerned for my welfare. Steam and sauna await me in the boy's room. Go ahead, call."

"I intend to. Don't barge in again looking like the Abominable Snowman."

"My favorite Himalayan freak, you know."

"No I don't. Go."

Morpheys went upstairs and she wondered whether she should offer him a ride to campus. Or after he left go and pick him up. Less intention, more by accident. With the clomp of his heavy workboots she'd hear him leaving. She dialed and the phone rang once.

"Hello mom, how are you feeling?"

"I had my wrist in that special sling all afternoon. Last hour I tried embroidery. How's your arthritis?"

"Fine."

"Doctor's appointment comes Thursday at Vassar Hospital. They'll do a bone scan to check for cancer. Doctor suggests it's all menopause and arthritis. Of course my periods stopped with the cancer so what do they know? Male doctors are so glib when they know nothing."

"Dad should take you to Boston. His relatives know the doctors there and he could find you a good female physician."

Kady acted as sounding board for her mom. She magnified mom's complaints against male doctors and diminished her scare of cancer. Mom had colon cancer, then her colostomy, and did without nurses at all. She changed the bags and scoured the sewn cavity herself. Kady protected her mom. Nobody said any harm of her. Mom had plenty of courage, but disease and pain saps anyone's strength. Kady knew from age 13 if she wanted her best friend healthy she had to help her mom through operations and recovery, and ever since she helped her mom talk about her ailments.

"Ride through the snowstorm was okay?"

"I got here. But late to see Barb Kelly off."

"That's too bad. I like Barb. Wind's blowing against these old farmhouse windows. I can't stay warm today. I'll get Bontecott to check the furnace. His foreman's got less to do winters."

"Warm up with a nice bath after dinner. Watch TV and read one of your romances."

"I wish I could sew more. TV's too stupid most of the time. You still got friends there?"

"There's Deb and Jesse to talk to. New guy named Morpheys I'm not sure about."

"These men in the program go to Paris?"

"No. Deb says it's just us twelve girls."

"Why don't you talk with this new guy if he's nice? I know you don't mention a guy unless you're somehow attracted."

"He makes me mad. No, he makes me nervous around him. He's shy too, so it's not his fault."

"Kady, if I could give you boy advice I would. Back in Dalhart, Texas boys were either wranglers without brains or Pentecostals praising the Lord. I left them alone so they'd leave me alone. Bontecott was older, even then, and from up north. I wanted to leave the dusty streets of Depression Dalhart. Not much choice between the glass cases of colored stones inside daddy's jewelry store and mom's excitement over cowflops and horses."

"We didn't exactly find high society up north, did we? Either in Old Saybrook or Millbrook."

"No, nor wanted it all that much. Wish I could work more. Have enough pain-free days to do home decorating again. Get out on a regular basis. Plan room schemes and think in patterns, fabrics, and textures. That was my life up north."

Kady saw Morpheys walk by, smile, flick the booth glass as he cracked open the door. Kady turned away, smiling too, in case he stopped to talk. He left quickly, pulling a wool skullcap over his ears and wet hair. Kady told her mom, she'd wait a couple minutes and ask if he wanted a ride.

"You might be polite and ask before he walked into the cold."

"I could, but he'd ask to start the car, and I'd have to ask him every night and day. I don't want that."

"Well go ahead, and do it your way. You always do, like Bontecott. Call tomorrow and tell me what happened."

"Okay mom. Try the motrin again. See if it works without wrecking your stomach."

Kady hustled into her warm coat, started the car, and let it warm up while she rushed back for the recital program. Wonder if Morpheys liked Bach? She liked the contrapuntal music. Pulling onto the road she saw the full moon over Lake Cayuga. It looked weird with the wind swirls in the stark lunar light. If he was halfway, she'd inch up behind him. He was nowhere in sight. She got to the Inn. If he ran all the way, he couldn't be here. Kady went in to see if he drank a beer at the bar. Over near the window she saw Deb with a few band guys and Kallini. They waved her over.

"Deb, you see Morpheys come in?"

"No, how come? After basketball, he refused a ride back and walked. He wanted to see the lake. He hoped the snow blew back along the beach leaving a place to walk. You see him play ball?"

"Good at the game. Frosted to death when he returned."

Kady gazed along the lake below the Inn windows. She saw the wide expanse of moonlit waters, hypnotic in their somber sweep, and she saw a solitary walker casting a shadow. Morpheys made his way along the Cayuga beach. The raving lunatic, she'd give him a talking to at dinner.

Then he wasn't there. She talked to Jesse about chamber music. Music at the recital worked a tone poem by Debussy. La Mer was beautiful. Then the bass violin played a somber solo from a Bach piece and she looked back and saw Morpheys staring as if the sonorous complaint shook him up. The look became all too familiar. He'd heard the viola piece in a Bergman film, where the wife returns to the asylum, troubled by visions. He had a Jewish neighbor play the same piece in a Long Pond cabin. Morpheys was ten years old. Talk about a song getting to you. He left after the solo, back to the library to read Rimbaud and write a poem he worked on with the moon, the lake, and the windy night.

For days Morpheys said nothing to her. Kady saw him in classes and heard he played ball every day and saw him once on a library couch beneath a lake window in the winter sun, fast asleep. Whatever he did then, didn't concern her. He was weirdly in his own world. What she told her mom when she called Thursday. Her mom saw the doctor, who questioned her sanity. Male doctors made her mad.

14

Marxist Party

Kallini made the Thursday session for RYM. Josh Steen in his full beard said maybe they'd forgive and forget if he made the scene. Else they'd come for him. Kallini sat in the empty room. All the furniture of Quinn's apartment removed for the meeting on this hilly main street of Cornell. Furniture packed in the garage like padding for a cellar bomb about to explode. In came folding chairs, stacked around the carpet, around Quinn's armchair where he sat in a long Nehru shirt and shades. He worked down cellar right up to the meeting.

Blacks from the Union at 320 Wait didn't show. Kallini got blamed. Since Kallini sent Lionel to Oakland, no other blacks wanted SDS help. With Zimbawe they'd gone more radical. No more Black-White connection. Not until this Revolutionary Youth Movement proved they could take pressure off the Panthers. Bring the war home. Fight the pigs patrolling Amerika's Black colony. Kallini heard the rhetoric before, but now it was gospel, slogan, and song. HO HO HO. Mao Mao Mao. He figured since the takeover of the Economics building and King's assassination the Black Union was on its own. Call its own shots. Why he sent Lionel west. Let RYM wither on the vine. More serious business shifted to GI Resistance.

He knew people in the group from Oakland, Moratoriums, and Chicago, some of them back to the beginning. But those rich enough to continue into their twenties took radicalism to an extreme. It became one more drug, like sex, like music, like all the psychedelics. Burn, Charlie, Dier, Quinn, even Rawley Johnson from Lawrence, Kansas, they all tried to be like Che, or Fidel, or Ho. They quoted Mao's redbook and Stalin. It was the Thirties' schism all over again. Everyone more radical, everyone the party line. Marxism ruled after peace, love, and participatory democracy wore out.

Kallini's back muscles pulled up tight and his leg thrummed with pain. Like he was on trial. Big room, expensive Persian, no Blacks, kids off the street, chicks with fists, and empty chairs. Quinn stared across the room at him. No more consensus. More splinter groups, more arrests, more violence made the high. Until felonies stacked up and radicals fled underground. Cadres of trained Marxists, bombers, hit and run. Kallini saw it like a prophecy. Further left they go, better for Nixon to dump all the blame on them. Repression coming. The war come home.

He knew Quinn meant to call him out. The RYM-rockers meant to excommunicate him. If he kept Joshua Steen he might weather the storm. Josh worked the Cornell CO program for conscientious objectors. Resistance against the draft got more difficult with a 19 year old lottery serving the army. Now they had to turn the army itself against the war in Vietnam. Connect the coffeehouses on each base of the armed forces. Quinn refused any partial reforms. All show for the Blacks, as the whites started another front here inside the Black colony of Amerika.

Kurt tried to defend himself against Quinn the Eskimo and manage a stand-off. Compromise solution was a curseword, language of politics opprobrium, and business the unforgivable sin. Stalemate coupled with ambivalence his possible ploy. Kallini could no longer rumba with the new regime, toking up, ganging up, putting on black faces of Panther brothers who rejected them as lily white, well off, sons and daughters, beyond anyone's command. RYM-rockers made ready for street fighting with the pigs.

Kallini straightened his crippled back, hobbled on a short leg over to Quinn's armchair, with his roll-ups of Acapulco gold, stuff Kallini stashed in his guitar case for leaving this scene. He removed Quinn the Eskimo's shades to his icy blue eyes. Like Quinn had the pale albino in his genes, his real name Luther Rene.

"Who among you casts the first stone?"

"Kallini, sit my man, we're all of us here good and stoned."

"Who among you doubts the FBI infiltrates our ranks, that the person toking next to you, he's the nark who nabbed your brother or your sister, and tells you, cool dude, fire the building, explode the bomb, and come with guns to riot in the streets?"

The groovy chick, Burn baby burn, came up to Kallini from behind and coupled both fists around his chest.

"You know me all too well Kallini. Time to get it on. Get on the riot gear and swing back to Czechago with all our rage."

Kallini managed to swing in her arms, while she held him up, and come back at her.

"One swinging revolution. One burning spear thrown. One wargasm shared. Rage against the pigs and warmongers and bring Vietnam home. But how do we know who's with us? How do we know who's really radical and who's really FBI. It's Nixon now. All the tricks. No more liberals to disappoint us. We know the new Nixon, he's the same old pig and the person next to you owns your file."

Burn took Quinn's shades for her own dark look, overfull Irish body and brunette hair, chick who slept with everybody like guys did and didn't give a shit who knew. She did her dance for Kallini. Who barely managed to keep his feet. But Prairie SDS'ers, from Texas to Kansas, for whom joining SDS meant taking a beating in their hometown, it was all or nothing. Rawley Johnson responded for them to Kallini's summons.

"So how do we flush out the infiltrator?"

"Rawley, let me tell you," She turned on him. "We screw them over. Drop tons of acid. Make them run the streets and throw teargas back at the pigs."

"Right on, sister. Let's start our own revolution."

Quinn wanted his shades back.

"Hey, what's Kallini trying to prove? That he's more radical. That he doesn't need to know which way the wind blows."

Kurt Kallini knew the trick of infiltrating the Movement.

"Just a weather report. So we know who stands with us and who collects info for the pigs."

Quinn took his shades from Burn. He wanted to get back to briefcases in the cellar. More and more he wanted his dark plans for apocalyptic death. The end to company. No one to speak to him of Dow and Dupont, and better living through chemicals. No more calls for Quinn the Eskimo. Make bombs, not sheets of LSD.

"Come on Quinn, groove together, fight together, make love together. You tell a pig because he can't party down the revolution."

"Burn's no fool," Rawley said.

"Nobody's fool, but yours."

"Burn, your sweetness I can't forget."

Kallini took his seat hoping this meeting blew itself up in smoke. Cadre groups spurned rational discourse. Like these rich, cursed kids could screw the revolution into another sphere of street violence. Take it higher. Take it mightier. Make its meaning, cosmic. Revolutionary highs where violence begets violence, wargasms of iniquity, targets of their parents offspring: corporate offices, banks, arms research on campus, and ROTC buildings. Their willing accomplices: street gangs, high schoolers, Vietnam vets on guilt trips, anyone with a grudge, without work, ready to wreck havoc since everyone was a target, most of all, themselves.

Rawley did his dance around Burn, Baby. He slapped a black hat to his thighs. Burn did her dervish of a dance right back at him. Joshua Steen amplified the scene with White Panther music from MC5, Kick out the Jams, mother___. Quinn rolled joints out of a machine, out of habit, passed by twenty hands, spread to a ceiling high with smoke, a cellar of bomb manufacture, a garage packed with an apartment's padded furniture. They were tight, solid, and packed to explode.

Joshua Steen cut the record and the livingroom echoed, raunchy smell of dope, heavy in too little space, party atmosphere. It was another diversion.

"We ought to have a marriage here. Like Arthur and Morgana, like Samson and Delilah to pull down the temple walls. Connect the plains cowboy with the Czechago chick and let the bastard baby kill or be killed in racist Amerika. Let it be a revolutionary wedding."

It was Josh trying to fit in with the new order. His maiden speech to this parliament of fools. Somebody from the way out West who saw dramatic theatre with its brief hour upon the stage, when words would be heard no more. Burn kissed her swinging cowboy, Rawley Johnson, and Blue Moon offered to minister to the couple. A last SDS rite before they took to the streets and the new year. They decided to drive all night to be at Nixon's inauguration.

"Dearly beloved we are gathered here."

Josh Steen put on Marrying Maiden. Brother and sister in harmony with violins. A Beautiful Day in flames with the whitest of winters in western New York.

"Anyone here who can say why this couple can do no wrong?"

It was a rep from PLP. One with the slight mustache. One with Marxist rhetoric for all occasions, and the straight look of an FBI infiltrator.

"What kind of sentimental crap, what kind of bourgeois bullshit are we here to witness?"

"Lighten up Bucky. It's all a put on, it's all a gag."

"No more marriages, Josh Steen. Only cadres of street fighting men."

"And women."

"Mao Mao Mao, marriage has got to go."

It was the minister of Maoist persuasion. Youth brigade to defrock all the ceremonious BS. Drown out logic without logic.

"No more marriages. No more children. Look at Quinn the Eskimo. Is he the 4th or 5th generation of this racist, manipulative, corporate killing machine, which bankrolled every war of the 20th Century. From the Philippines to Chateau Thierry, from oil fields to napalm in Vietnam. Guilt grows worse every generation. So it's a crime. This marriage is a crime. The offspring of this marriage is a crime. Because every white baby grows up to another link in the chemical chain, connecting Quinn with Dow Chemical. No more white babies. No more marriage."

"Shut up your puritanical rant."

Burn gave the Harvard Marxist a flip of her skirt over her behind. And Blue Moon blessed her indignity.

"You heard the logic. Admit the guilt."

"Go back to Boston, will ya, asshole."

It was Rawley standing up for his Irish lass. And Bucky did leave for DC and serious street protest with his fellow PLP. He let the twain be broken between him and SDS, least this Action Faction of the RYM-rockers.

Kurt Kallini and Joshua Steen sat through the mock wedding. Who wouldn't cherish a kiss from this bride? Only Quinn the Eskimo whose supply of LSD equaled Mosley on the West Coast. Quinn descended into his cellar refuge, chilled by company. Least Kallini managed to leave on terms of community. And he knew the FBI found the SDS refuge, from Czechago on. Agents in hip costume and righteous rhetoric reported what went down. Kallini had other business with his Uncle Carlo, support the GI Resistance, as campus uprisings reached a winter of discontent.

15

Winter Meltdown

Friday in class Morpheys sat by Kady, both of them down low, back against the wall at the couch-end. He had his thin copy of Rimbaud.

"Read this," he whispered to her. "C'est retrouve. Quoi? L'eternite. C'est la mer melee au soleil."

Kady nodded to him. "Tres bon."

"Rimbaud had visions. Cathedrals for factories. Eternities like a chip of moon cutting ice."

"You've been scarce after hours."

"Walks along the lake. Nights hiding out in the library."

"You're here to learn French."

"And read Rimbaud, to write you a poem."

Kady looked over at Trixie, happily sipping her latte, and telling Deb she dreaded her mom's arrival. Jesse listened without caring. Her brother called from Chase in the city. No one bothered with Morpheys rambling on.

David tapped a knuckle and thumb to his French grammar.

"Dig this."

Waters murmur to the moon,
Singing like a scythe,
Wintry silent tune,
Black and blue skies,
Swooning far too soon,
All that's dead has died,
Oh clair de lune,
Oh prodigal time.

"I like your style."
"I like the way your freckles shade the same color as your straw

blond hair, when you're surprised with something. The freckles darken when you're mad. Smile again and I'll translate Baudelaire."

"You're putting me on."

"No, I'm serious. It kills me I can't write you one good poem. Get the visions inside my head down on paper. Lose the nightmares, keep the dreams."

"You got clair de lune and prodigal time. Work on it."

"Work to wear away the rough edges of time until eternity."

Now she couldn't stop laughing, less shy, more amused. He played with words like he played sports.

"You this corny with Deb and Jesse, or Dana Dupont?"

Again Kady spied on the gathering, but no one cared they conversed in words charged like songs.

"You like to talk lit, don't you Morpheys?"

"Yes, when it makes time stand still, and mystifies the moment. An illumination succeeds, if it seeds the fields of time, momentarily. A sunny vision into Platonic caves of ice to melt the time between, then till now till eternity."

"Too weird for words."

"I'm working on your poem."

"Why?"

"To charm you. To make time prodigal with possibility."

"Well don't."

Mme. Rochelle never showed up so Mamselle got on with lab exercises. Repetitions got easier for Morpheys. He made real progress in a week. Class moved swiftly this Friday. During the 10:30 break students wandered outside to the veranda. Sun surfaced patches of grass below the snow. Aurora crackled with winter thaw. Temperatures steamed with spring…40-50-60 degrees warm. Students in shirtsleeves took coffee toward lawnchairs long bellied up in snow. Mamselle had trouble enticing them back.

To celebrate the winter thaw David and Deb winged a frisbee. Overweight Walter waltzed onto the lawn, wanting Kady to join them. It was a meltdown. Snow sizzled on the firepan into trinkets of tiny streams. Sun blazed like a warm smile, like the four Cartwrights of Bonanza burning onto center screen. Lawn grew misty green. Kady gave in. She ran wild as she had in prep school, as if her athletic grace made not only her heart beat faster but the sun burn brighter, and earth turn in tune to her fleet steps.

Mamselle heard by phone, let them go, and stirred by the high noon whistle she yelled "La liberte pour vous." Students cheered her. Mamselle's shy face smiled with her one warm reception. Walter called for a timeout. David turned to walk the waterfront to campus, and Kady waved to him with winded breath to ask where he went.

"Up the shore. Come along?"

"Sure," she said, coughing, catching her breath.

Her face flushed, scattered with freckled punctuation. Hair dribbled in curls over her grass green eyes.

"Did you see Mamselle beam like an idiot?"

"Yes, I was happy for her. She shared the excitement of one insanely nice day. And you Miss Athletics, what a whirling dervish you are, reveling in the frisbee spin. Sing music of the spheres and run with cosmic dance."

"Morpheys, the more you try to annoy me, the less I listen."

"I'm trying to charm you."

"Words are no more real than one sunny day."

"One's enough."

"And the exertion. For a week my elbow hurts."

"An eternity of damnation for a moment in paradise. Baudelaire."

"I want a smoke, a beer, and someplace to sit down. Then when I'm breathing normal again."

"Normal is not natural. You've been hiding athletic grace. You need to anticipate the dawn of cosmic dance, by practice and practice, and …"

"More practice," Kady responded. "Like the nutcase I had for track coach."

"Miss Athletics, I knew it. Coaches are abusive, but sports are wonderful."

"I need a smoke."

David reached in Kady's jacket for her Dunhills, and put them in his own. She grabbed his wrist like he sneaked a feel.

"The smoke of dreams. Let every woman be her own coach. Find the freedom of sport and it will set you free."

"Morpheys, don't piss me off. Running was fun, but don't pester me. You don't know sports at the Bennet School."

"Never the sport, always the coach."

Kady wanted to say, far enough, and leave Morpheys to wander the shores alone.

"Like sports are good for the new kid in school. "

"You, the new girl everybody wants to know?"

"Not close. Most traumatic year in my life, the switch from Old Saybrook."

She lit the Dunhill for which she almost bashed him. They stood near an ice age boulder like a burden nobody lifted.

"Kids can be cruel."

"What a horrible year. The ratty, stuck-up girls. The cold reception. At fourteen I was tall, gawky, with a face full of freckles. Not very sociable either. Running hurdles wasn't sport, it was work. Coach said it gave me a graceful figure as he winked at the debs. I survived. My mother didn't."

"Your mom?"

David laid a hand on her elbow where she hurt. She drew on her cigarette, ran fingers through her hair, and looked for flat stones as they walked along.

"My mom got colon cancer."

"Why you're so close to her."

The back lawns of the Aurora Inn came into view. Kady saw the debs on the porch in their best dresses. Like a summer regatta.

"I was her nurse for the five years she survived cancer. God-willing, she's better now. She finds days when menopause and arthritis let her live a life. I won't burden you Morpheys with any Catholic stuff. It's not cool to consider one's faith."

"It's cool you and your mom are close."

Kady took him by an arm like an escort.

"I wish faith meant a little more to me, but it doesn't."

"Damned atheist, aren't you Morpheys?"

"I suppose. You know Hudson Park, not far from Millbrook. We had a few girls in school that rode horses with the Roosevelt girl out there. Otherwise, prep school was pretty remote to us guys. God too."

"You're kidding."

"Football ruled our lives for Saturday's glory. Full grandstands of green and gold, mobbed and screaming, Touchdown! Touchdown! I still hear the echoes in waves on the shore. Hard to have God when you already got the power and the glory. Hard to have religion when football rules one's life and then is heard no more."

The girls waved to them from the white-laced balconies, especially Trixsie. Kady let go Morpheys' arm. They lifted magnums of champagne and clinked fine crystal to the beachcombers.

"The past stays with us," Kady said.

"The future too."

"Want to share the sun with the debs?"

He shook his head.

"Little room for Kady Bontecott at the Inn of social graces. And none for you, Morpheys."

"Go up if you want. I'd as soon walk on."

Kady took up his arm again.

"They're Millbrook types, all of them. Smile all rouge and lipstick and stab you in the back. Sit with their well-dressed moms, whom they despise, and drink champagne. Bitches, all of them, mothers and daughters both."

"Let the past go."

"Not me, Morpheys."

"I'd embarrass you in the fancy restaurant."

"Probably, with your cosmic dances and musical spheres. I'll take you to the Fargo, where far out hardly matters, least in Aurora."

David liked her. This Bontecott girl whose father fired his own. A big fight sent him packing. Dad said little more. He didn't mind farming, but no one owned him at IBM. Coincidence, this encounter with Kady.

The Fargo stood in stark contrast to the Inn. Girls at the Inn brought their rich parents and well-groomed guys to share cocktail talk and dinner courses. Only place not sedate was down cellar where the bands played. No frills dining at the Fargo. Outside stairs climbed above the garage pumps into two deep parallel rooms. One with spagetti cloths on the tables. The other with lacquered bar, TV, and pool table. Local kids lived at the Fargo, except for the townies in the band.

Kady chose a table looking over Lake Cayuga. David ordered two beers.

"Let me buy, I invited you."

"You buy next."

In return she offered him a long goldmarked cigarette. She cupped the match. A Dunhill cigarette milder than the Marlboro that scarred his lungs. Smooth luxury called up drinks like sloe gin and cherry pipe tobacco. He stared at the red and gold box, imported for the crown, LTD.

"Hey Morpheys, you're slipping off again?"

"To a Paris cafe, where a factory mirrors a cathedral, in the sparkle of sun on the lake waters. Puts one in a mood."

"Why the fuss with words?"

David shook his head and drank his beer.

"Me, I return to the Bennet School, to tutor until they let me teach. It's a job and probably a life. But Apollinaire and Rimbaud mean little more to me than Ronsard and Racine."

"But a little more."

"A line here and a poem there strike me as unusual."

"That's all?"

"God, Morpheys. Quit the Socratic questions. It pisses a person off. I asked what poetry means to you."

"A little more than sport, that's all."

Kady gave him the look she reserved for the society bitches. He was trying her patience. Calling on her to make an act of faith, as if once in her life for her mom, was not enough.

The one act of faith, from age 14 on, gave her patience to endure the prep girls and the guys who wanted one small part of her to reflect their performance. She refused. She endured sports with its stretching, laps, minute attention to steps before the hurdles and footing afterwards. She listened for some truth in the pulse and heartbeat and body bent forward into a headwind.

Then the girls basking in teen adoration and cosmetics found cracks in their confidence. Kady listened to their anxious confessions, guys and girls alike, and discovered this caste with cool connections, which built a wall to keep her out, crumbled to pieced together personalities. Kady learned her one act of faith made her in one way special. She was self-sufficient, she and her mom.

"Calling Kady, come back to me."

He put a hand over hers. She playfully removed her hand to slap his own.

"Then tell me why all the poetry."

"Kady, some poems punch a hole through the dull canvas skies. Through these rents in the social fabric come starlight and more permanent existence. A line of Rimbaud and a life of Francois Villon, prodigal with possibility. With the power and grace of a football game, without all the hoopla."

"Like poetry."

"Exactly."

"Sounds nice, David."

"It does."

"Like staring off into space."

"Else it's all material pursuit of sleeker cars, larger homes, and greater security. Nothing really. What's that French cliche?"

"Metro-boulot-dodo."

"Car, work, and sleep, that's it. Nothing, without L'eternite, la mer melee au soleil."

"No alternative?"

"None. The mad pursuit of bourgeois success, nothing. A better job and a better night's rest."

"It's a life."

"No, I don't think so."

"Then sports ruined you too."

"You think?"

"I'm kidding."

"Well, when sport fails to punch a hole and pour in poetry to the soul, then the eternal spirit sleeps. The big sleep."

"It's a life to me, David. Be a teacher. Then a wife and mother. I don't want illusions."

"You must."

"Why deceive yourself?"

"One must envision a life worth living. Then live it. Punch a hole in the dull canvas skies. Let in starlight above the tent of suburban streetlamps every four homes. If visions, then the rigmarole, the Metro-boulot-dodo, can be god-guided and magnanimous as the human condition."

"Try leaving God out of it, you atheist."

"Call the hole poetry punches through, God. Or the vision of God."

"I'm a Catholic, Morpheys. No mystic in search of meaning."

"Okay. Call the appeal of poetry, or the quest for philosophy, an act of faith."

"I can't make it, again."

The jangling door stopped their discussion. Kady turned to the husky boy and said, "Hi Don."

"Hi Kady. You guys coming to the Inn tonight?"

"Your big date with destiny. You guys are good."

"We're good, but we have to practice and tighten our sets. Kurt Kallini's good."

"He sings well."

"Not beautiful like you, but good. Bring your friend tonight."

"Sit down and meet David. David, this is Don."

David grasped the power handshake from Don, and said, "What's happening?" Don reminded him of his friend, Joey Gallo, the same sturdy build, and belly undoing the bottom shirt button. Joey ran his dad's Italian restaurant and played in his band TRAX, since ninth grade in high school.

"Hey have a beer with us."

David went to get the three bottles. Don worked in the ball bearing factory in Auburn. He said it was cool to study French and go to Paris. A second beer flushed a warm glow to Kady's freckles and elevated David.

"Shall we eat lunch?" Kady asked.

"Before we get stewed and stay all afternoon."

"Drive you two up to campus?"

They tottered, hands to the railing, downstairs into the fresh air and Don's fabulous Olds 88. The Cruiser when it worked, the Bruiser when the car failed. Don dropped them off on the square, surrounded by the brick and ivy buildings of Wells College.

The January sun cooked the lawns near 70 degrees.

"Want to see the Wells waterfall?"

"Sure. Skip lunch and live on a beer diet."

They passed the modern library cut into the mountain above the college square. Its cubist layers and jagged angles the abstract picture of mountain ledges. Modernity contrasted with the Federal style and also with the rolling hills banked off the finger lake. Across the playing fields David's feet raced ahead of him. He turned, detached from Kady. She shook her head, waved a forefinger, and said Non-Non-Non, a thousand times Non. Then she laughed.

"Okay coach, if running makes me graceful for the guys."

She paced like a fawn, easy and tall, across the meadow and through trees to a clearing in the woods. Moldering grass and leaves mulched the banks. Smell of melting earth scented like spring air. David heard the roar of raging waters from the meltdown. The falls angled the stream sharply around the mountain. A huge oak pinioned across the falls and a sturdy branch hung pendant over the abyss.

"You like the waterfall?"

"You recall me knocking on your pipes to compliment your singing?"

"Don't remind me, Morpheys."

"I had a nightmare of pouring rain, driving with a madman, and skidding off a bridge into waters like these below. Your singing saved me."

"Get off it."

"Really, another nightmare last night. I woke and wrote you that rhyme."

"You want visions, you want an act of faith, what you get is ten times worse," Kady told him.

"Don't I know it. Last night I checked out a mansion like the Wells Library. Like someone's estate beside a roaring stream like this one. Cathedral ceiling, dormer hallways, everywhere weird books and paintings and backyards of gardens glassed in all weathers. Like a library, like colleges seeking curious ideas, keeping artifacts too special for a Hudson Park boy. So I left. I saw what I saw, returned to my dad's car, his Ford Galaxy, knowing the mansion was far beyond me. Then you came running out, worried your father saw me inside, saying he can't see you here, and I said what's the matter Kady, I'm looking for you. You said you knew, but he can't see you here. I could barely hear you. The stream beside the mansion roared like this one over the waterfall."

"You want dreams, you get nightmares."

A strange mood stirred David. Almost a physical exhilaration as during football, him quarterbacking the team downfield, each play completed with power and precision. Today was different. This electric current connected the two of them. So different from his mental doldrums the past year. Times hopeless to an extreme, reading Dostoyevsky and Kierkegaard, searching for the abyss and the absolute bottom. This high felt physical and refreshing. They could do no wrong. The effective cause was Kady Bontecott. He walked on the branch above the abyss. Waters plummeted below.

"Here we are Kady. Waters of a life run by. This tree, bridging the stream, offers a view of the future, for a few moments magically time-free. Below us rumbles the abyss over which we feel more alive, the closer we tempt our fate. Let us tempt our fate. Let us make an act of faith."

Kady shook her head and waved her forefinger Non-Non-Non, a thousand times no. She had gone to the other side and beckoned him over. "Come on, let's go."

But she returned. She reached for his hand. Two of them perched above the falls spooked David. He held her hand and walked with her. Then kissed Kady on the lips, thanking her.

"Sorry, I nearly lost it with the rush of salvation below. Whatever that means."

He let go her hand. They smiled. It was a shared pleasure. They cut up through the dark harvest of pine trees, the floor soft and scented with evergreen needles. Another rise and David rushed up and around to ambush her, a childhood game of hide and seek, lost in the woods, lost in love with her. Kady enjoyed the diversion. Open before them swept the winter stubble of a farmer's cornfield. Across the long rows came a country road, and around the bend a Baptist church. Then the vineyards for grapes and wine of western New York.

They followed the road back down to the lake route and walked nearly five miles back to the French House. Kady's skin chapped red as a chill returned with late afternoon. Her freckles whitened the same sunny blond as her hair. The sun fired west over the lake, bright red and flaming out with dusk. Winter returned as if never gone. Kady heated coffee and then soup on her hotplate. She asked David if he wanted to hear Howling Wolf in his London session with the Stones. Kurt Kallini gave her the record. KK on the cover.

"Perfect end to a perfect day," David said.

He listened to the deep bluesy growl, pounding drums, Jagger's responsive vocals, and the screeching and soaring as Wolf and Mic Jagger traded riffs. Perfect except for this guy, Kurt Kallini, with black hair and beard, smoldering eyes, and brows that bunched. Kallini came to Kady's room before him.

"Kady, what's Kallini to you?"

Soon as he said it Morpheys knew it was the wrong question. Like her asking about Dana Dupont. But he told her everything because Dana meant nothing to him.

"He slept with my roommate, Barb Kelly. Him coming on to me, it gave me the creeps. I told him to get lost. Later he apologized. He came by the Townhouse and suggested I listen to his blues albums. He likes to talk about serious things, sort of like you."

"Where's he from?"

"He went to Berkley a few years back and works in some capacity at Cornell. Maybe with the movement. He comes and goes."

"His eyes look right through a person. First I saw him there was a resemblance between the two of you. Something in the mold of the face. Crazy right? First time here, I saw each of you for five minutes and I got this impression. Another dream my first night."

"It's weird too. Don, seeing me and Kurt together in the Fargo said, "You two look like brother and sister, him dark and you light."

Then Kallini said, "You see what you see, but don't believe your eyes."

"Can't fault his music."

"You should come to the Inn and hear them play."

"You mind I tag along?"

"Please do, David Morpheys."

16
Barb Kelly Calls

"Kady, C'est la telephone pour vous."

Mamselle came upstairs and knocked on the door. David leaped to silence the record player, and Kady pulled the plug.

"Jesus, I forgot to call my mom. That's her."

Kady saw David atop the stairs and then heard Barb Kelly's crying voice on the phone. Her face drained. She knew Barb made a big mistake.

"It can't be all that bad."

"How can I come back? I haven't a penny to my name."

"Well if it's that bad, have Lionel drive you."

"Lionel's in way over his head."

"Kurt Kallini said Lionel had business. That lying creep said you were fine."

"Kady, I'm not. All these black guys have guns and they're getting ready for Armageddon. That's what they say. Pigs gone to poke their heads in here any day now. I'm scared, Kady. Lionel's such a preppie he doesn't belong. You got to help me Kady. I got myself in bad."

"Call your parents and ask for airfare, at least to St. Louis."

"I can't. Go home and it won't be 24 hours before Mr. Eyes-of-God knows I'm pregnant. Dealing with my dad's no better than Lionel and this whole Panther thing. Kady, what can I do, you got to tell me."

"I'll go talk to Kallini. He told you and Lionel it was cool out there and it's not. He's got to do something. If he won't do shit I'll fly there myself. I'll bring you home if Kallini won't."

Kady was crushed. She made Barb a promise and what was she going to do? Few times had she really done something. Going to Paris was once and she wasn't there yet. Three thousand miles away to Oakland. Lionel was a creep, but not a bad guy. Just a black preppie from Rye Country Day, who turned colors at Cornell. Barb swore it was all

Kallini's work, behind the scenes. Kady was crushed.

David sat on the stairs staring at her.

"How can I help?"

Kady wondered how poetry, frisbee, and finessing the abyss translated into action. Invite him to fly with her to the coast? Or ride there in her VW? She thought not. Kallini made things happen, David didn't.

"Let's go to the Inn," she said to him.

The two of them grabbed coats and got into the VW. Winter thaw languished in the sinking sun over Lake Cayuga. Pungent vegetation still sweetened the air. It lingered on physically like desire. More a memory than meaningful. More a moment ago than time today. Button the brown suede and the Navy blue as the air shivered with sharp wind.

"Where did our day go?" David asked.

Kady gave him the godawful look he saw first picking up her huge canvas bag. She hurried and he held her back. Did she miss Barb Kelly because of him? Was this all his fault?

"I got to see Kallini. He better help Barb out. This is all his doing and goddamn he better do something."

Gone, gone, gone, David said to himself. He was along for the ride. An intruder in her car. Better keep his mouth shut. Otherwise, she'd freak out.

The band practiced downstairs for the weekend gig. Townhouse girls started the weekend early. Empty longnecks lit candles on the tables.

"Hey Morpheys, you cut out on basketball," Deb yelled.

He waved to girls he knew.

"Yeh, we played at the outside rim, you believe it? Kady, you're chalk white."

"I got to talk to Kallini."

"Don't even try," Deb warned. "Anybody says boo to him he goes ballistic. Don comes in a beat too early, or Lloyd forgets a chord change, he's all over them. Kallini wanted to kill Tim Burt when he left with his girl. He wants him out of the band."

Kady didn't care. Barb Kelly was her best friend. She grabbed

Kallini's hand, which jolted him around. He stared at her. The Nietzsche scowl of bushy eyebrows. His temper ticked like a bomb with imperfect music.

"Kurt, I need your help."

"Later Kady," he said, staring without turning toward her. He kept the one two three four beat with his free hand. Kady held on.

"Kallini, I need you now. Barb Kelly called, crying and about to go crazy with that Lionel creep you sent with her to the coast."

"I know her predicament."

Kallini slanted his fender bass to the floor, his eyebrows like ropes. Kady held on tighter, frightened for Barb and careless of his temper.

"Then do something about it. You owe Barb that much."

Kady and Kallini took center stage. Kallini kept a beat with drums and chords into his bass rhythm, prior to singing. He ignored Kady. He started singing the song directing the band.

Then he slammed his bass to the stage, wham with amped effect. Kady's white bird withdrew into his shadow. He looked at her speaking into the mike.

"I've done something about Barb Kelly, damn't. Now do something for your mom."

"My mom! What's my mom to you?"

Kady spoke half as loud as Kallini, but she was shouting at him and he at her.

"Barb Kelly called your mom because she couldn't reach you. Nobody knew where you were today. Your mom's going to Columbia Presbyterian for tests, so you got her to worry about. I took care of Lionel and Barb. They'll both be at Berkley. Both out of the line of fire. Both safe, secure, and back in school."

Kallini stepped back from the bellowing mike to stop the echoes.

"I didn't know my mom went to NYC for tests."

Kallini took her to the sliding glass doors. Last glare of sun streaming over Cayuga, their two profiles silhouetted.

"Listen, I'll take care of Barb Kelly, I promise. Even if I have to fly tonight to Oakland and bring her home. You probably know she's pregnant. Something her and Lionel need to work out. Give them a chance. That was one reason they took off for the coast."

"Did Barb want to go, or did you tell her to go?"

"Lionel wanted her to go. Let me deal with this mess. Your mom needs you, so give her a call. Let this cross-country soap opera work itself out, okay?"

Kady spun around, flustered. Her mom called and Kallini took care of Barb Kelly. Well he better. The right wires pulled her back to her parents. Where duty calls.

As Kady left for the phone, Kallini signaled to David Morpheys.

"Come on up here. You mind trying the chord changes on Sympathy for the Devil? Lloyd needs backing on the beat once he starts a lead. It's 4 beats on E, 4 on D, 4 on A, and back to 4 beats on the E chord. Simple as that. No Mike Bloomfield needed."

David's hands sweat and he dove them into his pockets. Lloyd strapped him into a Squire Strat. The Fender amp had two channels. Kallini kept his eye on him, and his free hand accented the beats. Four to sixteen again and again. David engulfed in the heavy sound reverb. He overheard his chords out there in the echo. Kallini stepped to the mike and started the song one more time.

Kady listened to a few verses. She waved to David, on the way to her car. Her halfhearted smile. David couldn't drag himself away. He'd always wanted to be in a band. Chord changes cooked a powerful drug with wailing all around. Like surfing a wave at Long Beach Island. In a center of a storm, which blows on by. And this was only practice.

During a break he ran back to the French House to catch Kady Bontecott. Tell her what it was like and find out what she planned to do. Things moved fast. Kady posted a note on her door.

"Bye Morpheys, be back Monday."

17
Kallini Works Wonders

"Kady, la telephone encore pour vous."

Mamselle shouted upstairs and David figured he better let someone know she was gone. Or maybe it was her. He couldn't hear what Mamselle said exactly. Maybe Kady called from down the road to set his heart at ease. She must be off to her mom's.

"Hello, David Morpheys here."

"I'm calling back for Kady Bontecott. Can you get her? I'm calling cross-country from Berkley and it's costing me a fortune."

"I'm her friend," David said. "Kady took off in her car. This is Barb Kelly, right?"

"You must be the elusive gent her mom told me about. The guy Kady's checking out."

"Well I'm her friend and willing. Hey I heard you weren't all that happy in California. Trouble in paradise?"

"Morpheys, I got myself stuck between a rock and a hard place."

"That's what I heard."

"I had no idea the revolution started. Black power with guns and pigs and more guns. I think Kallini got it straightened out."

"Kallini reaches out and presto, things are cool?"

"God that guy has long reach. He called this black dude at headquarters before he talks to Lionel. Kallini knows everybody. Whatever he said to Lionel got him hopping. He had us packed and moved out in an hour. Looks like we're living in Berkley, and next semester I'll wing a few art courses. Doodling's what I do."

"Then things are cool?

"Peachy keen."

"I can tell Kady if she calls, Barb's at Berkley and doing better."

"It still isn't paradise, but I'm fine as a fiddle. Glad to be out of that fix."

"Kady was worried. Ready to fly to the coast, that's a friend."

"No kidding! Remember what you said. So don't get upset with her and mom."

"They're close?"

"They're a pair. And Kallini's cool when he wants to be. You meet him?"

"Playing in his band I am."

"Luck then, dude."

"You'll call Kady?"

"For sure, and tell her big thanks. And tell her with my other problem, Episcopals can be as Catholic as Kady. You got God on your side Morpheys?"

"We talk long distance, like you and me."

"Not face to face?"

"When he calls."

"Again, be cool with Kady. Unless there's divine intervention, we'll keep ours a phone affair."

David laughed.

"Luck to you too."

"Peace."

David got back to the Inn fast and saw Kallini in the entrance light. He wanted to tell him everything worked out. As Kallini planned. There was a parked car of Cornell students.

"I only got a minute, Morpheys."

"Barb called to say everything was cool in Oakland and she's better off at Berkley."

"Girls cause a ruckus and they get a reaction. Barb got hers."

Kallini lit a smoke to lull his impatience. Jewish guy with an auburn beard and another with shades sat in the Fairlane. Longhairs looked the cross between drugdealers and Movement heroes. Not much difference.

"Barb's okay, now you fixed matters. Good going."

"Fix one thing and two others fall apart. Morpheys, you sit with Lloyd and Don and learn those chord changes. Lloyd can't do both, play rhythm and lead because he loses the beat. Take up the slack."

Kallini fingered his collar for the right button.

"Morpheys, I got business at Cornell. Black Union there and the Panthers in Oakland. Learn the songs and tell Tim Burt to go to hell. Takes work to do anything well. You know that."

"Hey man, we better go. Panthers mean to have our asses for their breakfast program. We got to deliver. Negotiate before it's too late."

Kallini gave David a half-hearted scowl, as if he were least of his worries.

"The chord changes to the songs, until they're second nature. We'll open next week instead."

Kallini was gone. Business, Black Panthers, and a band. A control freak among the flower children.

III
Whitebirds in Flight

18
Preps Got it Easy

David saw his big chance to be in a band. A whitebird of his imagination. Like football, like an education, like poetry, it solves everything for the time-being. If not longer. For one's very being suffers transfiguration. Then the normal life, whether Metro-boulot-dodo or material well being, rides a wave to an archipelago of islands awash in the greater ocean. Whitebirds of the imagination. No longer is one marooned on an island or landlocked on a continent. Freedom is a spiritual condition. Not free to do drugs, have sex, and rock around the clock. Not free to make big bucks and buy anything the heart desires. But freedom from excess of desire and cringing from fear. Live a life in touch with eternity. For the time-being.

Downstairs David worked with pimply Lloyd West. Heavy black glasses gave him a Buddy Holly look. Lloyd and Don let Kallini pester them because their one dream through school was to put together a band. They practiced doggedly. With Tim Burt they never got a gig and he got the girls. To them Kallini was gospel. When he told them they needed Morpheys, they taught him to play. Back on a team.

Lloyd let David take the Squire with him to practice chords. That's what he did. He strummed top bunk in the window over Lake Cayuga. Roommates made ready for Friday dinner at the Aurora Inn. Frat friends of Walter arrived from Colgate with plans to pick up chicks and get laid. Walter gave an abbreviated tale of the deer killed my car. He cut out Doug from the hick parts.

"And my brothers I thank you for coming to Wells and bringing me wheels to replace my GTO. Your wish is my command. Before we roll to the chicks at the Aurora Inn, let's talk."

Walter surveyed his roommates, guitar player and pipe smoker, and found them lacking.

"Doug, you don't mind. You know how frat meetings go. Nobody listens in. So take Morpheys, our longhair guitar-playing fool, and your wimpy Thunderbird up to campus. The library's open."

After the chatter of come-ons and T&A jokes, Walter cut loose Doug, who stuck his pewter pipe in his mouth and took off chagrined. The preps in blazers and ties reminded David of Babbitt boosters. Conformity of the frat mind annoyed him, and their money angered him. No concern for others or the world at large. Like a bluesman David broke free into the darkness, and Doug roared off in his silver Thunderbird.

He carried the Strat back to the Inn. Bluesman in the black night traveling Route 90. Cold was dry, and not uncomfortable. He sat in the cellar with a Schlitz longneck, strumming chords to the first set off songs. It was a juker night with no live band. Kallini was gone, and Tim Burt blamed him. An overflow of college rolls came downstairs. Girls like Deb and Trixsie came over to say hello.

"Kady's gone home, hey Morpheys."

"Sorry to skip b-ball today."

"I question your commitment."

"As you have every right to do. Deb, I'm sticking to it. Either you're in or you're out, and I'm in."

"Kady takes a shine to you."

"Think so?"

"Definitely. Only get used to her and her mom."

"That's what Barb Kelly said on the phone."

"She okay?" Trixsie asked.

David nodded, seeing Trixsie, better dressed than with debutants on the porch. Better cosmetics with her perfect nose, brunette hairdo, mascara eyes, and lips glossed. Another look and he saw why she was half asleep mornings. She rose at dawn to do her face and hair and clothes. With her it was cosmetic art.

"We Townhouse girls stick together."

"Don't let the frat guys tear you apart?"

"Trixsie likes the better frats, don't you?" Deb asked.

Walter shuffled over to introduce his frat brothers. One was goodlooking, with bootdockers and blazer, and already a bit drunk.

Boatdockers asked Trixsie to dance. Walter and his yachting buddy ignored Deb because she wasn't Trixsie. There was Steve Hancock from Hamilton.

Steve Hancock gave David an obligatory wave, as teammates a year ago. He had a kid's smile, good teeth, and bright eyes. He liked to be liked. He never took Morpheys as a threat, personally. Why should he? He got the quarterback position without a contest. Coach lodged him there. Senior had no real chance. Three freshmen came to try out. Coach said Steve had the better arm, and he played. Three seasons of losing football. Steve tossed the forty yard, down out and down, along the sideline, perfectly. Yet put no points on the board. He instilled no confidence. He failed to take charge, as if the team gave him support. He had the quarterback look. He had the Groton background. None of which counted. Except to the coach.

"Hey Morpheys, cool with the chicks, making time."

"Steve, rolling?"

"The brothers need a night out."

"Gathering of the AD's?"

"Sure thing, Colgate and Hamcoll. You still DKE?"

"No. Quit the frat and football."

"Too bad. Coach put the curse on you."

"One too many headbangers."

"Why I loft the football. Get it and throw it."

"Yea I know."

"Hey, who's the groovy chick?"

Jesse showed up and the brothers stared. It was her Goldie Hawn look. Petite, shortcut blond, small breasts in a pullover and jeans. Her profile was perfect as Trixsie, but she wasn't there to attract guys.

"What's up with Kady?"

"Gone home for a hospital run," Deb said.

"Be back Monday," David reported.

"Don't believe it, Morpheys. As likely Easter as next week."

"Not what her note said, Jesse."

"Every time Kady goes home for a holiday her mom's sick. It's this or that. Mom's not a hypochondriac. She's sick all right. Kady arrives at Wells and she has to call home, come home, and make a hospital run."

"But her mom's really sick?"

"Had cancer, has arthritis, and suffers in silence," Deb said.

"She's sick enough for nurses around the clock. Or Kady and her, together."

Jesse's sliver of an intelligent smile suggested sarcasm.

Deb confessed to David. "This is routine all through school. If Kady went to Vassar, she'd be living at home. Least here she has breaks."

"Her mom would be her Vassar roommate," Jesse quipped.

David stared at Jesse, always did, when he was with Dana Dupont. Her perfect body. Her quick wit. Lovely to kid her, be a buddy with her, and badly wish to cop a feel. Dana and him, same room, then the same bed, and Jesse there too. Steve Hancock stared at Jesse. Doug Bryant made it down cellar, piping cherry tobacco in his tweeds, and stared at Jesse, the perfect come-on girl.

"Barb Kelly said never get upset with Kady and her mom, they're a pair."

"Like us roommates," Deb said.

"A few years, sure, but a lifetime with your mom, come on."

"A lifetime sentence," Trixsie said, her arm tucked in her escort's arm. Guy with boatdockers.

"See her in Paris," Jesse said, "about February, enrolled in classes, settled in with her French family, and mom calls. Allo Kady, come home. My arthritis is killing me. Please fly home for a weekend. Be back Monday, right Morpheys? Home for a week…"

"Home for a month," Deb responded.

"Home forever," Trixsie said. Though Trixsie's mom never wanted her home. Too much competition.

David saw Steve Hancock put a hand on Jesse's shoulder.

"I think you're the prettiest girl here. Dance with me, baby."

"No thank you."

Jesse removed his hand.

"How long do you give Kady in Paris and Barb on the coast? Tell Morpheys, will you Deb."

"Kady has a week free after vacation. Let's give her a month in France. Barb's gone for good."

"And when does she come back, Morpheys?"

"Monday. Thus it is written."

"Monday, a week from now. Don't be naive."

Jesse kept talking, as the girls got a laugh, to make Morpheys wiser in the ways of Kady's world. He didn't believe a word they said. Guys don't take no for an answer.

Steve flicked his splash of blond hair off his forehead. He liked to be liked. He leaned over Jesse and returned his arm around her shoulder.

"Listen, let me buy you a drink. Whatever you want. Dinner if need be."

"Take your arm away."

"Baby, I'm going to stand here until you say yes."

The palm of his hand opened to say hi to the frat guys. Jesse grabbed his hand.

"Can't you hear we're having a conversation. I don't want a drink. I don't want a date. I don't want your hands on me. Get lost."

"Hey baby, let's share a table upstairs, you know, champagne, whore-durves, and our own conversation. What do you say?"

Again he waved his palm off Jesse's shoulder. Then Steve reached down and copped a feel.

Jesse squeezed his fingers until he winced in pain. He said ouch, bitch. He waved to the bro, returned his hand, and copped a second feel. Jesse pulled him down and punched her fist into his face. A welt bled on his cheek. Less confidence in his look.

"Call the campus hotline if you want a date. You want to get laid, go say hello to Candy by the jukebox. But leave me alone, goddamn't."

"What a bitch! What a lesbian bitch!"

He got Walter to inspect the welt under his eye. Walter said to cool it. Before they got thrown out of the Inn. Jesse shrugged, and went back to her conversation. Douglas stepped in.

"As a frat brother at ELS please accept Jesse's apology. She doesn't want to be with you. So be a gentleman."

Steve stared hard at Douglas with his tweeds and pipe. Then he glared at Walter to see who knew Douglas, and what the hell his problem was.

"Doug's my roommate here. But he's from Hamilton."

"Well he's an asshole. Let's try upstairs."

David played his Squire during the scene, a bit guilty he didn't take Jesse's part, like Doug did, a bit turned on too. Preps got it easy. Served Steve right to suffer and Jesse to smack him.

19
Kady and her Mom

Kady and her mom traveled to the City, like sisters, to see dinosaur bones in one museum and abstract expressionists in another. Kady's mom got her tests done. They waited for the results and a reading by the doctor. They chose a table at Mama Leones for antipasto and lasagna. Like they were Italians off the boat, Kady kidded her mom. Kady had Kallini in mind. As atypical a wine and spaghetti Italian as she could imagine. What would her Texan mom think of him? Or Morpheys if she bought him home? They passed days as tourists, seeing as much as possible, and shopping Fifth Avenue.

Thursday in the waiting room Kady wished to light up a Dunhill. Her mom wrung her knuckles, worried this doctor with tests in hand told her she had cancer again. Magazines plastered with Nixon, Vietnam, and flagwaving Americans. It was his inauguration. Kady read how Nixon planned to bring us all together, young and old alike, and recall the troops home with an honorable peace. Nurse in starched whites and cap like a modified nun's bonnet said Dr. Morton would see them now.

Older man about Bontecott's age with gray hair and his Columbia degree framed on the wall told her mom, "Please sit down."

Chairs in the office were of cloth and cushion, not the linoleum hard seats of the waiting room. He took the clipboard the nurse handed him, tipped his bifocals at a reading angle, seeing his patient over them.

"It says here, Mrs. Bontecott, you complain of debilitating pain in the wrists, knuckles, and elbows of both appendages. Often the wrist strap gives temporary relief, as does medication, but neither provides adequate resolution to your problem."

"Doctor," Kady interrupted, "she's worried to death she has cancer again."

"Miss, allow me to speak with your mother. Now Mrs. Bontecott, what makes you think the joint pain has anything to do with your colostomy?"

"Because the pain began shortly afterward."

"Let me assure you there's no medical connection. The two are entirely disassociated. In fact, I'm led to believe the pain is more a psychological response to menopause. For eight years your cancer shows no sign of recurrence."

"But I hurt," Kady's mom said sadly, resigned.

"You think you hurt," the doctor continued, "because you find menopause difficult to cope with. I recommend counseling. Also resume the wrist wrap and motrin. You may have twinges of arthritis, especially with wet or winter weather, but nothing an adult can't handle."

Kady gripped the underpinnings of her chair, as the doctor disparaged her mom. What if the metallic taste in her own mouth meant cancer.

"Why do you treat her like an infant? She ran her home decorating business. She's had children, miscarriages, and a severe surgery. She handles her colostomy, entirely herself."

"Young lady, I'm diagnosing your mom. Control yourself."

"Show some sympathy then."

"I'm her doctor. I tell her the truth."

"Then recommend a female counselor who sympathizes with her problem. You know nothing of menopause and nothing of her colostomy."

The doctor adjusted his bifocals to bring Kady into focus.

"Young lady, there are few competent counselors in the City and none in the Poughkeepsie area. Your mom receives the best health care in the world, so you can rest assured, a woman's sympathy won't solve her problem. Our team of technicians guarantee her recovery from cancer. Her pain, exacerbated by menopause, is more psychosomatic than real."

"Please list the female counselors for my mom, whether they're competent or not."

Kady caught herself before she put Dr. Morton in the second class.

"That will be all for today," Dr. Morton said to the nurse, who catered to his patients, after he left the room.

Kady and her mom saw a matinee of Long Days Journey into Night with Jason Robards, and returned to their downtown Hilton. High above the City they watched lights flicker like stars in the winter air. Talk time for them.

"Isn't it great, the City?"

"Beats Texas."

"What was it like for you mom, my age?"

Her mom told her again. Kady later told Morpheys how it was for mom and how it was for her. She'd tell him and be gone. Mom was her only real friend through school. Who else took care of her mom now? Kady kept a faded photo of her mom. There she was. A poised maiden of Dalhart, nowhere town in the west Texas Panhandle. Her mom was the blond girl in white cotton dress. She leaned on a porch pole of her dad's jewelry shop. The wind swept dull dirt and her bright dress against the shabby backdrop of her dad's store.

Katherine Lonigan stood on the porch listening to her dad's radio tuned to any faraway station that played Bob Will's Texas swing. It was the one lively entertainment. Radio KADY permeated her being and she could sing. Radio KADY rode the Panhandle winds, and she intended to travel far from this lonely place to somewhere just as lively as the swing bands she heard.

"Keep tuned, you hear now, to 99.9 on the radio dial. This is KADY and we play Bob Wills and his Texas Playboys, till the cows come home."

Kady pocketed the picture years ago from her father's study in the Old Saybrook home. The picture was her mom, and Kady was that 20 year old girl too. Her mom defied her dirt farmer world. Irish Catholic as cut stones. She walked tall and pride. Straight back softened only by her wispy hair bleached but not burned by the heartless sun of the western desert.

The girl Katherine Lonigan met and married a tall, thin, educated man named Evander Bontecott from the New Haven jewelry firm of Bontecott Stone. He was twice her age when he took her away to

Old Saybrook, where she was Texas Catholic and they were icy New Haven. Her mom lived in a coastal town on the Long Island Sound. Her mom took to business and decorated homes in the New England country style with warmth of fabric and subdued colors. It was her New England seen from bleak West Texas, and it caught on in the magazines. She had work but few neighbors.

Kady came with God's grace. Katherine tried three times to bear her husband a son. Twice she miscarried and carried a third to term only to find her son stillborn. Kady was twelve then. Her mom turned to her work and her faith and her girl Kady. They moved to the family horsefarm in Millbrook, New York when Bontecott ended his sales for Bontecott Stone.

There came the cancer to Katherine like the charged emptiness of a miscarriage, the gnawing antipathy that grows and decays. At Vassar Hospital the doctors cleaned her colon of cancer. Kady was thirteen, when she became daughter and nurse to her mom. She helped mom scour her cavity and she helped mom pray at Our Lady of Lourdes. Kady was unhappy in school, but her one act of faith changed her life. Her prayers for her mom's recovery were answered.

20
Last Revolutionary Alone

The Sixties ended. Kallini saw it coming. Prodigal time took a detour off the tracks, and everyone leaped from the train. What had begun as a mission ended with splintering, enclaves, and last resolutions. Everyone said, it was all but over, the Movement, the Brotherhood, but Kallini acted upon that assumption. After a week of meeting with all concerned: black, ghost white, and liberal Jew, the Movement ended for all practical purposes.

Josh Steen with auburn hair, hazel eyes, and wire rims brought Kallini a cup of coffee.

"Really, why send Lionel Dubois out west?"

"He had to go."

"But man, he was our connection to the Black Union."

"Now he's at Berkley."

"Where's our coordinated activity?"

"Nowhere, man."

Kallini drank his coffee. His detour was his uncle's business and Evander Bontecott. Cigarette smoke in the room fogged rational conversation.

"So what do we do?"

"They go their way, we go ours."

"And what is ours?"

"Fund the GI Resistance on every armed force base. Fund it with the army in Vietnam. Fund the outgoing navy and air force revolt, and stop supplies supporting the army there."

"Then what?"

"Wait. See what Nixon does. See if he means business. If he brings home 25,000 troops. Wait and see."

"Who says?"

"Word leaks out."

"Too tricky Dick?"

"Nixon is a strategist, a politician, for better and worse. We bide our time. Wait for his first mistake."

Another voice, hushed, spoke from the ratty armchair, from behind shades and ghost white complexion.

"Time has come for cells of activity. Student suicide groups of 1-2-3 units each, focos of small, effective units, dedicated to work separately, take instructions, do a job, and disappear underground."

"Get off the anarchist lingo. Nothing's gained without mass activity," Josh Steen parted ways with Quinn the Eskimo.

"Against our capitalist system, more bang for the buck. A guy with a gun and a job to do. A girl with a bomb and a target destroyed. Cell system works. Mass action misses the point."

Kallini stared at the seated dude with shades, who never moved.

"You're reading too much Kirilov, The Possessed. Anarchism leads to suicide. Way you label the cells."

"Frighten the hell out of bourgeois America."

"Brings out Middle America, saying, love it or leave it. You get war in the streets and special police in your cell activity."

"As you said to Burn and Rawley. FBI infiltrates the SDS, the RYM, why we need cadres with a purpose."

"Listen Quinn. We have infiltrators. Why not you? You have the connections with Dupont and Dow Chem."

"But I don't need the bread. I make the bombs, so it's my ass on the line."

"You invite KGB and FBI operatives to be as devious as you, they will, and they have much better training."

"I'm with Kallini," Josh said, wiping his wire rims with a red bandana.

"And Kallini ditched you."

"Meaning?"

"He sent Lionel packing. Along with Barb Kelly pregnant. Kallini knows we bear no more white babies into this WASP, racist society. Especially his own."

"Still time for mass activity?" Josh asked Kallini.

"With opportunity."

"Time for cells and resistance."

"Careful with the terrorist call. See the Algerians against the French and the Vietcong against us. It's the rest of one's life in hiding."

"Least you know which way the wind blows," the armchair voice said, taking a deep drag on his Turkish cigarette."

Kallini stared back. So much time they took putting together the global effort from Prague to Paris to Berkley to see the Movement splinter into lone rangers.

"Hey, hang on. Weather will be bad all winter. But Nixon is no brain surgeon in politics. For his first mistake we prepare one more mass strike, one more massive moratorium, one more try at open confrontation."

"Black and white together?"

Kallini told Joshua Steen, "Our paths already diverged. The Panthers want none of us."

"Reach out again."

"Prove ourselves with bombs and bullets," said the chair smoker.

"What can we do in the ghetto community?" Kallini asked. "Theirs is a grassroots program. They build pride where there's poverty. Guys like our Rye Country Day were like us. And they don't want us. Lionel wasn't radical enough. And we move on too."

"If Lionel's useless to the Panthers, why send him west?"

"Hope he gets religion, or he builds a political career."

"He's lost out there. Here we used him with the Black Union, who ignore us."

"They should. Time they know themselves. Cultural assimilation is a dead issue. Zimbawe sees the institutional racism and uses the issue.

"Lionel told us what was happening."

"And told the FBI too."

"You lie," Quinn said, as if he turned more white than his near albino skin.

"There's a leak. I thought it was Lionel. Find another, if I'm wrong."

"How would you know FBI?" Quinn asked.

"I got an Uncle Carlo in the city. Italian, you know. High up in the family where the FBI keep tabs on members."

"No lie, really?"

Quinn looked at Josh Steen, who nodded.

"Like my parents work in the jewelry district, his relations are Italian."

"And yours Quinn work for Dow Chem. Why we need to know you're not FBI. With all the bombs and dope you may get off scot-free when heavy shit falls like rain."

"Kallini, you know I'm not, and you know, any control over the Movement slips through your fingers."

"Movement has no leaders, Quinn."

"That's right. Only those willing to do what's necessary, and those like you, who don't."

"You have no political sense, Quinn."

"We're white panthers, and we're going to bring the war home."

"Panthers don't want violence. They realize the unified strength they possess and push for economic power where it counts, in their own communities. Like Zimbawe with the Black Union here at Cornell."

"Listen to you Kallini,"

Quinn slouched in his armchair and tugged on his shades.

"Big bucks for the righteous black man. You're compromising. Why the RYM wants out of SDS altogether. It's a chickenshit group. It's the system all over again."

The debate ended. It was Quinn's place and they left the last revolutionary alone in his empty room. Kallini looked to old friends in these burnout days, one last spark in the darkness. It was the end of the Sixties. All messianic hope extinguished. Nixon elected. Let Nixon be the focus then for one last hurrah.

And Quinn was right. Kallini knew the value of a dollar. Poughkeepsie streets and Uncle Carlo taught him that. Time he did business. Make a killing all at once. Evander Bontecott needed uncut diamonds to control his family business of Bontecott Stones. When the welcome dies here, go back to Paris. Go back to business. Fund the GI Resistance and the Brotherhood of worldwide revolution. Go back to Wells and his band, and take his mind off this dead end desolation.

He cleared out of Cornell. Prodigal time ended for these collegiate holdovers, doing doctorates to dodge the draft. They grew older without deciding on a life's work. They leeched as students, TA's, and Movement attaches. It was a cold Friday he hitched back to Wells two weeks after he left.

He heard from Mr. Jacobs his garage band improved in his absence. "They practice all afternoon, except the singer. They'll never be good, we both know that. But they get better."

"Time to bring a big Friday crowd down cellar, and see how they sound."

21
The Fool and the Clown

Kady and David took her VW to Friday dinner at the Commons. She'd come back a couple days, and they opened up and told all. Kady about her mom, and David about his dad's farmwork for Bontecott. They skipped the foolishness in their few days left. Plenty of room even for Doug and Walter. New manner of world at one with their own. Two in tune, love's like that.

The Fool and the Clown argued whose car, Thunderbird or GTO, had greater power. Doug rode Walter up to Skinneatteles.

"And there's my car sunning itself in the garage lot. Still disabled, crunched like a beercan."

"Needs a part."

"Needs an overhaul. Looks like I'm stuck in your pantywaist car."

"Walter uses my car for limo service, except when his frat friends come."

"Forget it Doug, it was two weeks ago. Next they come you can be head honcho, and every chick we pick up has to kiss your ring, to prove they're worth the rush."

"You're a real jerk," Kady told him. "Behave better."

"You are a real jerk," Doug agreed. "Like the way your frat buddy picked on Jesse until she punched him in the chops."

"He asked for a dance."

"He assaulted her."

"Douglas, you're so proud of your Presbyterian code. The perfect gentleman. It's as ridiculous as your Thunderbird. You know what I told the garage guy. Use this wimpy Thunderbird for spare parts."

Kady took Doug aside to get coffee and dessert. She heard how Walter cut Doug out with his frat buddies.

"He called Jesse a lesbian bitch. I felt like punching the cad if Jesse didn't. A gentleman's supposed to protect a lady."

"Girls at the Townhouse protect themselves, Doug."

David advised Walter to "cool it" for one more week. "Be nice to Doug. He's driving you places."

"Christ, don't I know it. But his moral codes. Loosen up baby. I tell him no chick wants a straight arrow. He's so conservative he should drive a Lincoln, not a muscle car."

"One more week we all split. Keep the peace."

"But that pewter pipe and tweed coat, my frat guys can't help but make fun of him."

"It's his father's code of conduct. He'll get over it."

"What the hell, one more week. Let the frat make him a temp. Like the idiot pledges whose parents get them in. We'll puff him up. Anyway my GTO's out another week."

"Not everyone's a born comic like you."

"True my man, Morpheys."

They sat with the Fool and Clown. Doug liked Kady. Walter told her jokes. Nothing else really mattered to David and Kady because they were in tune, together, to this new world.

22
Cellar of Sound

After dinner they walked from the French House to the Inn. The night was cool, not bitter cold. Lake breeze had a damp smell. No flurries whipped like needles in the icy wind. They strolled close with a playful nudge. Kady escorted him to the bar. Already the floorboards resonated with drumbeats and bass rhythms. Wall lamps and chandeliers tabulated bells with the cascade of notes from a guitar riff. Long mahogany bar burnished with bottled dreams. Gin, whiskeys, and liqueurs posed like a mirage against the mirror wall. Kady ordered two cassis. Her knack for novelty charmed David. Cassis created the melodic vineyards of French wine and poetry. With a Dunhill cigarette Kady enjoyed the "little luxuries".

David practiced afternoons with the band. He heard them start up and they sounded good. The cellar commotion heightened the shared conversation. Other drinkers displayed a mild hilarity, gesturing and laughing like swimmers splashing in shallow water. Music drew them to the deep. Everyone descended to the cellar of sound. The concrete wraparound of darkness, drab by day, pulsated with the flail of whimsical dance. David plugged in Lloyd's Squire and adjusted his eyes in the dim. Darkness made him nervous. He played as much by sight as sound. Dark sound like sex all around him. It was cool.

David stood beside Don on drums with the guitarist and Tim Burt on the other side. Don kicked back profuse with sweat. Tim Burt let go the microphone, his other arm tilting a Genesee longneck. The pace slowed. The tension heightened. Strumming a occasional chord, Lloyd with his hick look, tall and pimpled, stepped back to adjust his amp.

Then the surprise. Kallini was back. He stepped solo to the microphone. Acapella, he sang like ascending steps to a summit, "There is a house in New Orleans, They CALL the Rising Sun."

His gravelly voice growled, swooped up, and screamed viciously.

"It's been the ruin of many a poor boy…"

He silenced the crowd for the reverberation. Then he dropped into perfect tone, repentant and sincere.

"…and God I know I'm one."

The vocal imitated Eric Burdon, but who cared. David shut his eyes and saw the cavern cellar of Liverpool: the early Beatles, Yardbirds, Animals, and the Stones stepping out in their visions of Black rhythm and blues. The Thrill is Gone stopped dancing on the floor for people to listen. Sympathy for the Devil his bass dug down deep, created patterns which pushed Lloyd's lead and Don's drums to pulsate rhythm. Tim Burt stood aside and drank longnecks. He refused to sing harmonies and no one noticed him. David did all he could to keep his chord changes inside the chamber of amped sound.

Tim Burt left between sets, mad Kallini was back. Who cared. He went upstairs. Kady went after him. "No fun standing around," he said. "It's not our band anymore." Kady told him he was good, but he was too drunk to care. Two years out of school he headed for the factory shift and drunken stupor. The band had been his lifeline and Tim Burt let go the rope, carelessly.

David stared between sets at Candy, who returned for the semester. He'd been with her freshman year, for drugs and desire, sated. She bent an ear to the juker Ball and Chain then and now. Another kind of girl, very open and unusual because she didn't care what others said. She looked up and saw him staring. She came over.

"I thought I recognized you in the band. You're the guy with Kady."

"Good to see you back."

"Be good to her. She's a very cool chick, her and Barb."

Kady returned from her talk with Tim.

"Hey Kady, sorry about Barb."

"Tim's upstairs, crying in his beer, you know."

"Kurt's great, isn't he?"

"He sure is, but I'm sorry Tim and Eddie are out. Everybody's leaving."

"I guess, but change has got to come."

Candy touched Kady's arm.

"I'll talk to Tim and console him. His girl friend ditched him too."

Kady didn't ask if David knew Candy, but she knew. It bothered her. She sat in silence at the table. Jukebox played the Zombies and "Tell her No." She had not slept with anyone. And she liked David. It was a new feeling for her. She distrusted the overwhelming emotion.

David asked her to dance, and she said, "No, not now. I'm too upset about Tim Burt."

She left again. She asked Candy how she knew David. Candy was honest, and said sure. He was a quiet guy from freshman year, nice guy, but I haven't seen him since."

"Nice guy you think?"

"Yes. As Janis says, don't close yourself to love."

Kady returned with two longnecks. She reached for David's hand. He breathed easier with his heart hurting, thinking, there's nothing he could do.

"You spooked me Kady. Grooving along and then I'm stranded over the abyss."

Kady kissed him.

"I've learned a little about you, enough to trust you."

"Everyone has a past they're not proud of. Sorry."

They shared another kiss, longer, a bit awkward. One falls in love and falls too far. David strapped on Lloyd's guitar for another set. He watched Kady from the stage. Had he lost her? Kady's face with a bead curtain of curls over her eyes possessed a glow. It was the lighting, or him, doting on her. Then it was a Robert Johnson song. Kallini kept the tune slow, "Love's in vain," the sorrow turned bittersweet.

23
Last Time, Forever

The final week they shared a dialogue of smiles, a language of gestures, and a touch of hands like words. How was a long talk conducive to their short time left? They told their stories. In the other person mirrored the world, mysteriously arranged. With the group departure ticking days they walked the shores of the finger lake. Weather hit another cold snap. Ice sifted solid back into the shore hollows and temperatures dropped below zero.

The melt was a memory. The month narrowed to a final weekend. Pleasures shared arched like a Mirabeau Bridge from here to over there. Time between rushed beneath a frozen surface. David wished them together in Paris, but how could he master the cold air and fly to foreign ground? He was a poor boy in love with a rich girl. His wishful thinking was a white bird and a figment of his imagination.

Saturday afternoon it got so cold they drove to the state park, where they walked on warmer days. They sat in the car and heard radio tunes. Not the Fabulous Finds of the Fifties, but pop of the early Sixties. Day of the thaw this outlet stream rocketed over the falls and poured into the lake. Now it packed with ice in several jagged layers. The empty picnic table bellied up in snow. They dusted it off. The car radio played a song, "Hey Paula" by Paul and Paula.

He sings he can't wait till graduation day, and she says in her clinging reply about the same thing.

The song captured a time of steady dates in high school before boy and girlfriend changed. They grew up, went different directions and ran with different crowds. And nothing was ever simple or the same. Social change complicated matters. Hey Hey, the sadness of parting sang in strains of sweet melancholy. He held Kady's hand. Time was an underwater current. Prodigal time waited on them. Else these were stolen moments and all they had, white birds in flight in a cold winter of passing time.

"Song of sweet memory, you think Kady?"

"Not for me."

"An early Sixties when we had a date with destiny."

"It's a sappy song, Morpheys."

"Yes, it is."

Morpheys took both her hands to see her better. Warm them up. Cold grit a person's teeth. Kady's freckles baked spots on her red-chapped cheeks. They could be warm in the car, but here the air hung with possibility.

"You're dreaming Morpheys, and it's cold."

"I know. What if we met, and there was no draft, no duty, no demands other than making what we have work? What if we had lives ahead of us, together?"

"Hey Morpheys, we're not townies, you know."

"Hey Kady, I do."

"Well you are, probably."

"I am. And you're a girl with class and intelligence."

"A girl like Dana Dupont, then."

"No, not you."

"Not cute enough for a debutant?"

"You're beautiful. The way your hair falls like trinkets from your cap. The way your eyes are cut green emeralds, like Bontecott Stones. I'm mesmerized by your beauty."

She shivered, but let a smile flare all freckled and fine teeth. He continued.

"And no, nothing cute about you. You got a mind and you know what's happening. And nothing of the debutant. You're a pretty normal girl. For a pretty normal day freezing in a state park."

"While this boy philosophizes over a sappy song."

"And fearless in all weathers."

"Not a Dana Dupont, and not a Candy."

"Neither."

"Neither sophisticated nor sexy."

"Much more. You have integrity."

"What the hell's that remark? Integrity's a word for a business to invest in, and all this sappy Paul and Paula crap disguises the fact you don't want me."

She shook off his grip, rubbed heat into her hurt knuckles, arthritic and scaly with winter psoriasis. Not enough sun to keep her limber. She'd be like her mom, bedridden on bad days. If cancer didn't cripple her first. What about sex to save this relation with Morpheys, if that was what he wanted. Or he wanted an easy girl like Barb Kelly or Candy.

"I want you like Paul wants Paula, you know that, Kady. And you know what that means."

She slammed the car door, turned up the blower, and searched for warmth. David got in the passenger seat and grabbed her hands to warm them.

"Listen Kady, you have integrity. I'd lie, cheat, and steal to get ahead, to get out of town, to see everything there is to see. You're different. You know your own mind."

"Let's get back to the House. Call your friends coming to pick you up."

"They're in DC on winter study. Politics and all that."

"Let's go. I need coffee, hot soup, and a warm bath."

"The Paul and Paula, why not us? Why not all the time in the world? Why are we apart after tomorrow?"

"Forget it, Morpheys. Just shut up about it."

24
Eskimo Pies

"You told the FBI?"

Layton Hayze nodded his head yes. Emotional responses failed to register. He wasn't up to them. Like heat to nitro glycerin. Layton kept cold and damp for fear of losing what little he had. He sat in a folding chair center of Quinn's apartment. Quinn called to tell Kurt Kallini the FBI had the two of them on tape with a witness to boot. Come to sort out an exit strategy.

"You told the FBI or you plan to tell them?"

"Both."

One word was all Layton possessed.

"I don't blame you."

"Quinn does."

"He would. You work for him. For long as you been at Cornell. What's it, the second year of grad school?"

Kallini could not stand well without a chair to lean on or one to sit in. What with his short leg and the twist in his spine. Though he didn't want to sit and let Layton stand. Layton let beads of sweat roll off his forehead. He kept his hair short. He kept his scholarship. He wanted a career at Dupont or Dow Chem.

He made concoctions with Quinn with never a trip tried. In fact he was straight-arrow, waiting for his chemist degree, waiting to work for Quinn's family. Better living through chemicals. There was the hip irony Quinn reveled in. Layton wanted to improve himself and get ahead. The logo for him was literal truth. For him, the philosopher's stone.

"You okay? You want to tap a glass of water, smoke a Pall Mall, tell why the hell you want to rat us out?"

"Quinn has this chair on a trip wire."

"Ha. The Eskimo puts the freeze on us all."

Again the termite nod, the sweat, the pale skin of a chemist kept under wraps in Quinn's LSD cellar. Dark stronghold for funhouse antics. Damp and dead serious for casebombs waiting a destination.

"So I need to give Quinn his due?"

Kallini didn't bother to notch Layton's last nod. Layton Hayze was timed to Quinn's neurosis. Quinn on a hairtrigger more Maoist than his RYM partners. With Quinn it was one step beyond programmed Redbook, chants, and violent confrontation in the streets. With them Czechago ended one politics and began its polar opposite. Nixon was in. This year they planned to return to Mayor Daley's Chicago for the June meeting of SDS and for a fall retaliation.

Kallini descended into Quinn's cellar. Kallini recalled Morpheys' grandpa and his cellar. No father of his own he visited with his mom. Nana and his mom worked at Deeves Jewelers. Down cellar of Nana's house on Haight Avenue over from Vassar College, tools were taken from Delaval to concoct a bathtub still of gin. Cellar went right into the rock of the Haight and had that musty smell of the underground. Like he should sneeze and let the tiny grains blow his brains out. That cellar in the rock, this cellar. There down cellar and up St. Genieve's bloody cross of lightning, the virgin supreme over Poughkeepsie. Hell and heaven not far apart. Here Quinn had Layton Hayze on a tripwire.

Quinn worked in his musty cellar with a fan and humidifier on. He worked under one lamp, specially set for low heat, as his tweezers and tiny Phillips worked on a casebomb. He set wires to powder, to nitro, to dynamite. It was second nature to him and his family.

"Did you have a chance to shake Layton's hand?"

"He never offered."

"Pigs approached him in town. Offered him immunity. He gave up all he knew."

"He let them wire the apartment?"

"Yes. For a group called Cointelpro."

"You got information inside the government too."

"Layton told what he knew. All this means nothing to him. Like everyone outside the RYM, including you, Kallini."

"So your bird on a wire sang his song."

"You want to know who's infiltrated inside the machine?"

"Layton, he'll say anything to save his skin. After all it's nothing but heavy weather to him. He's filled with fear. And he's not furious enough to face squads of police and FBI infiltrators like you, Quinn, and your cadres."

"Kallini, you said Lionel was the snitch, and that was why you sent him to the Panthers in Oakland."

"That's what I said. And I sent your casebombs with him in the van to impress them."

"And the codes to the casebombs?"

"No."

"Kallini, you screwed us over."

"One acts according to his lights."

"You informed on us, not Lionel."

"I did not. They have ten times the reason to go after me than after you. And I got reason to stay clear of the FBI. My Italian relatives, unlike your connections, get very touchy with snitches and rats."

"Kallini, you got connections, coast to coast, only we don't know the nature of the game."

"End the war in Vietnam."

"No other concerns? What about an end to the war against the Black colony inside Amerika? What about your white skin privilege? End that too?"

"Remember I don't have the privileges of your family in the military-industrial complex. I'm Italian, with no family other than an Uncle Carlo, and no one to save my sorry ass when the FBI comes knocking."

"All whites have white skin privilege."

"Not like you, Irene."

"What did you call me, creep?"

"Eleuthere Irene. Not Quinn the Eskimo. Not Richard Lammont. But by the name of your famous French ancestor. One who learned the secrets of gunpowder from Lavoisier. One whose ancestor escaped to America when Lavoisier lost his head to revolution and the guillotine. Hail to you, Irene. As revolutionary, as LSD chemist, as bombmaker, as child to the merchants of death."

"Where'd you learn this bullshit?"

"FBI told me. No, maybe it was your dad waiting in the corporate structure for his prodigal son's return. Come back to manufacture napalm to burn fleeing Vietnamese children from B-52 raids on their villages. You're the only one with white skin privilege, the one with family influence, the one working with the FBI."

"Shut up Kallini, shut up."

"Why I sent Lionel to the coast with a chick I cared for. To take away your casebombs to the Panthers. To take Lionel away from your clutches on him. Show him real radicals and a real cause. I owed Lionel that much. Like you owe Layton Hayze that much."

"I sent them the codes."

"I knew you would."

Quinn clicked his tiny headlamp back on and applied his tweezers to a circuit that needed soldering. Kallini saw his forehead sweat the same as Layton Hayze. His skin had an albino complexion and his blond hair looked burned with peroxide.

"When I get to Paris I'll say hello to your benefactor who went to the guillotine when your relative fled to this land of opportunity. Listen Quinn, there's nothing for you here. Just walk away. Just walk away, Rene."

"Kallini, you'll get yours in two minutes if you don't get the hell out of here."

He exited into the pull down garage packed with all the plush furniture from the apartment. There was some cash stored here. For when his parents visited. Kallini heard movement upstairs and a door slam. The tripwire was a ruse. It was a bright day on the Cornell street, steep from top to bottom. Kallini breathed in the icy air. Despite his crippled spine and constant pain it wasn't bad to be alive, some days.

Josh opened the door to the Fairlane.

"Learn anything from Quinn?"

"Not a damn thing. Drive away before his apartment explodes."

25
Cornucopia of all Good Things

Last Saturday night on this planet. Several fraternity jerks returned from Colgate and Hamcoll, Walter's AD friends. They drank pitchers of beer at the Fargo. Walter entertained the table with his deer-killed-my-car story. Steve Hancock, who grabbed Jesse's breast, was totally out of it and totally obnoxious. Like an idiot salesman at conventions with a buzzer for handshakes and water jet in his flower lapel. He pinched girls as they passed and pleaded his drunken debauchery.

He pinched Kady before David came and she kicked him into the table spilling the beer.

"If you ever touch me again, I'll kick your face in I swear it. Why don't you frat assholes stay at the Inn?"

"They threw us out," Steve stammered.

Walter told him, "Cool it now before we get kicked out of town."

"Why did you bring him here?" Kady asked Walter. She looked at Doug at the same table and shook her head, why bother. Douglas saw where Kady sat. In his tweed Jacket he went over.

"Let me apologize Kady for those jerks. All the come-ons in the Playboy pamphlet it's trashy behavior."

"Look Doug, he's doing it again."

Kady got up to go help the girl, and the girl sat down beside him.

"It's a lonely freshman, lousy drunk as him, and she doesn't know to say no. Why bother?"

"Anyway, Kady, I'm leaving."

"Me too, as soon as Morpheys comes."

"I don't want to sit with Walter. His frat brothers are playing up to me. Then laugh with each other. Glad this is the last night."

"Me too."

David got there. He stamped the snow off his boots. He said hello and goodbye to Doug on his way out. This working class sanctuary suffered a frat roll. Kady caught his attention. She grabbed her sailor coat and gave Walter a dirty look, leaving. David saw her infuriated and didn't know why. Was she mad at him? For waiting on his friends, Early and Peter, calling from DC? For this afternoon and a sappy song? He followed her downstairs past the pumps and out into the falling snow.

"Did you see that shithead at Walter's table? Guy with the blond hair and tie around his neck. Son of a bitch pinched me as I went by."

"Steve Hancock? Let's go beat the crap out of him."

"I kicked him into the table and spilled his beer."

David guided her upstairs, saying, "Let's go back."

"I should have punched his head. Then kicked him in the face."

David bumped her again, and she slugged him in the arm, hard.

"Really Kady, it's the guy Jesse suckered two weeks ago. Let's go back and kick the shit out of him."

He enjoyed her anger, long as it wasn't against him. Kady gave up.

"Let's go."

"Okay."

"Why bother."

"Why not?"

"Careful Morpheys, don't piss me off."

"Sorry."

"Let's go to the Townhouse, okay. You're not playing in the band tonight?"

"No, I'm out. I was extra playing chords."

"Go play if you want."

"I don't."

A foot of powdery snow filled the streets since dinner. There in the Townhouse some sanity ruled. The girls were friends and free from bickering. Guys from the band shared some smoke they sold for Kallini. David and Kady sat on a corner couch. By the window it was dark. They watched snow fall in the hollow a streetlamp carved in the night. A radiant spot of calm.

"You reach your roommate in DC?"

"I did. Peter's there as legal intern. He liked it. What his dad wants for him. What Early Hayze does is anybody's guess. He's a DC kid."

"Somebody like Barb Kelly."

"Carbon copy."

"What took you so long?"

"Sorry. Sure you don't want another shot at Steve Hancock?"

"Let's go."

David made a slight move.

"And kick the crap out of him, again."

"And again," Kady smirked.

Don walked in with Deb and came over.

"I'm going to miss shooting hoops, Morpheys. Come to Paris and we'll play."

"Double or nothing."

"We're there till the end of June. Hamilton must get out in May?"

"Sure, give me a month to work, make planefare, and I'll be there before the Draft rings me up."

Kady looked at him, inquisitively. David decided he'd go back to school, that he'd work, and that he'd go see her in Paris. The sudden idea coalesced at once. Then seemed unreal. Much of youth has a dubious quality. To push a plan into action risks a life decided and months and years of interminable routine. Better a suspended animation. A cushion of time before the walls and empty rooms.

"We don't return till July so do it."

Deb put her hand in Don's pocket and shook loose change.

"You too Don. Come to Paris this summer."

"Yea right."

As wild as Don's fancy wandered with the drumbeat of rock stardom, he knew townies don't take flights to Paris. This was a rich girl idea. Don took Deb toward the fireplace where good hashish passed around. The smoke that fueled Don's dream.

Kady sat closer to David. Couch in the dark with the window full of snow and the streetlamp.

"You think about Paris after school?"

"I just did."

They didn't talk much. It got beyond them too easily. They

listened, attentive to the slightest tremor in the other person. All responses measured, meaningful. Edgar Winter mourned a bluesy tune, "Fly away." That was Paris, a white bird. Hours unwound for them, and they had not moved from the couch, from the calm of the Townhouse. Occasionally a word, a touch, an arm around her shoulder, which was enough. Make the most of time together.

At a late hour they left for the French House. Snow sifted knee high and weightless. No cars and the night stood still, sound proof and shock proof, like walking on the moon. Their two bodies arm in arm were stored batteries, receptive as a radio to waves in the vacant air powdered with snow. Like her mom's KADY radio born in love with the dry panhandle winds of west Texas. Now Kady. Radio waves pulled her places she didn't know and wasn't sure what to do. How was she to fill the expectation? The two of them, she knew, like radio ready to play whatever tune she wished.

Inside the House light made the air empty. David said goodnight opening his door and there discovered Steve Hancock humping a girl in Walter's bottom bunk. It wasn't the freshman chick. It was Jesse. "Jesus." Steve popped up his head and grinned an asinine smile. Walter wasn't around, but Doug stared wide awake from his bed against the wall. Tough trick the frat guys pulled on him.

"Hey asshole, what are you doing in our room?"

"It's okay, hey it's okay. I mean Walter's an AD bud and he said it's okay."

The jerk was too drunk to make sense.

"This is the guy who pinched you, right Kady?"

Kady tugged on his arm.

"Come to my room, David. There's an extra bed."

David agreed. Jesse, her business. "Jesus." The new world of their love needed a new orbit. So be it. Numb glow warm as anesthesia transfused his senses with the dream in his mind. Desire transported them away from worries what Steve did, or what Walter and the frat guys did to Doug. David took care to do as Kady wished. Favor her invite as she pleased, and not be a jerk. He undressed next to the other bed. Then heard her whisper with some hesitancy.

"You mind sleeping with me?"

"I'd love to."

"I've never slept with anyone."

"Me neither."

David stared until she smiled at him.

"You asshole. Turn off the light, okay.'

There are smiles of a winter night too. The weightless cold remembered of fallen snow. The pleasure waiting for the one you love to say it's okay. Then the warmth of Kady's widening hips and thin flat stomach pressed against him. The small of her back, the softness of her breasts, the talking of lips and darting tongue. The untold pleasure of touch took away all wish to sleep their final night. All new to them, the tender touch of a new world, begging to be born, in touch with eternity: the blue sea seared red with the rising sun, the new day, the novelty of incredible nuance, and always tomorrow. No memory's so cherished as the first time.

Next morning they woke to the assurance of a warm glance and warmer touch. By noon Kady packed her bags to go. David sat next to her on the bare mattress in the empty room. Winter sun streamed in cold waves through an uncurtained window.

Her big canvas bag like a cornucopia of all the good things and all the good times they had lay in Kady's room. Prodigal time and its possibilities zipped for departure. Leave something too valuable. Make yourself return in haste and regret with leisure. But Kady was packed and ready to go.

"See you soon," said David.

"Don't make promises."

"Expect loads of letters."

"Great time, okay."

"Expect me, knocking at your door."

"Got to go. You stay, okay?"

He nodded. He was mesmerized by her green eyes. One last glance and she was gone, gone, gone. There were no words. There's a silence full with time to follow and silence which is empty with parting. She told him, stay. With her heavy canvas bag in hand she drove off in her red VW.

IV
The Workings of Fate

26
Funereal Concoction Painted Red

"Douglas drives crazy as a mother____ in heat!"

Walter Rink rolled down his window and yelled at Morpheys walking Route 90 toward the Inn. Thunderbird reved beside him. Late afternoon sun screamed across Lake Cayuga. Doug stayed in town to pick up Walter's GTO on Monday. Walter treated Doug to Sunday dinner: cocktails, wine, gratuities included.

"What up with you guys?" Morpheys asked. He really didn't need a ride.

"I had books to return to the library, and Doug wanted to show me what his wimpy car can do. Then dinner and drinks on me. My GTO's twice the car. For crying out loud it's no contest. This pissant engine just don't have the pep. Come on, hop in."

David wasn't awake enough to dissent. He got situated in the roomy backseat.

"Okay Doug, let's go for a spin."

"Fasten your seatbelt, Morpheys."

David caught Doug's eyes in the rearview and they had the same glazed look as late last night. Tough trick they pulled on him. Eyes were all white, with the pupils washed out, drunk or something. Walter assumed watching was fun for someone like Doug, like frat guys sharing peepholes at the house.

Doug reved the Thunderbird engine and squealed piston lock and black tire mark along the wet cement highway. They fishtailed 3-4 ways before second gear kicked in.

"Slow down, shithead, till we're outside town. Cop will clock you and what does a ticket cost? Couple twenties. What it will cost me for dinner, so slow down."

Doug twisted his stiff neck and said, "____you, asshole."

His words didn't suit a straight guy like him. Straight arrow shot loose in free fall flight. He was ripped and his car roared away all inhibitions.

Then Walter's words sunk in. Slam on the brakes skidded them to a stop before the Aurora Inn.

"Kady said you waited for friends."

"Yes. Incoming from DC sometime near dinner. Come share a beer."

"We'll be back," Doug said.

Walter spun around with a weird look like he didn't know what to do. Doug was his ride to Skinneatteles. Humor him out of this weirdness.

"Hey order three beers and we'll be back once this wimp-mobile shoots its wad."

David watched them leave from the Fargo pumps, as he crossed Route 90 to the Inn. Doug turned down a plowed path for icefishing onto the lake. Where was he headed? Car on Lake Cayuga among the tip-ups of icefishing fools. Late afternoon burned east into his eyes. It looked like Doug shot his car, like an arrow straight to the far side. Car increased speed across the miles of iced over lake. To get a better look David ran into the Inn. Kallini at the piano gave him a glance. He promised Kallini his friends would give him a ride to Hamilton.

"What's happening, Morpheys?"

"Roommates of mine play Bonneville Salt Flats on the icy lake."

"No kidding. Let's get a look off the porch."

Kallini motioned to Mr. Jacobs to come open the sliding glass with his key. It was cold out where the debs drank champagne during the winter thaw. A few patrons lingered along the warm side of the glass.

"What's to see?" asked the owner.

"Nothing yet."

"My two roommates took a Thunderbird over the lake."

A cloud covered the eye of the sun, and they saw the car skidding sideways miles on the far side. A few sighs and groans of amusement escaped the spectators. College kid prank. More came out on the porch. Car spun 3-4 times and headed straight back at them. No one could say with certainty whether it moved east, west, or suspended in space. La mer melee au soleil, David thought, as sun and icy blue lake collided.

"Doug's gone nuts," David said.

"Watch and wait," Kallini said with resignation.

The car ran a beeline. Sun shadowed the refracting blue hood, half the blue lake on both sides. Doug was a meteor headed toward earth. He was kamikaze to a US destroyer. To the Inn where Walter and frat buddies shunned him. The Fargo they embarrassed him. The French House they f___ him over. With Walter in the Thunderbird Doug had his target in view. His mind was a reved engine cutting metal on metal with sheer lubrication of speed. His mind was a wasp's nest with one sting left.

"Horrible to watch the working of fate," Kallini said.

"That's what it is."

"The consequences of sin come swiftly home."

Crowd of patrons cheered the speeding bullet until it clearly headed toward the Inn. Cheers changed to screams and baited silence. They saw the plowed slope of lawn to the lake. They realized the unwinding of fate. Closer it came they saw the wider and thin body. More scream than silence. Thunderbird must be rocketing well over 100 MPH as it lurched out of sight, not out of mind. Glass shattered like a wedding, and the wood porch shook as the car crunched against the basement wall. Nobody saw a thing. They all sensed the impact.

Kallini knew deep in his dark heart this was coming to Quinn the Eskimo in his cellar refuge among his eskimo pies, where he would blow himself up, where he would end what he started, where Layton Hayze would flee for his life if he had forebodings what was coming. Kallini saw the workings of fate, there and here, at the end of the Sixties. Like a disaster waiting to happen because kids in RYM and Weathermen had gone too far into revolution. The worst they could do they'd do to themselves.

Kallini grabbed David's suede coat to come with Mr. Jacobs to the basement. Girl behind the bar called police and ambulance. Bottles, carafes, and champagne glasses fell to the floor. Downstairs every sliding glass door blown out. Glass shattered like starry dust. The engine smoked twisting on itself. Horn squealed relentlessly. Walter Rink's head shaved red and raw through the windshield. Impact emulsified brainmeal, limbs, and organs to a funereal concoction painted red. As David expected.

Doug cried laughing at a Playboy one-liner like he couldn't stop. He was seatbelted and badly bruised. Walter Rink lacked both seatbelt and life. Doug stayed at an Ithaca hospital for a week and a Scranton, Pennsylvania asylum the rest of his days. End of the Sixties for the straight-arrow and the goodtime joker. Over for the fool and the clown.

27

No Reply

February of spring term David bided his time. He read for classes and wrote Kady long letters. No reply. Winter hung on in cold snaps and blizzards. Seldom were temperatures above zero. Kurt Kallini moved into the Towers with Early Hayze, and the two shared smoke. Kallini called political meetings: a following of freshman radicals, eager to activate the dormant college hill, eager to push dope in the freshman dorm. Hamilton stirred with a steering committee and the pipe dream of a March on Washington.

Early's good fortune got them the towers. The three roommates lucked out senior year. The Towers overlooked the Hill of Hamilton College. Early had the lottery pick of apartments and the Tower was paradise. David recalled Early's big news. Early pointed his roll-your-own Topps cigarette like sewing with a thread of smoke. His eyes overladen with thick lenses, green tinted, eyes bulged, filmy orbs with small pupils, as if a layer of smoke sifted between him and you.

"It's the Sierra Madre of motherloads. Luck at last."

Peter with his full beard and cavernous eyes, said, "Place my speakers on the turrets and we'll blast the campus from our castle walls."

It was perfect for parties. High above it all. Then a prison of solitude. The Hayze, whose good fortune won in the lottery, lost in the Draft. Early's grades got worse and his worry turned to outrageous humor, drunken binges, and hitchhiking as far as rides took him.

Peter moved in with his girlfriend Cheryl over at Kirkland, the girls' college across the road. David saw him one class and afternoon basketball. Early spent days drinking coffee in the cafeteria. Then later at night the Hayze, Kallini, and a few freshmen radicals ascended to Early's room. The ceiling hung low with smoke colored Acapulco gold and political pipe dreams.

Days David had time and space to himself. For his senior thesis he wrote on the time lapse in existential literature. Titled: Prodigal Time. He worked to stem depression. Douglas got to him. Walter's death was no small deal. He dreamed of car crashes and drowning. Great damage letting go. Drop out and worse happens, his dad said. True enough. Graduate and go.

Find the bonanza of unharvested time: the sideways show in this land he was leaving. Because burn baby burn, the candles burn bright, and prairie fire redefines the tundra with green grass. Start a revolution. Phoenix rises from the flames, a renewable resource. Love searches the quiet aftermath in manifold desire. Double shot into space one comes back wiser and not the worse for wear. Prodigal Time: the best years of one's life, and why not?

Modern technology hurries one here and there. Years slip away. Art of living discovers the time lapse and lengthens the magic moment into eternity. David strayed into the seven year cloud sanctum of Mann's Magic Mountain, into the time swirl of Hesse's magic theatre in Steppenwolf. He returned to Dostoyevsky and his characters' seizure of the moment verging on crime, madness, and annihilation. Time all relative said Einstein, and eternity once experienced, space and time are no matter. Go to work, go home, leave town. Be at one wherever one is. Be useful in a worker's world. Find the precious trick of time. If world enough and time, one discovers the trick of two-timing a life, living above it all in the clear vistas of the awakened mind, and living a decent life with the person one loves. For nothing else matters once time has lapsed.

David withdrew into the solitude of a lonely room because the inner landscape of his senior thesis pleased him, this dreary dead-end of winter. Fewer people he saw, the fewer people he needed to see. His letters to Kady went unanswered. No reply. All my love in vain.

Mornings David saw The Hayze in the Commons drinking coffee black and rolling his Topps tobacco. Already on academic notice, Early quit sitting in classes. Waste of time, Early said. David filled his coffee thermos and tipped his cap to Early Hayze.

"Hey David, come share caffeine with the Hayze."

"You're up. About time. Sure you want to share the heights late night, with Kallini, and those freshmen?"

"Kallini's a guru of the open road. Like I've been places, hitching. But no place he hasn't been."

"School's the thing."

"So many more things to see than school."

"You're a poor boy like me on loans and scholarship. When it's over, you're done."

"It's over. And I'm done in. I'm off my niche on the tree and floundering."

The Commons were empty. Snow squalls twisted outside the vaulted windows. Early had a wrecked look. Film over his eyes accumulated. Water-logged pupils fished out of view in his bloodshot whites.

"Finish the thesis, graduate, and go."

"I can't do it. I'm played out. Nessen wants my work on Coleridge. Why him and the other Romantics failed to write good poetry after the age of thirty."

"Drugs and doping their imaginations."

"You wrote on Wordsworth and Coleridge."

David nodded. Early's fingers kept busy rolling a smoke, long fingers like a guitar player or an athlete. He was neither. Slump shouldered and pale Early had the scholar's look, animated by hyperactive talk.

"Got any ideas then? Got the paper?"

"Sure. They were blazing with the French Revolution. Catalysts for one another in the Lake District. Coleridge makes the fantastic real and Wordsworth mystifies everyday people. Young dudes shooting poems to wake the world from its doldrums, like Schiller and Goethe in Germany. Until the powers-that-be capped the French volcano, and Europe simmered smoke for a hundred years."

Early bobbed his head weaving smoke rings, the needle of his cigarette piercing the center point. He talked with the accent of his lit cigarette. He talked all the time scared of the solitude necessary to write his thesis in an empty room.

"Kallini compares Coleridge to the beat madness of Kerouac and Ginsberg."

"Okay, or the symbolist poets in the tailspin of Rimbaud's hallucinations."

The Hayze reeled off lines from Howl he heard Kurt Kallini tell him.

"Is that Kallini or the beats?"

"Both of them, and you too, Morpheys."

"The powers-that-be got things capped, they had to, with wars about to blow like an atom bomb."

"Beats flamed and simmered smoke. Now it's rock music, and the war in Vietnam about to blow the world wide open. Blow off that iron lid like a manhole cover. Make the connection to the starry dynamo. Top off the Towers and blow out into space."

"Dig it, Early, out of sight. Only write the paper."

"I can't, I can't get it down, I can't get started."

"Take mine for starts, but Early keep out of the smoke. You don't look good. Send off Kallini and his freshmen contingent."

"I can't."

"Don't do a Kubla Kahn. He tapped the hotline to eternity smoking opium and never wrote poems again. A cliff to see out into the ocean, and an abyss to tumble into. Really take care of yourself, Early. See you. I got work to do."

28
Hail to the Hayze

The Hayze fell from academic grace. By night clouds of smoke and days drinking coffee black. Talking out his senior thesis and putting it off. Inside the Tower sanctum of Early's room, painted black, with a parachute nailed to the ceiling to keep the smoke low down, four tokers sat cross-legged on floor mattresses. Early had a brother Layton in Ithaca doing graduate chemistry, who wrote him off. Layton caught him toking up in DC, warned him, caught him again in school with a buddy, Harry Heintz, and wrote him off. Harry's dad got the charges dropped. But then on Layton wrote off his brother.

The parachute recalled a ripcord adventure. Time he paid two hundred dollars to skyjump for the onetime thrill. Time he jumpstarted something in his life that stopped. He'd told the story to Kallini and the two freshmen. What the pilot said too. "Keep the chute kid, you deserve it." Then it occurred to him that his life stopped. He'd lost his niche on the tree. He was in free fall again.

He rapped with Mark, the freshman from Valley Stream, his blond hair tied behind, and Lester, the black dude from Queens. Now he added a new twist to his tale. What came to him like inspiration.

"See the chute, it goes with me. I decided to join the army and go airborn. Chute goes with me."

"Full of shit," Mark said. "You're putting us on."

The jean-jacket freshman reknotted his pony tail and looked to Lester for confirmation. Two guys from the City don't fool easy. Lester liked the Hayze and his line of bull.

"Lay off the man. If the Hayze says he's taking to the friendly skies, my man's airborn. Like the time he hitched through Georgia and those crackers clapped him in jail and crystal-balled his head. Now that's how crackers treat longhairs."

"But this is bullshit."

"The Hayze knows what's happening. He don't just blow smoke."
"Get off it."
"Let's salute our senior. Graduate and go airborn, my man. Just glad it ain't me."
"Lester, you can't think he's officer material?"
"Whitey don't want to be an officer. Let them lead off too far into the Vietnam jungles and PC's gonna potshot him."

Lester took off his shades and stroked the gnarled beginning of a beard. Kallini scrutinized the group and the Hayze in particular. What material he had to work with. The tissue of Early's intent weaved with his cover up. The Hayze flunked out. Facts and fiction had no separate reality. All one on the karmic wheel. Bhudda come down to do time with earthbound bodies suffering to be free.

Kallini wove magic into the pipe dream. Time of winter his crippled back gave him the most pain. Time when he had least to do. Shortened spine and epileptic tendencies were worst in winter, and he took drugs to walk upright.

Under Kallini's gaze the Hayze took heart and inspiration too.

"You know compadres of the Sierra Madre, Academia has the Hayze at rope's end. Wonder the Dean didn't give me walking papers at Christmas. He converted my scholarship to loans. So I'm deep in debt, failing, and facing the fact my next stop is Vietnam."

"Stay high," Mark said.

"Until the Draft catches my DC ass about midsummer?"

Mark and Lester shared a roach, while Early bared his soul. Plumes of tweezered smoke sucked up the nose. Early rolled his Topps tobacco. Thin penciled cigarette he fired and waved to accent his plans just made apparent.

Kallini nodded to Early.

"You got a good idea. Join the army and start revolution within the system."

Lester scratched his stubble, and said, "My man."

"Way I see it. I'm on a skid, and this skid takes me so far off the road nobody finds my sorry ass."

"But the army, they kick your ass sideways," Mark said.

"Whatever line of bullshit the army feeds me, hell I can take it. I'm no gung-ho athlete, but I can hack basic with a bunch of crackers."

"Crackers so dumb they don't know no better." Lester liked his black dialect because others did.

"Let them work over my body long as I keep my head on straight. Way I see it. It's like a bad skid on an icy road. You turn into the direction of the skid. Basic driver-ed. Draft comes after me so I sign up. Turn in the direction of the skid, dig."

"The Hayze has his head on straight," Kallini said.

Early's radical logic disturbed the two freshman, whose goals included getting high, getting rich, and at all costs staying in school. Let the Hayze take flight, who cared, it's his treasure of the Sierra Madre.

"Don't think Early Hayze is a fool signing up," Kallini told them. "See him as a hero. A soldier starting the revolution from within. No conscientious objector. Movement soldiers, they don't wave the freak flag."

"Hail to the Hayze," Mark said like a smart ass.

"The revolution comes when the collective mind of the man in uniform says, this ain't right. I won't board the planes for Vietnam. I won't slop in the jungles of the Mekong. Put me in the stockade, where the true soldier fights his own private war. When the jails fill to capacity, like Birmingham with Blacks, the war skids to a halt."

"Hail to the Hayze," Lester said in unison with Mark.

"Let the military go mad. Why are blacks forced to fight their yellow brothers? Shoot the white officers and the war's over. French and Russian revolutions began when the soldiers said no more."

"No more, no more war, Hail to the Hayze."

Kallini trained his freshman chorus. Early let his smoke burn to ashes without a single drag. The Hayze a hero. Mark and Lester leading student battalions in a March on Washington. Early rolled another and scratched a stick match. Blaze of flame in the fog of low lying smoke. Confession time.

"No marching band for me. I'm hardly American. My dad's from New Zealand and he arrived in DC with the push for D-Day. He'd been British Civil Service in Borneo. Some anemia he caught there, so he was fit to shuffle papers. Bad blood and he died of leukemia after I was born. I got the same bad blood. Doctor labeled me anemic. But if the movement can use me, who wants to live forever? Do something worth the trouble doing."

The two freshman stared at the Hayze, awestruck. He made no sense to them, but what a grand gesture. Valley Stream kid asked him for a pinch of Topps tobacco.

"We all live up to a father," Kallini said. "Even when we don't have one."

"Too true. My mom told me dad's stories of him in the rain forest of Borneo. The Empire counted heads."

Kallini reached over and laid a hand on Early's shoulder.

"I got no father at all. My mom worked a jewelry store in Poughkeepsie. I was on my own. You know the feeling. I got in trouble and into reform school. Some heavy black dudes from Harlem protected me. My mom died of cancer while I was there. My Uncle Carlo from the City got me out. Put me with the Marist brothers. I was no altar boy, but I learned the power of a strong community. Dude's got to belong to a group larger than himself."

"I hear you Kurt," Early said.

"To me the Movement is that group. Be proud what you do, Early. The Movement makes the whole world worth the trouble. I see you and I see myself. Times I was lost when I went on my own. Can't be done. We need something bigger than us. Trouble then has meaning."

Early let his rolled smoke burn to ashes, smolder away, and he rolled no more. The night of their winter colloquy came to an end, and Early Hayze had direction.

29
Black is Black

"That you Lionel?"
"Called out of my government class."
"Time to come home to Cornell."
"What's up, my man?"
"Zimbawe went too far. Whitby's in and so are you. Deal for the Black Studies program, it's on the table if you convince Turner, Northwestern teacher you met at the Howard Conference, to direct the program."
"Leave here now? Cause now I'm involved with the Panthers breakfast program and their ghetto school. They might take it wrong."
"They got your casebombs and the codes from Quinn. All they wanted."
"Well, I learned a few things, Kurt."
"You made your mark. Now return and complete what you started. It was Zimbawe who called out the economics prof for institutional racism. Him with the toy guns, the stolen pillows, the kicked over food in the President's office. He can be the radical; you the voice of reason."
"There's only reason and revolution, my man. Toy guns and pillows are bullshit."
"You want to refuse to eat with President Perkins?"
"What about real guns matched with revolutionary rhetoric?"
"You got your chance."
"Time slot to make righteous demands in a voice which speaks of worse violence unless right prevails."
"You been listening to Huey and Bobby Seales."
"And keeping a low profile."
"No reason to broadcast your intentions."
"Time's right, hey Kallini. What about Barb Kelly, want her?"

"She stays."

"Barb had a month of morning sickness."

"She's got her art. White chick cancels your influence here. Black is black."

"She's got a Marin County friend who looks after her. Teaches 7th grade, a Ted Westerbrook."

"Good, Barb needs looking after."

"Kallini, your kid?"

"No, yours?"

"I don't know."

"Let's leave Barb to her Marin Country friend. Best for all involved."

"Serious times for serious business."

"Not RYM, but for the Panthers and your Cornell brothers, yes."

"Zimbawe, he's not me."

"I know, Lionel. Time for your return. Leave Barb to her good graces. Leave her the van. Leave the briefcases with the Panthers. But you Lionel, take a plane back to Ithaca."

"You really think so? A plane. It must really be now."

"And no Rye Country Day."

"And no Kurt Kallini."

"No. Stand by Whitby because the politics fell into place. Reap what you sowed."

30
Exaggerate the Dialectic

Lionel worked with the Cornell College president over the summer with the Cosep program preparing students for a Black Union and a Black studies program. Whitby welcomed him back. He let Lionel introduce the president for an assembly and ask the first question.

"What do you intend to do about trustee funds invested by Chase in South Africa?"

"We will try to divest soon as possible. To be honest it's beyond my influence how trustee moneys are spent."

Zimbawe moved across the stage toward the podium. He collared the president in front of students and the speakers, like Adam Adonai. Kallini sitting beside Josh Steen signaled to Lionel, with his frail thin body of an intellectual much like the president himself. Unlike the husky Black man who latched onto the official leader of the university and gave him a good shaking. It was a shock. If Burn, Rawley, and Quinn had been present, their RYM would rouse a radical cheer. But Lionel allowed the president to compose himself and introduce Adam Adonai.

Then Lionel let the Black Union censor its own leader, its former leader. Zimbawe returned to the Brownsville ghetto to work with its teachers who struck for local control. Like many of SDS he moved from college to social problems beyond Academia. His departure left Lionel in charge, the voice of reason, but also a Black leader who learned from the Panthers. He learned reason, liberal compromise, and Platonic dialogue from his Cornell professors; from the Panthers he learned the skills of confrontation.

Zimbawe left a residue of ill will behind him. He labeled professors with charges of institutional racism. He nearly started the revolution back in December demanding complete control over Black studies with no white students in the program. His behavior harassing professors, students, and administration brought the judicial board into prominence.

Kallini advised Lionel how to resolve the cases and take credit for the Black studies program the Board wanted to pass. Then SDS managed a break in and confrontation with recruiters from Chase Manhattan. Similar damage and harassment of recruiters occurred, but no one got called before the judiciary board. Lionel saw the unfairness. When four Black students had their hearing scheduled before the judiciary board, Lionel had them refuse to go. Zimbawe already departed. The judiciary board ruled, the black students would be tried in absentia.

Lionel saw his opportunity. No one said they would appear, then everyone showed up. All of the Black Union members crowded into the hall. They dressed in leather and black berets. Lionel spoke to the board.

"Try us not as individuals but as a group. Since it's black people you blame. Not SDS when they do the same thing. The judiciary board as an institution judges black people different from whites. Therefore judge us. Not as individuals but as an offending group."

No one on the board knew what to say. For a month they sought a compromise. Trying the toy gunners and pillow throwers in absentia made no sense either. The board declined to make a ruling because of the intimidation. They were scared shitless.

So Lionel let the campus know about institutional racism. Exaggerate the dialectic so everyone saw, black and white. Lionel learned a few things. Like the SDS radicals forming the RYM, Lionel stepped beyond Kallini's control.

31

The Hayze is Crazy

With spring came a season of rain and mud. No sun at all. No sunshine and Kady Bontecott was gone. Trees budded in the subdued drizzle and April saw hard green shoots signal blossoms to come. Early Hayze ended his vigil of smoky nights and caffeine days.

One rainy Monday David arrived late to basketball, and Peter cut out from a game to talk with him. His cavernous eyes beamed with intensity. He had a trucking walk with arms and legs thrown out. He and the Hayze were roommates since freshmen year. One of those odd arrangements, and Peter accepted responsibility.

"Listen, the Hayze has gone completely nuts. Last night he needs company. Cheryl's away looking at grad schools, so I say what the hell."

"You go to the Pub?"

"Yeh, but first to the chapel."

"And get down on your knees to pray."

Peter sweat like mad, and his eyes shadowed. They'd been together on football, where they blacked their eyes in the sun. David saw his sarcasm didn't fit.

"Fog swells all around the chapel. You can't see a hand in front of your face. But the Hayze swears the stars up there are out and the steeple's a starry dynamo to the great beyond."

"What were you guys smoking?"

"What I asked, to kid him along. All the way up the pitch black stairs, Early talked about his dad and some tree-god of Indonesia called Aki. The ancient heavenly connection, Early repeated as we climbed the stairs. He kicks open a door and we're a mile high. All before us billows of fog. Like we're in a plane above the clouds. And the stars are out too, I swear it."

"You're putting me on. Like the Pimpmobile story for you gram's car. Kallini didn't buy into that one on the ride back from Wells. Of course his Acapulco gold christened your gram's clunker."

"No lie. This is gospel. The Hayze like Tarzan, goddammit, swings out on the steel-cabled lightning rod, and glides down into the fog. If he's not dead, I figure he's gone nuts. Like that Douglas character of yours. He's talking in a hollow voice, which should be muffled, but it's not. Like he's right next to me. He yells come on in, the water's fine. He's cracked up. He's whacked out. College sticks me with the Hayze freshmen year and I'm supposed to be his roommate forever?"

David had no smartass remark. It was Peter Bergman he trusted for his own sanity. Clean for Gene when David had no politics. This was a normal guy, who if he booked at all, would be like his father, the lawyer, and do pro bono work for liberal causes. His cavernous eyes had the crazed look when the two of them followed the Hayze hitching to Wells, to Ithaca, and once to Cleveland until 3.2 beer out of state let them down.

"Jesus, you didn't! You did. You followed the Hayze down the line."

"Damn right. I'm braindead. The Hayze has gone crazy and took me with him. God it was great! Far f___ out! Take me to the loony bin. Then we went to the Pub. That feeling, riding down the lightning rod stayed with me all night."

"You don't look sane now."

"We drank Milwaukee dry, and stayed high all night. The Hayze is crazy, and me too. Listen I got zero chance to get into law school with my grades, but I got no reason to risk my life."

"But the Hayze does."

"Come on, let's get in this game."

The Hayze was no mystery to David. He'd seen him hitching. Easier to act crazy than go over the edge. Early got worse from freshman year as the world got worse. Early languished like electric current with breaks in the line. Shoot the gap. What one does to tempt fate. Gaze into the Wells waterfall as into the abyss. It wasn't thrills for Early Hayze. Take a jolt and jumpstart time from his manic depression.

According to David's idea of Prodigal Time, the manic lapses were black holes of eternity. Once in, never out again. Douglas stepped in. Time amplified and space, spaced out with madness. No one drove through the wall in pursuit of happiness. Early Hayze did crazy things to scare himself sane again.

32
Take the Straight

All but the Blacks left for DC and a Dow demonstration. Especially Quinn who planned the trip to prove he wasn't in any way connected with his parent's industry making napalm. Then came the Harvard takeover against ROTC recruiters. When administration overreacted, students flocked to the radical's side. Including many of the RYM and PLP who reflected each other's methods and hated each other's politics. SDS lost its anti-war consensus. Kurt Kallini worked with the GI Resistance, not SDS, since there was no SDS consensus, anymore.

Lionel knew these SDS people too. He knew the Rye Country Day group and he knew that afterwards they were set for life. This time he acted for himself. In the past he asked Kallini for advice as his course TA at Cornell. He knew the setup. Zimbawe left because his actions were too radical. Or too poorly planned. But Zimbawe's actions as much as Lionel's planning got the Black Union, the Black studies program, and took down the college president from power.

So what was Lionel Dubois to do? Till now he took care to do the liberal, reasonable thing. Then the crude cross burning before the Black women's dorm. As with injustice on the judiciary board, this was racism, pure and simple. Not vague institutional racism, but violent intimidation. Black men had to protect their women. The case was clearly black and white.

"What are we to do?" Whitby asked him again.

"We do what they did to us. Three things."

Lionel had the groups' attention, by his silent delay, by making Whitby repeat the question, and by his response.

"First thing we act in direct proportional response to the intimidation of our sisters. Second we make that action as intimidating as the cross burning. Third we take over the Straight, the student union for the entire campus. For the intellects, for the jocks, and for science and engineering students who care less for politics. And when students and administration come, we enforce our occupancy by all means necessary. All the force necessary to intimidate the cross-burners and the lynch mob."

"All the force necessary," Whitby repeated.

"We prepared to defend our Black Union. So we're prepared to defend the Straight."

"You heard Lionel, we're in this together. So brothers and sisters, be prepared.

"All the force necessary."

"Lionel didn't get call and response. He got the will to action in the minds of the Black Union.

And they acted. Then Joshua Steen, left in charge of SDS on campus, asked Lionel what they should do. They should patrol the building, picket the Straight, and explain the reasoning for the BSU action to the media. Black action and white explanation. Lionel liked the dialectic. It had its own logic.

33
Blacks with Guns

It was dreary late April weather. They arrived at 3 AM in the morning and had to oust parents from their weekend rooms. Complaints called into the President. Complaints to the media. It was Parent's Weekend. Lionel wanted to cause equal disruption as the cross burning at the sisters' dorm.

Then they used the phones. They called home to their own parents to make them aware what happened and why they took the action they did. Before the media took over the reporting. They had food and phones and rooms, but administration turned off the electric. Public phones left them a means of negotiation. How long they stayed depended on nullification of the judicial decisions against their black brothers and investigation of the cross burning against their black sisters. Reasonable demands.

Precipitation turned to freezing rain on the SDS marchers outside the Straight. Campus police circled the building the best they could. Windows broke on the west side about two in the afternoon. Lionel thought it was an invasion by Ithaca police or Rockefeller's state police. They were scared. They took pool cues and broke chairs to the windows where about twenty frat brothers crawled through. The jocks were pissed off. Blacks took over The Straight where everyone hung out. Jocks wanted to oust them by force.

Lionel got in a few shots with a poolstick and got roughed up a bit. There were more black brothers than jocks from the fraternities and the fight meant more to them. Once the jocks were back outside they flung ashtrays and chairs and whatever lay in reach out the windows. Campus police converged. The frats retreated until they could return en masse. Lionel repeated, all the force necessary.

No one would cross picket lines or come past the campus police again. With the invasion from the frats, Lionel had guns he amassed in prior weeks smuggled into the Straight. Rumors circulated, the frats had guns too. Radio supplied news from SDS and Josh Steen explained why the Blacks took over the Straight. There was no justice with the judiciary board. There was a cross burning and an invasion by the frats. There was institutional racism. Why shouldn't Cornell resolve their problems peacefully? See what happened and what continued to happen at Harvard, violence and chaos. Not here. Let's change Cornell and restructure the university.

It was a charged situation. Negotiation with the dean of students occurred Sunday. They discussed terms of an evacuation. Kurt Kallini came with the dean. Electricity turned off. No phones. No refrigerators. No way to see the mess because darkness illuminated only the circle of guns, candles, and Panther berets. Kallini had helped broker a compromise in the McClaren case and convince the Catholic priest it wasn't worth the crisis. That was a year earlier with the takeover of the economics building. The week followed the death of Martin Luther King.

Now Kallini got asked to bridge the gap between black and white. Lionel was his protégé. Other professors in history and government liked Lionel's quiet intelligence and his ability to reflect their ideas. The dean of students knew Lionel was the leader he had to convince. Zimbawe departed to the fractured world outside the university. The dean wanted to save Cornell. There were issues and answers. Storming the building at Harvard got administration nowhere and now the Cornell campus gathered to support the Black students.

Kallini took Lionel aside to the broken cigarette machine. In the semi-darkness he gave Lionel the look. Kallini's eyebrows contracted. Time for the simple truth.

"You got everything you asked for. Take the Black studies program and leave."

"Did we get complete authority to choose professors, pick programs, and say-so over admission of more black students?"

"Of course not."

"Then we stay."

"What more do you want?"

"Our black pride."

"Meaning?"

"To run our own institutions without interference from a racist administration. To build our own communities without interference from a racist society."

"Never happen."

They returned to the table. The Dean told them of funds for the Black studies program, for an outreach into the Ithaca community, for a say in the choice of director and visiting professors. The Dean looked to Lionel within his circle of black students with guns. Lionel spoke.

"These are our non-negotiable demands:

1. Nullification of the judiciary board's charge of harassment.
2. Amnesty for the takeover of the Straight.
3. Investigation of the cross burning outside our women's dormitory."
4. Right to choose professors, pick courses, and admit students to our Black studies program.

Lionel glanced at the dean surrounded as he was by blacks with guns. The dean had come to end the violence at all costs. Before the Ithaca police came on campus. Before someone called in the national guard.

"Nullification will be the sticking point."

"It's a bankrupt judiciary board. No black members. No charges against the SDS when they harassed the Chase recruiters. It's institutional racism."

"I will take the demands to the faculty, but they will fight for academic freedom. They're still smarting from the McClaren case and the takeover of the economics building."

"It's institutional racism. Their call."

Lionel stood firm. He had other ideas. Inside the whirlwind he transformed the politics of compromise to the politics of willpower.

"The guns got to go."

"The guns stay."

"Please Mr. Dubois, be reasonable."

"A cross was burned to scare our black women. Jocks from the fraternities crashed into the Straight like Nazis to evict us. Racists and fascists threaten to shoot us down like dogs. Reason is lost on them. The guns symbolize our political will."

Lionel took the scratch copy of the agreement signed by the dean. "That's the deal."

"You're out in the morning."

"We're out when the faculty sign."

"I will take the demands to the faculty on Monday for a vote. If they do not agree, I will resign."

"Done."

The Dean got up to go. Kallini saw he was extra in these negotiations. He hoped none of the radical SDS returned from Harvard, particularly Quinn the Eskimo. This was a powder keg waiting for Quinn's match. One bomb exploded brings an end to the entire academic community. Lionel too had his radical agenda.

So much press and media arrived on campus because of the picture of Lionel and the BSU marching out of the Straight with guns held high. Bandoliers, shotguns, poolsticks, and Lionel head down, rifle carried low, without flare, as if it was the least thing on his mind. Guns upped the ante. They were badass black men guarding their women. The cross burning resulted in the guns.

Press coverage and the pictures portrayed a radical escalation. There was no cause and effect, no this, then that, only the black men carrying guns on an ivy league campus. What happened at Harvard was worse, but it had no shock value. Lionel wanted shock value. All the force necessary. They walked into the Sunday morning, into an alerted press coverage. Black men not marching to church, but as to war. The faculty took it for confrontation, for them to sign off the deal under duress, to capitulate as they had done with McClaren the year before. The Board listened to the president and he wanted the show done. Luckily they escaped near catastrophe with the frats and the blacks fighting for bragging rights. The president wanted peace at any price.

The Dean explained his reasoning to the faculty. How he promised to resign if they rejected the deal. That part of the faculty subjected to loss of academic freedom in the McClaren case refused to sign. Not under duress. Not until the BSU participated in the judiciary board. Not until the issue of institutional racism stopping impinging on academic freedom.

So by Sunday afternoon all came to a standstill. If Lionel led the BSU into the Straight, if he fought the fight against the frats, and if he marched them out with guns and changed them from the Black Student Union to the Black Liberation Front, what had they won? No deal. Again the harassment charges against the brothers and cross burning against the sisters. He could call Kallini and work on a compromise. Instead he accepted a chance to speak over campus radio and broadcast his message. At least SDS gathered the Cornell students in support of the BLF stand.

Martial law was in effect since the picture of the guns. Question he was asked by WHCU radio, whether any of the faculty supported them.

"Some. But there are members of the administration and faculty who are racist, and they will be dealt with."

Lionel mentioned the name of the president, the dean, faculty members on the judiciary board, and professors with reputations in the scholarly community.

"You have guns?"

"We have a constitutional right to bear arms and when black people use that right to defend themselves, it's called coercion."

"Anything that can be done?"

"In the three hours until 9 PM the faculty should convene and pass the Straight deal. After then, it's all on the line. Cornell has three hours to live."

The president set up the meeting at Barton Hall for everyone to have a say. The hall filled with ten thousand students and a hundred teachers. It was a huge fieldhouse used for concerts and athletics. Lionel let the SDS run the assembly. He expected them to put their bodies on the line and take over a building. Take some of the pressure off the BLF and put some white pressure on the faculty.

An hour later Lionel repeated his radio remarks. "We blacks are willing to put our lives on the line, so let the faculty know their lives are on the line too."

Beside Lionel in his shaded persona of black revolutionary stood his white counterpart, Quinn the Eskimo, back from Harvard to put the RYM at Cornell on the line beside their black brothers.

"Then let's back up Lionel EB Dubois and his BSU become the radical Black Liberation Front. Let's back him up with an SDS become the Revolutionary Youth Movement. Let's march out of Barton and take over Day Hall. March into night's martial law, and turn night into day."

There were rumbles in the crowd of 10,000 students. Pretty much all the frat structure had done penance, and they wanted to make amends. Much of SDS knew they got off scot-free for the Chase recruiters. If they broke martial law on campus and took over Day Hall, then white and black would have as much on the line as anyone. There were rumblings of movement from the great hall.

Kallini reached for the microphone on stage as he'd done before as rock musician, and as a TA lecturing in the government and history departments. He had no set speech. His time was limited to a few sentences before the surge started to become a tidal wave into the night, over to Day.

"Hey, let's not play revolutionary tonight. I mean, if you are really serious about change. Or do you want to act out some psychodrama? A confrontation for the sake of confrontation. You know, go with the black and white. Go into the night to Day. It all sounds like a script. It's too simple. So if you're serious for change, then wait till tomorrow. Wait! Now is not the time to move. Now is not the time to act out some psychodrama. Now is the time to be reasonable. The faculty convenes tomorrow at noon. If they don't vote to nullify, then I will be with you. At high noon, not now."

Kallini gave both Lionel and Quinn the look. Like black and white were the same answer, and that answer was wrong. Kallini had really done no more than delay the crowd. He doubted he had any effect at all. But he had his say.

Josh Steen helped him back to his seat with that odd hop he had. What made Kallini recognizable. Josh thanked him and returned to the microphone. The whole student body was ready to stay or go.

"I've been on the phone with the president. High noon tomorrow. Why can't we wait? We can. Why can't we act without marching into the night over to Day? We can. Why can we? Because we have already taken over the great hall here at Barton. Why can't we wait here all night and all day? Here we are. Here we make our stand. Here we are the Barton Hall Community.

"And what are our demands? Yes to the BLF and their black studies program. Yes to SDS and its housing program in Ithaca. No to Chase investments in South Africa. No to ROTC training on campus. And no, ten thousand times no, to the war In Vietnam."

Josh Steen got his cheers when neither Kallini nor the black/white alternative got this crowd's full consent. The right way he decided found the greater consensus.

"The Barton Hall Community will stay here until the faculty does the right thing. Nullification is the right thing. Then we need to have positive action. We need to restructure this university to make it over in an image of black/ white pride. We need to participate in this democratic change, not like the reactionary professors who cry for academic purity while there's institutional racism. Not like the radical night and day of the BLF and the RYM, new acronyms for a new nightmare. No, we want to participate in restructuring Cornell, and if we stay here till it's done, then we will have our redemption and our racial reckoning. Stay here and turn night into day. Make the Barton Hall Community the center of the new Cornell University."

Other speakers added to the Teach-in as the night progressed. Some did go into the night with Lionel and Quinn the Eskimo. Some grew weary after midnight. But half the ten thousand stayed and waited, and for them it was a transforming experience.

34
Kady's Blessing

Kady Bontecott traveled by train from Paris to Rome. Jesse came as her companion. There were student strikes in Milan and Rome where sixty thousand students had too few professors. There were union strikes for wages. And one of the larger communist parties in Europe. As Kady saw with the communist party in Paris it was a bourgeois affair. They marched in crowds down the Champs Elysee, but like the students they went home to family and a late dinner. Only in Czechoslovakia was the communist party serious and Russian tanks sent into the Prague Spring dealt with Dubchek, seriously.

The politics got beyond what Kady knew was a finishing touch to her finishing school education. Moreso with Jesse who missed her brother at Chase Manhattan. Much as Kady's dad ran her life, Jesse's brother ran hers. Even who she got to know. Brother heard she punched Steve Hancock, and Steve applied for a job at Chase. He came from the same Groton, Episcopalian crowd as did her brother John.

A life worth living, that was what David Morpheys talked about. For him it meant a lot more than it did to her. To Kady and Jesse too, a life worth living was one where they had some say in what they chose to do. Jesse's brother told her to apologize to Steve Hancock and say she was sorry matters got out of hand. Our parents know his parents. Kady's father expected her to come home this April break of two weeks from French courses and see her mom. Soon as school completed he expected her home for the summer, for the rest of her life. Her father expected her to take care of her mom. If she tutored at the Bennet school and then taught there, all was good. Then marry some teacher at the school. Her life, her father's business.

"So how are you without David Morpheys?"
"I forget how it was."
"Then how were you with him?"

"It was a nice month."

"That's all?"

"I mentioned to Deb. What if you met a guy who didn't take all your time and effort? With whom you could be yourself. Like with a girlfriend. You could tell him everything. Like about my mom, and not have him tell me what to do."

"It was that way with Morpheys?"

"No, but it was close. What's a month anyway?"

"Thirty days together, sharing everything."

"I liked sleeping with him the last night."

It was dark on the train car over the Alps to Milan. They watched the Cote d'Or on the way to Switzerland and south. They slept with the early evening and the April rain. Then the moon came up, hung about window level, and no one rode the boxcar except them. It was pleasant to share secrets late at night. Sort of cuddled together. There was no honest to god sleeping on an all night train to Milan.

"I bet you did, you slut."

"To know one, you must be one."

"Yea right."

Kady gave her a nod.

"I don't care for Steve Hancock one bit."

"You're so cute, Jesse."

"So what was it like?"

"Like all night awake and dreaming. All touch and feel, you must know."

"Must I? Steve Hancock was count to a hundred."

"I don't know."

"You have sex?"

"No."

"Why not?"

"The last night, that's why not."

Jesse leaned with her as the train swayed around a mountain curve down the Alpen slopes into the industrial valley of Milan. Like the Milano cookies full of chocolate. Which Kady liked. The little luxuries. So much better than Orioles. She lit a Dunhill cigarette and Jesse took a few puffs. Jesse didn't smoke. Kady brushed Jesse's bangs from her blue eyes as smoke made her cough. Strange how the moonlight illuminated the coach.

"Like I'd get pregnant the way Barb Kelly did. Already four months pregnant away at Berkley. Some guy named Ted takes her to see the Oakland A's play baseball."

"Is it Kurt Kallini's kid?"

"Barb doesn't know."

"That's Barb Kelly."

"But she wants her baby, black or white. Either Lionel with his black rap or Kallini with his scowl. I wonder how Italians will look to us after knowing Kurt Kallini. They can't be like him."

"Barb's her own person. The baby will be like her."

"Good luck with her father."

"Yea. So did you want to have sex with Morpheys?"

"I don't know, Jesse. So much sweetness that night. I want to now, sometime, but I don't see us getting back together. Every couple days he writes, all kinds of poetry and philosophy, and parts of his dissertation thesis, what am I to think?"

"He wrote long letters to Dana Dupont. She shared them with me."

"Did Morpheys love her?"

"I told you it was different. Like brother and sister, what I have with John, who calls from Chase in NYC. What I had with Dana until she left for Hamilton to be near her brother."

"He sleep with her?"

"The one night coughing in the room Dana got in bed with him. I got jealous and left. Dana came after me, telling me it was nothing. Just a lark."

"You liked Dana Dupont?"

Jesse fell quiet. Still the moonlight on her perfect face. The two alone on a train coming into Italy sharing secrets before the dawn.

"Did you like that Steve Hancock?"

"That was for my brother. A make up."

Kady fell quiet. It wasn't something she understood.

"I liked Dana and she liked me freshman year. We were roommates by coincidence. She was naïve about the attraction. She didn't know what to think. She had lots of guy friends too and I think she wanted both of us with Morpheys. Would that have blown his mind!"

"I don't know. It's way beyond me."

"Well I know."

Kady didn't know what to say in this situation either. Guy pinches your ass and you sleep with him for your brother's sake. Now her and Dana. She heard out Jesse because she liked talking with her.

"I love the way you listen to people, Kady."

"Yes I listen. Like with Morpheys. I write back short blurbs, an occasional postcard, because I can't answer in full. And what he writes doesn't respond to what I say. I don't know what to think with Morpheys. I'm just fooling myself."

"Don't think so. I saw the stunned look between you that day, him playing ball and us at yoga. That's love. That's the sweetness in the dark Dana and me had."

"It didn't work out?"

"She wouldn't admit we were closer than roommates, you know, closer than Trixsie and Deb, closer than you and Barb."

"Barb was boy crazy."

"Barb was open with everyone and everyone took advantage. Not like a girl friendship."

"That's what I want with David Morpheys."

Jesse held her by the arm. They had a talk. Girls talked all these matters out. Least girls Kady knew at Bennet and Wells College. It was no big deal. They managed to sleep until the train pulled into Milan with the morning. Then they shopped in the fashion stores. Best in the world unless they were fixated on the Rue de Rivoli in Paris.

They got a hotel room and the next morning a train to Rome to see the Pope. For her mom's birthday on May first Kady sent a papal blessing to her and hoped she'd get well soon. Hope springs eternal, especially in the eternal city, for Catholics like Kady Bontecott and her mom.

V
Mayday, Mayday!

35
Expansion of the War

Last week of April blew David's mind. Early dropped out for no better reason than failing grades. By fractured logic he joined the army before he got drafted. David shook his head. Go into a skid and veer in that direction? Enlist for Vietnam? Like leaning into a punch, David thought. Early's plan to resist the war from within was all Kallini's idea. To David the army was the wall with a draft door in and no way out.

Same week Early got his DC Induction notice and dropped out, Nixon stepped up bombing Hanoi and troops crossed into Cambodia. Nixon escalated the war. The March on Washington, smoke from Kallini's pipedream, erupted into a full blown reality on every college campus. The steering committee captured the college community and took over student government.

Onto the chapel stage walked Kallini's freshman contingent. Black dude with shades and gnarled beard took the podium. The place was packed.

"Nixon had his pigs shoot Black Panthers in their beds, and nobody cared. Nixon bombed yellow people in their rice paddies, and nobody cared. Now it's time we cared, time we gave a shit, because we're gonna be fighting World War III, if we don't."

Second freshman partying with Kallini had his say. He was jean-jacketed and his hair tied back.

"Listen, we students have a job to do and that job means we refuse Nixon's war-mongering. There's no time for politics. It's simple, we march on Washington. We lend support to the national coalition. We close campus and open shop in the nation's capital. We lead, we don't linger in debate."

Normal finger-snapping of chapel debate turned to cheers and footstomping.

"Okay, here's a visitor from the national steering committee. His name's Kurt Kallini and he graduated from Berkley in the far out West. Listen to him and let's go."

Kurt Kallini stood transformed. Typical clothes he wore were long black coat and cowboy hat with a peace band. Now he looked like a professor in his tailored gray suit. His shaggy black hair and beard he trimmed neat like a lawyer in court. Kurt's thick eyebrows and riveting eyes fired like flint and steel. He gripped the podium and stared: his eyes on the professors in front, his pause catching the back and balcony crowd. Snow drifted down the vaulted church windows, snow on April 30th, snow a month late off Lake Erie. Kurt fisted his knotted tie loose.

"Pretty hot in here."

Kurt removed the gray jacket and lowered his tie-knot until he looked the executive, dressed for a presidential advisor in the war room.

"Pretty hot along the Mekong and hotter in Cambodia. I think advisors failed to tell Mr. Nixon hot war in all Asia means nuclear war. Cooler heads should prevail."

He spoke calmly, but a tense edge razored his voice. Radiators hissed and steamed when Kurt paused.

"Shouldn't we cooler heads here at Hamilton have a say, before Mr. Nixon starts the next world war? Shouldn't this advice be a chapel concern? And political action too? Are these the questions to ask?"

The chapel crowd buzzed with whispers. Heater pipes knocked and banged, like organ pipes of protest and drums of destiny. Kurt elevated his voice and deepened his tone.

"Are these the questions to ask, and are these the questions we need answered? What do you think, you with the cooler heads?"

The professors begrudged him a nod of the head, while the crowd in the back and the balcony shouted yes and applauded. "Right on! Out of sight!" Kurt removed his vest and turned to collect his notes.

"I say we take a trip to see our congressmen in Washington, and have our say. If soldiers are marching, we should march too, we should march on Washington. What do you with the cooler heads say?"

Kurt tugged at his tie like it choked him.

"God it's hot in here. Let's go make it hot down in Washington."

Kurt took his tie off.

"It's time we hang Nixon with his campaign promise to bring the war to an honorable end. He's starting the next world war. It's time we hang Nixon."

Kurt slipped the tie-knot like a hangrope. Ranting cheers made him shout himself hoarse.

"Tomorrow is May Day. May Day all around the world, and that world hangs in the balance. Hang together with the Movement, or hang separately. Tomorrow may be too late. Mayday! Mayday! Mayday! Let's march on Washington, tonight!"

A normally calm Peter Bergman shook David and said, "He's right. The dude's damn right. Let's fuel the Pimpmobile and ride on Washington."

David caught the fever too. Chapel fever grew in every soul there. Snow fell furiously on April 30th. Mayday, Mayday. Nixon started the third world war, but students en masse fell like an avalanche upon the capitol to overwhelm the war effort. Hear the voice of reason. It was Peter Bergman, a soul possessed.

"Come on David, let the others march. We ride tonight. Get Early Hayze, our DC inductee. We'll take him and his induction notice and tell his draft board he can't go, because we ain't going to study war no more."

In a flash they had Early, and Early had his idol and everyone's now, Kurt Kallini. The Pimpmobile was warm, the snow dusted. They took to the tunnel with light at the end. Ride the night like a break-away in a football game, a run to daylight and dawn. Down Route 81 road conditions were terrible, well into Pennsylvania, but morning the snow subsided like a winter dream. There was spring air, sweet-scented near Gettysburg, and as they crossed Delaware a salty dog dampness cast its spell. Route 95 revealed budding trees and flowering bushes around the Beltway of Baltimore. Southbound, and Early delivered them to DC and across to the college campus of Georgetown. Trees hung summer full on nice neighborhood streets. The black iron gate draped a sign, saying, "Welcome, War-Weary of the World."

There was light at the end of the tunnel. Early had a friend from high school.

"Harry Heinz is cool. He's got us a place to crash. His dad was a special-ed teacher. Picture him in the Fifties with a pointed beard, definite beatnik type. He mentored us both."

"A look like that got the McCarthyites on your case," Kallini said.

"He helped all the kids in trouble. In fact, he saved me and Harry from a drug rap for smoking a little weed in the boy's room."

Harry was hip in bell-bottomed jeans and tie-die teeshirt. His beard was blond fuzz, and his heavy granny glasses gave him an academic look. Harry loved the tail-finned Caddie.

"Hey Peter, your car is cool. Call your cad the revolutionary taxi. Let me give you a tour of DC."

Kurt shook his head.

"I got to deliberate with the steering committee. See me after the tour, Early, and I'll introduce you. Power to the people, Harry Heintz."

"Far out, man. Far out."

Peter relinquished his keys. Downtown the skyline vaulted stories high. Theirs was tunnel vision. They craned their necks to see the sights. Harry spun curves and switched lanes, saying he was taking the revolution to the streets. He took them to a second floor Chinese place for dinner. His wiry frame packed away a fortune in food. David counted what money he had and checked the prices. This was a dinner gone south. Harry told him to come along.

"The place is expensive, isn't it Harry?"

Harry smiled his glazed smile, stoned and happy with the world.

"Don't worry, man. Early Hayze handles it. Always has, always will."

They passed the men's room, pushed open the posh doors to the parking lot, and Harry reved the caddie as Early hopped in. Peter shook his head. They were out of there in a flash of red tail-finned delight.

"We liberate our first restaurant, the people's free eatery."

No check, no tip, and no normal day. From snow south to mild sunset, space was a bold frontier and time a path of flight. Fourth floor Georgetown dorm viewed the capitol skyline, a bizarre aura of white marble and sun setting over the Shenandoahs. David stared starry-eyed at students rapping protest and marches. He watched constellations and dozed in a chair, till Harry took him to a mattress and he crashed.

36
Stand up, Sit down

Next morning Peter Bergman said they should see their congressmen. The right thing to do. Peter had on his double-breasted suit and wingtips.

"Heavy, dude. You're the spitting image of your old man."

"Do what you do. If I get Clean for Gene in New Hampshire, I can dress up in DC."

"Trim the beard and cut your hair too. You think politicos care how you look?"

"All they care about. They talk to constituents, not long hairs. Like Kallini said, I'll have my say. That's important."

"Yea, I guess. The sitdown seminar, we ought to check it out."

Peter trucked along and David rushed to keep up. Tunnel to the Capitol. Peter's Caddie was gone. It was Harry Heintz. Note read, "Early lent me the keys and your car serves the steering committee. Be proud, the Revolutionary Taxi's on the job."

Peter wasn't. He was pissed. Try the seminar, to find Early. They found him there. Kurt Kallini planned a demonstration for the bus terminal, where army inductees shipped out to Ft. Dix and basic. Same feverish look and bold eyebrows. He spoke crisp and dry, with little wasted emotion, no dramatics. Early was more alert than normal.

"Notice the Hayze over there. One brave dude. Early joined the army as a resister within the military complex. Revolution starts when soldiers side with the people. Begins at the Bastille and Red Square when soldiers become the people's army. Today we do our part to clog up the Capitol."

"How do we clog the capitol?" Early asked.

"Resisters on the north and south entrances sit down to stop your bus. They let their body go limp. Offer no help to the DC police carrying you away. Police are well trained. Don't expect rough treatment and don't offer any."

"What do I do?"

"With the bus stopped and cameras showing protesters removed to police wagons, you break out as many inductees as you can. Resistance from within. We want that picture on the evening news. Good luck, Early."

His shoulders slumped less. The Hayze had his day. David wished him luck.

"By 4PM I'll be a celebrity. Army will dump me in jail a few days and say the Hayze he's not military material. It's my ticket out. Make them discharge me. Beat the Draft, dig."

Idea of resistance appealed to David. It was nerve and action, not a lot of talk. Each person decides to sit down and do time in jail. Decision and action. I did this to stop that. Here the imposing moment to decide one's future. Jesus, he'd leave the country and live in Paris. Do it!

Peter located Harry Heintz, who threw up his hands to say, "Hey, shoot me. Couple dudes helping the Hayze needed a ride to the Rotunda."

"Then put the car to good use. Give us a ride to the Capitol?"

"Dude, let's roll."

Peter surrendered the keys and all power to the people. Early promised to pick them up after the debate on Cambodia. Harry Heintz, the hippest dude in DC, to the rescue.

Congress loomed large. Peter took to the stone steps with his purposeful walk. He lunged forward each stride, straight-backed, square-shouldered, and stiff-necked as a West Pointer. Peter worked hard, except on grades. He was sensitive to approval. From David, who liked his political optimism. From activists, who liked his spirited work and comradery, and from himself. Peter liked to be in line with this best appraisal.

Like his father the activist lawyer in New York City, Peter wanted change within the system. Get the government to serve the people. When inspired, he did his dad's agenda. Only his classes didn't inspire him. Work hard for others and himself, it's mutual benefit. It fit his picture of the good life, and life should be good.

Peter petitioned a page and asked for the office of his Westchester congressman. Peter knew how to get things done. Then the page returned and regarded David, as David, already nervous, regarded himself. His leather moccasins hid a hole in the heel, his Wranglers frayed and stained from the journey south, and his workshirt tucked too short for his arms. Slumped shoulders and face unshaved he was here to tell Hamilton Fish, Jr. what to do. His rep, whose grandfather and father had been bigtime in the Cabinet and the House. Tell him that David Morpheys says Nixon has to remove the troops from Cambodia.

Who the hell was he? Son of a farmer and IBM toolmaker. What a fool! Talk to Hamilton Fish, Christ he wanted to run and hide and join the army like Early Hayze. All in the moment David saw how stupid he looked, and he agreed with the page, stay put.

Peter returned in twenty minutes. He had his say. Arthur Townsend spoke to Charles Rangel of New York City and agreed. No joint resolution passed in Congress today. Townsend knew Peter's father. Just the votes were not there. Peter had two passes to the show.

"You see Hamilton Fish?"

David shrugged his shoulders.

"No matter. Fish is a staunch Republican and refuses to limit the war in any way."

David liked his friend's understanding. The page assisted them to balcony seats. Fifty to seventy-five congressmen stirred in dispersed conclaves below. Like Radio City before the Rockettes took stage. They gossiped and exchanged notes. Even when the joint resolution was read, they paid scant attention. Ted Kennedy and Eugene McCarthy made positive comments. Congress should assert its political responsibility. Congress declared war, not the President.

Senator Stennis rose in support of the President. His haughty southern drawl reminded David of standers in the schoolhouse doors.

"This is but an incursion into Cambodia, Mr. Speaker, limited in scope, its express purpose to clean out Vietcong arsenals over the border. The Gulf of Tonkin Resolution grants the President the power for such a sweep up operation."

Stennis continued his carefully constructed argument. He cited examples of presidents using war powers without an express declaration of war. In his bluff manner Stennis concluded in lawyerly fashion.

"History then approves the President's action, the Constitution approves the President's action, and circumstances warrant this limited incursion into Cambodian territory. For these reasons the President is right."

The balcony scorned the senator's speech. Chairman Agnew threatened to clear the galleries if further disruption occurred. The vote tallied. A line of congressmen reported to fill a quorum and have their vote recorded. The proposal was defeated, and few congressmen stayed to deal with daily business. No Webster-Calhoun confrontation. The debate and vote were for the record and nothing more.

Revolutionary Taxi waited among the black limousines. The red-finned phantasm said protest was part media event, another show like the Senate masquerade of meaningful debate. Harry squinted at them through his granny glasses.

"Hey David, you set your senators straight?"

"Ridiculous, Harry. Business as usual, right Peter?"

"The count was recorded. Some reps took notice. Change is a slow process in democratic government, give it time. We had our say."

"No way, no how. Change is a personal process. We saw hardening of the arteries. We saw a contraption to let off steam and cap tight its control. It's the machinery of night, as I heard Early say. Or was it Kallini?"

Harry drummed the wheel to a radio tune.

"Hey man, it's time we gave Early his sendoff. Let get to the bus station. Early's breaking out. On the Revolutionary Taxi, we got a date with destiny. Hold on dudes."

Peter tapped a front seat cavalry charge and Harry joined in, beeping, weaving through traffic, and skidding into a parking spot near the Peace Corps building.

"Velvet fist of American imperialism," said Harry.

There was a corridor for the buses to exit. DC police trained for protest. The tunnel to light went that way. Early stood near the bus with his hitching knapsack. They'd been places with him. Their guru of the open road. Peter wished him luck and gave him a pack of smokes. Early's fingers shook rolling his own.

Then it was time. Early said his goodbyes and went in. Across the street some bearded guy pounded a bongo and chanted like Hari Krishna. He drew a crowd and Kurt Kallini sat beside him. Someone said the guy with the scraggly beard was Allen Ginsburg. Kurt knew everybody and there was Ginsburg "Howling" for their generation. North entrance cleared of hipsters and hangers on. The newcomers shared long hair and colored clothes, but they were in earnest to stop the war by sitting their body in the way.

The bongos pounded from the Peace Corps and the police sanctioned a line, one side spectators and the other side, those prepared for nonviolent protest. The battle lines being drawn. Hey, stop. David was drawn to the imposing moment as it elongated in time. He had no senator to see. He had no Allen Ginsburg to sit beside. He had only his friends, and Early Hayze on his way to Vietnam. And others like him. David included. Somehow he lost connection with Kady Bontecott and that was sad. He had only his brain and his body. Sit down and have his say. Here today it counted.

Peter understood. He always did. "See you later. Good luck."

"Sit down and say no."

"If the worst happens, I'll be by the jail to get you out."

David sat with the latecomers on the ramp. Early birds crowded the garage doors of the bus exit. The sky above towered with clouds racing in a brisk breeze. The sun shone sporadically. The cigarette an older man named Tom Sanderson gave him settled his nerves. He viewed the crowd waist high. He was doing good, and scared too.

He readied himself like a quarterback plans plays for what the defense allows, then takes advantage. The old thrill returned, battling an opposition when the score counted, when his action mattered. It was time transfixed by spirit, the zeitgeist on the make, and his decision tied into predestined action. Do it and it shall be done.

Doors opened and DC police cleared bodies from the flat up the ramp. Prepare the way. They were professional. They asked each person to be carried or walk off. They were efficient. Half the sit-in crowd sat in a police bus. Behind the doors waited Early's bus. More protesters rushed to the north entrance for the confrontation. Here it was happening. The crowd surged with a new tide. The time was right. Just as police asked Tom Sanderson whether he'd walk or be carried, a police walkie-talkie said, "Exit has been effected from the south entrance. Discontinue operations."

The crowd surged and ebbed with news the buses rolled out the entrance to the rear. They'd been had. Tom Sanderson stood and squelched his burnt out smoke under his heel.

"I got to admit, David. I'm not eager to elevate my spirit and do it again. Nice to meet you. And keep the faith."

David walked away with the tail end of the crowd to the rear entrance. Draft buses traveled out to the main road, away from the pit where a sitdown blocked their exit. Resisters in the road sang, "We shall overcome." But they were too few to matter. The front bus turned off its engine. All according to plan. The police deftly lifted each man or woman from the route to the police bus. Pictures came in flashes of light, unreal, almost like a film about making a film. David was a spectator. The moment passed. Then he spotted Early Hayze with his bug-eyed face, no glasses, staring hopeless in a window. Military police sat surrounding him. Early was off to Ft. Dix, like it or not.

37
Fort Dix Breakout

Kallini hesitated coming to the RYM meeting. He won over the GI Resistance and RYM was not trusted by them. He'd have to detach RYM from the Ft. Dix Breakout planned by soldiers there. Quinn retreated into his cellar. Annual SDS get together came in June. Josh Steen refused to come to their church in DC. He had work with the Georgetown group planning peaceful demonstrations, anti-war work, and options for conscientious objectors. Many filed paperwork en route to Canada and Sweden. Josh said he'd take Kallini there and pick him up, but have no more to do with Quinn and their divebomber collective. It was Kallini's suicide mission. Get rid of RYM.

Events changed Kallini's attitude. He worked with Joshua Steen. And his SDS with a human face. But if it needed more radical action to jumpstart the revolution, it wasn't Burn and Quinn and Rawley who had the answer. Yet they had their plans too. Harvard, Cornell, and the DC moratorium looked like steps to stopping Nixon and his reactionaries before they reved up the FBI and this new Cointelpro group. What if Ft. Dix counted for more than a demonstration? What if draftees, Vietnam vets, and Movement people changed the mind of the military? This was the weekend for it to work. So Kallini came to the RYM meeting to make it work. His presence would deter the radical RYM-rockers.

Rawley and Burn met him at the door. Better times they would marry and present a couple to the world. Now smash monogamy was their slogan. In balmier days couples linked up with endless meetings and countless campus parties, while uncoupling completed the links from guys to girls to other guys. Now the orgy, the rage, and the gut-check. Rawley offered him a seat, but Kallini stood and watched. Let everyone see him, defenseless, come to plead with them.

Age 33 Kallini grew into another generation. His crippled back and leg left him without youthful fervor. He had no talent for violent confrontation and no appetite for the apocalypse. Sex and drugs and violence for them took on team sport. For them it raised revolutionary consciousness and dulled the cunning of acquired experience. This Action Faction embraced global revolution, and whatever helped the Black vanguard they would do.

RYM expected the army to rise up. They expected Blacks to shoot white officers. They wanted a Redsquare Mayday across the nation. They garnered support with women, high schoolers, and gangs. They called for the jailbreak. Next came involvement in the prisons. Czechago called them to confrontation. They got beaten up and they wanted to come back for days of rage.

"So you're off to Dix with us?" Kallini asked Rawley.

"To the coffeehouse crew of soldiers returned from Nam. They got all them black dudes. I know Cornell and Lionel got in the papers, but these dudes got guns and used them. We'll fuel the revolution with their rage. And their guilt."

"Burn going with the women's contingent?"

"She's got a bus full, but we'll see how it plays out."

Burn, Baby returned. She hardly looked at Kallini. They'd been a couple with her fresh from Catholic school and him from the seminary.

"So Kallini, you in for Ft. Dix? I mean, to destroy the place."

Level of animosity aimed at him. Somehow you were either with Burn and Charlie and Dier or you were the enemy. Rawley kept his Plains' generosity.

"I got a willing draftee to stage the breakout."

"Anybody we can trust?"

"Burn, I think so. It's the little brother of Layton Hayze."

"Layton Hayze told this Cointelpro group on you and Quinn. Layton's another snitch."

"How is Quinn?"

"Underground with his casebombs. He hates you and Josh Steen and Layton Hayze, so that's your standing with him, and us."

"But can we work together on this Ft. Dix Breakout?"

"Sure, you all know what it takes."

"Don't listen to Rawley. We ain't in Kansas anymore. We're fighting back, fist and sticks and boots. For now. Then guns and bombs, all means necessary."

Kallini saw which way the wind blew. As Josh told him the RYM, least Burn and Dier and Quinn, readied for the revolution.

"Burn, do we have a demonstration or a hara-kiri mission?"

"We're not afraid to fight."

"Cornell made gains."

"It could have made the revolution. Let the frats and the BLF shoot it out. No compromise. No more fear of consequences. Let the revolution begin at Ft. Dix."

Rawley took off his quirky country hat and slapped it on his jeans, ready for the dust off. He wore RYM's fighting gear: boots, padding, upfolded jeans, but the hat was Kansas.

"No more half way measures, Kallini."

"Charge like Custer. Same with both you and Burn?"

"Kallini, quit playing Rawley. No more white skin privilege. Vanguard out front. Or right behind our black brothers."

"No one follows you if it's kamikaze."

"We don't want no followers. We want vanguard and revolutionary cadres. Others are the enemy. Including you, Kallini."

"Josh works with CO's and they won't go."

"We don't want Josh Steen, and especially not you, Kallini."

Dier came up to Kallini. They'd been a couple and now she was with Quinn, and his cadre had one mission.

"Hey Kallini, how did you manage to tick off Quinn?"

"He's got a short fuse."

"You play him against his family? Enemy of your friend and that bit."

"We've been at odds over Lionel and his role in the revolution."

"No more odds. You are the enemy. You play people, Kallini."

"So it is. Then choose, women. March for the soldiers of Ft. Dix. Charge the gates, trash the place, and break out the draftees."

"We do what we do?"

Kallini looked around this Methodist church. RYM changed

too. No longer the hip clothes, dancing, mating. No longer the revival of party like there's no tomorrow. Now the enclave of critical discussion. Criticize the group, criticize oneself, and try for transformation. Weather-fries. Now the stormtrooper boots. Everyone lecturing someone slouched ashamed by criticism. Women a year out of college ripped into girls and guys from high school or gangs from Detroit.

Kallini pulled a chair up to one of their enclaves of discussion. Burn and Dier gave him the cold stare. They'd been conrades. They'd been lovers. They'd shared the rosy hues of the SDS Sixties. They'd shared the endless meeting and the participatory democracy. Like the warm embrace of Mayday come to DC, the smell of dogwood, azalea, and explosion of cherry blossoms.

Dier had widely popped eyes. A flower child gone sour with violence. In boots and battle gear ready to take up arms, the machine gun, and Quinn's bombs, hating any of her lovers unwilling to resist, to risk, and to accept all this as revolutionary, determined, and by all means, necessary. All else was bourgeois and benign. New left became the old left, again.

"You're the bastard who turned Quinn the Eskimo against himself."

"Sorry I touched his quick fuse."

"Shut up."

"Aren't you afraid bombs in banks and pig stations will splinter the Movement?"

Kallini looked into the faces of the young kids, not too bright, not too happy with their lot in life, but eager to belong. These were Movement women dressing them down.

"Shut up, peacenik."

Burn yelled at Kallini. Her with the weight of brunette hair, the beautiful body, the kind of woman like many of the men, who liked sex, and played their machismo game.

"This is the end, our working together?" Kallini asked. "This is the end of the Sixties?"

Burn called over Dier.

"It's over?"

"We can't cooperate anymore than we can screw together. Fight with us, f__ with us, or just f__ off."

Kallini zoned in with his bushy brows. He riveted his look on first Burn, then Dier, finally the naive mirrors of hate from the kids. It wasn't a barroom brawl look he'd seen in Poughkeepsie. Two hip chicks dressing him down. Kallini could be a blue pig with scutcheon in hand, Tricky Dick, or another backslider in this new power politics. RYM echoed Mao's redbook and its report of Third World solidarity. Amerika stood for imperialism and the black vanguard were a colony in the belly of the beast. Kallini had no face to them, no history, no backlog with these new kids recruited by RYM, pushing aside Progressive Labor. RYM took over PLP's chants and added violent confrontation. It was gut-check time.

Dier … Burn, please. It's all here for the taking. A march on Washington, the close-down of the college system, and release of troops from Ft. Dix. Action into Cambodia, an equal and opposite reaction in DC."

"Hey Kallini, shut your f__ mouth. You're out."

Dier, shorter than him by six inches, pushed at him as he stood up. He didn't have his legs under him and he toppled over a chair and sprawled on the church floor. A pain stabbed in his back and he spun on his stomach. New recruits sang a Maoist version of Yellow Submarine. Like Quinn, everyone headed underground. Dier gave him a boot jack in his ribs and said it came from Quinn the Eskimo. Group criticism moved onto karate and Kallini was victim.

Rawley came over to help him up. Kallini twisted his short leg with an ankle sprain. He feared Rawley might finish him off. Least he knew the Movement was at an end. Kallini who never had his health, and now he knew RYM meant him harm.

"Listen Kallini. Women are pissed off the way you talked down Quinn. He supplied a lot of love and drugs and we miss him underground. Sorry. We'll miss you too. Women are on a macho trip. Don't mess with them."

Kallini hobbled toward the church door on Rawley's arm. Rawley waited while Kallini negotiated the three cement steps to the street. Cherry blossoms scented the air. Kallini knew he'd be tied in tight muscles for months.

"Good luck, Kurt, with the Ft. Dix Breakout. We decided if Dix is not us, then it's not our bag. We fight our battles, but we're going to choose them too. No more Czechagos. Sorry we can't work together, but none of the mass movement really worked to end the war."

"Half of America is against the war."

"Not our half. New tactics and strategies."

"Old mistakes. And violence that violates the Movement."

Kallini held onto the railing for dear life. He had no idea how to get back to the Georgetown campus. He didn't want to ask Rawley and Rawley didn't want to say no. Outside the new cadres of RYM there were no farewells. Least the GI Resistance had a clear shot at the Ft. Dix breakout, with no RYM interference. He called Joshua Steen from a People's Drug. Go ahead with their plans for Ft. Dix and the March on the capitol.

38

Cosmic, Man

The major part of the program closed, David meandered the DC streets toward Georgetown. His mind was dazed. Unreal city. A store called People's Drugs sold him a pack of smokes. Had the place been liberated by a battalion of freaks named Harry Heintz? Unreal, beyond belief.

They ate in the college messhall. They paid two dollars, to pass on another revolutionary meal. In the college he and Peter drank beers. Like they traveled high speed through a spiraling, turning tunnel the past twenty four hours, and that was it. What to do?

David wanted to go home and work for enough cash to fly to Paris. If the fling with Kady Bontecott faded, so what, all things pass. Maybe she didn't write letters. He wrote her daily meanderings, all mixed up with poems and lunatic fringe philosophy. It was his thesis on Prodigal Time and it wasn't. He wrote Kady so he wouldn't have to finish school. He wrote to her in love with a memory. Unreal girl. Love for her was an illusion too. Or she didn't write letters.

"Hey Peter, let's go to Paris this summer."

"Funny you ask. Cheryl wants to travel Europe. In August we go to Greece. I told her my grandfather, a bigshot Episcopal minister, has a friend in the American Church."

"Where's that?"

"Paris."

"Yea, I got a place to stay, and spending money."

"How's that, David?"

Peter gave him an unsure look.

"No, I'm set. I'm working for a group called the Brotherhood. Les Freres des Pauvres. Catholic group Kallini knows. I wrote and they listened."

"Hey then, we're set."

Also set was an evening of entertainment at Memorial Park. Congress had been a slow show. Not here. Judy Collins sang of clouds and changing times and Phil Ochs parodied, "I'm glad to be an Okie from Muskogee." Speakers from the Chicago 7 labeled Nixon as phallic as the Washington Monument. Black Panthers rapped. Rock group named Rhinoceros blasted sound into the far out reaches of space. Then David Dellinger led a burning of Draft cards for a sendoff into the starry night. Only bringdown, Early Hayze tripped to Ft. Dix and he was unlikely to return.

Then the mammoth parade of protest down Pennsylvania Avenue. Busloads poured into the Capitol. Masses moved like the mountain for Mohammed. Sunny skies and a swirling humanity paraded the streets to the Jefferson Memorial and out to People's Park. Bands played and orators spoke and spring sang of Mayday in DC. Back at Georgetown they stared at crowds in the square reveling in warm weather as dusk fell.

Harry was gone since yesterday. So was the red-finned Caddie, named the Pimpmobile, renamed the Revolutionary Taxi, now with no name and missing in action. From their perch on the sixth floor they had a long view. Crowd below cheered Vietnam vets returned home with tales of atrocity. In the DC vista sun traveled west across America, while they planned to leave the States for Paris.

"So how come you're not pissed off about your car?"

"I don't know."

They looked near and far. First the tunnel vision of speed and now the vista of space.

"You know, David, it's pretty spectacular."

"Far out."

"I mean how Nixon crossing a border in Cambodia stirred up this movement. Like a rock in waters. Physics, it's action and reaction. As Kallini says. Cosmic, as Early says, how it makes us global citizens. And in a democracy we have our say."

"Careful with the BS. Nixon did what he wanted and however much we sing and shout we have no say."

"Yet we do. You see the red car way off there. It's Harry come back from God knows where with my car. It all works out."

Their eyes trailed Harry Heinz from parking lot to the dorm. He ignored crowd and speakers and walked by as if the revolution didn't exist, very unlike Harry. He arrived on the sixth floor.

"Sorry, I forgot you guys."

He took off his granny glasses with thick lenses and rubbed his thumb and fingers over his nose. Frazzled look with hair all over, and unwashed bellbottoms of two days ago.

"Sorry I took your car all the way to Ft. Dix. I thought Early would somehow get away and need me. No chance. Those MP bastards gave him a personal escort."

"How did he look?" Peter asked.

"He looked scared shitless. Bastards beat the crap out of him. His face was red and bruised when they stopped for dinner in Jersey."

"We didn't do shit," David complained.

"You know what I think?" Harry said. "I think Kallini set him up. I think Kallini wanted the confrontation for news coverage."

"I don't know," Peter said.

Harry Heinz, Early's one good friend through school, took it personal. He didn't know Kallini, only the Hayze.

"There was sure no break out. No way to save his ass. Early was my friend, like a brother, and I miss him already. You guys take care cause I got to crash. Sorry again about the car."

39
She Wrote me Letters

They returned to Hamilton Sunday without Kallini and without Early Hayze. What spooked David back at the Towers was a postcard in Early Hayze's room. From Kady in April it pictured the prison of Chillon in Switzerland. David read her script like Dead Sea Scrolls.

"Love your letters. Been traveling in Italy. Had an audience with the Pope…Right! Will I see you in Paris this summer? All my love."

That was it. Byron poem and a poor dude locked up in the prison of Chillon. That was enough. He ransacked the room. What spooked him more, he found the card among Kallini's correspondence. Letters from San Diego and Berkley planning a March on Washington, then a big summer blowout. They all wrote the Sixties was over. In the end is the beginning, one letter quoted Kallini. Next the GI Resistance to the war.

Then knocking around in Early's closet beneath unwashed laundry, clothes Early wouldn't wear again in Basic or the jungles of Nam, he found an airmail box of poetry books. Breton, Mallarme, Verlaine, countless others he didn't know. In the box he found more postcards and wafer-thin, airmail blues.

David took the treasure of the Sierra Madre to his room. Before he crashed on a late Sunday night David committed times then and now to memory. He cursed out Early Hayze and Kallini, who picked up mail and ditched it in a closet. Guys were unreliable. He cursed out Kallini's DC March and summer blowout because none of it mattered more than the Chillon postcard. For the three short letters and three shorter postcards Kallini could go to hell and the Hayze to Vietnam for all he cared.

2/2/69 Hey Morpheys. I didn't know Paris lay in a temperate zone and Gulf currents kept it warm in wintertime. I haven't seen snow in a month, really. Of course, I haven't seen sun in a month. Neither seems entirely natural. Reminds me of Old Saybrook over the ocean. Instead of blue skies and views like you'd expect, the color gray keeps each thing in separate cardboard boxes, like this one. You look at a slick red VW and see just that. You look at a boathouse painted slick yellow, see the rectangular cube, but not the red VW up on Route 1. Walk along the beach. The sand slips under your feet beige-y white and waves curl sparkling blue crested and white capped, but like a gray colored world it grows monotonous. It's a world wet, luke-warm, and cardboard boxed. I read your letter about the interminable snow blowing blowing blowing on the Hill, and hope you miss me like I miss you. Kady calling calling calling…

2/28/69 Hey Morpheys, I don't like letters. Writing them I mean. My mom calls me every day before dinner, Millbrook time. Her usual hour, not mine. Here it's nine at night and Madame my French mom flips out and goes flying around the second floor apartment to find the phone because it must be an emergency. I miss my music too. We got a phone for emergencies and no phonograph. Jacques Brel sings on radio, whoopde-doo. Kallini came with you to the Hill. Excuse me, I don't know Hamilton College and the Hill impresses me. What's higher: the Hill or the Tour Eiffel. Jesse and I got to the Tour Eiffel with French guys sweet talking in Anglais, Hey Babe you're so pretty, tu sais. Jesse says no way Jose. I don't think she likes guys anyway. We elevator up above the gray city and see the gray sky. I wonder if your Hill has a better view this winter. Wish I could see what you see. Wish I was there. Wish you were here.

3/22/69 David my dear I do miss you. I don't miss Kurt Kallini much. Let me get this straight. He came with you and Early Hayze and Peter Bergman back to Hamilton College up on the Hill up into the Towers, and he smokes talking up some spring march to Washington DC. Hard to keep up with Hill lingo, and harder to keep up with Kurt Kallini. I won't mention any rumor has it. Like when he visited my horsefarm friend Dhalia Richards. He can't play tennis much. One leg's shorter than his other. I drove him to Cornell and met Lionel who's now in Berkley with my best buddy, Barb. I hope names are now familiar from you to me and me to you. Jesse picked up a Larousse volume of Andre Breton I send along. Like your letters Breton writes automatique, nonstop, surreal beat, and makes no sense at all.

In the box are other poets, enjoy. I'd send along Dunhills and grape cassis, that I enjoy. I'd send along an invitation. Come to Paris, David, and explain what your letters mean. Particularly, on Prodigal Time, lapses in time, and imposing moments. Come to Paris. There, I made the invitation. Four weeks in January were a sunny memory in this gray drizzling city of more museums, stores, cafes, tours, bridges and sights than anywhere in the world. Rather depressing, your missing it I mean. There I said it. At least in a letter. Bye to this white bird, please send one in return.

4/10/69 Dear David by the time you get this postcard we should be gone. We, includes Jesse and me. Paris has got the best of us. April break takes us to Switzerland and sunny Italy. Your last letter wrote more about Kallini, and your friend Early Hayze joining the army, but didn't say a thing about coming to Paris. In January I didn't mean to ask, but I did. Didn't I? We do nothing but tour Europe. No classes. Not for two weeks. Postcards fit my terse style and limited repertoire. Now on postcards. Less expectation. Fewer frustrations. Nifty trick, postcards. Mom calls. We talk. All is said. You write. I write. Letters make no sense. I hate writing letters I do. Postcard: This is Paris and wonder of wonders Le Pont Mirabeau.

4/25/69 Dear David. All roads lead to Rome postcard. Roma spelled backwards reads Amor. Eva backwards read Ave Maria. You know I love you. Maybe I never said it. I didn't intend to. But Paris and the Alps and sunny Italy, respectively, look gray and high and a bit too Catholic. Wish you were here. Of course. If you were here I'd be back in Paris. So not here but there. I'm mixed up. Calls to my mom connect us. With us, meaning you and me, letters and cards don't bridge the gap. It's a time lapse. They keep us apart. Mirabeau, deja vu. Never to return. I know you know the poem. On Mayday we return to Paris. Return, never to return, which is it?

He saw clearly now. Kady wrote him. Not much, but she cared and he'd go to Paris. All he had to do was go. Find work for planefare and go. How could that be a problem? Only possible problem, Kady didn't care for him. But she did.

He heard talking in Kallini's room. It was the freshmen, Mark and Lester. Not the Hayze of course.

"Hey Morpheys, you guys got back too."

"What's happening, Mark?"

"Packing up Kallini's shit and sending it to DC. What the man said to do. Then we're home to NYC before dawn."

"Can I get a ride with you to New Paltz?"

"Leaving in ten minutes, get ready."

The college voted to close. He'd write his senior thesis over the summer. The March on Washington closed Hamilton College. He was on his own now. Go live with Kady in Paris in a prodigal time.

Late Sunday night in a Chevy Camaro they rocketed like a bobsled down the luge tunnel of the New York State Thruway. Headlights hardly outran their motion. Blondhaired radical with hair knotted and his black brother, Lester, rushed home.

"Hey man, sorry to hear about the Hayze," Lester said. "Dude wanted to break out and it didn't work."

"What's Kallini up to in DC?"

David wished Mr. Valley Stream paid more attention to the road at 90 MPH. He'd been with Doug and this was no joke.

"Beats me, the man goes places normal men need a ticket and ID. I heard he had dinner with the underground SDS, to see which way the wind blows."

Like some slingshot they lunged around cars here and gone. Grand slalom on a Sunday night. Counting coups on the warpath, some crazy game, as Mark shouted Yippee! and Lester said Yippie-yi-oh. Past Albany a trooper clocked the car near one hundred and Christ, were these dudes surly. Mark with his Long Island accent complained he just passed some slow bastard. Trooper kept his composure and ticketed them. All the way to the New Paltz exit Mark yacked about the sombitchen cop jacken them around. They churned up a new head of steam and David shouted watch the exit after which warning they spun around the ramp, slowed as David leaped for his life, burned rubber in each gear and were gone.

The screech and speed tracked David's memory until a four-thirty, chilly silence settled down like dust. It had been months. The wonder with Kady, the endless winter, Mayday Mayday, looking for the light at the end of the tunnel. He was home. Call his dad, and twenty minutes his Ford Galaxy came. What a difference with his father. Slow and steady waiting for the dawn. His huge hands made little electric jerks holding the wheel, and his forearms clenched to quiet his shakes. Dad had a week of work at IBM.

"So a graduate of college, good."

"Got to finish my senior thesis."

"You'll do it this summer. Got plans?"

"Find work, make some money, and fly to Paris to see a friend."

"The Bontecott girl you met?"

"Yes."

40
Strings Attached

David drove first thing into a Pay-less gas station near the Riverview Bar and took down the Help-Wanted sign. Boss was early twenties, David's age, short, blond haired kid in search of his American Dream. David started that afternoon to learn the first hour was unpaid training. Pay-less said it all. Gas caps, wads of bills, unleashing hoods, sweeping and meter reads, these were stock and trade. Pungent fumes filled his fantasies, and tedium knew no end. Grease, oil, and gas patterned with dirt his jeans and his tied back hair heated in the sun. His dad said a job is a job. Why else call it work?

Bill, the kid entrepreneur, sat in his booth keeping books with rides to make sure Pay-less priced one cent below his competition. Scrawny high schooler toked up when Bill left. He returned and David caught his reprimand.

"Hey Morpheys, how come the pavement's unswept? You spread sand before I left. I don't have to watch over you every minute, do I?"

An irate asshole with bad teeth pulled in. He lost his gas cap.

"Yes sir, certainly," Bill told him. "Let me put a Pay-less check in your hand to buy a new one."

With his smile and locks of blond hair, Bill knew why he wasn't further ahead in the game of life. College kids like David got the breaks. He deducted ten bucks from David's salary for the gas cap.

He had David ride a pizza up to his house. His airhead wife told David to set it in the kitchen. Two babies played in the pen. TV played to Sears furniture all one cheap pattern. Her ranch carved out of a hill plot with twenty duplicates. She didn't thank him. She and Bill worked too hard to keep up payments. Bill toed the line on company policy. His mortgage and credit card belonged to the company. Kid Galahad of the gas station saw David didn't buy in. One's job, home, and family positioned a man in his town.

"Hey, with your smarts and correct speech, you should know all I know in two days. Trouble is your sweeping and toilet cleaning stinks."

A week on the job and Bill fired him.

"Why, for Christ's sake?"

"You don't fit in. You need constant supervision."

David shook his head. With the pothead kid Bill was boss. The paycheck was pay less too. It took another week before he got a job with Hudson Printing. After a safety seminar they put him to work: third shift, nighttime, eleven to seven. When he left for work, dad snored, his hand twitching now and then. His mom drank beer and smoked cigarettes until Johnny Carson. TV kept her company. Her time to relax after a hectic day running programs at the YWCA.

Her new career in community programs paid David's tuition. David got out of town. Parents sacrificed for him in college. Townies lived in town. Like Bill they worked a lifetime to make it in Hudson Park. Or like his two friends, Joey Gallo and Flash Gordon, who pulled all the strings to avoid Bill's set-up, found strings attached. Nobody else got out of town. Why David went to college.

Italian boss Sal Giordano showed him punching the timeclock. David heard the roar and crunch of the paper cutters. Rattle and hum shook everything under the ceiling intestined with ductwork. It shook the cement floor, the unpainted concrete walls, and rattled the sheetmetal like drum cymbals. It shook the windowed employee room including the coffee, coke, and candy machines. Even the people smoking on coffee breaks looked all shook up.

Sal put him on a far assembler. He shouted above the roar. His head tilted into his wide shoulders. Sal had no neck.

"David, you stack Lew Gordon's machine, cause he knows you. It ain't complicated so you'll get it right away. We got a good safety record this shift so don't stick your fingers into no machines and we'll be happy as hell."

David began his education on how books are made. Forklift deposited eight bins on his raised stage. He carried 48 cartons of fifty pound pages from loading to the cubicles. "Keep the cubes full," Sal's one direction. He inserted 8 separate cartons of double 16 pages into the long leviathan of a machine. Rattle and hiss as the leaves sorted. Glue squirted into the wrapped binding. Then chugging, shearing, and shucking out back to back four volume piles. Packers combed the product from the conveyor to the forklift. Glad Tidings. The process propagated an enormous number of "Good News" bibles. So be the good book in a machine age, product of the machinery of night.

Two hours until break passed with nervous haste. David rubbed shoulders with fellow employees smoking in the lounge, but noise made talk intolerable. By lunch his shoulder and back muscles strung tight. Harsh lights bleached the whole place white. Heavy black night hung low over his drooping spirits. Time stilled and extended the tedium of lifts, the repetition in books and faces, and the grinding noise knocking, knock-knock, knocking on the cerebellum of his brain. At five AM he slept on a box ledge for a split second fifteen minute lull between whistles. Time until seven tuned with dawn humming behind the vaulted windows painted black.

Sleepwalking days. Same books every night. He steamed into gear as others simmered to a stop. Night in and night out he drove to the factory, punched the timeclock, and worked against the roar. No escape. No nothing but the black encasement of ceiling, walls, and floor. Weeks passed. Hurry sundown, come sleep, and bring salvation. Darkness was all around and he was sinking down. Time lapsed.

41
In the End is the Beginning

Next Friday at five Joey Gallo, best friend in high school, called. David didn't sleep that day and sought something to purge this time lapse.

"Hey David, my man, B-ball game at the old Marist gym. Can you come?"

"Yes, let's do it."

"We haven't seen or heard boo from you. You're hiding out!"

"Working nights at Hudson Printing. Got to stash away money for a plane to Paris."

"Flash heard the bad news about your draft number. You staying there?"

Joey Gallo lucked into a draft number of 358, a stay at home number. He was free to pursue his music and hitch up with TRAX or run his father's restaurant or marry Sue Gordon and settle down. A problem solved is a problem earned. Too many solutions.

"Stay in Paris? I don't know. Unless the girl I know there ... Who knows?"

"Hey hey it's all weird. Same with Sue Gordon when I ask her. Why don't we shack up and get married?"

"Why not?"

"She finished community college. Now she says this place is a drag. She wants to go to Albany and photography school.

"She shoots great photos, why not?"

"Where's that leave me? My Uncle Carlo and a cousin Kurt Kallini offered a loan to fix up my old man's dive for me. Go to Albany and do what?"

"You got a cousin named Kallini? Dude with black hair and real piercing eyes?"

"You know him, Morpheys. Kallini's eyes burn a hole through you."

"Great musician?"

"One step below me. Why don't I go on the road with TRAX again?"

"Why not?"

"Jesus, I don't know."

David knew the road didn't suit Joey. He'd tried the ten shows a week grind, got sick, drugged up, and came back, swearing to Sue, he'd never do it again. He'd work his dad's restaurant. She'd shoot weddings for Jewell Photo, and they'd be happy together. Paul and Paula stuff. Except Joey pushed more dime bags over the counter for Flash than he served spaghetti dinners.

"Let's play ball, then."

"Yea, life's a bitch, then you die. I got Memorial weekend off, and Sue's got a wedding. Let's tie one on."

"Sorry, I got work on the late shift."

"Then tomorrow."

"Maybe."

"Come on, it'll be a blast."

"A wild weekend."

"Yea man, catch you on the flip side."

"See you when I see you."

"The gym at seven, then. Arriva-dirty."

The old Marist gym had block walls and high ceiling laced with duct like the factory. All six baskets balls pounded and bodies flailed. Gym reverberated with pitched yells, twenty bouncing balls, and echoes soared disembodied to the vaulted ceiling. The gym steamed with May heat. Sweat poured profusely. No one starred except Don Bliss with long shots and driving dunks. Once they were football stars. Now they were out of shape. They strove for stardom with competitive zeal and knowing they fell far short, got down. Rebounding became push, shove, and elbow. Joey bodied Sue's brother Flash Gordon out of the lane. Game stalled with hacks, cuffs, and complaints. Flash stole the ball from Joey, mauled him, and charged to the hoop. Joey sprawled flat on the floor.

"Asshole, how'd you like me to run over you?"

"How'd you like to try?"

They pounded and pushed some more. Then Joey had enough. It was Sue's brother, and Flash was out of control.

"What the hell, it's too hot anyway."

Sport was no longer a life and death matter. They mourned its passing magic like mortality. What else was worth it all? They retired to the Riverview Bar. Where former football players sat like old men. One time you were the talk of the town, and a year later one of the extra people who lives there.

David talked with Mickey Jones, center to his quarterback, who transferred from Trinity to Annapolis to fulfill a father's dream. Mickey puffed himself pale, chainsmoking. Annapolis with polished shoes and math facts for battleships wracked his brains until a break was a smoke and his education a joke. He stuck to it, year to graduate, years in the Navy, and a career. David at quarterback sneaked a touchdown against rival Arlington behind Mickey Jones.

David talked with Ken Kribek, hey "bones", coaches' names for ends with nothing but wiry speed and fantastic hands. They were ends, then David quarterback. Ken caught everything David threw him.

Ken told of a heroine addiction he sweated out in Guam, "yea man, after Vietnam", tripping on guard duty under Oklahoma skies, and a buddy who got his ass kicked by "Niggers" near Ft. Bragg.

"Get off the talk, Kenny."

"No, it's different than Hudson Park. You got to walk with buddies and be ready to do some shit if you're jumped by nigger gangs. The whole town's a gang war between niggers and white GI's."

David got to the booth with Flash and Joey Gallo.

"It must have been something I didn't eat. This diet's a hassle. Try managing a restaurant that makes no money. Forget it will you? The fight I mean."

Flash pulled his shades down with engaging coolness.

"My fault, Bro, and Joey, you're like a brother to me. Forget it you say. Forgotten."

"Nothing happened."

Flash notched his shades up and peered at David Morpheys. Flash, one shade too cool for his buddies. His grayish eyes glazed over, the kind that hypnotize girls. His sister Sue Gordon had his eyes, but she had the photographic eye. Flash got any girl he wanted, he got high all the time, and he made unrighteous rolls of money dealing drugs. He was a cool guy, and then his brother Lew came home dead from Nam, and he was cold. They worked one summer on a Millbrook farm, but time lapsed on their friendship.

"So brother Joey. Our college grad with his bachelor of bullshit met up with Kady Bontecott and Kallini too. Morpheys, you're connected?"

David managed a smile.

"Yes, I know them."

Flash took a long drag on his Kool cigarette.

"You're connected with Kady Bontecott. Nice long-legged girl. Remember our farmwork up in the country where the water tastes like wine. And my farmgirl, Dhalia?"

"Some farmgirl. Millionaire parents with a horsefarm, indoor pool, and a mansion way above it all."

"I screw them rich and poor. Now Kady lived a mile down the road. She was visiting relatives in Texas, or maybe you'd met her sooner, or maybe me."

"Don't be an asshole, Flash."

He got tense, then let it pass.

"Okay Mr. College, she's not my type. She showed up after you left. Kallini too. We played tennis. My chick Dhalia plays to beat hell, Kady's okay, and Kallini hobbled around. Me, I play every sport we poor kids play and faked it a little. Far better than Kallini. I laughed at his game, but he doesn't take a joke."

"Me neither," David said. "What do you know about Kady?"

"Kady drove him to Cornell."

"He lived there."

"That's what I know. Kallini's a part of Poughkeepsie, connected you know. He played with Joey's band and Question Mark and the Mysterians when they came to town."

"He's good."

"No, he's bad. But Kady was a hip chick. Least I thought so, but what do I know? I don't have a BS degree."

It was getting late for David. He had work."

"Well Morpheys, tell us more tomorrow."

Joey said, "I'll pick you up at noon. Be cool, another Memorial Day weekend, like high school."

That night Lew Gordon, Tom's father, moved David off the lift for a new kid. David packed books. The change unnerved him. Tired and tanked on a few beers, he wanted routine work, zombie work. Packing books took a hectic precision. Take the books filing in fours with one arm, two arms, and pack them left hand, right hand on the crate, until it filled and forklifted away.

Make no mistake. Tedium endured until an edition stacked or the machine cracked up. Workers never cracked up. They just quit, tanked up and hollowed out. One's nervous system played a nimble extension to the machine conveying cut books to bookshelves. Then a nervous breakdown. David handled the endless line coming at him, the incessant rattle and hum.

His brain buzzed as if for a breath. What connection between Kady and Kurt Kallini? Home to Hudson Park, it was hard to get out of town. Stylish Millbrook and downtown Poughkeepsie connected too. Mysteries meant for college discussion, not for the factory floor.

Here reigns Tedium, monarch of monotony. A lithe Haitian girl in quality control ruled the night. She stood motionless amid the humdrum of third shift madness. Her tawny skin shimmered, tanned in the harsh glow. Egyptian empress barged down the river Nile to its deep African source. Night is the Nile and nobody knows where it begins. In the end is the beginning, Kallini wrote. Over were the Sixties of our lives.

Her sight launched a silent raft for his mind. David fought the flailing fours of pulp fictions and Good News Bibles. Witness to bookmaking, from creation to consumption. And Kady Bontecott, was she waiting in Paris for him? Was his plan for planefare and flight to France an illusion? Townies back in town stay in town. J'ai trouve la beaute and je l'ai injurie and je l'ai trouve amere. Rimbaud in deepest Africa selling slaves after writing poetry, no more nevermore the mystery, why Rimbaud was no more enamored of the night.

David flipped a pile of fours like a pick-up pack of cards. The multiples spewed out and backed up the line. Soon the machine cracked up. He tried to fix the tangle. He reached wrong and a metal repulsar buried its nail into his left hand. Blood spurted down his fingers and over his palm. Sal and Lew Gordon rushed to the scene to save their safety record.

Shop steward wrapped David's hand and got him to the emergency room. He waited an hour for the blood to stop. Bleary-eyed, caffeine addict of an intern saw the hand swollen, but not damaged . Bad gouge, that's all. Glad tidings, he could go home.

42
Time Lapses

David was a week out of work and he saved nothing. Two dead end jobs. Plan to earn planefare and fly away, a pipedream. Hudson Park daunted him. Too many ghosts blocked a townie's way out of town. Flash Gordon, fellow quarterback, pushed drugs in Poughkeepsie and Joey was caretaker of his dad's dive in the Guinea Ghetto. Damn, Joey had been a musician one step from recording his band TRAX, and they had made it. Now he waited on tables for Sue Gordon to marry him. David and Flash shared football stardom. Too many ghosts in town. Hudson Park daunted him.

Joey arrived. He asked David to share a tab of acid with him.

"What do you say? We go to Poughkeepsie, buy some eight tracks, and then groove out to Millbrook. There's a cool retreat near the Bontecott Farm. Where Flash takes Dhalia Richards. Part of Tim Leary's estate. Perfect."

"Sue working today?"

Joey nodded.

"Saturday's always a wedding. She'd have to block time for me."

"Then photography school in Albany?"

"I can't stand it. If she splits, I don't know what to do."

"Wish I had your draft number."

"You know what to do?"

"No. I got a girl in Paris. Who knows how it works out?"

"Drives me crazy. When did the good times stop being good?"

"Damn if I know."

David recalled the good times of high school: travel to the City to see Hendrix, glory of football, illusions of grandeur with write-ups in the paper. Better left unsaid. Ghosts of good times gone by. Forget the good. Forget the glory. Townies stay in town.

"So David, split the tab."

"I got too much on my mind."

"Forget it all. Live in suspended animation. Be like skipping school. We'll meet Flash and Ken Kribek and breeze over town for the Memorial Day fair."

How many times David and Joey searched town for something to do. Town drew them back in. No chance for a decent job. What had his college education got him? Draft number sent him to Vietnam. Would Hudson Park be any different when he returned? If he could talk to the Hayze, tell Early he needed a ride down the chapel lightning rod. Tell Peter Bergman he needed confidence to get out of town. Tell Joey Gallo he needed to jumpstart time from this manic depression, from this time lapse.

His mom spoke from the door. She'd asked what happened to his hand.

"No big deal."

She wanted him to go to the church supper. On a Saturday night, she must be kidding. His mom went to church because her Baptist mom had gone. One connection left to her Binghamton childhood. With the YWCA job and two sons out of the house she saw less reason to go.

"You can take two pies over to the church?"

"I guess so."

David looked at Joey who nodded. They all had parents concerned for their welfare.

"I'll ride along, Joey, but reality's already too much of a trip."

Get good and drunk he'd like that. His hand hurt. Joey drove him over town. He was a friend who trusts you forever because you did crazy things as kids. They shared high school, they shared Hudson Park, they shared this dead end, where Sue goes off to Albany without Joey, while Kady was in Paris and he'd never get there. Water had gone under the bridge. He was drowning in his dreams.

Sun shone hotter than hell off new white siding of a Reformed Church, built 1700. David put on shades to lessen the glare. Stained glass scenes of shepherds beside still waters. The pulpit was empty. Sundays were interminable sermons. He read books. Reverend

Everett had mild eyes and droning cadences. At the fire department they kept his sodas in the cooler. It struck him during the Christmas bazaar second grade that the reverend played Santa too. Overall, a nice guy. Never a charismatic speaker, but a nice guy.

His mother told him about the scandal in church. Congregation dismissed the reverend because he fondled the Lashley girl. He didn't believe it. Loretta Lashley got pregnant and her mom asked the reverend to counsel her. He came and when Loretta cried he comforted her. Mother was the dressy type who abandoned the Reformed Church for the Episcopal on Easter to show off her clothes. Loretta was a flirt who got what she deserved. Congregation wished for a more eloquent minister, and they buried the poor bastard. David knew it wasn't true.

Two pies in hand David left the cool sanctuary of the church, for the hall and kitchen. Ladies like Mrs. Lashley and old Mrs. Sisler made themselves busy. They inspected everyone's offering for the church supper. Mrs. Lashley bought platters of cold cuts from the deli, she wore high heels even here, her bosom a cold and imposing battlement to oncoming age. Beside her Mrs. Sisler waddled with her rouged smile and sweetened cakes. Churchladies grew fat and flattered themselves, chastening the ungodly. When David set down the pies, they smiled all lipstick and said how nice.

Ernie Runkel came from the kitchen, knife in hand and pipe spewing smoke. He was the man in charge of pie cutting. David hated him. He was David's scoutmaster. Late one night he lectured the campfire of fathers on the greedy Morpheys kid. David bagged down with kids his age.

"Mind that kid don't grab the best tent, the bigger share of everything. Kid wants to get ahead of everybody else."

David had wronged the shuffling, hard-boned Ernie Runkel. Other kids smirked and said, "Ernie's got it in for you." He played the perfect scout to prove himself and spite Ernie Runkel. He became Eagle scout and hated the rope tying, the organized outdoors, the stupid slogans. He did it all like he did church on Sundays. He swore once he got loose of this bullshit he'd never pitch a tent or bend a knee again.

With Ernie's arrival, David tucked his identity behind his shades, sweeping his hair back with a bandaged hand. But they fastened on his parents before he was left the building. Mrs. Sisler exclaimed, "Isn't that the Morpheys boy?" Mrs. Lashley said, "His mother should be ashamed, his coming to church looking that way." Indeed gone for good, David bet old Ernie said, "Even in scouts that boy thought he was somebody special, such a swell-headed kid." Damn the whole bunch of them. There was Joey in his Dodge Dart. David looked forward to a day away from all good people.

Joey puffed a Kool cigarette on David's return.

"Sure you don't want half a tab. Be a wild weekend."

David laughed and felt better. Sure, why not.

"Share the wealth. You forget your problems and I'll forget mine."

Joey split the wafer thin communion chip. Lottery sendoff to ethereal dreams, offering salvation. They took off in Joey's Dodge Dart with its push button transmission. Push button trip, they sped toward Poughkeepsie, and mass confusion. There in the tired factory town, its main street of shambled stores sinking unwept before the malls of South Road, the chemical reaction occurred. Catalyst of high sunshine spotlighted the wispy clouds careening across oceans of blue, and earth revolving at speeds greater than the flat building tops. Terra Firma was a trick term of relativity. Slow down to get off for a day, weeks, months, years, and you can't. Time lapses.

Joey maneuvered into Tape Tapestry, where David unshuffled a slimy bill to purchase a Hendrix eight track. Tongue-tied, total frustration, no words can say. Joey proved adept at calculation. His pudgy face like modeled clay looked guilt-ridden. His handlebar mustache should fall off. They rushed through a swirling breeze of passers-by, strangers on an orient express, each face a mystery and a clue. Rushed to safety of a Dodge Dart.

Tape cartridge slid into the deck, clicked down, and as the car idled, the distant hum of feedback gained intensity like the bee buzzing of a reved up fiddle electrified until it spilled across the speakers, then juggled back and forth like a slinky of guitar wired vibration, to hell and back. The Dart lit out on Broadway. Suffocating heat cut loose through the open windows. The breeze sang with a voice in double backed harmony, speaking of a journey to Electric Ladyland.

The three-floored stores kaleidoscoped with incredible color, fauvist like wild beasts, and not the faded ads on dull brownstones. Dead ahead loomed Roosevelt's post office of Depression stonework, WPA project modeled on old Dutch architecture. Out lower Main the black faces sweated and swooped across concrete to netless rims. In the Italian section of spagnoli shops, old men in black suits sat like flies on park benches. Past the Gallo Restaurant. Yes, it was a dive. Yes Joey wasted time, while TRAX made it big. Get out of town. Too late, time lapsed.

Same scenery of Marist and Hudson Printing, the route 9 of Payless and river estates and the schools of fifteen years, were already memory, unreal and back in time, surreal and painted like backdrops in Hollywood movies, not aching with loss anymore. Backroads crossed the parkway into Millbrook, home of horsefarms like Bontecott and Richards and the estate of drug guru, Timothy Leary. Simply drive out of town. So easy to do.

Quick stop at a dark roadside store to buy beer. At Herm's store the attendant had one eye. Old shriveled Cyclops foretelling horror and cannibalism. Herm inspected ID, his bad eye squirming with indignation. Longhairs invaded his store and he sold out.

Joey and David took a walk in the woods. The religious retreat near Timothy Leary's estate. Over an ancient millstone time paused while its slow waters pearling the cement brink, dappled in sultry yellows, rich greens, and blues alive in liquid fire, then crashed like cataracts into the gurgling stream. They sat mesmerized, returned to simpler times.

Joey said, "This is where Flash brings Dhalia. Sometimes he helps out Bontecott's men when Dhalia's dad doesn't need him."

Flash saw Bontecott once. Tall grey-haired guy was cold as ice.

"Flash always worked hard."

"He's trying to get off drugs. We talked of taking the program."

"Once Flash makes up his mind to do something."

"Yea, he's determined, working two jobs. I'm trying to make the restaurant work. Just need a little help. Just need a word from Sue to turn my whole world around."

"All you need is love."

Joey Gallo cracked up. Morpheys and his sarcasm. Good to have him back in Hudson Park.

"You and Kady Bontecott. Forget her old man. Forget how rich he is. Love is all you need."

David shook his head. He could tell Joey nothing of Kady Bontecott. Tripping was like treading water, like his nightmare in the muddy Hudson. A chemical reaction that can't be controlled. Tread water until every nerve turns numb. A failure of faith.

David wanted out of the woods. Nothing was natural anymore. He was riveted on tracks that took him far away. Away from football glory, from scholarship, away to Vietnam if drafted. Then back home which daunted him. Kady wasn't here in Millbrook and neither was he.

"Let's get the hell out of here."

No words can tell. Intelligence was a breech of faith no factory work could mend. Say kind words to his friend who lost his girl. A friend so like him because a ghost of his former self. No turning back and no such thing as God for us. No words can tell. No words can forgive intelligence like a beehive of thinking, no going home. Years of college changed everything, and nothing.

There was no slack anymore. The Dart roared hellbent back to Hudson Park. David had nothing to say, nothing connected with nothing. Joey drove to the greenhouse where Flash worked weekends. There was Kenny, back from Vietnam, drugged out, flinging flowers and badmouthing niggers. Kenny's army experience of heavy drugs and racism ruined him.

Wind inside the greenhouse scented with fragrant cuts. Luscious colors curled with radiance like perfumes and liqueurs. An acid rain drizzled in David's harried mind, crawling vortexes all dissoluble. His muscles twisted like reptiles, long tailed lizards, all knotted, all naked. Gangrene pulsated beneath his bandaged hand.

"Throw the football to Mr. Quarterback. Come on Kenny. Your brain isn't completely dead."

"You throw it to him. You guys were quarterback."

"That's it Kenny. Don't expect me to be a buddy when we go down lower Main to kick some black ass."

"Quit goofing on me. Blacks are okay in Poughkeepsie. It's army towns where they gang up on whitey. You don't know what it's like."

"I'll tell you what it's like, you're braindead."

Flash fired a pass at David. The leather ball looked silly and David dropped it cold. His sensitive hands had no touch at all. His brain vomited up flung projectiles, none mild, none pacified.

The foursome played horseshoes. Lifting the shoe, lunging it to arch one and a half turns and slide onto the stake was far too many functions for David, and he begged off. They rode to Dairy Queen and the guys feasted on chicken wings and burger deluxes. David had no hunger. He stayed taut, chainsmoking, the air grating his throat. Then onto Community Day and its circus of rides. They loved whirling dervish rides, hawking games, and funhouse. David was ashamed. Meet somebody, and he garbled words from the troubled syntaxes of his brain.

By dusk the guys retired to Gallo's, where Joey's father and Uncle Carlo stewed in the congenial juice of family relations. An Italian restaurant when most Italians left the neighborhood. Lower Main palled, as did poor old Poughkeepsie. As night came, the acid ate clean the black holes in his brain. Time lapsed, and lapsed, and lapsed. Come today. Come Memorial Day, last of the maydays. If DC lifted his spirits, Hudson Park buried them.

Joey climbed another peak of insobriety. They loaded the Dart, as in high school, to go barhopping from starry night till dawn. Never let a good buzz go by, for the weekdays pound like hammers on the brain. Night was alive and paradise five miles away from whatever bar they tried.

At Club 44 the music pounded. Joey, Flash, and Kenny drank chasers after their beer. The shots left platinum rings on the mahogany bar. Joey was a drunk. His face bloated, his body swayed, and his eyes rang with blank excitement. The first drink was too much and the last drink never lasted. Before the band's final song, Joey lit the 140 proof Wild Turkey liquor. He swept his arm like a showman and drank the whiskey warm. Lights came on.

Three o'clock and closing time. Joey staggered to the car, and when the Dart failed to start Joey's head fell against the horn. Flash pounded him on the back. Joey surged awake and started the car, lit a Kool, and slammed car and body into gear. Off they stormed across the river to Highland and the Circle Inn, in another county where bars stayed open till four. David passed countless faces he knew from high school, all washed out in barlights and booze. He drank somebody else's drink, sorry. He walked into the ladies toilet, with an apology. Barlights came on for closing time. The dregs of beer and the ghosts of memory. He wondered where he went wrong, why he was so wasted.

Barkeep washed glass after glass and stacked them. In the four o'clock light David saw his brother staring at him.

"About time you noticed me little brother. I had a watchful eye on you and you're a pitiful drinker. You're not cut out for the high life."

"You coming home this weekend, Robby?"

"Me. Hell no. The weekend's but half over. I'm waiting for Bus to close his bar and pick me up for the racetrack. We go to Saratoga this Sunday. Make some money. Lose some too. You want to come little brother?"

"No Robby, I got to go home."

"Go then. Thought you were in the bag for good."

David followed the guys out to the Dart, like ghosts gone wild, returning to their tired forms. Ken stayed in Highland for an army meeting. He was back to Ft. Bragg. Flash kept at Joey to wake him up. All across the Mid-Hudson Bridge he shouted.

"Hey Ralphy-mouth, give me the pump, come on, give me the pump."

Big joke. Graduation night and Joey drank much too much. He jumped from the car over this same bridge, crying give me the pump. David drove him to Vassar to have his stomach pumped. Big joke. Same bridge David went over in his dreams, same damn bridge to nowhere. Joey swerved between curbs and the center line, swung out and scraped his Dart against the railing, fireworks and metallic sparks, then swung in to grind hubcaps against cement, until he slowed down.

They got out to see the damage. David gazed down into the vortex of muddy river sluggish under the bridge and a full moon. It was a drop and that was all. Damage to the car was minimal. How can you damage a wreck?

"Tell your sister Flash, she can kiss my ass if she leaves Hudson Park."

"She can kiss my ass too. And yours Morpheys?"

"Why not?"

Joey got into the Dart a bit winded. And he drove with some dexterity home. Flash fell asleep. The weekend was all but over. Sunday was a day of rest. Days off were freedom and flares rocketed in trench warfare to fire up the town. David waved Joey off. See ya, thanks for the lift. Gone, he saw the setting moon, hollow in its ghostly fullness, overfull and faded out, shorn like their ghostly selves of all significance. They existed in their time. Then it was gone. Time lapsed.

43
News from Kady

Four on a Sunday afternoon in David's shaded room his dad told him to get up. What a dead feeling. Sleep without having rested. The same muggy heat saturated the room, without the sunshine outside. Dad turned on the light and said Mr. Bontecott came to see him. Guy Dad worked for on the farm. Dad dressed in his patched khakis for working his garden. David dressed in yesterday's clothes. His grimy hair and day's growth looked bad. Through the curtains he saw the white Cadillac of Mr. Bontecott. Dad spoke to the seated man, partially visible through the tinted windshield. He couldn't keep Bontecott waiting. What news from Kady?

"Hello, Mr. Bontecott, I met your daughter at the Wells winter study."

He wanted to speak first. Kady's father stood tall, erect, and grey-haired, the grandfather type, though his Sunday suit removed any congeniality. Dad was taller. Only he hunched in his gardening clothes.

"Good afternoon, David. Your father told me of your late night out. Sorry to startle you out of bed."

His words carried a subtle stroke of condemnation. His glance considered David and found him wanting.

"Your father says he worked at Bontecotts, but for the life of me, I can't recall his face or name."

David's mood shifted from shame to annoyance. As Flash said, a cold character.

"My daughter asked me to deliver a letter to you personally. Why she didn't send it I don't know."

David recalled the stash of cards and letters he found with Early Hayze.

"Here, take it. I'm glad to make your acquaintance and your father's for a second time."

"Thank you so much."

He shook Mr. Bontecott's hand, who winced and excused his arthritis. The Cadillac backed from the driveway, and David rushed the letter open.

5/20/69 David, This has got to stop. Time I took this business in hand to figure out what the hell is going on. Letters from you tell of Mayday in DC and wish I were there. I wish you were here. You wish I'd write and then I write and you wish I'd write. You ask questions. I ask questions. You give answers. Letters don't fit. We write and write and don't connect. Why my dad delivers this letter personally. Come to Paris. Love to see you again. If you can't come, I'm sure you got invited. All my love, Kady.

Dad smiled and put an arm on his son's shoulder.

"What do you say I help out. Graduation present. Money for the planefare. You worked a month and see why it's called work. Go, have a good time because these are the best years of your life. If Bontecott's girl can be in France, so can my son."

David let the sunshine soak in after a month in the factory dark. Memorial Day and the machinery of night, now the ghost of memory too.

"I'll write my paper and graduate, if it's the last thing I do."

"I'm sure you will."

David saw dad's forearm twitch and pull his proud smile awry.

VI
Parisian Dreams

44

Phone Connection

Nine PM Kady's mom called. Her French mother knew emergency calls came late in the evening, from police or the fire department.

"Hello mom, what's the news in New York?"

"Bontecott met your boyfriend, David Morpheys. He woke him up at four on a Sunday afternoon."

"He's not my boyfriend."

"He must be more than a mere acquaintance since he's flying over to Paris to see you."

"Did he say he was coming?"

"Bontecott assumed he was. So happened his dad worked the farm, after the war I believe. If I'm not mistaken, his wife was pregnant when they left. Some blow-up about hiring the foreman's son. Bontecott said he had a temper."

Kady recapped her mom's comment.

"So you're saying, David drinks to all hours, he's an atheist, lazy degenerate son of an intemperate father who cared little for his wife's condition."

"You exaggerate."

"You're right. He is my boyfriend, and we're madly in love. The kind of romantic love no ocean-crossing, no disparity of background, and no language or time can keep us apart."

"Kady, you do exaggerate."

"I didn't ask Kurt Kallini to come visit me. If I asked, perhaps dad would make a call on him too."

She disliked sarcasm with her mom. It wasn't fair.

"Bontecott already knows Kurt Kallini. I do too."

Her reply gave Kady pause to listen, then think.

"Kallini said he worked for dad. He met you in the hospital when you had cancer."

"Is that what he said?"

"That's all I asked. He showed up at my novels class. He works with Les Freres at Gobelin, and wanted to know how I was doing."

Kady waited for her mom to share what she knew of Kallini.

"Well I won't say a thing more, like I did about David."

"Why not? Like I'm going to say Kurt's my boyfriend and we share an impossibly romantic love. Or that I'm sharing my Paris semester with any number of guys, and inviting more over."

"Please don't."

"I won't."

"So you don't, I'll tell you Kurt was a seminarian. His duties included counseling at Vassar Hospital. No, that's the wrong word. He listened to cancer patients. Most of us realized we'd soon be leaving our families, and endure incredible pain, before passing away.

"That's gruesome, mom."

"Well it was the truth. And Kurt was good at listening. Your father liked him too. Bontecott's strong suit is not sympathy with sick people. Kurt has that touch. Please don't go into it with him. Such conversations are of a private nature."

"I'm surprised."

"Don't be."

"Well then, I won't mention a thing to him, or to anyone else for that matter."

"Thank you, Kady."

"Tell me how your wrist feels. Any better?"

"No, much worse. I had Bontecott make me an appointment at Helen Hayes Hospital. Their specialty is bone disease. It may be osteoporosis, if it isn't cancer."

"It's not cancer, mom."

"They can't see me for a month, so Bontecott will take me to Boston first. I wish you were home to help out."

"Yes mom, me too."

"Honestly Kady."

"Dad will have to do."

"Yes, he'll have to."

45

Kallini, the Chameleon

Kallini called on Kady another June morning with her Faulkner class ended. The professor with a nifty bowtie repeated his first Faulkner quote. "Entre le chagrin et rien, je choix le chagrin." Which would Kady choose? Grief or nothing at all. She walked across Luxembourg Garden to her French mother's apartment. Nothing, Kady assumed, meant routine life without strong emotional context, a married life where the wife searches for herself, rendered invisible. Like Eurydice in Cocteau's film, a shadow of herself.

Like her mom. Like mother, like daughter. Kady feared that forever caring for mom's illness, without life of her own, made her invisible too. Like a cancer invisible inside. Metallic taste in her mouth. Pitiable hours of soap opera boredom bleached her mom's proud Dalhart complexion. Pale with pain. Then there was Grannie Lonigan with her earthy humor running her Dalhart ranch. Her mom lost her Dalhart balance come north among the yankees of Bontecott Stones. She lost her vitality and felt nothing, but pain. And nothing, like an alienation effect, caused her the pain of a staged existence. Kady chose le chagrin. Good grief, she thought, and smiled.

In the midst of her meditation on grief and its numb absence, Kallini caught up with Kady Bontecott. June sun swallowed up the morning mists. Paris grew brightly lit and more sultry as summer wore on.

"Kady, I wanted to talk to you. I got news."

She turned to see Kallini, dressed in spiffy clothes: beige slacks and suitjacket with tie. His wide collared shirt open two buttons. Twice now he met her after school. He'd invited her to dinner at Gobelin. Kady declined as she expected her mom's call. Any number of reasons. He surprised her less this morning.

"What news, Kurt?"

"News that David Morpheys' coming. I heard from Joey Gallo, my cousin in Poughkeepsie, he's coming this week."

Kady considered her reply.

"That's good."

"Since you left, I kept an eye on David and his friends at Hamilton."

"David kept me informed."

"Yes, he's quite a letter writer."

Kady wondered how he knew about David's letters. She got up from the garden shade and walked where sun lit her straw-blond hair.

"His friend, Early Hayze, showed me a paper David wrote on the romantic poets. It was good. His critique convinced an old section man like myself to accept his view. David has a scholarly, may I say, poetic attitude toward the Movement. He took part in a sit-down procedure. He wasn't arrested and hauled off to jail only because the buses took another route."

Kady returned to the park bench. She and Jesse met Sorbonne students in the bistros.

"Every student has a tale to tell of the 68' rebellion."

"They want the class system ended. Academic exams separate students into elite and menial careers. Those chosen by exam are the same percentage of haut bourgeoisie better prepared for the exams."

"I can't judge their courses."

"Extremely academic."

"We girls don't mix much with French students."

"I know. Yours is an enrichment program, theirs a weeding out process."

"Least you didn't say, ours puts a little polish on a finishing school education."

"I didn't."

Kallini dressed in his refined French clothes smiled perceptibly. It was an improvement on his black attire and Nietzschean scowl. Kady smiled back.

"It's probably true."

"I got news on David's friend, Early Hayze. How he gets along in the army and how he's getting out this summer. Would you tell me when David arrives?"

"He should be here tomorrow. He called my mom at 4PM to ask how she's doing. Manners, no less, and then got my number. He and a friend, he told her, want to visit me."

"I got him work at the Gobelin freres. He'd want to know."

"He needs a job to stay."

"How's your mom?"

There Kallini crossed a line. Even if he cared for mom during her cancer, Kady's relation was pretty personal. Kallini's tact let him subtly alter his approach.

"I hope good weather in New York helps her."

Kady nodded.

"And I didn't mean to be personal about David. Pass on the news to him and Peter Bergman about their friend. Tell David he has work at the Gobelin Brotherhood."

Kady agreed. Kallini gave her the Gobelin card, which she slipped in her shoulder sack. She gave him her French mother's number to use with care.

"Already she's upset with my mom's call at 4PM, New York time, which is 9PM here."

Kallini offered Kady one of those soft Parisian handshakes, which pleased her, then bothered her a bit because his French manners were too good. Kallini had the chameleon in him, whose array of colors all touch cold.

46
Plans

Kallini hurried off to consult a doctor friend from Dijon, who worked the Gobelin hospital. Antoine told him more about Kady's mom. Whether her arthritic pain was cancer or just menopause and aging bones. Kurt looked after Kady as a favor to Evander Bontecott. Kady's mom had been on his mind since his Marist days as death and dying counselor at Vassar Hospital. For years he watched Kady grow up. Recently he talked with her. Kurt's business was with Bontecott Stones.

He saw nothing wrong about her little dalliance with David Morpheys. If not him, another boy comes along. He read Kady's letters to keep tabs on her semester in Paris. Nothing special. Bontecott preferred she come home directly and care for Katherine. He needed his peace of mind to manage the jewelry import and distribution business.

Doctor worried Bontecott about an impending stroke if he refused to let up. Antoine's advice was do what he liked doing and avoid frustration. Paris had plenty of old folks, called viellards, and Antoine's practice was gerontology. Antoine was primary care doctor for the Freres, whose raison d'etre was care for old folks who survived the war.

Kallini's concern this summer was finding new couriers to carry goods from Turkey across Europe for his Uncle Carlo, and couriers to carry product from Amsterdam to Paris for Bontecott. Uncle Carlo talked of crossing over into stones. Kallini's connection with the two older men was different. Uncle Carlo was family. Bontecott was a chance connection who used Kallini because he found him capable taking care of his wife. With Carlo, trust was total. With Bontecott, trust came with his competent handling of various affairs: helping Katherine through her illness, keeping tabs on his daughter's doings, and only with gradual and successful efforts, the import of diamonds.

Kallini figured with the influx of Arab, Turkish, and Slavic workers, his normal couriers across Europe did fine. Customs checked few trains thoroughly. To Paris and Amsterdam he sought soldiers on tour from the German and Istanbul bases. Inside the PX paraphernalia of cigarettes, radios, and tech equipment, most all of Bontecotts and Uncle Carlo's goods could transport to Montreal and then across that long US-Canada border where guards were bribed effectively.

Kallini thought he'd use Early Hayze as a GI with a recent ID. Better if he got dismissed this summer and he'd have him in Europe for his long range plans. The GI Resistance Movement took strength in Germany. It was the only Movement Kallini believed could end the Vietnam War. A California friend, Mike Emmett, who'd been to Vietnam with the war's beginning, marines in Da Nang, wanted to fund a coffeehouse on every military base and infiltrate the Navy leaving from San Diego, where he and Julie Chambers lived. Old and dear friends he trusted.

Kallini didn't know the military. Sure he could persuade the hip or rebel soldier to translate easy money into the language of cool rebellion against an Imperialist system, and so on. But Kurt knew Early Hayze and his friends. Better you know a person the less chance of a slip up. He saw how it would go since earlier this year, and he knew everything took time and precise planning. His body crippled with polio from childhood let his mind think in a long range strategy. That fate unwinds in the fullness of time.

Then the beating from Dier and Burn. The breakup of Sixties' friends in the Movement. Joshua Steen went to the SDS June meeting, but feared the worse with RYM and the PLP and Quinn's new group of Weathermen. Did they mean him further harm? Did the FBI Cointelpro monitor him? Better security with Akim in Gobelin. Kallini recovered in Paris. Unlike many in the Movement he had alternatives. He had Uncle Carlo and Evander Bontecott. He had the GI Resistance Movement. With the end of the Sixties Kallini turned on a diamond and he was back in business. Bring the diamond trade to Uncle Carlo. Bring proceeds from the business to the GI Movement.

47
The Imposing Moment

Time transfixed, rubber bands. David bought a pack of Gaulois and a token for the phone. Nothing the woman said made sense. Rapid phrases fell like stars.

"Allo, est Ka-di la? C'est David."

"Oh, vous desirez Ka-ther-ine. Un moment."

Yes, desire was the mot juste, Flaubert.

"You there Morpheys? Sorry I sent my dad to hassle you. Desperate measures you know. You're probably hungover from the planeride. Say something, please. Don't let me rattle on, Morpheys. The Madame is looking daggers at me for tying up her line. You bring your friend Peter?"

"Yes, he's here in St. Antoine. We slept off the hangover and now comes culture shock."

"You're in St. Antoine then? Oui, Madame. Bientot, oui. Madame needs the phone to call her husband about a Fernandel film tonight. St. Antoine in twenty minutes, okay?"

On the phone Kady was familiar. Her nervous humor. Oddly square cars meandered in the circle. No white lines to direct traffic. They elbowed for space like pedestrians. This was Paris. He returned to Peter in the room and prepared to meet Kady again. Winter at Wells College was a million miles away. Meeting again was no easier. He stared in the tarnished mirror, and spaces of silver offered little reflection. Time fled so fast. He combed back his wet hair and clipped his Racine mustache.

They ambled to the arch of the St. Antoine square. Peter ordered a coffee in the tabac, and David watched the metro stairs. It was an imposing moment. Seeing was believing. Vision already played with revision, and he was nervous.

He watched Kady rise from the underground. With her jaunty

stride and hair frizzed in the evening breeze and her canvas satchel flung over a shoulder, she was a sight to behold. A good feeling. Time and tide had been met, and overcome. He spied on Kady from behind the tower as her green eyes scouted the street. KADY played swing music. She stood tall and pride like the picture of her mom on the dusty streets of Dalhart. He came behind her, grabbed her satchel, and whispered.

"Allo Ka-di, we meet again."

They held each other, uncomfortably. David took her hand. Her eyes glazed green beneath ringlets of hair swaying like head curtains. She stepped her tennis shoes on his moccasins. The least contact rocketed them. All memory and emotion merged in the girl who let him hold her hand and look at her. A world away, he saw nothing and heard nothing since winter. He didn't see her, they were too close. He stepped backward and marveled it was really her. He wanted to backstep in time and watch her rise, like Eurydice, from the underground. But that meant losing her.

"Christ, you startled me when you grabbed my shoulder sack. Want to know my first reaction. I wanted to yell, stop, thief!"

"I watched to make sure it was you."

"Who'd you expect Morpheys?"

"Eurydice rising from the mists."

"Get off it. I'm nervous enough as it is."

"Me too."

Her freckles fluttered to livid sunspots. So he reached an arm around her to introduce his friend. From the bistro came the easy moving presence of Peter Bergman. In his stride, radiant brown beard, slacks and sweater over his wide shoulders, Kady saw the ebullient America she missed. David touched their two shoulders with names. He made short work of manners, both of them knew were necessary.

"So what's in the canvas sack, Kady?" Peter asked.

He had a jovial flair without judging anyone. There was spare weight, his clothes loose, not baggy or ragged, a lenient manner, and no arrogant bone to his body. Class without consciousness. Kady liked him.

"A bottle of Beaujolais."

She smiled to be friendly, first for David's sake, then with Peter's good will.

"Ah ha, David. The girl you missed these many months meets us with a bottle of wine. Scan this for significance. Is this proper in Paris? The plane may have whiplashed us across timezones and confused our moral bearings. May Paris encourage drinking and who's to say, dancing in the streets?"

Kady smiled back at David.

"This puritan questions my moral character. Tell him, David, I am de bon famille."

David saw Peter's drift into the ridiculous with Early Hayze. This was mild in comparison, a gentlemanly intent. They tested a shared sense of good breeding, of concern to Kady and Peter, less a concern to David, of no concern to Early Hayze.

"Okay Peter, this is St Antoine. Where Defarges drank the wine and spilled the blood of aristocrats. Pour the wine, Kady, to celebrate rebellion in our world. This is Bohemian Paris."

David checked her bag for the little luxuries, and sported the baguette and camembert. Peter's eyes lit up. He was impressed. Kady saw she had won his heart by fine dining. They had cups for wine and broke bread with cheese. David sat beside Kady on a park bench, as Peter poured them wine.

"Salut," Peter said. "I tip my beret to the new revolution."

David saw his jaw drop. A black-caped Kallini rose from the subway and greeted them.

"And hope and pray, we don't get fooled again."

Kallini knew the next line.

"What the hell ... when did you get here, and how?"

Kallini told Peter he should drink the wine first. Peter swallowed his and passed the cup to Kallini. Then he sat on the bench, broke off a crust of baguette, and shook his bearded face.

Kady felt some trepidation, as if called upon to account for Kallini. David detached himself.

"Guys, Kurt has news of your friend, Early Hayze."

David raised an eyebrow, mystified by this turn of events.

"Yes, he's on his way out. If not from Dix, then from Ft. Bragg. One way or another he gets his discharge within a month, two at the latest. He's getting along. We have training officers friendly with the GI Movement and they're taking care of him."

Peter was light on his feet, pouring more wine for Kallini.

"Here's to the Hayze. Him and I shared good fortune since freshmen year, on campus and off. Great then, he's on his way out."

"He'll be discharged by the Woodstock celebration late this summer, guaranteed."

"Any letters Peter?" David asked.

"Yes, one. Early wasn't optimistic. Your several contacts, he mentioned them, but there were plenty of gung-ho recruits and cracker sergeants on his case."

"That was Basic. Best he keep a low profile."

"Best he never joined," David said, staring at Kallini.

"I guess you're right. Better he attended to business, got the grades to graduate, and flew to Europe like you two. Better he had a clear mind and firm will to do what's good for him."

David removed his wire-rims. Sun set with the ironic glare of Kallini's cool logic. Paris had distortions similar to Hudson Park and Kallini's Poughkeepsie. So this is Paris: this one ramshackle, time-saturated section of the city.

Kallini, back to the sun, told David, "I contacted a Marie Montfort at Gobelin, and she's got a job waiting for you."

"No kidding, thank you."

This was Kallini. With razor precise logic to lance Early Hayze's faultline, factual as fate, then offer promise of dawn fresh sun at the Jersey shore. Was he manipulative? God yes. He constructed a wall hard as stone and opened a double doored gate with easy access to the desired sanctum. David needed work, as he had in Hudson Park and failed miserably.

"Can I interest you and Peter in dinner? Snacks with Kady and dinner's on me. I know an Algerian cous-cous you'd like, and David can see the job setting in Gobelin."

Peter agreed. David said okay, and Kady came along.
    They funneled down Metro steps. They swooped through compressed doors. It was the fast-track of the Paris underground. David sat beside Kady, opposite Peter and Kallini, and they desisted from talk. No conversation inside this weird wind tunnel, boxed windbags, roaring oceans, from silence to elevated speed to full charge, slow and stop, switch at Bastille, cross the river Seine, below the Pont Mirabeau in deep excavations underground.

48
Let's Be Bold

Kady on the rush to this someplace else, noticed her canvas sack stained red with blood like a fresh hemorrhage. Sorting the Faulkner texts from the half pie of Camembert and baguette crumbs, she saw the broken bottle. At Gobelin terraced an uphill district, hooded in origin with a medieval order of monks. They went to an Algerian restaurant, back of which Kallini lived on a top floor surveying all Paris. The owner of the bistro, Akim, had eyes as precise as Kallini's. David was gone.

Across the street Kady saw one security light and David's silhouette at the window. She was sad with the speed of events, especially the cool control of Kallini after a few expansive moments with her boyfriend. Do over again? Don't invite Kallini. Go see David and say sorry. A Citroen skirted her, headlights off until it reached the intersection, then flashed on headed to the hospital. Cars without lanes, lights, and it roared past almost hitting her. She took David around the waist, intent on reading the Freres sign. He looked back pleased, calm again.

"How are you, David?"
"Tres bien, like this place."
"Lonely four months of courses here in Paris, I missed you."
"A lost four months."
"You understand?"
"Perfectly."

He pulled her close to summon up testimony of two hearts in the flaxen smell of her hair. The kiss on dry lips swearing we're together here and now, please believe me.

Kady let go a laugh, like of course, it's you and me. I knew it all along.

"Sorry about Kallini coming along. He had news of your friend and invited himself."

"He had news, and a job for me."

"That's good."

"Perfect. I need work to stay in Paris. Else the Draft takes me into the army."

"That's bad."

"Come tomorrow with me, will you Kady?"

"I'll help if you want."

"Speak the words when I falter. That I'm afraid of, failing to find the right words."

Kady nodded.

"Job's crucial. Words and work enough to keep body and soul together."

Again she nodded. If he wanted work, then work was here.

"See the doorplates. Tous les miserables sont bienvenus ici. Says to passersby which side of the street they're on. I like the sign."

"Kallini's on the other side?"

"That's what I think."

"Me too."

"His designs for people are never simple, never unselfish. Sure, nobody's are exactly. But the marvels he makes smack of manipulation. Like much of the world. Take the college degree and cash in. Use grades and college name as key to open some big company door, like IBM. Or never go to college and manage a Pay-less gas station. It's the same what-can-you-do-for-me policy. Make the company more profit than they pay you. Fit in. That's the way the world works, and Kallini's a bit too worldly."

David turned in the security light and took the two hands of Kady Bontecott. Keep contact between flesh and her remembered image. Keep the faith. Whatever the world works into the deal, contract signed, shit wages, desiccated success, a limited life so similar to one's neighbor the sad reflection makes all mirrors bewitched. None of that materially matters, one misplaced numeral forward or backward, because Kady's green eyes see some wonder just as tangible in him.

"Let's be bold," he told her.

"Let's be together."

Kady heard David agreeing with her. She saw the Paris of possibility he saw, and sensed a solution. Their dialogue of ideas touched fingers and palms. Short talk assured them. Peter appeared.

"Hey, why did you guys leave me with Kallini? Jesus, he's got dynamite hash. Back of the restaurant there's all arabs in caftaned hoods like ghosts in the moonlight."

"Sort of spooky?" David asked Peter.

"Real spooky. In the courtyard, up the stairwells, up six floors to Kallini's room. Black curtains separate his balcony from the city. What a view! See the river and the bridges, Pigalle and Montmartre, is that right Kady? Then St. Chapelle above it all."

Kady said he had the geography down pat.

"Well Kallini pointed out the sights."

It was time for dinner. The patron named Akim bowed before Kallini, who genuflected back, and guided them to one of the four tables. Kallini introduced the place.

"It's a family place. The Hakim are from Algiers. They terrorized a French imperialism and won independence in 1958. The hyena call came as prelude to the unexpected bomb, while their eyes remained impenetrable. Like the sands of the desert, an eerie passivity. What we face in Vietnam is what the French faced there too."

"Dien Bien Phu, hell in a very small place," David quoted.

"Terrorism means to defeat the invader to their terrain. Bomb Hanoi and Cambodia to no avail. Hakim in every land cry vengeance, their eyes dry, their trilled scream everywhere and nowhere to be found, as bombs explode all pretenses of imperialism."

Akim carried four steaming plates of cous-cous, a rice dish seeded with pieces of meat and vegetables, and spiced with a fiery hot sauce, still light and dry. A carafe of clear liquor graced the table, and Kallini filled their glasses. With a motion like crossing himself Kallini drank it down, and Peter did the same, visibly shivering from the effect. Kady tasted it and coughed and shook her head. Peter grinned with Kady.

"It's a shot of lightning like vodka or schnapps."

"The Algerians call it desert thunder."

"Like I said, right Kady?"

"They drink three glasses with cous-cous, before to foster courage, during for fire to meet fire, and afterward as sign of victory."

"What's for dessert," Peter asked.

"Later comes a light wine and hashish."

For Kady lapin was too gamey. She preferred beef bourguignon. Don't Muslims avoid alcohol? Kallini arranged the potent liquor for them alone.

"So why your change of clothes, Kurt? You're all spiffed up."

"One dresses in Paris," Kallini told David.

"You look like a street priest of the world revolution. Like the Henry who said Paris vaut une messe and turned Catholic."

"I am Catholic."

"I think, therefore I am."

"I believe in the universal religion, like Akim's sword of Islam, therefore we prevail."

David shook his head no.

"Prepare yourself, David, to say mass for the sake of Paris."

David drank his desert thunder, and said, "for the sake of Kady."

"Atheistic communist," she laughed.

"Here I stand then with Martin Luther. Every man his own minister."

Kallini shook his head.

"Luther revolted for politics and a litter of children, and among them are Calvin and Cromwell, cold will and cannonballs. After them, bourgeoisie and the machinery of night."

David marveled at Kallini's mind. So many talents, so little warmth.

"Time for Catholicism to absorb its protestant heresies, as the Hindu way of life took back Buddhism. Come into the fold, Morpheys. All one world religion. No birth of new faith. I have a bastard's dislike for being born. Quell the vicious cycle of birth and death. Let the karmic wheel come full circle back to the true faith."

Peter waved a hot hand from the cous-cous.

"Akim, more desert thunder for our friends."

"What about Christ?" asked David. "How do you match his message of salvation with Buddha's withdrawal from the world?"

"Be careful what you say of the bastard son bathed in divine spirit."

"I don't like where this conversation's going," Kady said.

"Sorry Kady, to speak of the ultimate mystery man, in terms vulgar and divine."

"What my mom and dad never argue, religion."

"David has questions, okay. Christ suffers, dies, and reigns supreme. Left hand of God with his fiery swift sword. Last incarnation comes in judgment, in flames like a nuclear blast, revelation of truth in tune with eternity, too terrible for the ears of mortal man. End of the Second Millennium brings holocaust and collapse of countries till from the ashes is born world unity, the universal church, the Hindu multiplicity of matter in the infinite one."

Peter called for another round of desert thunder. David pondered the universal ideal. True heavenly city like Paris. Yet it wasn't right with Kallini. Too much a cul-de-sac of dark bondage and age-old terror. Kallini poured and David palmed his glass shut.

Peter said, "Up with this desert thunder ritual. I'll be a terrorist in no time."

Kallini kept his cool, with David's inquiry and Peter's sarcasm.

"So Kady, how do you like Gobelin?"

"A different part of Paris," she admitted.

"The hilly district. No grand boulevards through here. It was never leveled by the architects of modern Paris, nor commercialized like Montmartre."

"I've got an eight o'clock exam and my French mom wants me in by ten, sorry."

Kallini made her an offer.

"Let me show you the Latin Quarter. An hour or two we can see the sights and have you back home."

Kady said okay, and they took off with Kallini.

At Luxembourg they walked the bright-lighted boulevards. At a cafe they drank demitasse of espresso. Jugglers and old monkey-grinders entertained for spare change. Elegant couples strolled from

Racine's Phedre at the Grand opera or the ballet of Rue Pantheon. Kady placed her hand with David. An evening warm with lilac scented the air. Spacious streets and gentle breezes swayed the trees. All was right with the world as they walked toward the island of Notre Dame.

The cathedral too was impressive. Notre Dame towered above the island of old Lutece, stone battlement of gothic religion. The corners squared and the buttresses soared above modern contrivance, up into the heavens, their flight arrested by twisted-faced gargoyles. Inside Kallini bowed down and his mood grew somber. Kady performed the rites of her Catholicism. Peter and David stood mystified by the candled incense and stained glass. The magnitude of structure in brick and spirit. Kallini's gothic ideal of the universal city. Peter said it was a fitting climax to an evening of robes, Kallini in his black cape among the white moors. They parted company on the metro.

49
Sacre Coeur

Next morning after her Southern writers exam, Kady left the Latin Quarter. She wrote, of course, grief was the only choice possible. Was not all Catholicism an affirmation of life over the pagan pleasures: killing at will, lording it over the weak, and the hunger of instant gratification. As for the barbarian Gauls and Greco-Roman culture, decadence. Kady used her western civ course to place French Catholicism at the heart and soul of Euroculture. Its faith countered the dialectic of enlightenment, revolution, and Marxist ideologies. David liked philosophies.

Her thesis then, defined grief as living for the family and community, if not for the individual herself. For the Southern women like Flannery O'Connor, Eudora Welty, and Katherine Ann Porter the grief converted the individual to artist and suffering to social regeneration. Kady particularly liked Porter's precious jewel anecdote. In reply to a question at a reading, she said her stone pendant, though it hung more like an albatross of luxury than a cross of faith, represented a woman's craft, the years it took to refine her art, Virginia Wolfe's room of her own. Women worked for not only the generation of babies but the regeneration of society. Kady sent her Grannie Lonigan in West Texas a pendant with the anecdote. Her husband John, the jeweler, saw in her the precious stone.

Nothing defined the individual ego full blast for gratification, forgetting the dynamic self and the social fabric, which women engendered for men. Nothing brings nothing: the tribulation of sin and tedium.

David sat at Akim's bistro across from the Freres foyer. He looked sleepy drinking coffee, amused by the novelty, and confused by the language he needed for work.

"Exam go okay?"

"Whoopde-doo."

"I'm trying to wake up."

"Ready for the Freres interview?"

"Ready for the guillotine, mon amie. Parlez francais, parlez francais, n'est-ce pas?"

"Oui David, tu est nerveux."

"Nerveux, nerveux! Moi? Non, pas moi? I'm petrified."

"Allons-zi. Pas de probleme, pas de tout. Sois nonchalant and let's go."

As they entered the foyer, the desk person, hearing Morpheys' name, hurried them to a short blond girl. It was Marie Montfort, who did three things at once: talked to very old folks, served dinner, and asked David questions to fix a Biarritz trip for the viellards. On the Spanish border it was Bernard's vacance, who was from the Basque. Marie saw David had little French to say yes, pack his bags, and go. He referred to Kady for further explanation. Marie began to tug on Kady's heartstrings to help these poor old folks. They needed two more youth to assist in the care. Please come along too.

At once Kady, who planned a week beyond David's arrival, needed to search her overloaded heart and stare at these wheelchaired, spindly, slovenly viellards. They weighed on her sympathies, unlike her well-mannered mom. They wished a nurse for bedpans and cleaning soiled garments. Her mom would never be as bad as them. Was this what David planned for her, to be another bedpan person, while he carried luggage? Like her father who refused contact with her mom's sickness, cul-de-sac stitched closed, his sympathies closed too. Let his daughter do the dirty work. Her mom's disease her own.

Marie Montfort looked into her lost soul, counting loose change of how little Kady cared. Make the effort for her mom, maybe, but not these gnarled, bony-fingered viellards. No, Kady wanted to shout above the sloppy, slurping hubbub of the dining hall, I won't go. Her face chapped red, bloated, molten, misshapen with shame, her freckles crispy bacon bits upon the yokes of her sallow skin.

"Vous voulez allez?" Marie asked again.

"Non! Mais David, je ne sais pas...oui peut-etre."

She looked at David, scared of both her inquisitors.

David saw her frenzied face. The look, hands off. He saw Marie asked them both to go. He saw the two of them working together, saw Kady almost in tears, and decided no. He clutched Marie. He sought the words.

"Moi, non, aussi. Mais plus tard, oui."

Marie took out a jot book and pencil from her stained apron. She wrote down the address for the Richard Lenoir group, with a vacance to Troyes beginning of July. Marie hugged Kady and shook David's hand.

"Alors, mes jeunes amis, a plus tard."

"D'accord," David repeated. "We agree."

Marie bent over an old woman, mealy-mouthed, no molars, and cut her food in pieces. The viellard grinned desperately. Kady stared nauseated, recalled her mom's incontinence, her sallow complexion, recalled her disgust as a teenage girl with menstruation. Menstruate and Metastasize. The sex banter at the Bennet School ... and how she did difficult tasks because the difficulties of caring and school and track were easier than guy stuff, until she believed it impossible to have sex and be friends with someone. Too much tension: the regret, the guilt, the recrimination.

"Come on Kady, let's sit across the street. I shouldn't have dragged you along. My job is my job."

He ordered from Akim a couple coffees. Kady dried tears from her eyes and tangles of hair.

"I ruined your plans to stay in Europe. Get a job and all. Get to know the life of the people."

"No, my job comes later."

"What came over me I can't explain."

"No need to."

"It's too complicated. Too messed up. Way too melodramatic. You saw me make a fool of myself."

"No."

"Go back to Marie Montfort, who's young, competent, and not a crybaby like me. Tell her you'll go to Biarritz."

"Later, plus tard."

"Really, go."

"Took me months and miles to get back to you."

"No, go. One stupid month, what did it mean? We slept together because I begged you. All pretend love. God, don't let me get maudlin as Days of our Lives. Mom and Kady crying because they're so damn lonely, so out of it, a couple of freaks from Texas."

David sipped his coffee when Akim brought cups. She saw how it was. David masked his face in sympathy. Soon he'd ditch her and get about serious business. Akim left.

"Hey Kady, I'm not going."

"Suit yourself."

"Whatever happens, I'm here in Paris because I love you. I really do. One sure thing. I could be in Canada if we never met. Guys like me don't travel to Paris."

"But you're here."

"It wasn't easy."

"Kallini got you a job, take it. It's a solution to your problem."

"I don't have problems. Only possibilities with you."

"So what do you do?"

"Be with you."

"Really?"

"Yes."

"D'accord. Be with me."

Then David smiled at their solemnity. Words turned to tunes or literature. Words hung in the air like incense.

"David, I can't work with those viellards, not now. They're too much like mom, only way more miserable."

"I saw it. It's less complicated for me."

"How's that?"

"No mom like your mom. Any work with people beats pumping gas and factory work."

Kady nodded.

"I got a cold cold heart. Their misery doesn't move me."

"Like my mom moves me?"

"Yes, no."

"You see that Marie, how she cares. My father makes money and cares for nothing."

"You should be with your mom."

She peered at him through her tangled hair. Akim's espresso was weirdly scented. Distilled with hashish or tinted with mint, who could tell. Arab Muslims and desert thunder.

"My dad shuts down with my mom."

"No," David said.

"He should show a little sympathy."

"Yes."

Kady took a sip of coffee and her stomach turned.

"And you, what do you want, Kady?"

"Some time together. A life worth living."

Akim kept still eyes on Kady, like she should be veiled. Other robes wanted to walk by her and wouldn't. She wanted David and she wanted out of here. Away from the vacance, and Akim's penetrating eyes.

"Let's see what happens."

"Okay, let's."

Kady liked the way David said let's do this, and let her decide. Crying like a baby made her feel better. The coffee ruined her stomach. Yet none of it mattered. She wanted this gangly guy to hold her till the pain and the pity passed her by.

"Take you to Rue de Rivoli shopping, okay Morpheys?"

"Okay."

"No more of Kallini's gargoyles stoned like ravenous beasts on Notre Dame?"

"Okay."

"Let's eat crepes and gateau and drink cassis."

"Now you're talking baby."

"And see Les Impressionists in the Jeu de Palmes."

"Take me to your Monets."

"Street artists in Montmartre, nightlife in Pigalle."

"A day, a week, a month. Okay, a life worth living."

"Happy for a day, Morpheys."
Kady took her shoulder sack, stained with wine, and they were off.
"Yes, happy together."
"Name that tune in five notes."

David took the tunes, like poems and philosophies, to punch holes in the tedium and see through the curtain on let's make a deal. Moments come along, too perfect to last, too good to be true. Believe in them. Like Baudelaire and Pascal bet the bank, and risked an eternity of damnation for the ecstasy, the elan, the epiphany to last. A life at best strings together enough of these moments for a life worth living.

Kady gave him Rue de Rivoli's swirl of fashion and its soft sighted impressionists. A five o'clock light washed the angled steep streets of Montmartre. Whimsical clouds latticed the sky. Buy wine, baguettes and cheese, chocolate and ripe fruit, and feast like workers on their way home. Evening breezes cut the day's heat. Demitasses sparked a luster of consciousness to the slumberous tides of city and sky on the hillside. Evening mixed shadows with the streetlamps.

Then Kady took him above it all. Sacre Coeur: whitebird of the sacred virgin soared gentle and forgiving over the city of Paris. She told him Notre Dame ministers iron faith amid the grim fear of death, while Sacre Coeur counsels a calm piety. He converted for her sake. Paris vaut une messe.

White marble minarets, elegant on a hilltop, like the Alhambra. It lit the night sky without shadow. Kady sat with him on the warm steps, hand in hand, and they watched the dazzle of city lights flickering in the breeze. In the foreground Pigalle's strip blazed with movie marquees and beautiful putains. The Follies Bergeres a hundred paces from the virgin, her simple heart unappalled.

Vista of the city landscaped in sky and they sat side by side. Time lapses. Time rubberbands. Then it's time transfixed in the flex of eternity. Her loving eyes lost and found him. David flung the best of himself to the well wishes of the world at large.

"We should live a life while we can," Kady told him.
"What about your mom? You're worried about her."
"Paralysis in her joints, some new complication."

"Kady, you should go and be with your mom."
"You don't mean that."
"I'm not entirely sincere. Love's like that."
"I may have to go."

He stared into the citylights like shimmering specks of fireflies, and asked himself, what if this was the last night.

"The tests show nothing. July she goes to Helen Hayes. My father's there for now. My mom needs me, but damn, I need a life too."

"Yes, we do."

The illusion of love was Paris that night. Two lovers conquering a place in time, like Norsemen come to pillage and plunder stayed in Normandy. David imagined traveling with Kady. A journey east. Tonight, all was right with the world.

50
Only the Messenger

Kurt Kallini startled her at the Luxembourg metro. She didn't like it one bit. So what if he helped her mom face death and dying ten years ago? Kady faced living a life and Kallini startled her.

"Sorry for the scare, but I had a phone call from your father. Your mom's tried calling for days. She's not well and wants you home."

Kallini's black cape and browed eyes gave the misty night a weird shape. Her mom needed her. Why the messenger bearing gloom?

"Why the black cape, Kurt? It's theatrical."

"Keeps off the rain. There's a mist falling."

"Hardly."

"Your mom say I was a Marist seminarian?"

Kady nodded.

"Brothers conferred orders on me, but I wasn't ready. I ran from their offering. As one Catholic to another, I wish I accepted the call. The black cape's my secular robe."

"Really, Kurt. I'll call my mom to see what's wrong."

"Know why your father called me?"

"He's joined the Brotherhood and wants their secret codes."

"What?"

"Their secret handshake, you know, the ring of the knight templers?"

"Joke with me. But no. He did charitable work with the Marist brothers for your mom's sake. What your dad does he does in private. Your mom's faith motivates him to do charity. Your mom's faith, it's like yours, Kady. You're both good Catholics."

"I'm no Marie Montfort."

"Nobody is."

"My strong faith, the strength of character thing, it's a crock. Truthfully, Kurt."

"Well, your father called, your mom needs you. I'm only the messenger."

"Thanks, I'll call her."

Kady shied away from Kallini. The metro stop, and his sudden apparition unnerved her. Of course she'd call her mom. Hear how bad she was. Yes, she'd come home. Any day now because she had no life, nothing.

"Anything I can do for your family, tell me."

"Okay."

Kallini descended into the metro, then spoke up from its cement causeway.

"Catholicism has a universal message, and we faithful bring brotherhood to a sinful world. Good night. Go with God."

51
Metaphysical Imperative

Kurt Kallini had zinging pains each step down into the metro. He'd sat on a cold bench too long waiting for Kady. One leg short made stairs difficult. Early physical reality for Kallini was polio and epilepsy. Orphaned on the streets of Poughkeepsie he learned physical weakness. No dad, and his mom worked for the Jew jeweler named Deeves. Once he turned teenager there was no one but Italians in the street gang to protect him. He refused to help them break into Deeves.

He saw them rape a girl on Lower Main. They pushed him out with the battered girl. She scratched at his face, screaming, scarred for years, and he fainted from trepidation. His head raised he saw the roller board of the paper man with no legs two feet high. An old face at a toddler's height. He was shaking when police came. The girl admitted nothing, but the police took down his name.

They caught Kallini outside St. Genieve. Fist broke his nose cartilage. Kallini crippled up and bled into his eyes and mouth gazing into bright spring sun above the chapel cross. His first vision of the virgin, and his first epileptic fit. Vision bleared with the taste of blood. Him to the Highland Reformatory. Uncle Carlo saved Kurt from his captivity.

His mom died of a brain tumor. His Uncle Carlo put him in a military school and then the seminary. He was unfit for the streets of Poughkeepsie. To survive, to overcome, to control by more subtle means became the one obvious fact of his life. The metaphysical consumed the physical. Captivity came as second nature to him. A bastard child he never knew physical freedom. His polio-deformed muscles and epileptic unfit nerves offered him no moment of peace, no childish sleep of oblivion. Physical presence was his first prison.

Hours on a wrought-iron bench waiting for Kady. Evander Bontecott, calling him, grew more crotchety with age. Doctor warned Evander of a stroke. Told him to limit stress. That meant get Kady home to care for her mom. Evander was a man sickness made sick.

"Okay Kurt, you understand my problem."

"Convince Kady to come home."

"At once. Please."

"So she accompanies your wife through a battery of tests to distinguish bone cancer from arthritis and define what level of osteoporosis has set in. Is that what you want?"

"Yes, exactly. I'll hire nurses if doctors tell them what to do. I'll hire a psychiatrist if that's what she needs. But her mom needs Kady's support."

"I'll talk to her. Urge her along."

"What's wrong with her sitting on the plane tonight?"

"A western civ test tomorrow."

"Sooner Kady's home, the better for her mom."

"She's got a boyfriend."

"Well you impress upon her she can't gallivant around Paris. Her mom's worried to stay overnight in Boston. Make her responsible."

"You know Kady. She feels guilty, this long away, but it's simply human nature at her age to have a boyfriend."

"Fun and games are fine if and when her mom's better. Kady finished her education and has a job tutoring at the Bennet School."

"Okay Evander, I'll persuade her. And get a Marist brother to come counsel Katherine."

"That's more your expertise."

"Faith's important to her healing, medically and mentally."

"You know what you're doing. In two weeks I need you back here to talk business. I learned your Uncle Carlo's one import item. He called me. He told me about the Hasidic side of the jewelry business. He seeks a way to end his one import. Come back and tell me what you think."

"Won't the new business upset you, you know, the stress?"

"Not when it's planned out and successful. You run a business, it doesn't run you."

"This business with Carlo has complications."

"I can handle business. Since the Thirties I worked for my father and brothers. Low man on the totem pole. I road Teaneck to West Texas, selling every small timer on Bontecott stones. Why did I do the roadwork? One sloppy affair. In New Haven after college. But I digress. An old man's youthful fling sounds silly to someone your age."

Kallini said nothing.

"I'll share some stories with your Uncle Carlo. I'm sure he has peccadilloes too. Anyway it's my business to run now, not my New Haven brothers."

"I'll take care of Kady for you."

"Good. Tell me when she's on the plane."

Kallini didn't want to hear of Evander's youthful fling. His crippled leg pained him in the misty night. Nothing good comes of a tawdry affair. Barb Kelly was six months pregnant, the other side of the world. Some high school teacher named Ted Westerbrook took care of her, perhaps to marry her and make matters right. Nothing good comes of the sin one commits. He should know.

52

Lapse into Darkness

David arrived late in St. Antoine. He saw Peter lounging at the hotel door, disgruntled. Peter went to the American Church, David with Kady, and they left the key in a potted bush outside the door. Which the concierge moved behind the glass. They were outside looking in, all night.

"So Morpheys, you wanted Paris on five dollars a day?"

"It was a cheap hotel. Let's break windows and batter down doors."

"Laugh about it. I've been sitting here for hours."

"What do we do?"

"Beats me."

"Let's get Kallini. He owes us after the Towers."

"His place gives me the creeps."

"Let's walk that way."

They walked downhill, Montmartre to Bastille to the Seine.

"Nice to get high and all, but his talk on Jesus and revolution and Judgment Day, now that was weird."

"Him in Poughkeepsie's weird. Him in Paris is ten times weird."

"Got into my dreams. Robes, stone eyes of Akim, and Saracen blades sashed to rope belts."

"But him in my home town. He's cousin to my high school buddy. He's got an uncle Joey Gallo doesn't talk about. And he visited Millbrook, where Kady lives."

"You know more than me."

"To know anything makes everything about him suspicious."

"Especially what he did with the Hayze."

"Tell me."

"We need the Hayze here. How many times did he get us out of tight spots?"

David chuckled. Then kept up with Peter's truckin' to the Seine.

"How many times did he get us into tight spots? Freezing in Skinneatteles as freshmen, and him paying off the waitress for a hitch. Actually, we paid. Somewhere in Ohio in the rain, and the 3.2 beer solution."

Peter got laughing too. Always a good soul.

"Too bad David, you didn't shimmy down the lightning rod with us. That's one up for the Hayze."

"Save that for some reunion, far in the future, when toil and trouble has burned away."

"Damn Kallini. If we never let him in the Pimpmobile, back from Wells College, Early would be with us."

"How come?"

"Early's normal way. He'd written papers the last week possible for every last class. Done enough to get by."

"His way, yours too."

"Tell me," Peter repeated.

Summer to wait on law school applications, already denied, waiting for one vacancy, one string pulled by his dad, else poli-sci work.

"Cross the Mirabeau Bridge, okay. My feet are killing me."

"Kallini messed with his mind."

"Let's hope Early gets out of the army."

"That's right. And goes along to get along. Like he always did."

Hours walking and words lapsed. They walked into private lanes of thought. Peter's undaunted stroll lagged to a trudge of steps. They stalked the Latin Quarter with mist falling down. Cafes closed at two AM. One wrong turn, one lost key, and the sky turned foreign and heavens blanketed tight. City lights off. Solitary bulbs above a family business. The barkeeper upended chairs and mopped the grimy floor. Prostitutes behind the opera dispersed. Night grew speechless and they left, apathetic to passers-by.

At three in the morning they reached Gobelin. No lights above Akim's bistro. No passage into the courtyard. They didn't pelt Kallini's windows with stones.

"David, let's go to Concord and sleep on a chair."

"Let's go to sleep in the Metro. Lie over a heat vent with a Figaro for comfort."

Peter gave him a dead look. More weary than annoyed. Sarcasm was corrosive, once conversation wore thin. At the airport terminal they jackknived on short plastic seats. Loudspeakers haunted them with flight info. In an hour they left bleary-eyed to an impending dawn.

Raw deal, this shutdown of night. The war warranted this evasion. How to get on with one's life? The old irony grinned: to get on with one's life meant to get off to Vietnam. No deal. Their vigil of friendship wore down. They got on each other's nerves. And Early got on and off with his life.

Smell of croissants and baking baguettes spoke fluently outside the boulangerie. Rumbling vans jolted the cobblestones as they unloaded milk. Coffee compressed in shiny chromed machines. They parleyed a few francs into a steaming demitasse. Mist evaporated. Sunlight cut rifts in the cloud cover. They got to the hotel in time to see the 6:30 doors revolve open. They watched, hungry for sleep, as the potted plant came out for air. David called Kady to postpone their day at the Louvre and drink deep in adoration of the goddess of sleep. Sweet sister of slumber, forgive us our sins.

53

The Lumiere Switch

Kady arrived at their shabby room at four in the afternoon. David and Peter yawned. She turned as they dressed. Flush sun streamed through the window. The hop and skip of kids playing percolated upstairs from the courtyard.

"I hope you guys don't mind a new neighbor. I've come to stay." Kady blushed.

"I mean, I got the garret with its view. If I crouch below the rafters."

"Great," whispered David, his Racine mustache all one smile.

He picked up Kady's canvas bag, the cornucopia of all good things, and lugged it upstairs.

"You okay with this, Peter?"

He saw Peter taken back. He drank a sip of red wine Kady brought and broke off the end of a baguette.

"You two sleep here. I'll go upstairs. One night and I'm off to the American Church. Let's party."

"Kady, you okay with this?"

Again the blush, and shaking the straw-blond ringlets from her green eyes.

"Yes, I stored my luggage at Les Invalides for the plane."

"Okay, good."

They found a neighborhood Chez Louis for dinner. They kidded Kady about her shoulder sack, stained red with spilled wine. They smoked her Dunhills, marked LTD, British crown. Kady ordered beef bourguignon for them to share. They ate well. Then another carafe of housewine with bread and fruit and cheese.

"More sightseeing?" Kady asked.

"You guys go," Peter said. "I'm keeping the key close in hand. No more night journeys for me."

"Let's hang out," David suggested.

Another night, if Kady meant to board her plane. Short time together. Not days, weeks, and months. Hours together. He pressed the "lumiere" switch foot of the stairs. Another culture shock. It allowed a lull of light to last a short interval, then lapse into darkness. To each person the timed switch allowed light enough to see by. If one dallies, if one doesn't seize opportunity, then shade palls his path. He gropes among dull shadows to reach an empty room.

Another night. It wasn't a party mood. An hour they mused through books and today's Figaro and drank wine. The studied silence bred familiarity. Peter picked guitar chords on the small Guild he carried to Europe, and David played harmonica. They sang old songs, too loud and too late, with a fitful singing to wake the dead. Someone pounded on the door and left. They heard footsteps on the stairs. David looked out the door and the lumiere switched off.

Kady toned the first verse of Amazing Grace, clear and acapella, how sweet the sound. Like her singing of Whitebird along the winter pipeline. Memory resonant like snow flurries atomized in the moonlight. Grace in the moment multiplied the short time. Another night. Later Peter said his goodbyes. He was off to the American Church for a next day of work.

Kady and David sat shyly on the bed. He held her hand and helped undress her. Her red sweater and cotton shirt, and tresses on her shoulders. He kissed her long on the lips, then the tendrils of hair, and moved his hands down her back. Kady opened his denim shirt and pressed against his tense muscles. They faltered, another breath, a sweet dying like winter under a meltdown sun.

"We should go all the way."

"All the way?" Kady asked, to stem the hysteria of the here and now.

"On the journey east."

"What's the journey east?"

"We travel east to discover the world and who we are."

"Skip the preliminaries, and just go?"

"Travel together into the wide expanse, watching and waiting for the whole world."

"The whole world watching?"

David smiled. Yes, the whole world watching.

"Just take off and go?"

"Not home, but the journey east. See what there is to see. See for the two of us. Two for the Road, it's an old movie. We don't tell anyone where we are, until we know what it means, a life worth living. Then we can return."

Kady smiled too. She carried her bags to a guy's room. She knew what she was doing.

"Not just spend the night together?"

"It's not enough."

"I don't want to go home."

"But your mom's okay?"

"I didn't call my mom. This one time."

"What do you say to a journey east?"

"What do you say to shacking up? Spend night after night in bed. Say there, we've done it. Easy."

"Skip easy."

"How far do we go, David? East, I mean."

"Tripping over time zones coming to Paris, we're on the journey east. How far can we go? Speaking and thinking in French, another time zone. Then in German, further and further east."

"How much time?"

"We press the lumiere switch. See how long the light lasts. What time do we have, Kady?"

"You mean till guilt-tripping over my mom gets me?"

"Give me your guilt and give me your regrets too. All of you. Soft touch and arthritic bones. And the manners I lack. All your hopes and fears. How much time? How far can we go? All the way."

"Morpheys, don't complicate matters. I'm nervous enough as it is."

"No rush."

"Act in haste, regret at leisure. That's my Grannie Lonigan talking. Dirt farmer wisdom."

"See, another thing I don't know about you. I don't know Dalhart, Texas."

"You should. One place and one person, more like me. My mom fled West Texas. Every summer I yearn to go there. A flat panhandle welcome. My Grannie rides a horse and runs a farm. She lets her husband John do his precision work, cutting stones. Grannie has passion, my mom sadness."

"Another time we can go west and let the sun set."

"Day by day. I fear we won't have the time. The lumiere switch it cuts off pretty quick."

"The journey east, it's day by day. We'll take each day traveling as if it's the last we see one place and time. Raise consciousness and collect memories. Know one another body and soul."

"You think it's possible?"

"I don't know until it's been tried. Want to try?"

"Let's."

"And shack up too."

"Okay."

They lay together. He loved Kady's sweet ache and wetness. All anatomy sparked excitement: moist lips, touch of feet, thighs winding together, muscles straining, the soft breast, and flat stomach. Words of love as vows of constancy, crests of waves rising, billowing, crashing upon the sands of time. The flesh and bone of benevolence.

VII
The Journey East

54

Fountainbleau

They took off telling no one. Subway to the outskirts of Paris. Breezes whispered and towering sky dwarfed the high rises outside Paris. First hitch in a sleek Citroen took them toward Fountainbleau. They checked bags in a cozy two-story restaurant inside the castle walls. Room was no bigger than the soft bed with a window view of castle battlements.

This was the journey east: a hitch, a hotel, and afternoons to see the sights. They walked into woods outside the castle gate. Insects buzzed and birds sang as in a Watteau painting. They ran fleet as deer and dallied in June grass with the euphoria of previous lovemaking. High tide of cloud-works drifted above them.

Cadence of march and stomp of boots invaded the woods. A battalion of soldiers in baggy fatigues and black berets, one of whom, tall with shaded glasses, spoke to them.

"Je vous demande pardon. Ne derangez pas."

"Qu'est-ce qu'il ya? What's happening?" David asked.

"Ah, Americains. We play soldier here. Have a good time, au revoir. Nous sommes en marche."

It was sneak attack and soft invasion. Martial maneuvers pieced neatly into a mosaic of turreted walls and the stucco hotel shuttered with redwood. Novelty knew no bounds. Patterns of perception formed to absorb new scenes. They had dinner, a walk about the quaint town of Fontainbleau, and then plans for another day. David went upstairs for the Larrouse map. He returned to tables occupied by soldiers.

Kady conversed with a soldier whose back turned to David. Her eyes glowed like a Renoir girl. Her blond hair, sunlit in June, sprayed wisps of curls about the contours of her narrow almond face, the nose perfect. Then her freckles tan-spotted across cheeks and nose like camouflage.

David took the third chair beside Francois, the soldier who stood to introduce himself and shake hands. He had puddly filmed eyes behind his tinted specs, like Early Hayze. Yet he was taller than David, with graceful movement, different from the athletic armor of Americans. An intelligent bearing in green fatigues.

"Pardon my curiosity. I saw you in the woods today. Your liberty intrigued me."

"Francois travels to Quebec," Kady said, "to study North American politics."

"Politics has a mauvais nom, Ka-dy. Perhaps diplomacy is the word. En francais, c'est l'art du possible."

Le mot juste, David thought. Francois corrected Kady's intro to his advantage. The uniform and his suave manner bothered David.

"Then Francois, how do military drills, you know, the shoot and stab, the pillage and plunder, prepare you for diplomacy?"

Francois rolled his eyes, hardly apparent with his tinted glasses.

"Ah David, you are another mad American. I know several at the Sorbonne and they too are mad Americains. Especially my friend, Kurt Kallini."

"Kallini," David said. "Yes, we know him. More mad than the normal American. Kady knows him better than I do."

"And I don't know him at all."

"The old folk see you different, as naive and good-willed, as benefactors in the wars."

"Not ugly Americans?"

"No, pas ugly."

"Obviously, you're intelligent, why the army?"

"Vietnam has depressed your patriotism, like us with Algeria. Military is service to one's nation, the duty for each citizen."

"But the idiotic drill?"

"Play soldier, that's all. Every citizen, rich or poor, Parisian or provincial, gives a year to his country."

"Just a year?"

"A year for everyone. It lets me meet my countrymen. We drill, yes, but we perform communal service too."

"A year's not much, unless there's a Vietnam." David's proviso.

"Compris, agreed. Service to one's country because it provides an education. And service to one's country takes the form of opposition too. One's conscience is not always the politics of one's country."

"Compris, on the year of service, Francois. You are a diplomat."

"Enough of politics, though. Where do you travel?"

Kady showed him the map of Europe.

"Let me show you a route across the heartland of France."

They agreed. He selected Troyes and Dijon as two beautiful cities in the Cote D'or, the golden countryside. He ordered wine and penciled in the route for them. Friends of his in accents Kady couldn't follow called for his company. He was a favorite in the outfit.

Plans made, David and Kady retired to the quiet of an upstairs room. Noise below sounded like a fraternity free-for-all. It was a billowy bed. Any night together meant the tantalizing touch and the knowledge of passion. Gloria in excelsior and shout out every night.

55
Troy Burned

The next day hung overcast. Young kids rode them to the route and left them there. It was a wait. By noon after jambon sandwiches in the magazin, a truck carted them over forested hills to the factory center of Troyes. Industrial smoke increased the gloom. A two mile walk from town to the hostel gate they saw what looked like a fortress in Indian territory. On the heavy wooden gate, well-bolted, hung a sign saying closed until four o'clock. Scribbled almost like graffiti were the words, "porte magique." Like the magic doorway in Hesse's Steppenwolf. Entrance not for everyone, for madmen only. They were mad Americans.

To kill time they backtracked to a country cafe, drank coffee, watched by darkly dressed provincials. At four they entered a wide open gate to an encampment of buildings, lean-to's, shower stalls, and a modern dining hall with dorms. No one there but a cook who served them a rice dish at six. A few attendants arrived and ate at a separate table. They were ignored. So not every hostel and not every town was magical. It was a change of weather, and Kady's elbow hurt more than usual.

Evening air was sweater cool for Friday, June 20th. Overcast day and a lambent haze of dusk, this longest day of the year. Outside they heard the hilarity of a gate crowd. There entered a rabble of hip dressed kids in party mood. The band arrived in time. Local allegiance of rockers and groupies opened bottles of wine and circled picnic tables about the large lean-to. Music fired up an overcast dusk, which blazed into endless night. It wasn't the acoustic nicety of Jacques Brel, but drums and a baseline rocking out. They peered over the partiers at the magic gate into the cavern of performers.

Kady saw him first. His base rumbled like an earthquake under Kady's self confidence. She was on the run from duties owed her mom, much as Francois owed duty to his country. Dark-browed gaze from the base player alerted her guilty conscience. He pointed his finger after a baseline rift. Then David saw him too, peering at Kady, as he saw Francois eyeing her the night before. Too strange the coincidence. Mood changed as he stood to the microphone. More Sympathy for the Devil.

The band was cooking. The lambent Midsummer Night smoked the few bulbs in the band lean-to. The campfire crackled with the festivities. Friday and they burned the midnight oils inside the walls of Troyes. Next song changed to more French mood music. Kady took David to a picnic table. She leaned on him. Darkness fell over their plans like rain. They sat silent, struck speechless. Kady grappling with her guilt and the duty it imposed, and David with jealousy this guy came between them.

Then Kallini settled his hands on their shoulders like a master of festivities.

"Bonsoir, my partners in crime."

"Jesus!" Kady shouted. "What the hell you doing here?"

"My question to you. What brings you two through the magic doorway?"

"We're touring Europe," Kady said.

Kurt continued his interrogation. His voice modulated between grilling Kady and greeting her. He ignored David.

"Your departure was sudden, and unexpected."

"So what?" David asked.

"Kady's mom went to the hospital without her."

"My dad's with her."

"Yes, he is."

David interrupted to ask Kallini what happened at the Magic Door.

"It's a meeting of the tribes. A celebration of fire. Ancient Gauls danced ecstatically with the fully bright sun. July 4th and Bastille Day are secular uprisings, while tonight is a firing of the spirit, a religious rite. All that's missing is firing of a Druid maiden. Interested Kady?"

Kady ignored him, riddled with guilt.

"Seldom see the French rock out. They're too refined."

"Don't let it faze you, David. Rocking out goes on round the world. It's revolution time. Sorbonne students tipped cars and set them on fire in 68'. We turned Chicago into freedom capital and Daley's police battered back. This week in Chicago the SDS meets to retaliate against the pigs. Their national convention."

"How come you're not there?"

"Persona non grata. Group called the Weathermen took over."

"So you're on sabbatical from the Movement, like Hamilton this winter?"

"One step back and two forwards."

"Timezones away."

"Yes, but this summer the time's right for an August bash. Hope Kady comes back to the States by then. You too. This Troyes burning is small talk."

"How did you hear about it?"

"I'm here every year. Glad you two travelers made it. Well, I'll get back to business."

"Mom doesn't need me."

"No, your dad's there."

"For once."

Kallini nodded.

"Be careful you don't get lost on the way back to Paris."

Again he ignored David. Kady tugged on his arm.

"I'm going to the dorm."

"Let's both go."

But it wasn't the same. Though the dorms split for boys and girls, there was no one else. They lay together in a single sleeping bag. They were alone. Warm bodies, distant minds. Kady's duty to return home and help her mom. How long continue this journey east? Flee from Kallini and flee from herself. David tried to turn off too, but the base beat pounded into the night. So many songs he played with Kallini at the Aurora Inn. Finally he slept while Troyes burned and Rome rose from its ashes.

Morning the sun shone clear and bright. No one greeted them in the cafeteria. Kady discovered a shower stall and told him the water soon chilled, so hurry. Lean-to's were empty and no sign in the courtyard of any midnight rambling.

"You hungry, Kady?"

"Starved."

She kissed him, wet lips, her hair toweled in a turban.

"No one then."

"All gone."

Kady got her shoulder sack to see if she had half a baguette and cheese. David found big Marshall amps with a Gibson in the guitar case. If nobody surveyed the damage, why not play? The wired sound shot like a covey of larks in Bah-Bah-dum-Bah, down three notes like stairs, cross the three note chord, bend, twist, and warble the high note cry of Sunshine of your Love. He played till Kady lay her arms around him and pressed soft flesh into his turned back. Time to travel. The lead was solo and they were two for the road. Old movie he saw at Radio City.

Kady's guilt lifted with sunshine and a shower. All David needed was coffee. City of Troyes Gauls sacked in the night and burned to the ground. They closed the heavy oaken gate, no magic door, and walked a brisk two miles into town. Then the route sign to Dijon pointed into the golden countryside. En route to the journey east they followed the sun.

56
Midsummer Sunday

Dijon was a long jaunt. Space on the map hardly narrowed after several rides. Then a truck catapulted them halfway by noon, and another truck took them over big hills topped by forest and down valleys full of blond-haired wheat. The sun screamed heat, dust clogged pores with sweat, but they moved on the map. Kady had a way with drivers. She made small talk, lit their Gaulois, and located radio rich with accordion music. They liked the company, these crazy American kids.

Late afternoon they made Dijon. It was a hostel at the university. Kady asked for directions, but the midland accent was too staccato. Relax a little, David said. She bought them two Tobler bars. Coming from the magazin, they saw a white van pulled to the curb. Guy with crinkly hair waved them over.

"Where you going?"

They dressed too American, everyone knew them.

"I'm Antoine, can I take you there?"

David slid open the van door and tossed in Kady's big canvas bag. The guy had twinkling eyes when Kady offered him chocolate. She sat up front for small talk.

"Where did you learn English?"

"San Diego where I studied for a doctor. Then Hawaii. Many Americans were kind to me."

He toted the tired travelers to the university, then offered them a ride into Switzerland. He was off on vacation into the Italian Alps, where his family had a summer home. He left at four tomorrow, same spot, if they wanted to go. Antoine handed them a card from his wallet. His hospital number if they needed help. They signed on for Switzerland.

Rooms, showers, and a hearty meal of roast beef, mashed potatoes, and gravy of sorts served them well. They read in the lobby. David had a book of Kafka stories to practice his German. Kady read Le Monde. The university had summer courses, and few travelers used the hostel accommodations.

"How long's our luck going to last?"

"Day by day," David assured her. "Time begins new each morning. We're on existential time travel and the journey east."

"The route with Antoine takes us thirty miles from Geneva, what do you say?"

"Choose our destiny, Kady."

Kady went down the hall to the girls dorm. A short time later David followed, tapped a stealthy knock, and they had the night together. The French overlooked the rigor of hostelry. It was a German invention for stout-hearted hikers and road-weary bicyclers touring the land, Valer-ee, Valer-ah, with knapsacks on their backs. Not a big canvas bag, her cornucopia of the little luxuries, that Kady took along.

Sunday in Dijon they toured downtown where mustard factories closed. High towered cathedral tolled the church hours. Cathedral lorded over the five story town. The sky overcast again with somber clouds. There were rains coming. Kady wore her somber face.

Moody rivers widened for them to cross. Sunday had its routines for Kady. David didn't need a day of rest when the journey east stalked the eagle's nest of the rising sun. But they waited on Antoine. He promised a ride into Switzerland.

"Why not go to church, Kady?"

She didn't want to talk about it. She had nothing but "the look" for David Morpheys. The travel took away her routines, the little rites and luxuries, which made life bearable.

"You're Catholic and it's Sunday. I'll keep you company, it's as simple as that."

"No, I can't go."

"Come on, share the light with a sinner. You and Kallini are too secretive with the church divine."

Kady glared at him. She couldn't help herself. She didn't want to think about Kallini.

"Come on, I don't mind going. Do us some good."

"No, I'm not right for church."

"Sure you are. God is all places: the sky, the mortar and brick of the mustard factories, the human heart. Even within the walls and ritual of the church."

David made broad gestures to include all God's creation, but hovering skies confined his reach: the two of them, the town square, before the towering cathedral.

Kady's eyes were wet beneath her ringlets. Dark circles from poor sleep.

"Why go on?"

"Sorry about Kallini and the pantheism."

"I can't now. God wants total confirmation. One confesses and loses sin in prayer. In the Eucharist one belongs to Christ. Now I can't."

"Can't what?"

"I can't give myself up. I can't simply say I've sinned and start over, fresh in faith."

"Come on."

David held her weariness, but she explained.

"It used to be easy, so simple, to confess everything."

"Tell me."

"I like too much what we have going for us."

"Me too."

"You're different. You decide what to do and do it. Whatever the consequences, no regrets. I'm not like you."

"Why not?"

"One gives into God."

"Give to religion what belongs to religion, a Sunday service."

"It's more complicated. I want to be with you and I want my own life. While the Catholic faith asks for total surrender and I can't."

"Total surrender, it's too much. Follow the dictates of your conscience, sure."

"We all have to surrender ourselves to duties we owe others."

Kady had tears in her troubled stare.

"We should do good the best we can."

"That's not the church."

"Your church, it's too much. We can't abdicate choice. We can't bow to an organization and its collective decision on how to live. But that's me. Faith is foreign to my make-up, while it sustains you, Kady."

"Yes, it does."

"And faith means going to church, so do it."

"I can't. Not now, today. Too much tension, seeing Kallini come between us."

"He left, luckily. We're back on the journey east, far as Switzerland, if Antoine shows."

"Let's leave. Tomorrow will be easier. My mom depends on Sundays."

David swung an arm over her shoulder, she an arm around his waist. They had each other. What they learned on the journey east. They ate sandwiches at a shop, returned to school for baggage, and got to the meeting place by 4PM. Same bench as yesterday. They ate Toblers, wondering if Antoine arrived, good to his word.

Sure enough, the white van skidded to the curb. Antoine with his carefully combed beard and wiry hair smiled out the window. He got the door to assist them. He was short, maybe five foot four. The bearded head, strong arms, and wide shoulders suggested a larger person. Leather luggage contrasted with an open boxed stereo, speakers, and record stacks. Kady rode shotgun since she spoke French better. David sprawled on the carpeted floor and read record sleeves when they took off. Byrds, Big Brother, Quicksilver, Grateful Dead, Jefferson Airplane, and Spirit--the whole Filmore West crowd.

"You got good taste in music, Antoine."

They routed into the Alps.

"Pride of my California memories. Pre-med my vocation, and music my passion. Friends still send me albums."

"We got to get there, Kady. Prime scene of psychodelia, but a little spaced out for us on the other side."

"I think you are right, too spaced out. Like one lives in a new Eden."

Far out look twinkled in Antoine's eyes. Kady noticed when he talked he didn't look at the road.

"Too spaced out with surfers, skiers, dune buggies, for every terrain a new species. Life is meant for service to one's community, with one's job. The rest is secondary. This doing your own thing."

Kady agreed, but the van wandered into oncoming lanes. She gave David a what the hell's up look. Eighteen wheelers roared down from the Alps. David saw the situation and switched places with Kady. Let her try to sleep. Antoine wanted attention, and he talked twinkling his eyes, smiling, frowning, and waving his hands freely. The van wasn't a Parisian cafe, so David pointed to the road.

"Listen Antoine, I'm all for the betterment of community. But society needs individuals, n'est-ce pas? Someone to say no to the organization. Say no to the herd mentality. Then like islands across the ocean, like steppingstones, so individuals. Service is of all sorts."

David was pleased with his dialectic. To every idea there's an opposite, competing idea fit to make the first a more perfect whole. This journey east signaled an intellectual adventure. See the sun rise on ideas, even as night sifted down the French side of the Alps. The road zigzagged up the mountain. Antoine parked his van near an old stone church. Its French congregation dressed in peasant garb danced the circle, and fireworks lit the jagged clouds pulling over the mountain.

"Look, my friends. End of midsummer weekend is always the best. My people dance and fire the night a final time to celebrate the son of God's coming. These are my people, the simple ones for whom I became a doctor. It's the age-old community one serves."

"You got it made, Antoine. Your common sense sees things in extraordinary ways. Doing makes your ideal of service to one's community a reality."

David and Antoine, like younger and older brother, understood the dialectic. They fueled at the mountain intersection. Kady rummaged through his albums with a perplexed look.

"We should all journey together south to my parents' summer home. Come to Italy. Be my guests and travel this night the route Napoleon took to free the peoples of Italy."

Antoine's offer kindled David's enthusiasm. Freedom was a spontaneous flow of new plans, when minds met in foreign lands and found kinship. He saw Kady with her look. A nervous "No! No! No! a thousand times No!" Only for real. A look like when Antoine drove like a fool.

"Hey Antoine, our plans are set on a journey east, on a hitchhiker's orient express, sorry."

"No shelter this trip, but I know a Bill Cougar in San Diego if you ever travel to the coast."

David stuck the card in his Kafka book. Address of a Free Clinic on Mission Boulevard. He jammed the book in his back pocket.

57

Passage through the Alps

They dropped out thirty miles short of Geneva. It was 7PM on a steep incline, rain clouds darkening, wind gusting, light rain already. Whatever was on Kady's mind, with no church at noon and no further at dusk, David needed to know.

"Are you crazy, or what? What's up? Why refuse a ride in this weather?"

Then he saw the bewildered look in Kady's eyes. It wasn't her stare of defiance or the look of contempt she had for fools. It was her tapped-out look. It was time to be the Hayze and take charge. Be a guy and take care of her because she was scared.

"Sorry, David."

"Kady, guillotine me at the neck. I'm sorry too."

"You know what happened? I saw a Robert Johnson record in Antoine's collection. Cover had KK in the corner same as mine. A coincidence? I didn't think so. Him at Troyes and Antoine at Dijon, it gives me the chills. And his driving. And me, I'm phobic, that's all."

"Some coincidence."

He held her crying in the rain. He took heart. Clouds hung low and ominous and rain poured down hard. David, drenched by rain, waved at a diesel, and it stopped for them, thank God.

"Merci, Monsieur," Kady said, wiping her face with a red kerchief. She lit a Gaulois for the driver and one for her and David. She inhaled and coughed. Their wet clothes simmered in the cab like smoke fogging the windshield.

The driver jolted though the gears, engine grumbling for greater pull up the steep stretch, wipers flapping rain, a slow ten miles. It got more dreary, evening darker with rain, the engine overdrawn. They saw nothing, and hoped the driver saw better.

They climbed higher than David had been before, when the dark clouds opened like curtains, for the truck's passage over the Alps. Road leveled above the clouds. The misty cover fell below their cruising height. More daylight returned. No rain. Further below the clouds, dimly seen, there cut the cavernous path of the Rhone River flowing south. Breathless, they peered miles down to this Hudson of a river like wide awake Rip Van Winkles after years asleep.

The sight took them a moment out of time. In flight like the white bird. Into the all, the wild blue yonder, heavenly city of the imagination. Music was means of flight into the cloud cover. Nature was too. They were a body in motion, toward eternity. David drifted above it all: mountain, valley, language, custom, human conflict, for a time at peace with the whole holy world. Divine vision, for a second shared with God in creation. All fit, or meant to belong in the long run. If the same eyes saw, then as now. He held Kady's hand, wet and warm, pleasure in this moment of peace on earth. She was happy. The moment already in motion theirs to share for all time.

The road tilted, and the truck barreled down a winding road, back into thick cloud cover. Within minutes they reached the route outside Geneva. They hustled in heavy night, again the steady rain, into the misty lamps and Tudor-styled streets of houses lining the cobblestones. First woman they asked listened carefully and helped them along. She contacted a car and saw they were driven to the hostel, and they arrived minutes before closing time. A clerk processed them, directed them to separate girls and boys dorms, and 10pm shut down the lights for sleep.

58
The Movement Ends

For Kurt Kallini everything let go. One meeting ended the Movement. Joshua Steen called and told him how RYM, now the Weathermen, heisted SDS.

"First they walked out when the Panthers made fun of the PLP with a remark about "pussy power."

"Why?'

"To bait them. Another remark about their white skin privilege."

"Good then. If RYM walked out, then either PLP or RYM is out."

"The PLP. They were only in SDS for mass troops to support their Marxism."

"What about Rawley and Burn and Dier?"

"They returned on Saturday night with a manifesto. It's marxism with a revolutionary face. It's PLP rhetoric with Rawley's groove to make it all sound cool and logical and necessary. It sounds like SDS but it's the Thirties hardline. It's deja vu. Like my father told me, never let the marxists take over. Well they took over."

"We knew it was coming. Desperate times bring bad politics. Nixon makes mistakes, the Movement commits suicide. Let's link up with the GI Resistance. That's the only way to end the war."

"What can we do about SDS, Kurt?"

'I wish I knew. Start a life. Hope when Quinn finds targets for his bombs, we're not with his lunacy."

"You don't mean to tell the FBI about Quinn?"

"No. But we need time away from him when things blow up. That's the way the wind blows."

"Kurt, the SDS had been my adult life."

"A new life's coming to us all. Get religion. Get a job."

"Work for my dad down on East 46th Street cutting and selling diamonds with the other Hasids."

"Place to start a new life. We could find a way to fund the GI Movement, that would be significant."

"You got to be kidding. Remember the Barton Hall Community? Remember the March on Washington?"

"The Movement took the country as far as it means to go. You don't end war, end racism, or free speech."

"You don't?"

"You move in that direction. And everyone moved in that direction together. Some gains. Now the Weathermen and Panthers mean to put an end to parts of human nature. Can't be done. We are who we are. Return to religion because the revolution has been a drug and it's over. It wasn't won. We only moved America from right to left."

"You think?"

"Best we could do. Let the soldiers assigned to fight the war come to their senses and stop the war. No revolution starts until the soldiers in the army switch sides. Nixon has FBI, CIA, and the entire executive branch with him. The army of volunteers and drafted soldiers, they have no stake in dying for a lost cause, a goddamn mistake. Everybody after TET realizes the war in Vietnam is just that, a terrible mistake."

"You coming back?"

"A month or so."

"Good."

"Then, Josh, connect with your father's diamond cutting. I told you about Evander Bontecott and my Uncle Carlo. We'll do business until better times come. Use the proceeds to fund the GI Movement. See if the soldiers stop the war. But the Panthers and Weathermen aren't going to change a thing with guns. Too many guns and an organized FBI against them."

"The Beatles' song?"

"Which one?"

"Revolution."

"And Let It Be."

Antoine called from his parents place in the Italian Alps. He let Kallini know that Kady spooked. She saw albums Kallini had given him. They got out thirty miles from Geneva.

"They say where they're going?"

"After Geneva?"

"Or when they'll be back to Paris?"

"No. David spoke of a journey east."

"The idealist, and Kady the guilty sidekick."

"Well, looks like I wait at Gobelin. You got a week of vacation?"

"Yes."

"You know Francois Searcy?"

"A l'ecole together. His family's very aristocratic. Old French with political connections."

"Can he be trusted?"

"It depends."

"How?"

"Like DeGaulle. He's an egoist, but with an ego that contains all of France. And if you're within that charmed circle of his ego, then you are family."

"I prefer people whose ego have more material considerations. Or simply religion, like you and me."

"I understand."

"Compris."

59
Swiss Happiness

Kady slept poorly. Her arthritic elbow, which signaled rain, ached all night. Hostels wake early. She showered and soaked in the hot steam. Hot water removed the dirt and grime, days on dusty roads and standing in the rain. Some luxury tour. Her mom spoke of Dalhart, Texas as a dirtwater town where the hardest chore was to stay clean. Panhandle winds blew dirt in windows, in doors, and into the pores of one's skin. With hot water and fortitude a lady survived this trial by dust. Her mom minced no words like "prim yankees" and no emotion showed in her voice. Her pride was cotton dresses, an upright figure, and beautiful face. Her mom never let dirt and farm fortunes deter her.

Kady gussied up in a rose patterned dress, combed the frizzies from her hair, powdered the black circles under her eyes, and found low heeled shoes deep in her canvas bag. Dirty laundry she stuffed in her wine sack and looked for a washing machine. The desk person gave her directions downtown.

Clothes in the machine she found a tabac and a pack of Dunhills. She smoked one with a demitasse. Same metallic taste seeped up from her throat, her sour companion, worse since they left Paris. Some ugly food she ate on the hitch poisoned her. She needed a nice dinner, else her stomach cried bloody murder.

She discovered a park with a Lake Geneva view, and sun evaporated the early morning mist. She had to show the lake to David. He got a kick out of scenery. Mountains drenched in rain livened his spirit. The way he raving during these long hitches. He must be nuts having so much fun.

She remembered his playing basketball, his naiveté in movement. And she liked his excitement on the move across Europe. But the metallic taste in her throat, her joints ached, and she needed a good night's rest. As if exertion and stress opened her up to mom's disease. The trip told on her.

Her clothes washed and dried Kady walked uphill to the hostel. He wasn't awake. The healthy maniac probably slept twelve hours, ready to go, say another twelve hundred miles. She hoped not.

Nothing to do. Kady normally said a few prayers and wrote her mom a letter. She needed to write, but what to say. Hi mom. I've been sleeping around with my boyfriend, great time. I hope doctors find bone cancer to be the source of your pain, and not menopause. If doctors are right, you're a crazy hypochondriac, and if you're right, you suffer a righteous time dying. God it's horrible to think about, let alone write it down.

Dad stays detached, like it's none of his business. He's the old man. Your mom enjoys the first fruits of old age. His sense of humor. Him and Kallini gave her a real pain in the ass. So self assured that women should deal with their problems. Kallini says have fun and then go home, it's all the same. KK on the record. Antoine in Dijon. Jesus, maybe even Francois. Eyes on her everywhere.

A hand rubbed her shoulder. Shaking herself, Kady pictured the piercing eyes of Kurt Kallini studying the tabloid of her confession. What a shock. She saw David, drowsy, saying he had to shower before breakfast. Nine o'clock, and she had the whole day to ditch these doldrums. At the breakfast of pancakes and sausage David ate heartily. Kady had a few bites and the metallic aftertaste.

"I got us some smokes."

"Thanks."

David leaned back and enjoyed the Dunhill.

"You didn't sleep well?"

"No."

"You're tired from the rain and the KK sighting."

"Ache in my elbow. Better weather, beautiful lake."

"The road gives and the road takes away. Hanging above the clouds was something else. Different from surfing waves on a ocean too huge for mastery. But we made it over the Alps, what do you think? We make meaning on the journey east."

Kady shook her head.

"I'm boring you, carrying on."

"Not at all, continue."

He was an athlete and sought grace in movement. Now ideas and the journey moved him.

"What I mean, we make meaning by living a life. Decisions, choices, like that time I sat down before the buses and said no to the draft. We make meaning, existential meaning, and build on it."

"Not exactly the life worth living, in my view, but a life."

"But a chosen existence."

"You're onto Sartre and Camus, David. It's alienation from conformity. It's acceptance of the human condition. It's commitment to our fellow human beings, that's Malraux, as the professor explained."

"Yes, yes," David agreed. "We create our humanity."

"The French professor said, existentialism was a wartime ethic. By commitment to a cause a defeated people assert themselves as individuals. Then in their assertion they are not defeated. There is common cause."

"Oh yes, you got it Kady."

She saw she stepped on sacred ground. Like religion for him.

"It's an ethic for wartime, David. Not the devotion that keeps two people together, or a family."

"No, it's not the ethic of family with two cars in the garage."

David had to get coffee before the kitchen closed. She refused a cup. She saw David changing in his letters to her, and changing again. Was it their attraction or the journey? If she worked changes on David, what changes did he work on her? The cure for what ailed her. Or catalyst to her guilt.

"Now is wartime in America. Youth of America are an occupied country by the Vietnam War. Each individual makes decisions by choosing an existence. Kady, I choose you."

"I'm listening, especially if listening keeps us from hitching the roads, anytime soon."

"You want to stay? Slow down and see the sights?"

"Then I choose you, Rousseau, free and easy in Geneva."

"Let's hide out in Switzerland."

"Let's lounge by the lake."

"Time in Switzerland will be breathing space for us. How many years you want to stay?"

Kady flicked hands full of fingers as numerals for a lifetime. Good enough. The sunny wharves of Lake Geneva aired out the mysteries. They swam at the city beach and washed away the dusty roads. Kady wanted fancy dining with wide windows above the village square. An egg and cheese soufflé soothed her stomach. Male waiters served with faultless flair. They watched children gambol in the park. Rousseau fled this orderly existence to seek romance and ideas on the journey east. It was his hometown.

Another day's travel took them over the Alps to Bern. Between rides at midday the high mountain air made David a solitary view. He saw down two miles to goats and cows battening on valley hillsides. Clear, clean air increased the massive uplift of land, Montanas of land so high and vistas so vast, terra firma swung weightless in space.

Bern spoke German and David worked more on language. The Aare River cut the village into two hillsides. One side caverned with an entire shopping district underground. Winter was solved. They watched the Tiergarten one day. Round stone pit with bear cubs in constant combat separated by housing from older bears. Perfect family arrangement. The rainy day they stayed in Bern for the museum. David stared at the medieval paintings of Mary, the canvas worn and paint chipped and sallow. Art evoked a faithful splendor. Different from the cheeky girls of Renoir or the ballet dancers under Degas' gaze. The girls were all women in love, marvelous mystique and the paste of paint.

Onto Zurich they stayed two days seeing the old city. Touring for David became hallucination. Days buried under levels of culture stacked like musty library shelves new opened to light. Centuries stacked on streets. Not just Renaissance grandeur, but medieval alleyways lined with cobblestones, Roman aqueducts engineered, and barbarism of Hun camps on the hillsides. French and German reveled in his dreams. Time, space, and language came unpinned for him.

And Kady's elbow got better. The hostel beds were comfortable, they ate leisurely meals, and less wear and tear of travel as they toured. She had fun, marveling how much David raved at everything he saw. Cultural hunger and overload. Swans of Lake Zurich pirouetted on the lawns. David stepped among them to soak his road-weary toes. One scurried after him and he ran like hell in bare feet. Long craned neck snapped at his arches.

"God they're like snakes with bodies and legs attached. Slithering serpents with mobility."

Kady laughed and later David laughed too.

They laid out the map that evening for a side trip to Lake Lucerne and Byron's Castle of Chillon. Postcard Kady sent him. Short tour, a postcard trip. But beside them sat a gnarled old bicycler, who was deaf and dumb. His bony finger traced a route into Bavaria en route to Vienna. Where the old man went.

David pictured them forging ahead too. Go into the heartland of Europe. A day to Munich, stop, a day to Vienna, stop, and forty days and forty nights into the Baltic, toward Turkey, the fertile crescent, Iran and India, no stops, and why not eighty days on the Orient Express cycling God's creation.

"You're a lunatic, David Morpheys."

"Guilty as charged."

"Better slow down."

"Can't stop. We got to go, man, go."

"Somebody new inside you?"

"Every day."

"We had fun, didn't we this week?"

"First gear. And mountains are special like moments of happiness, like a Swiss time lapse."

"We didn't stall out, did we."

"No, but see us as two old codgers with gnarled hands and around us sit grandchildren. Your arthritic finger follows a grey line through Bavaria into valleys of the blue Danube. Journey east, for the memories."

"Morpheys, I'm too weary a soul for the journey east."

"Think of the memories my old soulmate."

"Let's dawdle and eat bonbons. Lie back and watch swans swim Lake Zurich."

"Damn the swans, Kady. Damn them, medusas of the lake."

"Plenty to see at Lake Lucerne."

"Kady, to us Americans, it's all new. Our souls age in golden countryside, misty mountains, culture and paintings, myth and legends, time creased like the upheaved earth. We age ten times faster on our journey east. But no further until you say the word: two for the road. Then go man go. Please Kady, say the word."

60
Stolen Kisses

David's ravings swept her away and Kady resigned herself to hitching the road to Bavaria and Munich. She woke to routine packing of her big canvas bag. The long hitch. It weighed heavy on her. David ate a big breakfast and drank cups of coffee and clicked his cup to hers, "To the journey east!"

Same metallic taste convulsed in her throat. She gagged all over again, sick to her stomach with self loathing. She hid her distress and said she hated breakfast. A good cigarette covered the taste and Kady breathed fresh air en route.

David hummed a tune, played harmonica, tread lightly on his feet. To her it was a difficult morning. Like a day after high school and she had a run-down of laps and her joints ached. Only by force of will did she run her routines. Or like Sunday mass, and this was Sunday the second week away from Paris. She had prayers to say and no heart to give them meaning. She hated this parched feeling. David praised the clear skies smiling on their journey, but the summer heat hung with oppressive humidity. Miles away from Zurich they waited in vain. Too far away to return. Hours under the hot sun convinced Kady this was all wrong. Munich was three hundred miles away.

Noon arrived with the great ride in a red convertible, top down, and a jet set couple dressed like Cannes film fans. Driving air frizzed her hair and roared in her ears. Jet setters breezed along with swerves worse than Antoine into the Alps. They crossed Swiss, Austrian, and German borders. The triangle. David's pointy finger scrawled across the map. Lake on their right looked deep blue like the cloudless sky, at peace, while they careened corners and darted eastward.

Metallic taste convulsed her throat like carbolic acid. Kady was sick. She tapped the driver to get out, amazing David, as their sports car sped off. She walked into the trees, vomited, and felt no better. She repeated David's favorite German, "Hier stande ich, Ich kann nicht anders." No further, David understood. He was nice about it and all.

"If you're sick, we're stopped. It's about a mile from Lindau, the map says."

David rubbed her back and neck.

"My stomach's wrecked. Let's go."

David carried her bag and she let him. It was Sunday, when she always called her mom from college, even in Paris. Two weeks and no call to her mom.

Lindau was a Bodensee spa and the major tourist spot for three countries. All central Europe went to the lakes, like Parisians went to the coast. Early vacationers filled the town. Kady found a phone and called home. Her father answered.

"High time you called, your mother needs you home."

Then her mom spoke, and she sounded bad.

"It's just like the cancer all over again. The tests in Boston knocked me out. I can't eat, I can't sleep, I'm incontinent. Kady, come home and help me."

Kady said yes, what else could she do?

David agreed she did the right thing. Best he could do, he did. He found train reservations that night for Freiburg, and from there the route went to Stuttgart and Strasburg and back to Paris on a Monday morning. David arranged it all, while she slept in the cool breeze by the Bodensee. His spaced out, sleepy-eyed soul materialized into an efficient person. He saw what to do and did it. She liked this competent side of him.

The break in the journey east wasn't so bad. On the train they leaned together and found solace in the smooth swaying. Paris was a familiar place. Coming into Gare St. Lazare, the skyline of six stories was human scale. Paris was Switzerland, sanctuary for young lovers on the run from the adult world. It was like home. Kady rested in the Tuilleries while David found them a room up in Pigalle, where nightclubs quieted by day.

That afternoon they saw a Truffaut film called Stolen Kisses twice because it was cool in the theatre. Night and neon greeted them. Kady recovered from her twenty four hour flu. She had her ticket home for tomorrow. No metallic taste gagged her, no tinge of pain, no lingering nausea. Purged of remorse she revived from a five hundred mile trip when all she could do was puke in the jiggling toilet. It wasn't a great room in Pigalle for a last night.

"You better?" David asked.

"Much, thanks to you."

"Come sit on the bed."

"No place else to sit."

"Sorry about the cramped quarters. The tourist office has a skewed perpective of suitable rooms. It's small, stuffy, and hot even with the window open."

"Least it's got a window."

"Now who's the optimist?"

Accordion tunes skipped from the dancehalls with the screech and exhaust of Citroen traffic. David uncorked a nearly full bottle of wine. She sat on the bed with bad springs and sipped burgundy. David played harmonica. Slow bluesy rendition of Sonny Boy Williamson.

"You want to sing?"

"No, my voice doesn't suit the blues. Too flighty."

"Too beautiful. Such clarity of tone deserves champagne."

"Always with the compliments."

David sang verses. "Going down to the station, catch the fastest train and ride. If my baby don't want me, I'll have to drink myself stone blind."

Kady passed him the bottle between verses. She drank half the bottle on an empty stomach and it all went to her head. Nice rosy feeling grew in her. More wine and "Rolling and Tumbling" caused banging on the wall from the concierge's office. "Alors!"

"Give it up, else we'll be sleeping in the streets."

"Then come closer, darling."

She kissed him and removed his round spectacles. David unbuttoned her clean cotton shirt. The wine and travel and all, got Kady tipsy, and she felt very fine. She let him undress her. The lovemaking was different than other times. It got to her and Kady let the surge deep inside her rise to his kiss. Urgent upsurge and madness and she tensed her brain, her spine, the whole contortion of her being. Too excruciating, the sweet sweet pain.

Kady caught a breath. All extended she felt the tense rushing to meet his own. The rushing of streams over the Wells waterfall eager to reach the lake. What a melting moment of bliss. Then sleeping with his heartbeat in perfect time to hers, their breathing together as one person.

She woke with the dawn, a little hungover, and very much at peace. It was such a small room after the vast expanse of Europe. The room looked worse in the sunlight. She kissed David, who opened his dazed eyes, smiled, then fell fast asleep. She managed to save her flats and paisley dress and clean underwear for the planeride. The hallway looked worse than the room, but it had a shower. She gussied up best she could. Time until David woke up and showered she spent walking from Pigalle up to Sacre Coeur to pray for her mom's recovery, and a quick prayer of her own.

On the metro to Concorde she told David to come home with her.

"Meet my parents, then be nearby in Hudson Park."

"I'd be in the way. Until you know how your mom's doing."

"Write me letters then."

"Not again."

"I know. I hate letters."

At Concorde she checked her ticket for a two o'clock plane. The sun shone bright. She asked David to share a couple drinks in the air conditioned bar. Sense of distance across the tiny table for two. Kady looked different in her paisley dress. The male waiter brought two cassis and deftly leaned over to set down the drinks. He was immaculate in white jacket, articulate in his subtle movement, and far too suave for David. The cool grace of a performer between them.

Time and space grew vast. She belonged to him, and she got ready to go. For weeks they shared every waking and sleeping hour. Now they numbered minutes. Like a last kiss was a kiss goodbye.

"Somehow I believed, Kady, we traveled into the dawn. Road always rising before us."

"The journey east, it was wonderful."
"But what more?"
"We'll come back again."
"Well, I'll make money this month with Les Freres, enough to bring you back."
"David, I'll come back on my own. We'll both work for Les Freres and we can go as far as Munich, even Vienna."
"And further. Around the world, let me make plans."
"I got to go Morpheys. Turn around for me to leave."
"I wish your mom well. Tell her she's got a lovely daughter."
"Not another round of name that tune."
"Go."

When she went and boarded the bus to Orly, he saw her go like water under the bridge, swift flowing like time, a place and time young hearts never know again. He should have gone with her.

VIII
Season in Hell

61
Spiritus Mundi

Little Kallini could do. Bontecott grumbled, why he ever let her go to Europe. Kallini's trip by car to Troyes aggravated his back condition, and the painkiller Antoine ordered made him sleepy. He closed his black curtains on Paris and waited for the summer heat to pass with nightfall.

His metaphysical imperative worked poorly. Meditation brought little relief. Heat and the whole world magnified the moment to its physical presence. Gone for how long that marvelous sense of mystery, when the timeless world worked its miracle on the here and now, when the Movement was a drug, when hard work with the Freres and Uncle Carlo and Bontecott connected him with the spiritus mundi, the whole worshiping world, and his nerves and muscles were at peace.

A week later Kady called from Lindau and told her mom she'd come home. Boston tests proved inconclusive with osteoporosis and cancer. Kallini sympathized with Kady's mom. Arthritic, menopausal, and depressed, the three word diagnosis given Bontecott for his wife's condition.

Kallini disliked his role as go-between. The way he inveigled Kady and her mom back together for the summer. Women kept in captivity. Already working women like Marie Montfort broke off from the Brotherhood. They had their own agenda. Burn and Dier gloried in their greater role in the Weather machine. Kallini stayed in Paris until Bontecott, his wife, and Kady worked things out.

Kallini had oblique conversations with Uncle Carlo, who waited to summon him home for a deal with Bontecott Stone. There too he wanted the older men to do their preliminary negotiations. Uncle Carlo knew Kurt was prone to periodic pain. Worse since the beating from Burn and Dier. The deal between Carlo and Bontecott had risk and advantage. The influx of Hasids to Crown Heights after the

Holocaust brought stonecutting skills from Eastern Europe. With Joshua Steen he wanted to trust them. Use this Brooklyn-Catskill network to import and distribute greater quantity of stones. Carlo offered his finances to gain respectability.

Kallini had business to do. He needed to increase his connections in New York. He needed to find additional couriers incoming from Europe, especially during the rush season of Christmas when baggage searches were lax. Kallini waited on Bontecott to set his house in order for such a deal.

62
Gilded Guilt Trip

Traveling back to America took more than eight hours, train ride included. When Kady arrived her dad and mom had never moved from study chair and TV couch where last she saw them. She buried in sand as soon as greetings and guilt trips ran the gamut of what was new.

From her Boston tests Kady's mom came home exhausted not only from the routines, the runaround, being wheelchaired here and there, while dad stayed in his car and hotel, but also because the tests took drugs to search and disturb her tenuous body chemistry: barium enemas, catscan liquids, causing nausea and incontinence.

Kady's mom got sick from the tests, and her father returned home with a brittle tenseness, nerves like wires electrified by a lightning overload, afraid of sympathy. He locked himself away with texts on the diamond business, detective novels like Mickey Spillane, and his twelve year old scotch. Both sick parents vented frustration on her and called it love. Kady called this weary business, a gilded guilt trip.

She helped her mom into the bathtub and took her soiled undergarments to the hamper and her backlog of dirty clothes to the cellar washing machine. There was a maid who came several days to clean house, cook meals, wash clothes, but her presence disturbed both her father who left to check his racehorses and her mom whose incontinence looked to her like guilt and sin. Soon as Kady came home these chores devolved upon her. They dismissed the live-in nurse from Vassar Hospital, once Boston said the tests resolved nothing: arthritic, menopausal, and depressed. Male technicians searched every nook and cranny. Now Kady had come home, her mom, nauseous and incontinent, was totally dependent on her 22 year old daughter.

Kady returned to soaping her mom in the tub. Already this morning, a day after sitting in a paisley dress served chicken cordon blue, David across the table mal a l'aise, sad, and increasingly distant, Kady knew this routine never ends. She helped her mom throw up and flushed soft boiled egg on toast down the toilet. She helped undo her loose nightgown and slip off her soiled undergarments and wash the diarrhea from her mom's intestinal hole after her rectum was sewn shut from colon cancer. She changed her bag for antiseptic new ones, washed the clothes caked with shit, and realized the bathwater was already unclean.

Washing her hands over and over took on a phobic repetition, like Lady MacBeth, sleepless and insane. Kady preferred the exotic image of maternity with its great evil and sexuality, as her pleasures palled before the trivial routines of cook and clean and increasing care it took to nurse her mom. Kady and Katherine Bontecott belonged to Millbrook with its horsefarms and private school.

"How's the hot water for your arthritis, mom?"

"Pretty good. Thank you darling. Nice to have you home. The Vassar nurse told at great length how silly her patients were at the hospital. She liked coming here. I didn't tell her how much harder life was fifty years ago, like her other geriatrics. She wanted to transfer to childcare, and next year have babies of her own."

"So unfair to you."

"She was a nurse who hated nursing. I told Bontecott anyone would do, and he didn't bother. You'd be home soon. I thought a couple weeks ago, then. So I didn't chat with the nurse, and she never stopped complaining."

"Well I'm home now. You want me to change the water and make it warmer?"

Soaping her mom mixed the turgid color with a chalky brew along the surface. Kady's stomach was none too well.

"No dear, this is fine."

"Let me do it."

"If I were well enough to go live with Grannie Lonigan, I would. My sisters offer to help."

"How's everyone in Dalhart?"

"Their children are young John's age, and most are married and live nearby. Why I left Texas I don't know. Old John is unwell."

"What's wrong?"

"Lung cancer. That's what cigarettes do for you."

"How bad?"

"It's spread beyond his lungs. No one expects him to last the summer. Cancer is a killer, only it takes its slow, sad time with me."

"Come on mom, don't get morbid. Let's get you out of this tub. Then into clean clothes sitting up in bed."

Much as it pained her mom to stand, Kady showered her clean. It was sad to see her body, and the ravages of age. She saw her mom's paunchy midriff and sagging, pinched buttocks. So unlike her picture. Tall girl straight as the upright post to her dad's jewelry store and disdainful of the dusty Dalhart streets because she planned to be gone. Thirty years later Katherine longed to be back. Sisters promised care for her crippled old body.

Kady affixed the new colon bag not as neatly as her mom or her nurse, but once a day for weeks and months and years made for competence. A clean nightgown, and the Japanese kimono Kady bought her mom on Rue de Rivoli let them sit and talk in bed. As though Kady never left for college. Once Kady tutored at the Bennet School, she knew part of her schedule included care for her mom. Duty accompanied by guilt. Her mom and Millbrook.

63
Work was Job One

July burns hot in the city of Paris. David sensed only Kady's absence, as if the levitation of the plane left gravity the powerful force, pulling down. He heard the metro burrow beneath his feet. Either see Peter at the American Church or start work for the Freres. Work was a step down from his high minded visions. All matter and human endeavor seen from the mountain top as god-guided dispersed in the steamy maze of city streets, in the turbulence of cars and crowded humanity. Concord was in riot. With Kady, there removed the gateway to visionary power, the mastery of mind over matter. Heavy was the word.

The rigors of work offered no enchantment, but work was job one. David opted to see Peter Bergman, whose Episcopal minister said friends flocked to Peter's fourth floor room. David knew how quick Peter acquired friends, but the tribal activity surprised him. Kurt Kallini was back in the picture. His dark eyes less ferocious in the French milieu, attuned to the tenor of place. Kallini filled the high ceiling with his all consuming presence. He had hands on everyone, and never touched a person. David took notice. Never touched a person. Eyes that bore into one's intentions. Mind that handled one's wishes like horses to ride. Kallini's presence disparaged his own. With Kallini came two unusual characters.

The elder guy introduced himself as Christian.

"How do you do, Da-vid?"

A left hand swirled a column of smoke from his black ivory pipe. Short forty year old guy, dressed in a fashionable vest, and eager to please.

"We have been waiting for your return at Boulevard Richard Lenoir. Kurt, my long time friend, told us you wish to work for the Freres."

David shook Christian's limp hand. Fashionable French handshake exerted no pressure. Christian had funny little eyes, which gleamed, as the pipe returned to his pursed lips like a parakeet to a perch.

"Merci Christian. I come to Lenoir after my visit with Peter."

"Yes, Peter offered us his company for the Vichy vacance late in the summer."

"Sure, I'm in. Clean up work here lasts a month or so. Then David, we're back to the U.S. of A. to see Early Hayze. It's all planned. We'll make it the communal thing in Vichy. Cheryl agreed too."

Peter shook his hand, hopping around, full of energy.

"What do you think?"

"I don't know what to think."

They heard the squeal of brakes and tires skidding on the street. It signaled a muffled and awaited crash, shattered glass spilling over the time lapse.

"Jesus," David shouted.

Christian shuddered, rippling a line of smoke from his ivory pipe. Peter said it happened like clockwork at the intersection. It killed him at first. Now he was used to it.

Kallini's eyes kept an imperturbable glare, as he passed a joint to the white-robed, Algerian kid in the windowsill. David knew he was there, white robe in the white frame, never moving, but lost him in conversation. The kid was a handsome teen, his olive complexion and short black hair prominent in the frame. Kid stared at him without looking. Those still dark eyes alive like the jeweled eyes of a snake cool behind glass. Crash occurred and the kid heard it like a wave hurled on the beach, a phenomenal crash, heard at once.

"It's necessary I go. Somebody must be hurt at this corner everyday. Suffering of others makes me sad."

Sweat showed in Christian's wrinkled eyes and his pursed lips like fish were wet with the shiny pipe in the orifice. Kallini and the white-robed kid went with him.

"A bientot, Da-vid. We wait for you."

"Glad you're back, glad they're gone."

"What're they doing here?"

"I got bored. Maybe this vacation will work out, who knows. How's Kady?"

"She was sick, some kind of flu. And her mom, you know. Kady was worried about her all the way. Sickness is all nerves, anyway."

"Funny you mention nerves because Early's are shot. Breakdown after bootcamp. Kallini says he should get a medical discharge."

"Kallini has hands on everyone's business."

"I know."

"He's here regularly?"

"Talks with the minister. Takes me places. He says Early has a free ticket to come to France, whatever happens."

"I don't like Kallini. Especially the whole deal with the Hayze. When's this Vichy thing?"

"Late August."

"Well I got to get to work. Be independent."

"But not independently wealthy."

"Enough to get by, till Kady returns. You should stay Peter, be expatriates in Paris."

"No, it's not for me."

Peter set himself in the window's sill like the Arab kid. Then raised himself on his arms and peered down where the last accident spilled glass.

"It's limited here, what's happening. For all its faults I got to get back to the States. Hope my dad gets me into law school because polisci's a bunch of grad bullshit."

"No Vietnam, huh?"

"Not me. You?"

"I'm here for good."

"Get your thesis done?"

"Sure I got hundreds of pages on the transcendental moment in modern lit, all notes and critique, passages of my poetry, no organization whatsoever. It won't cut Dijon mustard."

"You going to graduate?"
"Promised my dad."
"Me too."
"So start with the Freres?"
"Got to, yes."
"You live the good life traveling?"
"God yes. Time only passes when you live somebody else's schedule. We lived life intensely and put time on hold. That was the journey east."

Peter gave him a get-off-it look.

"Oh sure time goes by, but there's no tedium. Burst full speed into the moment of truth. In spirit, be above it all. Then time is relative to the vision. The senses accept the whole truth as holy, as miraculous in the moment."

"Your thesis idea?"

"Yes. The seer and the seen stare like gunfighters the moment before the explosion: poised, decisive, confident on the verge of death. No death ever comes living a life intensely. Like a Cape Canaveral rocket one bursts from earth's restriction, one flees the grip of gravity into the all of space, released, weightless like the white bird in flight, like Rimbaud."

"Who?"

"The visionary poet, seer and seen, when sea and sky, time and tide, are all one. The moment for Rimbaud is a spiritual bill of rights. One whiff of eternity and freedom from time can be recreated any time, any place, and once found, never lost in this lifetime."

"Too fantastic, Morpheys. Can you get room service on this trip?"

Peter flicked his eyes like a loony.

"Just pick up the phone and dial the Twilight Zone. Dee-Dee-DEE-Dee… Dee-Dee-DEE-Dee."

It was good to laugh away the time like college roommates. Nothing too serious. Long as they recalled life on the Hill and its four year interim. David slept on the rug in Peter's room and left for his job early the next morning.

All depended on this job. Make money to bring Kady back. Make an impression to bring Kady back. Survive when his draft number came up. Stay in Paris. Make a life for him and Kady. And someway make the journey east an abiding part of his stay in Paris. Work was job one.

64
Godspell and Last Tango

Metro stop between Bastille and St. Antoine, and David came up to one of the big boulevards of Paris with its parks and trees and benches between coming and going traffic. Inside the foyer window of the Freres David saw faces of old women in their seventies, stocking legs in heavy shoes, sweaters and long dresses, some fat and some spindly, and a few old men wearing black suits, berets, and wooden cane dandled between their legs.

He opened the glass doors and greeted Andre, the secretary, with her small cubicle of privacy. She too was in her sixties, but force of character deterred aging. She stood erect, her head bird-like, detached from the dole of affection given old people. Her eyed squinted saying, "They all expected him," then radiated with the sparkle of false diamonds, careful to appraise each person.

"Oh Germaine," she twittered back to the kitchen.

Out from the pots and pans waltzed a cigarette smoking old man with a carefully clipped mustache, wavy grey hair, impeccably dressed except for the apron. He wiped his hands and smiled graciously. He was but five feet tall and dipped lower with sloping shoulders, as if weighed down by his luxurious wave of hair. He zig-zagged on Sammy Davis legs. The comedian, malgre lui.

Christian rushed into the doorway followed by Bernard, saying, "D'accord, le beau enfant va pas en haut."

The beautiful child. Bernard was young like David, energetic, with work to do. He yelled through the office, "A plus tard, David."

Christian recovered his poise by putting the shiny pipe in his pursed lips.

"So Da-vid," he said in French. "You have met Andre and Germaine?"

David greeted each in turn.

"Bien sur, Christian. A travailler, then."

"You like to accompany me around the quarter?"

"D'accord."

In the basement the walls shelved with canned pates, breadstuffs, vegetables, and bottles of wine. Christian filled two bags of food for old folks they intended to visit. This was the work. Morning air along the boulevard kept a wet coolness under the spreading trees. In the buildings the air was damp, and the top apartments seethed with humidity. July heat was here. Old ladies were happy to see them. "So gentils de vous to come." They were polite, well kept, with a roomful of family pictures.

The round of conversation followed a pattern: talk of food, the nice work Les Freres do, a shared knowledge of the woman's nephew or grandchildren, the heat is terrible, and full circle to thanking the two for their gentilesse. David as American they thanked for helping the French in two wars, as if he personally liberated the streets of Paris. Flood of news in the Figaro and Le Monde raged against the Ugly American, and how the US risked world peace by expanding war to all Southeast Asia.

Lunch they took a tin of hot food to Mademoiselle Patin in her squalid room. She sat in a ragged chair, hair frazzled, baggy-eyed in a blue sweater, and long dark attire. They arrived, and she salivated for dinner. She worked her gums inside her flabby cheeks. They helped her hobble to the table, saying over to them, "Vous etes tres gentils, tres gentils", breathless, then hoarsely whispering, "tres, tres gentils." Christian squinched his narrow nose against the smell. Same expression David saw when Bernard spoke about "Le beau enfant." They left with yesterday's dishes.

"Christian," David said, framing his French better, "She needed help more than others. She's very sick."

"Too true. Twice this week she defecated over the room. Terrible mess to soap everything. Somebody at least comes from Gobelin to change her clothes."

"C'est bon, what you do."

"Someone has to."

"But you're a good person to do this work."

David felt the compliment fit. Christian thanked him. David understood the art of gentillesse, manners. Christian invited him that evening to see Godspell, in the Latin Quarter, and during intermission actors served the audience wine. Christian cornered the handsome Jesus and told him David hailed from New York City. The actor took his wide-eyed adulation in stride. Then asked David.

"Excusez-moi, Monsieur, did you see the play performed there?"

"Sorry, wish I had."

"To compare, Monsieur."

"Your production is particularly good. And thanks for the wine."

"That too is part of the production."

Christian detained the actor for an autograph. His beady eyes followed the pen's movement, his narrow nose close to the pen and program. French people got closer to their fellows, like the Italians at Joey Gallo's house, where David spent time in school.

"Oh tres, tres bien."

His lips squinched and he kissed the words as he spoke. David decided he was a forty year old kid in many respects. But the work was important.

Next day they visited more of the trapped women and David understood the daily rounds and type of conversation. It was nice work. He liked helping, and he enjoyed the new world of Paris. If only Kady stayed. He worked for her return.

Christian was too gentil, always stopping for a demi tasse or a glass of pernod. He took David to the Bertolucci film, Last Tango in Paris, when he heard David talk cinema. He nudged his elbow to say, "tres erotique, n'est-ce pas?" He was uncomfortable with Christian. He agreed the sex scenes of Brando were brutally erotic, the last reach of nihilism.

"Ah, la verite."

On the metro Christian said, "When all is nothing and nothing has meaning, religion offers solace."

"The church banned Last Tango, n'est-ce pas?"

"Yes, the church has one policy, and many doors."

David nodded, but didn't understand.

"Five years ago I underwent analysis and I live on better terms with who I am."

Christian accepted himself and his Catholicism. Religion to him was tenderness for old people and young people like David, and the sentiment was to his liking. As they climbed the stairs and keyed open the upstairs to the Freres foyer, David questioned Christian taking care of him and paying for everything.

"You do too much for me."

Christian retreated behind the reserve of gentilesse, and said, "Bon nuit."

65
Heavy was the Word

In one week Kady made her mom clean and neat, cooking meals her stomach kept down, managed her incontinence, and Katherine was up walking, almost as strong as before her Boston tests. Then came the cancer surveys, blood tests, and more probing and prodding at Helen Hayes; resulting in several days of nausea, puking, and dependence on Kady's round the clock care with weeks to put her back on her feet. They offered no clear diagnosis for her aching bones and suggested Johns Hopkins for further tests. Bontecott agreed. They scheduled the first week of August, but Katherine with Kady's help delayed further tests till she was stronger. Wait till September.

Kady was apprehensive for herself. Like care for her mom caused cancer in her. Her period was late. Not that she missed the intense pain and headache. She played tennis every day with Dhalia Richards. She received airmail blues from David every few days describing Paris and making her world, depressingly mundane. Her bones ached more as her mom got better. Kady got out of bed with nausea so bad throwing up was marvelous relief. And she wanted to be sick.

The alternative was full of weedy possibility, a garden of happiness, a forest of fears. She needed David home from Paris and fearful to ask if he said no. David's airmail blues told tales of Les Freres. After two short replies, Kady gave up writing. Replies ruined the routine which kept her free from thinking, and worrying.

David walked the rounds himself, giving him the freedom to come and go as he pleased. Near Peter's room was the Musee de Cinema. From early afternoon until night he watched Eisenstein, Goddard, Bunuel, all classic cinema for a franc apiece. His eyes mastered the dark: the raptured vision of celluloid reels, cut, mixed, rolled like magic on the white wall. Bogart as bad guy. Jean Paul Belmondo sneering, breathless, life up in smoke, shot in the back, are you the cop who killed my brudder. Working class crashing on apocalypse down Kremlin steps, and her molester's head severed rings the chapel bell. Only the breaks to pay another franc disturbed the nonstop vision. David subwayed cross the city, Paris at night a steady cinematic roll, all grand scenes ghostlit with dark breezes swaying the trees. Spotlight moon seen suddenly up an alleyway.

July heat steamed early that morning David took food to Madame Matique. Boulevard swirled with stores and cars, his eyes sweeping camera scenes, then cutting a still of black-clothed men rolling boules, pigeons like spectators. What can't be seen side angle to timeless space, stillness and peace, a single tree like sculpture on a mountain in mist with a cool stream on a slope, oriental, rococo, all zen wonderful? Yet it was summer in the city.

He located the numbered building, Rue de Grace, rational numbers and intuitive search. Inside the courtyard the sun sifted decay of old stucco for an ambience of dust radiant in the light. Ground floor housed the labor of workshops, tool repair buzzed and crackled, noise swelling the heat like an impending explosion, the steampress laundry increasing humidity.

Upstairs on the top floor the grating noise elevated temperatures. Flies darted at odd angles and black spotted the stucco walls. Plaster chipped off boards, wood rotten, the studs warped in the threshold. Rimbaud syncopated steaming shops in the crucible of the senses and distilled illusions of turrets and ramparts of medieval castles. Alchemy of word and perception. David saw a crummy apartment. The heat paralyzed old folks staring out fatigued faces, all too real, with doors open. David was too rational. The intuitive search an acquired sight. Oh, to be blinded like the savage cyclops.

David knocked for Madame Matique. She opened to him. In the bright sunlight she hesitated, red eyes to focus, pupils filmed over with age, watery, and her birdlike face drawn and wrinkled. A week ago he brought her food and brought back Bernard, always efficient, with a doctor. Her spindly frame in painful motion asked him to come in. Did she feel better? Her whisper of a voice, suffering, asked for no sympathy. She didn't complain. She didn't beg for fellow feeling. Only the inevitable to come quickly.

Yes, she was worse than last week, you know, the heart is bad, her hand trembled, the worn dress covering her heart. She asked David to bring Bernard and the doctor again. Pain held her heart tight, grim reminder now is now, without slack for memories or illusion. She trudged to the kitchen to store the sack of food.

Across the corridor a woman sewed in the shadows. David couldn't see the face. She sewed methodically, one stitch, another, a third, lapsed a moment to shift the garment on her lap and stare out the window, then back to her needlework. David saw a robin silhouetted feeding her young and then a serpent toying with a palpitating bird. He saw old Atropos, cutting edge of a last stitch. David told Madame Matique he'd bring Bernard and the doctor. Heat roared like a furnace deafening the dark room.

Not until the weekend did David learn from Bernard that Madame Matique died.

"Her poor heart gave out."

"I heard Mme. Patin suffered a stroke."

"Yes, with all kinds of paperwork due."

Bernard, leader of the Lenoir group, wrote poetry and played flamenco guitar. Now he was all business. His voice leapt in tones, his hands lifted for emphasis above his head, like throwing rice at a wedding. Extravagant gestures and courtly manners.

"Always paper," David said.

"Funeral forms are fantastic, I fill them out for days. So absurd."

David nodded.

"Death is real though."

David agreed, letting the realization shadow his illusions.

"Sorry for Madame Matique, very fragile and very brave."

"Yes, poor as she was, she kept her dignity."

"Ah David, an American with heart."

"And you Bernard, a Parisian with time for papers and sympathy."

"Yes and no. I am Basque. Land in northern Spain no one knows the origin of the people or the language."

"Fooled me. Ah, the flamenco guitar. I assumed you were Parisian, seeing how hard you work at the Lenoir Equipe."

"You work hard too, David. Stay on with us. In weeks you have visited all the viellards and we are always behind. The work agrees with you. You don't mind the sadness, the details of organization, nor the relations with suffering veillards. And the old folks like you."

"The Freres take all comers to help the aged. It's a duty of the young."

David saw himself like Christian, the Belgian, and Bernard from the Basque country of Spain.

"I will stay on as long as you'll have me. As foreigners we owe a part of ourselves, a working exchange, for living a life in Paris."

"C'est tres bien. You stay with us."

Then he invited David to come to the Freres chateau for the weekend. A group traveled there to clean rooms for an August vacation.

"You should come en vacance and see what joie-de-vivre a month in the country gives the old folks."

"Bien sur. Glad to go. Now and in August too."

"Then bring along Kady. I heard from Marie Montfort of the gracious girl. As a couple stay in Paris for many years. It is a good life, don't you think?"

"Certainly. This weekend then, out of the city heat. As this year, out of the turmoil which is America."

"D'accord, David."

David signed on with the Freres. With Bernard and Marie Montfort whom he respected, not with Kallini whom he distrusted. Make a life for him and Kady. Work was a priority.

In the van with Bernard and David were two high schoolers, Mary and Daphne, very perky in the red-hot heat, talking, talking, talking. Then Jean-Luc, the law student with money, and Jean Pierre, the philosophy graduate at the Sorbonne. The girls chattered two seats back, and the two Jeans disputed logic of the Napoleonic Code, inflexible to changes from the '68 revolt.

Weave of conversation knotted David's attention. He closed his cinematic red eyes from a late Friday night and slept on the way. The heat smoked into a dim fog with drizzling rain for the two hour trip. Late afternoon haze diminished and darkness fell early, with red headlights narrowing in the night. David awoke from crazy dreams on arrival to the chateau. Again the bridge dream, and his fall into the muddy Hudson.

He woke to the stony spaciousness of an aristocrat's country estate, the towering monument of an ancien regime shrouded in fog. Like his Vanderbilt Estate in Hudson Park. Bernard and the group entered the kitchen behind the chateau and cleaned the sinks, dishes, and table there. Then into the grand salons on the ground floor. Guests of the viscount ate in a salle de manger with frescoed ceilings, the room half the size of a gymnasium, and danced in another salon with polished oak floors. Marbled stairs spiraled to the second floor where each guest retired to a room with fireplace and salle de bain. Tall Jean Pierre checked the huge oaken doors to see they were bolted secure, before everyone dispersed upstairs. Bon nuit, toute le monde.

David's magnificent room lodged above the door and foyer. His chambre suited a dutchess with plush velvet curtains the length of a cathedral window. Over the bed lay a burgundy spread and below a counterpane of red velvet. Pillow rolls provided cushion against the oaken backboard, and the overarching canopy curtained the bed, same red color as the whole decor.

David was worn out. More than a month he traveled, worked, and holed up in the cinema to turn day into fabulous night. Sleep was a soft raft on the wide waters with a horizon of blue skies and blue seas, alone on a wide ocean with the bad feeling he was not alone. He sunk into the billowy bed. Masted raft dipped perilously into the ocean swells, plummeting down a skyscraper's depth, down like a whitebird, gasping for air below the blue. It scared him because he didn't thrash for the surface. Underwater and sky he saw a muted sun, and all the elements of water, air, and fire transfixed. His body to earth did not belong. He was disembodied soul.

He slumbered awake and stared restless at the red-curtained cathedral window. Glow in the texture goaded him, as if fire burned in the night and his chamber locked like a vault. There was the source of incandescence: red light filtered as through stained glass. Time stilled. Fumed with ominous smoke. The fire which agonizes and refuses consummation. Hell's own image. Then he fell into a fitful, dreamless sleep and an hour later woke once more. Night was dark and dreadful quiet. Good God, the glow was gone.

With the first light of reason David dressed and opened the curtains. Fog cleared and dripped jewels on the dewy grass. Center of the lawn sat a lake and the road circled the water. Further beyond was mowed grass, parcels of wheat, rye, and fields of clover, and afar the layered hills with squares of green corn and blond wheat growing full toward harvest. It was the Cote d'or near Troyes he and Kady traveled. He welcomed the peaceful view like a Poussin landscape.

Down the marbled steps he met Bernard en route to the manor farm for a pail of fresh milk and warm baguettes of bread. This breakfast bounty reminded David of his dad's dream of farm life. Work hard, eat well, and live long. His dad had the right idea and David longed for home. The milk had to be boiled. There was rich coffee and they dipped thickly-buttered bread into bowls of cafe au lait. The cheery girls chattered away. The two Jeans disputed law and logic. It was all talk to tune the ear to humanity.

Morning was Sunday work housecleaning. Time to attend mass in the town church and hold hands with farm folk during the peace of God. This genuine faith in one's fellow man. He thought of Kady and said a prayer for her mom. One for his parents too.

Most of the day he worked the polisher, buffing wax on the oaken floors. The slow sweeps made the shine deeper and rich with the perfections of old wood. Sun angling into the salon softened the shine and blessed the work with holiness. He waxed the long marble corridor, slow patient labor, which lasted the afternoon and left him satisfied. The chateau regained the dignity of its architecture and the group felt good with its Sunday work.

The ride back to Paris was a long one. They stopped for a meal in Troyes. Then the rain resumed, and not a mist like the trip here, but a downpour which narrowed the reach of headlights. No one talked on the way back. The return brought weariness to everyone. Back in

Paris the summer night was hot and rainy, with lamplit streets where light had little effect. Others lived elsewhere in Paris so they dropped David off at the foyer. The schoolgirls wore dour faces and waved weak goodbyes. Good will gave way to heavy night.

David mounted the stairwell. None of the keys unlocked the Freres apartment. He tried the ring of keys again and tried knocking to no avail. He hoisted his bag and turned to the foyer downstairs. Floor above he saw the flowing white robe of Kallini's Algerian kid.

"Pardonnez-moi, Monsieur. Ou est Christian, vous savez?"

Kid's French was foreign. David understood the robed teen asked about Christian, who left for Brussels.

"Pas ici. En vacance."

The young Algerian approached him. The stairwell light was still on. The boy reached out and cupped David between the legs, saying "Vous voulez?"

Hands full, David was stunned, then angry. He swung his bag into the white robes of the Gobelin boy and pushed him hard into the stairs. Timer up, the stairwell darkened, but David saw the knife, like a film still, he saw the knife flash from the robes and slivered eyes flash from the dark face. "Le beau enfant."

David fled downstairs into the driving rain and across the boulevard. No one was on the street. He stood under a store canopy. He stared at the Freres foyer for half an hour. No one was there. A few passing cars, windshield wipers and headlights, and the empty streets again. David took heart. He returned to the foyer, wary of a white robe. He left his bag upstairs and found a mattress and blanket in the cellar. He hung up his wet clothes and slept badly. Heavy was the word.

66
Commune of True Believers

The old man Germaine arrived at dawn. He was already coiffured with his wavy hair perfect. David dressed in damp clothes. He asked how Germaine slept. Manners first. Germaine, this short rickety man, had long hands and fingers.

"Vous etes tres sympatique, Da-vid. Je dorme mal. Les vielles toujours dorment mal."

Germaine waited anxiously for the dawn. He said old men seldom sleep.

Andre came in with birdlike eyes and rouged smile. Always efficient she had another key for upstairs. He found his bag next to the door. He tried to sleep. The courtyard buzzed with disembodied voices. Four times hourly the metro train rumbled beneath the building, its hollow sound, the busy soaring of planes at Orly terminal. Wake, get away, get away, now! The groan at regular intervals broke the surge, loud enough to deafen the time lapse, ingest the trite business conducted above board, toil the time to its tenth part, and dive every time grumbling this may be the last time: monster of a city too massive, too inhuman, for the souls swallowed in its wake.

Awake, on edge, sleepless, David decided to work, watch cinema, and get down on the street. In the lobby he saw Andre, ever watchful, and she signaled to him, insistent he come inside. She pointed to the phone. He wondered if it was Peter, wanting to shoot baskets in the church gym. He'd rather it wasn't Kallini. Andre hawked his attention. As he opened the door, she said, "toute de suite, c'est Les Etats Unis."

Kady calling for sure, his stroke of luck, lightning in the darkness.

"Allo," he blurted out, forgetting to speak English.

"Hey Frenchie, it's Joey Gallo calling. I got good news. Me and Sue, we're getting married. We want you home for the wedding. Tom's got to be best man, brother-in-law you know. And we'll all be together because Lorraine's home."

"Jesus, good news, Joey."

"And we got money together for your ticket."

"Great."

David had to focus on Joey's voice.

"I'll try to make the big day."

"You can't miss it. One hell of a party."

David couldn't connect Joey's puffed face with the people around him. He missed home. Kady, especially. A month away was too long.

"You still there? Listen we all want you home, especially Lorraine. Ticket money, we got it. We know you're poor. And Flash he's off drugs since he went into treatment."

"Great."

"You didn't know? Sue's happy, and says she wants to settle down for life. Come on, everybody's here, so you got to come."

"Okay Joey, I'll try. And I got a small salary to pay you back. Congratulations."

David hung up and said merci to Andre. He left in limbo between two languages, between duty and desire to be gone, between here hellbound and what's happening there. He hurried to the metro. He needed to think. He knew going home was best.

You go through school with guys and do crazy things together. He and Joey tanked up a six for the St. James dance. Ninth grade at the Rock Ledge Market. Wintry cold so the beer shivered their fingers before the alcohol fired their blood. They hitched from East Park and a cop in an unmarked car stopped.

Holy shit. They ran like hell past apartments and down the power lines, and out of trees near Pine Woods. No cop spoiling their party plans. Same cop stopped them hitching again. Run, stop, think twice. Both he and Joey waited in the backseat cage while the cop called in their names. Clean slate. He rode them to the dance. No better story to tell your buddies, hey Joey. A memory belongs to the two of you. You go different directions after school. Still your buddies are part of you and you owe them.

A nagging tightness in his chest bothered him. His heart beat a mile a minute. Best be gone. He'd return with Kady. Of course he had to. Write his senior thesis. Escape the draft. Go see Peter Bergman. He'd know what to do.

Peter saw him coming from the fourth floor. On arrival he saw Kallini too. Same window as the Gobelin boy. There was Kallini, curator of cosmic effects. David disliked him. Kallini climbed down from the sill. No cape and only his wide-sleeved shirt open to a gold cross.

"Coming to look for you, Morpheys. Akim's son wants to stick a knife in you."

"He better stay away. Nobody accosts me, you hear?"

"Be cool."

For once when David moved toward Kallini, he saw the smolder in Kallini's eyes extinguish to the semblance of reason.

"Shit, he's there for that old bugger, Christian. Forget it."

"Hey David, the Hayze is out. Let's get back to the States and see him."

Peter tugged on his beard, sensing David had enough. Then Kallini gathered himself.

"My advice, David. Split from Paris and go meet Early Hayze with Peter. We got him out."

"Nervous breakdown?"

"He's okay. Big summer concert too, at Woodstock, and then all you return for this Vichy vacation. Bernard and Marie Montfort are the good people in charge. You and Kady will like them. Take a break from Paris."

"Form the commune of true believers," David said.

"Until the war ends it's a better world here."

"Say Kallini, don't you show up for Joey Gallo's wedding?"

"No, Poughkeepsie's not cool for me. You know it's my hometown?"

"And a prophet's never believed in his hometown?"

Kallini hesitated a second time since David met him. Piercing eyes ate like acid into each other's plans and grooved their meandering with meaning.

"No, I can't make Joey's wedding."

"Well, I'll be there because they're my buddies, like Akim and his crowd are yours."

"Akim's nobody's friend. They tolerate me because I'm useful. Nobody crosses their tribal lines. The Berbers are bombthrowers. But I'll tell Akim you meant no harm, okay?"

"I'll take care of myself."

"Then you're alone. Better to belong, you'll find that out soon."

"Then it's a choice. While you got buddies you belong to them."

"I got to see Akim anyway. Peter, say hello to Early. David, tell Joey Gallo, best of luck."

Kallini was gone. Morpheys was gone, soon as he took care of business. And Peter had two weeks left of work at the American Church.

"I'm flying home Peter."

"Paris ain't the same without Kady."

"How'd you know?"

"How wouldn't I know?"

"Sure, you got buddies you belong to them."

"Yea. Then we'll be back for that Vichy vacation."

"Good to get a last look at the States, what do you think?"

"I hope the Hayze is okay."

"Me too. One last look at America. One last goodbye."

67
A Hoodlum in My House

Uncle Carlo called him for a meeting at his brother Joseppi's restaurant. Joey cooked dinner from sauce to pasta. Joseppi had no connection to the life Carlo made for himself. Just family, glad to see him and Kurt.

Their cousin Marie came across with them in 1924, the last year of legal immigration. Her parents were dead. Her father died in the army campaign ten years earlier, and her mother from grief. Carlo and Joseppi looked after their cousin, selling jewelry for a Jew dealer. She kept her accounting job during the Depression when they had no work. Marie followed her boss Deeves up to Poughkeepsie in 1934, barely 20 herself. She had work, they didn't, so she was on her own.

Five years later she got pregnant. At age forty she died in a few short months from cancer. Her kidneys failed, and Kurt Kallini was in the Highland Reformatory. Uncle Carlo had him released for the funeral and put into a military academy, then Marist Seminary. He made a major donation to the brothers. He made his mark in the City during the lax wartime, and in the Sixties he used Kurt to their mutual advantage.

Carlo with his connections to Hasid jewelry cutters, like Deeves originally, saw import of raw and semi-cut diamonds as a lucrative, less dangerous endeavor than his Turkish import. Naturally he looked into Kurt's connections, his working with Evander Bontecott. Carlo made the first overture to Evander. He wanted expertise in stones and offered his Hasid connections. They both liked Kurt Kallini. Carlo coveted the nice clean business of jewelry wholesale. To be respectably American suited Carlo's wish.

Kurt poured Carlo a glass of burgundy wine and sat opposite him. They looked over the Poughkeepsie train station. Traffic commuted to the City. Nights it became a decrepit, dirty, and dangerous city with petty drugdealers picking their feet in Poughkeepsie. Kurt and Carlo knew the causes and effects of their occupation.

"Kurt, I'd like to meet your other patron, Mr. Bontecott."

"I'll call him."

"He has a list I sent him of Hasid cutters."

"Joshua Steen's father."

"Yes."

"It make sense to Bontecott?"

"He sees how greater quantity of stones, cheaper prices, and wholesale across the country brings us both greater profits. His brothers retire from Bontecott Stone with nice homes in New Haven. It's Evander's business."

"He was never averse to importing diamonds through my European connections."

"No, he has no silver spoon in his mouth. He was workhorse for the family business. An Irish girl he had an affair with, a cleaning girl in the office, and she threatened to sue in court for seduction because she was under age. A youthful indiscretion, and he lost his family benefit. He traveled as salesman from New Haven to Poughkeepsie across the country as far west as Texas, where he met his wife, Mrs. Bontecott."

Kurt said he knew her to be a fine lady. He waited for Carlo to make his point and knew Carlo made a wise move.

"Would you prefer meeting here in Poughkeepsie or there in Millbrook?"

"At Bontecott's convenience, and where he chooses to meet. We come with the need. Not of course for money or connections, both we bring, but we need his garment of respectability."

Carlo ate the pasta with sauce Joey Gallo made him. He enjoyed dinner. He agreed with Kurt's assessment of Evander Bontecott. Carlo knew class structure from Naples. There his father hated the army campaign against Austria. He was forced to fight for the aristocrat officers and died in a mountain campaign against German soldiers. Bontecott with his breeding may not like Carlo's class.

Kurt between them made a difference. If they were on distant sides of the great river of commerce, Carlo would muddy the waters to bridge the gap.

"Kurt, I agree with you and you with me. We are of one mind. Call Bontecott."

When Kurt called from Poughkeepsie, Evander had scrutinized the personal and business risks of an arrangement. Kurt's call was opportune.

"Hello, Kurt. I was hoping you'd call. How's your Uncle Carlo?"

"We call to arrange a meeting. We've eaten dinner in Poughkeepsie."

"Tell Carlo we may meet at my Millbrook home this evening. Of course, if he's tired or drank too much wine with dinner, then another night."

"One moment, please."

Kurt conveyed the information to his uncle, who dabbed a napkin to his lips, nodded yes, his pasta finished.

"We can drive to Millbrook promptly."

"An hour from now okay with you?"

Bontecott had bourbon set out with a carafe of water, and red wine. He freshened his own drink.

Kady left to play tennis on her neighbor's court, about 7PM as the sun let up and there was an hour for her match. Up and around the horseshoe drive came a black Cadillac. To her surprise it was Kurt Kallini, who opened the car door and offered a hand to an elderly gentleman.

"Kady, please meet my Uncle Carlo."

The elderly gentleman with his gray mustaches, thick neck, and barreled stature, shook her hand graciously.

"Miss Bontecott, honored to make your acquaintance."

"Thank you for coming."

Kady felt silly in her short tennis skirt. Her father came to the door.

"I hope you enjoy your tennis game. We old men waste time on business, while you take the pleasure of a warm evening."

Kady walked to her friend's court, thinking Kurt's uncle an odd sight at her father's home. Her father lorded it over the shorter man, as he came down the steps to shake his hand. He placed a familiar hand on Kurt's shoulder, as if their meeting was a common occurrence. Kady was perplexed and played a poor match.

Evander took them into his study, and Carlo accepted the bourbon, mostly with water. It was not his customary drink. He liked the stylish mansion and said so.

"The home decorating was my wife's doing. She was professional, and several of her homes appeared in magazines like Country Living and New England Home."

"Very stylish home. Thank you for inviting us. I told your daughter off to play tennis I wish I were in my youth. Here to walk the grounds, ride horses, and play sport. Millbrook reminds me of the hills around my native Naples."

Carlo placed a housegift of canolis beside the red wine, then took a seat beside Evander. Bontecott thanked him and said his daughter loved sweets. He'd save a canoli for his breakfast coffee.

What Evander remarked was not Carlo's squat stature nor his old world mustaches, nor the ethnic differences of food and drink; instead, he noticed Carlo's suave manners, dignity, and his scrutiny of the room. How much they were alike surprised him. He planned to reject the bulk of the business and use Kurt Kallini's expertise on a freelance basis. Meeting Carlo made him reassess his position. Kurt was over thirty, never rash and always subtle. With him Evander sensed the disdain of the younger generation. With Carlo he was at home. With Kurt there was tension in his house; with Carlo, agreement.

"Carlo, I thank you for coming. Your connections with Jewish cutters would facilitate the time and cost between import from Europe and distribution to stores in the hinterlands. They have a separate delivery system, another valuable asset. And your cash resources solve any other problem of import and distribution."

Carlo listened to Evander's tone of voice. It was an accurate assessment. His tone said a moderate no thank you. Carlo expected condemnation of his connections or a refusal to deal with an Italian peasant. None of this prejudice spoke in Evander's voice. Years on the backroads selling product accustomed Bontecott to the facts of business: one face for the family and another face for making profit. He liked Carlo Kallini and ignored how he made money.

Bontecott drank bourbon. He asked if his guests preferred red wine. Then he continued.

"All your connections, Carlo, are of value to me. They would help with import, cutting of stones, and distribution wholesale to retail. For reasons of health I ask for only your partial help with Bontecott Stones."

Carlo asked Kurt to pour him a small glass of wine. Wine and pasta and canolis went together, for his digestion. Habit and age are good companions.

"Kurt does well working with you and with the Jewish community. They have a locus in Crown Heights with international branches to their family. Jewish folks are connected and spread out. It's their nature and their history. Though I'm no scholar like Kurt."

"I work with Kurt already, for personal and professional reasons. His learning the business benefits us both."

"Yes it does. Mr. Bontecott, let me tell you my needs, since you have told the nature of your own. Since you have not mentioned my Turkish import, I do. Else it muddies the water. I want the respected name of Bontecott Stones, as it lends support to your jewelry business."

"For Kurt's sake as much as your own?" asked Bontecott.

"Yes, as much. And moreso, since I am an old man."

"But the name Bontecott tarnishes like old silver."

"Understood, clean and dirty water mix and are no longer clean."

"We cannot gloss over your past, Carlo."

"Take Kurt, not me. All through Kurt and I'm removed from business. As Kurt learns of course and you trust in him."

"I do not, excuse me, I can not relinquish control of my business to Kurt, much as I trust his competence and respect his dedication. I can't give him, either alone or as your agent, control of my affairs."

"Again I understand," Carlo said. "He is young in much he does. As his uncle trusting him like a father, I wait on his maturity. Trust him as he proves himself. Trust him until his partial success assures you to trust him more fully. As you grow older. As we all grow older."

"Sorry Carlo, I'll never trust Kurt as you do. It's not my nature nor my preference."

Carlo got up, as if he meant to leave, their business completed. He nodded to Evander Bontecott. He walked over to him and said a few words in his ear. As if a confidence between two older men, which did not concern Kurt Kallini.

Bontecott gazed into Carlo's sympathetic eyes, and Carlo nodded again. Then Bontecott looked into Kurt Kallini's eyes and some synapse in his brain exploded. The frayed sensation of nerves, and he knew sin just as certainly as he knew what Carlo Kallini said was true. He could not contain himself. His arm crashed down upon the table spilling red wine on the Turkey carpeted rug. It was the Irish maid all over again.

"Get out please. Leave my premises, please."

"Thank you for your hospitality, Mr. Bontecott."

He left Kurt in the room and walked to the Cadillac. He met Kady at the door, face flushed from her tennis game, and said how young and free she looked in her sport costume. They were not the words he wanted, but Kady understood. Carlo sat in the Cadillac and waited for his nephew.

Kady stood there sensing something was wrong. She heard her father shout from his study, "Get out! Get out of my house." She had never heard her father raise his voice. He was always cool in demeanor, cynical, and never emotional over business. What business did he have with Kurt Kallini?

Kallini left her father's study. He wasn't himself. The weird way his black suit hung on his straight frame, shoulders slumped, confused Kady. A very alarming look, as if he came courting and her father refused Kady's hand in marriage. Her mother came from her upstairs TV, top of the spiral staircase, to see the disturbance in her house. It sounded to her like a break-in by a dark-colored burglar. She saw Kurt Kallini, her counselor, and wished he had time to speak with her. Her parade of troubles passed through Dalhart, Texas onto the desolate prairie of a lifetime.

Kady and her mom heard Bontecott's weird voice ranting from his study, as Kallini left.

"Get that hoodlum out of my home, please, somebody please, take him away."

Neither of them knew what to do, as the black Cadillac left for Poughkeepsie. Bontecott's behavior was way too odd. He slammed the study doors and drank bourbon mixed with less and less water until late that night.

68
A Live Worth Living

Bontecott apologized to Kady and her mom. He said he was sick. His doctor in Millbrook said it was nothing. Don't drink so much. He went for a series of procedures at Vassar Hospital: EEG, MRI, and machines with absurd initials to test brain waves and body neurology. Her father showed sympathy for Kady's plight, as he learned of his own health.

"I know you're doing much of the work for your mom."

"Lots to do."

"How can I help?"

"We need a housemaid a few days a week. Would she disturb you too much?"

"I don't think so. Months ago it did, before you were here. But after this check-up, the tension went. Whatever happened, I can deal with it."

"What did you do differently?"

"I detached myself from business. Let the New Haven family, with their lawyers and accountants, run the business, not simply the showroom."

"I think you're right. Less tension. Better for you and mom too."

Kady never talked to her father as an adult. He never let her, without heavy sarcasm. The night Kallini came and left was so weird. "Get that hoodlum out of my house." Of course Kady had her backlog of incidents with Kallini, but this was different.

It perplexed Kady, who had problems of her own. David wrote her a short note, period. Basically it said, he flew home for a wedding of high school friends. He felt obligated to be there. He meant, not for her, for them. He wrote of another vacance the end of August, where they needed young folks to help out. They paid him a slight salary. His friend Peter Bergman said he'd come. David asked her too, indirectly.

It dawned on her David came home. The wedding was this weekend. Kady called his number in the Hudson Park phone book and there was no answer. His family lived summers at a camp in Schultzville. The name stuck with her. On a map it wasn't far from Millbrook. Drive there, but not in the white El Dorado. Her VW was in the shop for repairs, for an engine overhaul. Hurry them along. This was Friday and she wanted to see David today. This sex thing made her eager to drive to Schultzville. It stirred her up. She avoided the word horny.

No car but her father's. No friend to cruise Poughkeepsie, except Dhalia Richards, who left for Cape Cod. As speedbumps riveted her road, Kady got more excited. Anxious too. She was a month late for her period. She wished to be back in Old Saybrook, a girl of twelve among her relatives of New Haven. Talk of mood swings. She had mood swings worse than David's poetry. Crises et elans, words he used. Mood swinging mind and imagination like a jet airliner sweeping on wings of poetry. Go see David. She missed him and he was home.

To top off this freaky Friday, Grannie Lonigan called from Texas. Old woman with little time for worries. Grannie rode horses around her farm at age 70. A woman who joked, cursed, and cried a full life. Kady answered the ringing, hoping it was David.

"Hello Katherine, this is mom. Your sisters wanted to call. Bad news, old John died."

"Grannie, Kady speaking. Mom's upstairs watching her soaps. Sorry about Grandpa John."

"I'm only sorry the old snort didn't wait for me. So your mom's wasting time whining over the soaps? Have her come to Dalhart. We'll put her out of her misery. Are you still cooking and cleaning for her?"

"Sometimes. Dad's getting a housemaid."

"Way they're rolling in dough, why not servants to wait at your mom's beck and call?"

"They aren't easy to have around the house."

"Your mom's the young belle of Dalhart. Miss Fancy Pants had her sisters do the chores."

Kady smiled. She knew Grannie joked her along. They could be laughing and crying in her big country kitchen.

"Sorry to sass you about your mom's laziness. She was my Miss High Fashion before she was your mom. She can't be completely the honey bee queen, seeing how she raised you to be sensible."

"I like to hear how mom was beautiful, it helps."

"Why don't you run off and visit me in Texas? Love to have you at the funeral. That doesn't sound right, but that's the way it is. Christ, the dead go in the ground. I got nobody but young John around the farm, and he's off teaching college. Hardly ever home. You still there Kady?"

"Yes, Grannie."

"You don't take anything I say personal about your mom. I know she's sicker than a dog most all the time. I seen what cancer does to a person. God knows I have. Wastes a body away until dying's a relief. Let's get together at the funeral, say a few days, in case you yankees like a real fandango to brighten up your lives. What do you say, girl? Don't talk much, do you?"

"Grannie, no one gets a word in edgewise with you."

"I know that. Nice change from your tight-lipped mom, who can't stop dreaming she's Miss Dalhart, 1940. You're not stuck on yourself, are you?"

"No Grannie, I'm not beautiful like her. Like she was."

"You are too. Just she can't abide two raving beauties in the same house. Let her sisters slave for her, she did. Miss Dalhart, 1940, and a parade of people to curry her favor. She thought Bontecott would take care of her. You got the work, didn't you? Kady, my advice, come to the finest funeral in three states and two countries."

"I'll try Grannie. If I can get my boyfriend to go."

"Bring him, young woman. Bring a couple guys, one for me too."

"Okay Grannie. Let me get mom on the phone. Sorry about Grandpa John."

"Well don't get me moaning again. Drag your mom away from romance TV so I can talk to her. Bye now."

Kady set down the phone and picked up plans to travel to Dalhart, Texas. Get David to go. Get her VW from the garage. Herself, she was ready, if not for travel, then for the woman Grannie had been these 70 years. A full life there and unbelievable tedium here. She couldn't bear it another weekend. A life of tedium. Texas tolled the alarum bell. It rang a wake up call for her physical being.

Kady wanted that physical being to be her. At Old Saybrook she let her family Bontecott from New Haven be her. The sound of that waveless ocean, her groans of I'm lonely, so lonely. The move to Millbrook isolated her. New girl knew nobody at the Bennet School. Running track exhausted her. Nothing but athletic practice and religious prayer. At Wells College she wanted more of her physical being. With Barb she had a friend and with David the physical being that completes a person. Like Grannie Lonigan she wanted a life worth living.

Kady took her father's car and drove to Schultzville. Up the Parkway onto Pumpkin Lane to a creepy general store, where a polio-armed woman told her to cross Fiddler's Bridge, onto Camp Road and drive till she saw the Morpheys' sign and a circle of camps. She met David's parents. His tall father's arm shook a bit and his shorter mom made a pot of coffee. They drew her directions to the church in Hudson Park, and she got lost. It was evening before she found the church. The wedding party left for a steakhouse and bar and the wedding was at two tomorrow. She was exhausted. It wasn't David getting married, so why get upset. No reason for all this tension. Not for her father, not for herself.

Okay, impulsive action proved a failure. She met David's parents and told them about David and her traveling to Texas. Okay with them. Mr. Morpheys treated her nicely. He joked about funerals and weddings coming together, old people dying and babies born. She saw why David worried about his dad's health. Well then, let David call her. She'd spend Saturday hurrying along the mechanic on her VW. Then she'd be ready to go to Texas.

69

Homecoming

Of course Lorraine was his partner walking the aisle in Friday's practice. Not six hours back from Paris his head reeled from gravity-free flight. Lorraine held his arm to keep him in line. David heard from his mom Grandpa lay in Vassar Hospital after a stroke. Mom said go see him. Wedding of friends and funeral of his grandfather. His dad had the shakes. It was Rimbaud's saison en enfer, only it belonged to him, like his buddies.

"You and me next, David?"

David was wide-eyed from flight, from his mom telling him of Grandpa.

"No, David? Just spectators of our hometown friends?"

"It's sure a sight to see."

"Remember us, the Inseparable Six? The drive to Hendrix and Janis Joplin squeezed together in a car, and now we're all grown up and still together."

"Jimi and Janis died."

"Don't say that."

"But Flash unlocked himself from the trunk, drugfree, thank god almighty. Glorious resurrection."

Lorraine shushed him. Time Flash, her cousin, asked her to bed. Time the Poughkeepsie cops came for Flash and he locked himself in David's trunk. Time Lorraine asked David to sleep with her, pack her stuff, and take her home.

Hudson Park's mail lady, Lisa Avalon, talked to them, chewing gum.

"These guys of ours, they're always ass backwards. So Flash, you asking me?"

"Asking you what?"

"To be yours in matrimonial bliss. You tried the rest, now marry the best."

Lisa was never stand-offish about sex, innuendo, or eating. She kept her bad girl Italian figure, and barely kept it in her skimpy halter top.

"I got the milk," Flash said. "And I want the cow. Damn give me the whole herd."

"Go f__ yourself. I take back my proposal."

Flash stood six foot five, football rugged, with his handsomely dark face and long hair. Lorraine shared the joke with Lisa until Flash grabbed her back in line. Then she got back to David Morpheys, her boyfriend in high school and ever since, except for a break here and there.

"You're quiet. Tired from the planeride?"

"Yes, that's it. Off kilter. Ears damped."

Flash stood them up, and the line was stopped. He grinned at them over Lisa's shoulders.

"Hey Flash! From drug bust to wedding fuss, get a move on."

Flash put a hand over his gray glinting eyes, not for shame, but looking beyond the practice to the party and getting Lisa alone. Flash walked on.

"David, tell me what you're thinking, will ya?"

"My own funeral."

Lorraine looked at him weird and gave his arm a tug, to snap out of it. The priest ran through the vows, ring exchange, the kiss, etc., and their exit from the church. They were off to a dinner party at the steakhouse near Marist. It wasn't far from Regina Ceoli. A fine American meal and open bar. Lorraine danced with David. He saw where this night went, and wondered how to hold off. He needed a night's sleep and not with Lorraine. He needed to call Kady. He needed to go see Grandpa kept alive on the machines.

Lorraine knew they were grown up. She was over Lawson McLaren and she was over the ridiculous things coming between them. Her first boyfriend always held her heart in his hands. Flash said Kady Bontecott was with the horsey set in Millbrook, rich girls on horseback with their own tennis courts and pools. David didn't want a rich girl like Dhalia.

Tell David she loved him. There was no more fooling on her part. Lorraine kept touch with David during the slow dance, reminder and rehearsal for later on. She wanted words telling her where she stood.

"David, it was me who asked you home."

"Really."

"Course you came for the wedding, but for me too?"

"Of course. It's time to connect again. Be there for one another. I'm afraid touch and go will be our routine. The number of mistakes we made, sort of dooms us to half a life, as friends, when we were like Joey and Sue."

He'd meant to ask her to Hamilton after a freshman year apart, but never did. Too much water under the dam.

"Why can't we be Joey and Sue, again?"

David picked up time to swirl a waltz around Lorraine and clear his head. Like he was still in flight.

"We were once like Joey and Sue. More than friends."

Lorraine smiled with her gorgeous eyes, her full body. They had loved one another all through school.

"I hear you pulled Flash out of the fog. Joey says you're a saint the way you took care of him getting off drugs and into AA. A saint the way you set up Joey and your cousin Sue. The whole wedding."

"Sainthood's not me."

"Nor me, Lorraine."

"And none of us are saints."

"No, but it's good you were there for your cousins, Sue and Flash, Joey too."

Lorraine pressed closer to him as he swayed from her. She wanted what she wanted, an answer, what the years meant to them.

"You serious with this horsey girl Flash knows?"

"I think so. She's the first girl to make me feel the way we did in high school. The wish for nothing better the next day than see you in class. Any time you left you took the whole world with you. As Kady did, returned home a few weeks ago. As you did freshman year in

Florida, with me too ignorant to say the words, don't go."

"Say the words now."

"Then what happened and all that sad time between us. We had it all and we had nothing, except loneliness and regret."

"Why not have it all again? It's as easy as say the words, same as Joey and Sue."

"I don't know. Only six hours ago I traveled all day and it was still day when I got home. Now it looks like darkness never ends. I'm all mixed up. My grandpa had a stroke, I should go see him."

"Sorry."

"He knew it was coming."

"So us together again, what do you think? No time lost."

"I don't know. All of us look patched together. Too much happened in too few years."

"Be thankful we're still together."

"Maybe we're too close. Too little space here in Hudson Park. We can't dance away without stepping on toes. We left. We're all sort of inbred. Especially Flash annoyed whenever I'm home. Joey and Sue never left, and I wish them the best."

"And us?"

"I think we already had our chance."

Lorraine let the song and dance end early. She wanted a daiquiri.

"Come on David, nobody in a right mind wastes a free bar."

He agreed and got a Schlitz. A month sipping wine with meals and champagne for occasions left him temperate. Drink cold beer and join in with his buddies. He belonged to them.

Lorraine had one dacquiri and then another, dancing with Flash. She asked him again about Kady Bontecott. Was she the girl for Morpheys? Flash asked if she forgot his bothering her at the apartment they shared. She had saved his ass with Jimmy and Jerry. That he didn't forget.

"Blame my proposal on drugs, please Lorraine."

She nodded to the gray glint in his eyes.

"Or blame it on our being too close for too long. All kind of odd ideas creep into my mind. Things I can't tell anyone. You know."

Lorraine wondered if they were inbred in some weird way. Another daiquiri and she cared less. Flash apologized and she forgot his transgression. He was family. The folks wished everyone luck and went home. Gloom and doom settled in like the fog. What kept her here in Hudson Park? Sue had photography. All the glamour stripped from Lorraine and she was alone. The rest wasn't enough. Not New Paltz, not her friends, not even her mom and family. Life faded away like a photo negative from the glamorous picture she remembered. Sorority life at Gainsville. She'd return for law school.

But she was closely tied to David Morpheys. When she moved closer to him he moved away. What kept them apart, her or him? The more intimate the more David imagined some glorious life, far away from here. Her too. The glamour and the glory. But this time it was him. She interrupted his beery tale with Joey about a cop car arriving at a ninth grade dance.

"David, why do think you're better than us?"

It was her drinking voice and she drank another dacquiri.

"I don't Lorraine."

"Yes, you do," Flash lectured him. "What we do with our lives you see from way above us. College boy back among the townies. That's what Dhalia calls us. Vassar girls too. That's how Kady Bontecott sees me, Dhalia's townie. Good for a laugh and a screw."

David didn't see how he earned this criticism. How he became the outsider. Flash always had that antagonism. Sue and Lisa never talked long with him. Only Joey and him were close, and not anymore.

"Hey," David threw up his hands, "I'm not better, I'm different."

"But what makes the difference better?" Lorraine asked. "Why do you need so much space? Why the need to get away from us?"

"Come on Lorraine, let the guy breathe," Joey said. "He's hardly back from France. We asked him to leave his job and hurry home."

"Why should he think twice?" Flash asked. "I mean, after all we've been through. I mean with me, we had a trip to the Maine football camp, we got broken up in football, drug trips too. We worked near Bontecott's farm and who do you think hooked him up with his rich girl? Now he wants to dump Lorraine for her."

"Shut up Flash, you asshole."

Lorraine hurried off for another daiquiri. David got mad. Flash knew how to tick him off, and they all had enough anger to burn up years of friendship in a single fight. Tell Flash what was up.

"Hey Flash, get a life. We're all at a time we need to get a life. It's got to be different. Can't help but be different. And I miss you guys, really. You belong to your buddies. You guys are what Hudson Park means to me, at college and everywhere else. But it's a small town and we got to leave it behind, if only to better appreciate it."

"Townies, all of us then," said Flash, with sarcasm, and a bit of bitterness. "And we got to listen to another goddamn graduation speech."

Lorraine returned with drinks for her and Lisa, whose thick lips pursed on the decorative straw. Inbred in some weird way. Lorraine drank and no longer knew where this started nor where it was going. Joey too, saw a blow-up coming. Not before his marriage day, he swore. David asked Lorraine to dance.

"Sorry Lorraine, I said the wrong thing."

"Forget it."

David agreed, glad to be off the hook. He said the wrong thing and got what he deserved. Blame the planeride. This was Lorraine. Flash escorted Lisa from the classy steakhouse back to his apartment, clapping Morpheys on the shoulder.

"Good to have you back home, college boy. Have somebody new to pick on."

Lorraine held onto David's arm, as she did at wedding practice, more to steady herself now.

The wedding went off as practiced. Lorraine Shanessey assumed David returned for her. The way she wanted him. Come home from Paris and start over again. She dressed in a low-cut gown, her eyes sparkled, and her Clairol blond hair made her pretty face beautiful. She had gorgeous eyes. After so many breakups David and Lorraine were friends, with so much shared, wild times growing up fast, much too fast.

She went to U of Florida and him to Hamilton. They left Hudson

Park and returned different people. Somehow they never were the same as high school. She became a glamour queen and a Southern belle. She fell in love with a Notre Dame guy with rich parents near Chicago. She fell in love in the Florida spring. He had a sports car and he bought her beautiful clothes. They went to great parties. He was a jealous guy and he beat on her.

Afterwards when they came home summers, David and Lorraine were friends. For David she was the girl he grew up with. They saw Hendrix and Joplin together, they went to the Jersey Shore together, they fell in love and fell into trouble together. The wedding and reception they all had a good time. Let the previous evening be forgotten. They took a limousine to see off Joey and Sue to Disneyworld.

They stopped the limousine at the Holiday Inn. The plane left the next day. Flash took Lisa Avalon to Disneyworld too. She barely kept her bad girl figure in a bridesmaid gown. Joey and Sue had a restaurant to run, which Carlo Kallini provided money for a restoration. And David sat with Lorraine on a hotel bed. She told him all that happened to her, about Douglas McLaren, and what she learned. She still loved David and he told her about Kady Bontecott, what she meant to him.

"This Kady Bontecott, it's a serious relationship?"

"Yes Lorraine."

"So how's Paris?"

"It's beautiful like everybody says."

David left his answers incomplete. He didn't mean to. He didn't mean to be reticent with Lorraine.

Joey and Sue said goodnight, and thanks for everything. Flash Gordon leered at them, waved Lisa's postal cap, she was Hudson Park's postal lady, and wore her blue shirt. Lisa showed off her lace bra, which Lorraine complimented. Flash pulled Lisa back into their room.

David was left alone with Lorraine. Cool air conditioning and the moon hung low over the Hudson River. Lorraine said again she still loved him. She cuddled beside him, close and warm and easy. It was too easy with her. Good times in Hudson Park had come and gone.

David promised mom to go see Grandpa in the hospital. Go, else you won't get a chance to say goodbye. He saw dad with the shakes. So much at home falling apart. So much at home settled a bargain with the way life was and can't be again.

    He woke early and left his friends a note: go off to the airport without him. Good luck. He had business to attend to. He hitched to Poughkeepsie in his wedding tux. Better to go formal to see his grandfather off. At Vassar the nurse directed him to geriatrics. Really Grandpa was dead, stretched out on white sheets, off and already gone. David wished the stroke had killed him. It took everything but a heartbeat, machine managed, the catheters like snakes, his breathing diseased.

    There in a white frock, all gnarled, his skin brown-spotted like rotten fruit, lay his grandfather. Who showed him how to fish the lake for bullheads, eels, and snapping turtles, creatures of darkness caught on setlines over night. Each breath rattled his whole frame. Each breath shook his bones. Each breath stretched further the skin pulled tight over facial skull and hollowed eyes.

    His was a death mask. Awful sight he saw. Let him go, dear God. Let him go and lose himself in darkness.

    Please end this season in hell.

IX.
Winding Road to Woodstock

70
Two for Texas

David called Kady. Parents told him she called, came by, looked for him.

"Kady, I missed you. Sorry not to call. Got hung up with obligations."

"We all got duties. Dad's helping more with mom."

"Great."

"Give me more time until her next set of tests in September."

"Heard you want to go to Texas."

"What do you say?"

"Give me twelve hours and we'll go."

"Great."

"Had to say goodbye to high school buddies. It's goodbye to Hudson Park too."

"Tell me about the wedding later. 7AM tomorrow okay?"

David gave directions to his Hudson Park home, where her father visited him.

"Last long look at America. Then years in France on what salary Les Freres provide. It's been lost time without you."

"My VW should be fixed."

"Lost weekend. Now I'm good to go."

"And I want to see my Grannie Lonigan who raised kids and grandchildren. She's so full of life. Such a cool old lady. You'll like her and she'll like you. As much as I do."

"I do, like you. Love you. Let's go across this country and see all we can see."

"But stay in Texas, okay David. See my Grannie. See my life. See if we can make things right between us."

"Two for the road then…two together…two hearts beating in time…"

"Enough, David."
"Or too much, from Blake, and proverbs of hell."
"Go to sleep."
"Sleep enough in the grave, Rimbaud, an eternity."
"Then we're two for Texas."
"Deep in the heart, my love, goodnight."

Kady's voice hung notes of happy hysteria, like the first time she crashed into the French House. Lovers meet new minted, minds immaculate with wonder. David wanted her. Her voice sparkled pictures of unparalleled promise. Her somewhere was Dalhart, Texas.

Kady came early to say hello and so long to his dad, off to work at the IBM toolroom. Kady saw his shaking hands and wired old arms. Then he lifted her high for Chet Maziewski, his ride to work, and Chet was impressed. She turned red, laughing hysterically. Mom smiled in the doorway and didn't cry till the red VW buzzed like a motorcycle out of sight.

Kady recalled her first trip west. She was twelve and had to go. Grannie welcomed her. Grannie saddled two horses and rode a hundred acre route around the homestead. She cracked jokes about the flat ass land and how the winds whipped the lid off west Texas. She told Kady how her mom riled the boys as she herself had, but your mom never gave in. Your mom suffered from a mile high dose of pride.

Asked why Grannie gave in, that's what she wanted. John was a lean wrangler, who outrode the locals at the Dalhart Rodeo, whose pensive, precise demeanor threw her for a loop. He learned his father's jewelry business. He gazed into watchsprings and shaped diamonds, unperturbed by the raucous cowboys, bothering him. John Lonigan was his own man, and Gram was his woman. Your mom never gave in. She hitched her pride to Evander Bontecott, and lived a solitary life. Kady liked how Grannie raised her children and ran the homestead. From Grannie she gained strength to live a life. She had it all worked out in her mind.

David settled into the trip out New York 17 to Binghamton, and down 81 in Pennsylvania. He played harp tunes. She fluted her voice and David dropped an octave to a steadier beat. Kady enjoyed her melody, as the harp burst a bluesy flourish in the breaks. Let her and David be happy, like Grannie and wrangler John, dead and gone.

Cloudy weather covered the funnel of sky between pine mountains. Eighteen wheelers rocked the VW as they whipped by. David dozed after reading her portions of Leaves of Grass. Raindrops pulverized dusty streaks on the square windshield. Wipers cut through the waxy film, which defracted the view. Kady concentrated on the line, as passing trucks sprayed water and swept the VW. She slowed to a side rest area. The queasy grip in her stomach acted up. Then subsided.

David awoke without the roar in the car and lit a smoke. Kady felt the world dark and abrasive, needle pine mountains, purple skies, and hurt like pulled muscles gnawing at her stomach. Like a cancer metastasizing. The Marlboro steadied her and she smiled at David, sweat cold to her forehead. He wasn't with her yet.

"What's up, princess of the pike?"

He pushed the wavy hair behind his ears, and refitted the black cowboy hat she bought him.

"Rest stop."

She grabbed his hat and dashed for the bathroom. Kady must be exhausted. So many reststops, and she returned all wet.

"Care for coffee?"

She shook her head in disgust. Straw blond hair and cheerless freckles. Her face drawn and undone. It was the route to Munich all over again, and she jumped out her VW rather than go on.

Turn back? Turn back to what? For David home was haunted by the ghosts of high school. It was another life already lived. Return to what? Ahead beckoned the wide open West of his imagination, Dalhart, Texas, but also the Coast, the ocean, Hawaii, and the Vietnam War, from whose abyss, David did turn back, with one last look at America, backward to France, for there'd be no draft for him. Yet he was drawn on, drifting, doomed.

David hugged Kady in the enclosed VW space, rain pounding down, and kissed her.

"You okay?"

"I'm beat. That's all. You drive, while I curl up in the back."

Baggage moved to shotgun and blankets to the backseat turned down. Space for Kady to rest.

"Wake me up when you're done driving."

"Texas or bust. Sleep tight."

Ohio on Route 80 was outer limit to the Appalachian chain. Mountains became hills and valleys. Sun cut clouds on the horizon and rain slanted silver, drizzling like glass. Farm country of wheat and alphalfa and rye carpeted the flat miles. The land lessened: the sky expanded. Clouds rolled, spread, and vanished in thin blue air. Daylight lasted longer the faster they sped across Ohio, past Akron, and down Route 71 to Columbus.

Curvature of the earth created time. Pioneer dream hearing Eden like bird and insect chatter. The virgin land ever in sight over the horizon. His watch read after eight. Full sun blared like Chicago horns. Corn crowded both roadsides: ears of gold, silken beards, green stalkers swallowing the super highway, looking backwards.

After nine the sun touched down, orange globe rolling before him. David veered southeast on Route 70 toward Indianapolis and St. Louis, gateway to the fabulous West. Kady slept back of him. The sun set off to the side. Night suffused the rim of the skybowl. Stars like a million fireflies patterned the heavens above unknown seas of space. David dreamed he sailed an ancient Phoenician, pursuing western adventures, seas of merchant ships and plunder. Westward special, conquest of open space on the lunatic fringe.

By dawn David intended one destination. Reach the Mississippi, once end to civilization. Now his dateline East to West. He swallowed down inside the endless white line like a lizard's tongue, his carbuncular lights spitting white, searching for race memoranda. In the wake of the eighteen wheelers, he drifted close like Ahab after Moby Dick. He worked the VW over 65 and all was space suffused with spirit.

He was Huck sweeping down the river or Mark Twain roughing it out to silver mines in Nevada or Lewis and Clark climbing northwest by badlands and Puget Sound. The Voyage of Discovery. The VW like a lawnmower cut a swath, burned up highway and spewed death and destruction in its wake. Forward into terra incognita, Columbus colliding with the continent, mind over matter, wheel turning wheel and tires rolling the concrete strip. Doors of perception open wide like madness. Like the night a single cover over the blazing dawn.

Kady slept day into night and back into day. Longer than the trip touring Europe. David worried about her. He was wasted. The rearview mirrored dawn's early light, twenty miles from St. Louis. Kady called for a reststop and coming out she was sick, wrung cheeks yellow and eyes bleary red. Her freckles were a fright.

"Don't you give me that sympathetic look. I threw up and I need a cup of coffee and something to eat."

The sun came up and early mist smoked the river. They saw the archway of St. Louis and crossed the Mississippi's eddying current, southward flow of muddy water. Redundant to stop at MacDonald's. Coffee with a smoke, and Kady put her head on his shoulder.

Halfway to Dalhart she wanted her Grannie for some answers. She rested after a night of dreams. In twisted patterns, her mom held her and cried "never leave me" and her father pulled mom away saying "Let the two have the house" and the two were her and Kurt Kallini, waving goodbye to her parents. Weird dreams, twisted like her curled body in the VW. Safer to be awake.

"Feel better?" David asked.

"Awake. Not rested, but better. Let's stop here in the heat of the day. Find a room in St. Louis, with air conditioning and a soft bed."

"Rest a while. You got some color in your cheeks."

David loved her green eyes tangled by strands of hair. Her freckled look undaunted by what comes along.

"Don't lie to me. I look like hell and need a shower."

"Me too. Maybe we can share one. You know, west from here is desert, cowbones and cactus. We should conserve water."

David gazed at her, and Kady smiled, like she had nothing else in mind.

"We should stay together, David, and not run off again. Sorry we didn't stay in France, working for Les Freres. Where mornings we'd wake up together."

Kady said what she wanted to say. She didn't believe the "you and me forever ideal." Marriage for all her Wells friends was unreal. Living together was real, better. David looked off like he was shy or shocked. Why didn't he say something?

"Kady," he said with the wistful stare she liked. "I saw a movie at Radio City. I was 14 on a school trip. The Rockettes were the show, off there, on the stage, elsewhere. Anyway the movie moved inside my mind, away from out there. Like you Kady. You moved in here. Inside the way I think and feel. The movie was a love affair, Albert Finney and Audrey Hepburn, their meeting and marriage and children, and through the whole trip they stay the course. The movie was Two for the Road. Why don't we stay, two for the road?"

Kady loved him. David defused her weariness. She trusted him. They made love in the shower tub, and there was fullness like sun shining after a storm. They were tired and slept the day. They lay smooth skinned like silk sheets.

They woke to ride route 44 to Oklahoma City and route 40 to Amarillo, fifty miles short of Dalhart, Texas. David had a sub sandwich and Coke for her.

"Sleep better?"

"Once my stomach settled and I slept in sheets."

"Good."

"We can drive without the heat at night."

"Ready?"

"Let me drive now."

"Do it, but don't overdo it. I'm good too."

They took the beltway and hit rushhour traffic. Kady complained about a shake in the steering wheel. A thousand miles caused creeks in the machinery. They were miles from Springfield to remold moveable parts. Two hours down the pike the wheel rattled. They passed Springfield.

"Should we check it out?" David asked.

He had no idea about mechanics and neither did Kady.

"Come on. Things are fine. We'll give it an overhaul in Dalhart."

A good hour to sundown. David read Moby Dick. Women make decisions same as men. Liberation put Kady at the wheel. His mind was elsewhere, in a weird firestorm on the Pequod's mast. Ahab snuffed out the eerie glow along the harpoon: mind over matter, and common sense too.

Out from a gas station twenty miles south of Springfield the steering wheel jittered and front tires shook. BAH-BAH-BAH...BOOM!... BOOM! The VW skidded toward the shoulder. Four hands grasped the wheel, until the car rattled to a stop. Front tires blew out. Flat road rubbers and depression of the spirits.

They called a tow truck and road with the mechanic. They felt safe, the trouble done. Garage guy talked baseball. Mickey Mantle was born down the road in Commerce, Oklahoma. This Cardinal fan said the Mets made a stir. David didn't know it. Baseball had been a childhood obsession. He got far from sports as meaningful to a life worth living.

Problem was tire alignment gone awry. Mechanic took them to Best Western for another evening. They needed the rest. He called back and the VW was ready. They encountered the bad breaks of Missouri.

With new tires and new day they charged in a land rush across Oklahoma. It was real dry land bleached by sun under wide open skies, one farmhouse per horizon, the West incarnate. They reached the Panhandle of Texas by nightfall with miles to go to the New Mexico border. Dalhart was that Texas bordertown, last stop on the lonesomest stretch of Route 66.

Late Saturday night they arrived at Grannie Lonigan's house, who bustled out to the VW and wrapped her arms around Kady. Sharp green eyes and frizzy white hair like tumbleweeds, she was Kady's spitting image, only age-old. Ghost of a farmhouse and 3-story barn loomed from the deep blue heavens, haunting milestone of human effort.

Grannie took them inside to sit down. She whirled cups of coffee and a tray of pies before them. David liked her hectic carriage, propelled more from her wide hips and sturdy legs than Kady's light feet. Absent were the graceful shoulders and still face of Kady's mom in the photo. Grannie was all movement and no pose.

"How the hell are you two kids doing, traveling cross country?"

Grannie smiled keenly. Her nasal twang pleased David no end, and he smirked between bites of apple pie and heavy creamed coffee.

"Just fi-ne," Kady said in imitation.

"Well I never been east of Tyler, Texas with the pretty roses they grow there, but I been clear across to San Diego. John took me a few years back. Picture him, will ya, David. Never did stray from the jewelry shop, 'cept Sunday for a ride round the farm. He says I'm tarred of Texas. Before I die I gone to see the ocean. John who never spoke more than two words and never gone further than rose festivals in Tyler gone to see the ocean. We saw it all right. It was a bee-u-tiful sight. The sun sets red like a ruby stone, he said, below the blue waves. John sure appreciated bee-u-ty. Made him happy, and he died peaceful."

Fitful energy for David faded with the food. Grannie walked him upstairs and told him not to bother with John's funeral tomorrow.

"Just sleep late as you want. And thank you for bringing my Kady. She sure looks bee-u-tiful, like a ruby over the blue ocean. Two of you have a happy life."

David thanked her.

71
Vigil Night

"I always ex-aggerate my Texas drawl when a yankee's company."

"David hates to miss a thing. He was wide-eyed the moment you opened your mouth."

"Bontecott never came back."

"Dad's a New Englander, for sure."

"Well Kady, glad to have you here. This is like the vigil night of my own dad's laying in. I'd prefer it that way. Women get together and the wife washed her husband's body. Womenfolk stayed up all night until the preacher come by to say his words."

"Catholics like it proper and in church."

"Yes, but the Baptist pride was a night of wailing one's heart out. Not John's Irish Catholic way. His way for the girls, but I'd like to stay the night if you don't mind. I won't cry."

"You cry all you want, Grannie, it won't bother me."

"Won't bother you none, I'll be. Maybe you got no trouble worth crying for. Got a good looking boyfriend, who loves you, given half a chance. Don't be your mom now. It's a man you want, not some nice house and Cadillac and servants. Don't do this David a disservice. A guy willing to hop in a broken down car and ride you to Texas should be proof."

"He loves me, Grannie. Trouble with him, he wants to see the whole world before he settles down."

"Wrangler type. Good rambling man, then honey. Some men got to wear out horses because they got a rage to live, too strong inside them."

"Like John?"

"John wasn't the wrangler type. All his life smacked of precision: his Catholic religion, cutting stones, even his damn cheapness with accounts. Lucky he was a stickler with himself, not me. My family's farm and he liked it that way. Two horses pulling the plow. Why I'd want to mind your business, Lord knows, he'd say. I got my way and he got his, with love and children and shared pleasures between. Million ways to have a good marriage if you a mind to."

"David has to settle down. This Vietnam War make matters for guys his age difficult."

"You'd think the government mind its own business. This is America, isn't it? What business we got half a world away? I hear young John talk. My John he minded his business, let others mind their own."

"David expects his draft notice soon. Then live in France, long as the war lasts."

"Well don't fret much. People here in Texas are fed up with young men coming home dead. War won't last long. Nixon may be Tricky Dick, but he's a politician. LBJ drug his ass home to Texas because he didn't end the war and should have."

"Draft causes David to drift. Stay in Paris. I suppose there's work there for us. But I get tired, worn out, and sick to my stomach caring for mom. In Paris the work is nursing and caring for about twenty old folk worse off than mom. I don't think I can do it."

Kady's eyes filled with tears.

"Old folk like me?"

"No, of course not. You take care of yourself and always will."

"Honey, there's something you ain't telling me. You ain't sickly like your mom. Or too dainty to wear out with a little work. What is it?"

Kady cried her eyes out, not Grannie.

"I'm sorry Grandpa died."

"Shush! He had a good life. Cry for yourself. It's your mom working you? That Bontecott? Live your own life. Leave them for a couple years, and let those Yankees fend for themselves. Let them know you're not only grown up, but gone. Old folks can't leech a young one's life. Leave them. Go to Paris, or stay here with me. Is that it?"

"That's part of it."

"Have more pie and coffee. You looked peaked."

"I can't eat. I throw up every morning, other meals too. It's my mom's cancer."

"Cancer hell, you're pregnant. And praying to sweet Mary and about fifty saints you're not. Honey if you are, you are. Tell David. Get his help. Hell! Live here and no one will ever hear of David Morpheys until the war's over. I need help on the farm, and young John's away. Tell David."

"I can't tell him until I know myself. What if it's mom's cancer?"

"It's not girl."

"I got to know for sure. I mean, how do I know he wants a baby? How do I know he's responsible enough?"

"No man's responsible until he needs to be. Tell him, David will do fine."

"He'll do like my father did. Say it's a woman's business, not his. You know having me dropped my mom's womb and caused her problems. Colon cancer because of me."

"Bull...shit, Kady! Your mom had about four miscarriages trying to bear a baby boy for that bastard, Bontecott. Sorry to swear at your father. But it's not fair to you."

"Babies were my mom's problem."

"I bet David's a lot different than your dad. More like my John."

"His father was a farmer. No kidding, he farmed for dad until things didn't work out and he went to IBM."

"David will do fine. Farming the land's in his blood then. I got a farm. You guys stay here."

"I'd like to, Grannie."

"I need you and you two need a place to stay."

"Still too early to know for sure. How my stomach feels I'm scared to death it's cancer. Like mom."

"Shush Kady. Without a doubt, you're pregnant. Always happens this way. Old man dies and a baby is born. That's the Baptist in me talking. Time people start crying, some young girl like Kady Bontecott says she's expecting, and ten of us women and as many men get real happy to help out. It starts again. The circle unbroken."

"Don't start singing Grannie. Else I'll join in and wake up David."

"Singing songs to wake the dead, preacher says."

"Cheer me up, Grannie. I wish living back home was this simple, this right."

"With Katherine, simple was never sophisticated. Don't be that way."

"I'll try, really."

"And tell David, first chance you get, hear."

Kady slept a few hours until she heard Grannie doing farm chores, and preparing her black dress for the funeral in town. Both of them ready, and Kady rode along with Grannie in a Ford truck, no less.

72
Selling David the Farm

Texas sun heated David's upstairs room into the dry nineties. He got up to ask Kady what's happening. She was gone and nobody home. A note on the percolator said turn it on and pies are in the pantry. Coffee and pie in hand, he opened the kitchen screen for a daylight look at Dalhart.

Outside was a three story barn, sign up high in black letters, The Lonigan Homestead. The barn towered over the kitchen and the sky dwarfed the barn. Western skies revived David's sense of awe. The wide world mirrored his imagination, with endless stretches and rich possibility. Lonigan farm owned a hundred-sixty acres of horizon with no other farm on the flat earth. Such was Texas in the Sunday quiet of an August day.

David wandered in the barn to talk with the animals. Riding horses were hitched. Cattle must be on the range.

"Hey dude, you're up. What's do-in?"

Voice came out of nowhere. Out of the upper reaches came a Wah-hoo, Wah-hoo, baby!

"Hey David, dude. Wanna share some smoke?"

A headful of blond hair peered down from the loft.

"Hey man, I'm hardly awake. What are you up high for?"

"Coolest place on earth, except Chichen Itza inside the Mayan temples. Barns are the best we Texans can do to reach the sky. Grannie said you was a language whiz and we should get acquainted."

"You John?"

"Twice removed from the John they're burying today."

"How come you didn't go?"

John swung backwards down the ladder and shook David's hand. In boots and hat rimmed with snakeskin and shoulder length blond hair, John was an odd wrangler. He was five foot eight, cleanshaven, and sharp green eyes. Only he was older than David, nearly thirty. John tilted his hat back to ponder an answer.

"Let me see. Paraguay Indians burn their dead. I saw that in the Peace Corps. Kind of gruesome. It's not Catholic ritual that turns me off, it's the body dressing. All gussied up. So a dead body don't look dead. More like waxed fruit."

"Got a Grandpa on machines. Alive and dead at the same time."

"That's gruesome too. Just I don't like Old John gussied up."

"I see."

"Hey Grannie said to take you riding. Show you the farm in case you want to buy it."

"Don't you want it?"

"I got work at WTSU, teaching Spanish. Got no time to care for the homestead, and Grannie too."

"Jesus, I never been on a horse."

"You'll like the ride. All ranching is, riding around."

"I worked a summer bailing hay and chasing cows."

"Then there's nothing here you can't handle."

"Skies are something else."

"Let me show you the riverfork of the Mustang and the Carrizo, we'll cool off, and then past town, you'll see the Rita Blanea. It's old John's Sunday ride."

"Ride around for his funeral?"

"Yea, and show you the place too."

David was nervous as hell mounting his horse. Animal was a massive force under him, and John's horse kicked up dust down the field road. On the flat fields grazed the longhorns of Texas cattle drives. The bump of the horse countered his natural rhythm. Lucky the horse followed John's over the gullied terrain near the highway.

"Don't mind the darkness beneath Arterial 87 because the horse is used to it. Be cool."

And it was cool in the tunnel. Dirt road turned to glop from the hooves of cattle. Walls were wet slabs of concrete. Sun shone in a square somewhere further on, but the tunnel was black. Overpass of cars echoed in the chamber. Horse surged and snorted, and clomped steady.

Gone to the funeral. Tomb of blackness, until the square of light at the end of the tunnel. Concrete craggy walls and puddled mud. Overhang was no more than a foot over his head. Short time, thank Jesus, before resurrection came.

"Thought you'd like that. The Tomb of Tut."

Over the rise David saw the rivers fork and they looked like streams. In dry land water magnifies.

"Problem on the farm, David, you should know. River comes close to flooding the tunnel, springtime. Grannie complains to town and county. No help. It's the state's business and they don't care if our cattle drown."

"So your WTCU job better than this one?"

"Better but insecure. I got the job as a grad student when the old signor died. I slipped in midyear and they got nobody better, yet. I can't get tenure without a doctorate and if I take the year to get it, they'll find somebody better."

"The Catch 22."

"Exactly. Why I sell you on the farm. It's a sure thing."

"You sold me."

"Then it's time for you to get serious?"

"If the war was over, maybe I'd teach school too. What else can you do with an English degree? You up for the Draft?"

"No. Vietnam wasn't big when I joined the Peace Corps and when I returned, local draft board considered three years in Paraguay, time served."

They watered the horses, and David was sore returning to the homestead. John had his Bronco 4-wheel drive out and asked David if he headed back to New York. He had friends who needed a ride.

"I heard your Grannie tell old John visited San Diego. I'd like to see the coast. Say hello and goodbye to the country before Europe. We hitched the Alps and this guy Antoine gave me an address. Someone he roomed with in college named William Cougar. Want to come to San Diego?"

"For old John's sake?"

"Sure."

"No. There's a big concert in New York. Friends in Austin wanted a ride, but if you're on to San Diego, they'll find another way."

"Let me talk to Kady. She has the word on where we go, it's her car."

"Okay."

The funeral party left church for a daughter's house in Dalhart. Kady returned to the farm. David strolled out to greet her with a hug as the VW sputtered up the dirt drive.

"Service okay?"

"It wasn't pretentious. Grannie cried. Sisters all got her laughing about John's trip to San Diego. He tried body surfing, for the hell of it, Grannie said."

"Let's go there. See the coast for ourselves."

Kady saw his far away look. It scared her some. It told her David was on the move. Reason comes on the far side of a man's madness, Grannie said.

"What did you think of young John?"

Kady wanted to change the subject from the take off and leave scenario.

"John nearly killed me riding the horse. I hurt standing and sitting."

"Did you like the farm?"

"The tomb of Tut."

"John show you the tunnel?"

"And asked for friends about a ride to New York. Ask you, I said."

"He did. He and his Mexican girlfriend want to ride with us. He's so cheap he doesn't want miles on his Bronco. Grannie said cheap he inherited from her husband. Old John kept accounts of everything, even sticks of chewing gum. Actual ledger. And he didn't drink or smoke because it cost money. Cheap but fair."

"Then John wanted the ride?"

"Yes, his way of asking, for friends. I'd tell him we're too crowded."

"Your decision."

"What did he tell you about us staying?"

"You mean buying the farm?"

"That's John's way too. See if you buy the idea. Grannie said we got a place to stay till the war's over."

"I missed the point entirely. What do you say we come back after the coast?"

"Trip there and back?"

"One last look at America. See the country, ocean to ocean. What do you think?"

"I guess we go. Else you'll regret not going."

"Okay Californ-i-a, gold country by the deep blue sea."

73

Townhouse

Kallini needed to see Quinn and Dier in their NYC townhouse. He saw Joshua Steen first in Crown Heights among the Hasids who helped Uncle Carlo. Then he and Josh saw Quinn.

Quinn co-opted the Movement, the SDS, even the antithetical PLP and RYM. How'd he manage the takeover? His politics latched onto the Maoist line and the Marxist underpinnings with its weird logic of other times and places. It was a matrix to turn the ramblings of Movement ideology into an LSD trip. There was no Movement or SDS ideology, other than statements applicable to the multiversity, whether MIT or Michigan or Berkley. When SDS started the anti-war march in 1965 their small group exploded with recruits on every campus. A meeting of minds and connection of male to female to male held together the small band of early SDS who didn't want leaders to read the parking meters.

Same Dylan song for the Weathermen. Quinn with his incredibly rich family got himself richer with manufacture of LSD and charismatic as a Timothy Leary with his Harvard background. Rich to richer and radical to extreme. Then with Weathermen taking over the SDS apparatus above ground Quinn moved underground as they pushed the limits of his action, the extremes of his confrontational rhetoric. Move from campus where they made a difference, from the moratoriums and marches on Washington where they won a majority of Americans against the war, to streets of gangs and high schoolers and unemployed workers. They wanted a mass army returning to Chicago for the conspiracy trial. They wanted confrontation. They were white freedom fighters like the Black Panthers.

Quinn came to the door looking albino white like the most badass black mother.

"Kallini and Josh Steen, you two still know my NYC digs. Means I have to move out of the Village."

"I'm over the bridge in Brooklyn."

"And Kallini, where do you call home?"

"Paris place called Gobelin, with Akim and his Algerian family. I wanted to come offer you asylum."

"A safe house from the FBI?"

"Their Cointelpro will locate you when the bombs explode."

"I figure when the bombs explode at military installations, pig stations, banks, and ROTC buildings, this townhouse goes up in smoke too."

"Movement means moving further and further into revolution."

"Yes Kallini. At Cornell you never understood. You always played two sides against the middle. There is no middle anymore. Why you and Josh are reactionaries, why you're the enemies, why Kallini, Dier and Burn kicked your ass in DC. We had that gig at Ft. Dix all set for a jailbreak and you got involved in our plans. Like Cornell where you two took over the ten thousand. Barton House Community got reforms, when confrontation would begin the revolution."

"You still see one explosion turning the trick. And everyone bent on revolution in Amerika. It's not going to happen. There are small steps forward. Conditions here aren't the conditions for Robespierre and Lenin and Mao. You can't spark the explosion like dropping a tab of LSD or lighting a fuse to one of your kin's devices."

"Why are you here, Kallini?"

"I came for your girlfriend, who kicked me after she pushed me down. I wanted her to know I'm okay."

"Dier, Kallini's come for an apology."

Short girl, about five foot four, who worked the auto unions with her union family and one of the originals at Michigan. She'd been in Cleveland with an ERAP project living in a single apartment, an urban commune of shared identity with students and oppressed poor. She'd gone to Cuba and worked in the fields among Castro's workers with Che and Lin Pao and other heroes of the Third World revolution in her head. Dier looked past Kallini to Joshua Steen. A former boyfriend. One of her sweethearts before the shared orgy smashed monogamy.

"Josh, I got a tape recording of your Barton Hall speech. For Quinn it's reactionary, for me it was moving."

Joshua looked around the East Village. With lofts and townhouses it wasn't Crown Heights. What a letdown to be back with his Hasids cutting diamonds and reading Talmud.

"Nice of you to say, Dier."

"It's the truth. You always had a sweet way moving a crowd. It's an art form."

"You guys better come in," Quinn said. "See an FBI agent in a hip getup, you can never tell."

Dier made a pot of coffee. She took Quinn's austere townhouse and made it livable. Nice couch and chairs and endtable. Other rooms and floors made ready the revolution. This flat she waited on friends. And fewer were the old friends Quinn wanted to meet. She let Kallini take the blame for the reactionaries and Quinn's queer turn to solitude. But it was her social makeup.

"I came to make amends," Kallini said.

"We're off to a project in Pittsburg. Already we enlisted street gangs in Detroit. Make ready for the showdown at the Chicago trial of Bobby Seale."

"You're what's left of SDS?"

"We're the action faction, certainly."

"Listen Dier. I wanted to show you I'm okay. Things got out of hand."

"We can't work together."

"Come to Woodstock for the celebration. For old times sake. For a last meeting of the tribes before the shit hits the fan and the streetfighting begins and the felonies file in the courts. Before you have to go underground."

"Kallini, you always saw things with a raw cynicism."

"If you succeed, I'll say the rest of the Movement turned chickenshit. But prepare for dark times. And if either of you need a safe place outside the States, I have one with Algerian terrorists in Gobelin. District of Paris. Akim and his family know what it means to live in a cadre of cells, to live underground. So I come with an offer to share, if not the confrontation tactics of the Weathermen, then security outside the States with The Brotherhood. Okay?"

"We'll be here till the last bomb," Quinn replied.

Kallini looked at Dierdre Hartford to see if she was suicidal as Quinn.

"You, Dier?"

"We will fight for victory. See white privilege fighting in the streets of Chicago. See us raise a mass army of 10,000 like Joshua stirred at Cornell. See that mass army ready to close the army bases and take over the city streets. It's revolution time, Kallini, and only you peace-creeps seek safe houses. Let the FBI come after us. We're more intelligent than them."

"See Butch Cassidy and the Sundance Kid?"

"Josh, that's our favorite film. Shoot em' up and flee to the compadres of South America."

"But who are those guys?" Kallini asked.

"Yes, Kallini, the pigs on the street and the pigs in the FBI are coming after us. But we'll stir up a mass army of radical protest, and find safety in numbers."

"Come to Woodstock, everyone will be there."

"No more time for love and peace, we tried it, and moved on."

"Okay, I made the offer. I wish you luck. Along with Josh."

Dierdre Hartford gave Joshua a last loving look. She had those naive eyes of girls on a mission. She had incredible energy. Her whole life had been organizing. First unions, then Movement, and finally the Weather-women for Pittsburg.

"Joshua, we're going to miss you."

"Why not let me back?"

Dier looked to Quinn, who shrugged his shoulders. At Cornell Josh had been his impresario. No one better on the social side, the political meetings, who loved the group as much as Quinn his solitude.

"Please join us."

Kallini was mildly surprised.

"I thought you wanted to do business for The Brotherhood."

"Sorry Kurt, it bores me. Especially back with my parents. Who wants to go home?"

"You can never go home again," Quinn pronounced. "Especially us with parents in the military-industrial complex, with a generation connected to what we mean to bring down, by a mass movement if Dier has her way, or by bomb for bomb, until the napalming of villages comes home. One, two, many Vietnams."

"Guess I go."

"Kurt, we're finally on our own. Wish us luck."

"Josh, make your luck, the three of you, this cadre, your collective might. Yes, fare forward."

It was the best a breakup could be. Dier, Joshua, and Quinn at their Greenwich Village townhouse, coming closer together, living for the action, for the exciting highs which made the Weather machine function, and with fate falling like darkness over village, Chicago, and the nation. The end of the Sixties. The end of time.

74
Pacific Ocean

David and Kady left Dalhart on the southwest diagonal of Route 54 to pick up Route 40 again in Tucumcari. Sun had trouble setting over the flat land. When it did, the land got dark quick. In the mountains of New Mexico Kady sacked out cold. Route 40 hit the mountains and did high twists and low turns past Albuquerque. Up and down without a moon, the headlights of little help. Pueblo Indians in their mountain reaches. The night road veered all angles. Lost in the wake of the white whale. Or like Coronado, his search for the seven cities of gold gone wrong, his travels to end in despair far from home.

Gallop and into Arizona came a stretch of Navaho land, flat and easy to ride, until the Rockies rose high in the night. Seeing nothing, fearing vast drops, David's ears popped after Flagstaff, the turnoff south on Route17 for the fabulous new day of Phoenix. There Kady called for a reststop and a blanket. She had the mechanic turn off the faulty heater for summer, and it was cold in the car.

To Phoenix took the rest of the night, when the sun dawned bee-u-tiful over the desert. Like a cross the VW ran north-south with sun stretching its shadows east-west. They found a Phoenix motel with a swimming pool, as if a chip of the vast blue sky fell to the cool water pool. What a night of extremes, as he shared the soft bed and air conditioning with Kady. They slept like spoons and her warm touch in the cool air kept David up awake.

Phoenix was nice with its dry heat. The sun baked the air and shadows collected cool and dry. Its museum displayed Indian art, elaborate designs in shapes of Islam, other dwellers in the desert. Nowhere was there sweat and dirt. All was sun-bleached and pleasant. They saw the sun set from pool chairs and got to bed early. Kady was weary from the wake, David from the drive.

In the morning Kady drove the final jaunt of their western journey, down to Route 8 and across the Mohave Desert. Here were the sands of time, eternal white wastes, silent under the sun. No matter what one's troubles, whatever pain and scars, here like meets like and is justified. Land of prickly cactus, Gila monster, and tumbleweed, where little is human.

The car heated. Its red metal blazed like a meteor past stops of Stuckeys to Yuma. Elements hard and inhuman reveal reaches of the stoical spirit. Sixty miles to El Centro the VW, ill prepared to climb the Sierras, baked and steamed. Its lawnmower engine showed virtue topping the heights, which sloped gracefully to the Pacific Ocean. An overheated car got them to the coast.

David followed his card address from Antoine to Pacific Beach. From a rainy night high in the Alps the address took them half way around the world. Palms lined Mission Boulevard. The address was the Free Clinic. Attendant called, "Hey Bill, a couple to see you."

Out came Bill Cougar, thick black hair banded by what looked like a Quebec fishing belt his dad brought him years ago. Apache black hair over his wide shoulders that filled the portal crosswise. His bronzed neck was massive, like a huge lineman on David's Hamilton team. His massive hands clasped together, jeans and boots beneath his doctor's tunic, Bill shook David's hand.

"What can I do for you two?"

David was taken back by his stillness and his size. He passed him the card.

"Yea Bill, this guy Antoine from Dijon, France said to look you up."

"You got that card from Antoine? That's what's bringing you here?"

David shook hands and introduced Kady.

"Ah Kady, you remind me of the roadrunner. Guy who runs The Brotherhood, Kurt Kallini."

Kady nodded. She scouted her eyes around the clinic. It wasn't much, and her stomach gripped her.

"We're from New York," David said. "We're from the other side."

"You're welcome to the coast, wherever you're from. Friends of friends, we're in this together."

Bill chucked his tunic in a hamper, and looked long and hard at

Kady. There was puzzlement in his turquoise blue eyes. "Just you look like the Roadrunner, sorry."

Just as Kady feared. This trip west included "the hoodlum in her father's house."

"Kallini's back from Paris. My friend Joey Gallo told me he came to Poughkeepsie."

"I knew he'd return for this Woodstock thing. Last Brotherhood bash, then Kallini's back to Paris. Some commune in Vichy."

Bill looked over their VW, and said to follow him to the beach. They could crash at his place. Up Mission they drove toward La Jolla with streets alphabetical by precious stones. David thought that got to Old John on his last trip from Texas. Stoned streets he told Kady, but she turned quiet. They drove a street past Tub's Tavern, and parked near cliffs and a long wooden pier jutting into the Pacific Ocean. What a view of sun hovering over the cresting waves.

"You got here in time. Same spectacle every evening."

"You connected with Antoine and Kallini?" Kady asked.

"The Brotherhood's their business. We're West Coast. Sit and relax, I'll be back with Tubb's Tuesday night special."

Kady sat shoulder to shoulder with David, and he hugged her close. She didn't trust this Antoine card, but Bill looked okay. Waves crested way out there, high and white, roaring with a running start and crashed, broke churning and foamed upon the sand. Then the undertow filtered the sand like miner's gold back to the sea. Sandpipers tripped daintily at top speed treading for food along the tow. This was no Old Saybrook on the bay. She liked the look of the Pacific Ocean.

David held Kady's hand at the journey's end. Crest, break, and tow repeated forever. The sun touched the watery horizon out near Hawaii or Tahiti or the Sea of Japan. If it wasn't for the war in Asia, David would settle here beside Kady. The wide world whirled before his eyes. Backwards, he thought, was the only way to go. Sorrow shared a big part of the rapture. Why his life drifted with the Draft threatening him. Why there was no place to rest.

When Bill returned with dinner, only the warm fervor of sea and sky floated over the Pacific. Dinner was three paper plates of taquito rolled meat, refried beans, jalapeno sauce, and salad covered with blue cheese dressing: the Tuesday special for seventy-five cents. Three bottles of Olympia beer squeezed in Bill's hand, massive as the mit of David's dad. His father's shook with Parkinsons.

"It's a feast, Bill. I'll never eat it all."

"I'm sure me and David can eat what you don't. Or leave scraps for the gulls and sandpipers."

Kady swigged on a beer and left her food.

"Our crowd at the clinic leaves for Woodstock in a week. Want to ride with us, our own gypsy caravan."

"Hey, that's great," David said.

"But Kady, you're welcome to crash at our place long as you like."

"I like it here," Kady replied.

She scraped her refried beans on David's plate, and Bill looked her over again.

"You okay, Kady?"

"Fine Bill, tired from the trip."

"Crash as soon as you're ready. Our casa your casa."

The stay in San Diego was paradise. Morning and afternoon David played football with Bill and other beachcombers. In the sands there were runs splashing into sheets of waves, passes that rocketed into the blue, diehard blocking and pass rushes clawing at the quarterback.

The Clinic kept short hours, and to supplement the luxuries of van and beachhouse Bill worked nightshift at the La Jolla Hospital. Days they watched powerboats skim high speed across Mission Bay. The Padres played in the sunny desert. The museum housed the fresh colors of Georgia O'Keefe and moonlit deserts of Ansel Adams. The Glass Menagerie staged in Balboa Park. Bill and friends were such good company they wanted to stay forever.

75
Woman's Day

Kady liked Bill Cougar. He had intuition few doctors had. Few doctors who weren't female had any.

"Hey Kady, come to the Clinic and we'll check out your stomach ailment."

"What time?"

"Between two and seven. No wait, and we know it's nothing extraordinary. So we check to be sure."

Kady came by at 4PM when David played ball with the beachcomber band of burly guys. She saw his arching spirals on the tilted beach. He caught footballs like a visiting seabird poised on his fingertips and crashed from the circus sands into the sea. He was free and having fun. The unfairness of being female. David dropped by her sunbathing as if she were his personal fanclub. She should tell him, make him responsible. A check up and then a heart to heart.

"Woh! This is the way life should be. Played out like a game under an ocean of sun. Played in complete earnest because it's only a game. None of that coached crap in college. No playing favorites here. No coach here to pick the Groton kid because his family has money up the wazoo. No rich kids here to get the breaks. No scholarship with strings attached. This is football, about as free as it gets. This is it."

Kady weighed the chip on David's shoulder. With his "every rich kid gets the breaks" speech he implied her father's money. No freedom in college. No freedom in the system so he simply quit. All this draft evasion added up to one thing: he drifted. The self-involved life. Good for him. Not so good for her. Whatever deal they made, it wasn't fair to her. She left for the Clinic.

Bill Cougar gave Kady no wait time in the lobby. Given half a chance she'd leave.

"Come in Kady. David playing football?"

"Yes. Crazy to kill somebody. Hope nobody gets hurt."

"You going to the play in Balboa Park tonight?"

"Yes."

"I'll tell Janey. We'll be late, after work. Listen Kady, we both know you're two months pregnant and not real happy about it."

Kady stared at him, then around the room.

"If you prefer because I'm a man and all, you can talk to Janey Tower. She'll be here and I can go play ball."

"Who's she?"

"She's a nurse practitioner at the hospital. She's been with her mom."

"And if I'm pregnant?"

"She can give you options. Woman's movement is big on the coast."

"Let me meet her, Bill. Makes sense to talk to a woman. We didn't expect a baby, which is terribly naive on my part."

"On his part too."

"Now I have to decide what to do, not him. If it's cancer like my mom, I don't know."

"Let me run the simple tests, okay?"

"Then I'll talk to your girlfriend."

"Don't say girlfriend, we're equal partners."

Janey Tower came in. Bill, a 220 pound desert butte of a man, looked sheepish. Bill introduced them, and Janey hugged Kady instead of shaking her hand.

"Mind if I let Bill go play with the boys."

"Go ahead."

Janey wasn't pretty with her large teeth. Her big boobs flopped in her cotton smock with square pockets for hospital stuff. Janey Tower was a big buxom girl who didn't give a whiz bang what men thought of her. Reminded Kady of Barb Kelly, and how she wished Barb would be with men. She'd called Barb's number in Berkeley, but no answer. That worrled her too.

"So you're knocked up and not sure you want to marry the guy. Is that right?"

"If the tests say so."

"They will. But the tests won't talk as brazenly as me. Have a DNC before two months. You're hardly the worse for wear."

"An abortion?"

"Drop the word. It's got too much baggage. It's a simple procedure. In and out. This is California, land of the free, even if Governor Ray-gun and his conservative cowboys sit in Sacramento."

"Abortion's legal here?"

"Till three months, simple operation. It's one option for us women in the movement who want control of our own bodies. The other option is time honored. Badger the guy who knocked you up into any marriage at all: then sit home barefoot, pregnant, and in the kitchen. If that's the life you want."

"You think marriage is that bad?"

"Maybe your parents are the perfect married couple, mine aren't. Mom's back teaching school because my dad decided at 40 he needed a young chick to soothe his male ego. And teachers get paid like nurses because it's women's work. Taking care of kids makes it babysitting."

"Your parents still together?"

"Hell no. Divorce laws are lax here in a common property state. Men can run off and women can get a job. We women need to be political because the personal is political. We need to rule our lives and control our own bodies. We're a majority, you know."

"How long for me to decide?"

"Most women spend all their lives never making a decision. A DNC and be home free the same day. You come stay with me. Up to three months of term even."

"And Texas?"

"That's southland and southern belles. Procedure puts a medical person behind bars there. Where a backstreet abortionist takes a coathanger, causes a hemorrhage, and kills you."

Kady got frightened. Idea of cancer never left her, despite Janey's optimism.

"And New York, Paris?

"More liberal. New women's movement comes out of Paris and the student revolution. You probably read Simone de Beauvoir, and her

Sartre's existentialism?"

"My boyfriend wants to return there. Draft causes men to drift out of the country."

"Well they got problems, and we got plenty of our own. We can't depend on them."

"I know what you're saying. Even the best guys think of themselves first. Not including Bill."

"Include him too. Kady, you got choices. Come to one of our group sessions. You'll be surprised what we talk about: pregnancy, contraception, abortion, that's only one topic. Why do women hate their bodies and think themselves ugly? Why think what men think? Practical issues too. Credit cards, bank accounts, and careers."

"We should take care of ourselves?"

"Let us help. Personally, I never imagined a man providing for me. Bill can't satisfy my every need, and why should he? Hey, things aren't going to be easier for men and women, but things are going to be better for women individually and in groups. Yes, let us help you, and you help somebody else in the sisterhood."

"Well I like the idea, Janey."

"Why don't you stay in San Diego? Let my mom find you a job teaching French in one of the schools."

"You're really talking me into it. We got to go back to Texas to say goodbye to my cool Grannie who runs her own farm."

"I'm impressed."

"Then David and my cousin John talk of going to the big concert at Woodstock, where Dylan and The Band record."

"Cool. Me and Bill are going, and ten or twenty local San Diegans. Come along on our Spanish Caravan, but stick with us women."

"Great, and thanks again."

This big girl with a big heart put her arms around Kady and hugged her again for health.

76
Sunday Service

David was glad Kady checked out her stomach ailment. She didn't eat much and threw up often. He was worried about her. What if she had the cancer her mom had? And Kady spoke in a defeated voice, as if now was already past. She wanted to stay together by the Pacific, or back in Texas, or even Paris, France. Stay one place with regular work. Stay together and settle in.

David told Kady about Vichy, France. All their friends together until the war was over. With Marie Montfort and Bernard from the Basque country. Make the commune idea work, if not here like Bill Cougar and his people, then by the waters of Vichy. Kady asked why the hell not here, but she knew his draft alibi.

"So beautiful here," David agreed. "Paradise returned to the desert earth, with Bill Cougar in California. We should return, someday soon."

Here and now reality they left behind. They drifted on the winds of change, on the road back to Woodstock.

Epic trip on the journey west became a race back east. They climbed mountains and dipped into the desert to Phoenix. They raced across the southwest to the flat Panhandle of Amarillo. Into Texas they rode facing a rising sun followed by stormclouds spilling rain as they slept. John Lonigan opened university rooms to the gypsy caravan, as he opened his heart to compesanos in Paraguay. Brave action, which cost him his university position.

Wednesday they rested and traveled by night to OK City, and made the Mississippi axis by morning. Again the VW tires shook. This time they stopped for an alignment, while Bill and friends raced on to make the Friday night start of the Woodstock celebration.

Not until Friday did David and Kady leave St. Louis. It was hot going across Illinois and Ohio. By night they were both so tired they slept in a reststop till dawn. State trooper told them to leave. Saturday dawn found them driving Route 90 on downtown streets of Cleveland en route to the New York Thruway. East then on Route 17 as the day turned to thunderstorms across the rolling hills of western New York. The car sputtered crazily through Jamestown and Olean, past Elmira's glass and Binghamton's shoes. Kady tried to sleep in the dark rain, but waked for a reststop near Roscoe.

There they learned the roads to Woodstock backed up. Something big was happening in the small town of Bethel. Hippies from far away pitched camp at the Roscoe exit. The New York Thruway was closed. Some kept coming and others soaked and happy made their way home. They told tales of rain and mud and beautiful music. David determined by dawn to be there.

By flashlight he tracked a map road from Roscoe to Fremont Center along the Pennsylvania border of the Delaware River. Hills were high and valleys low, and only a new chip of moon fostered hope. Kady fell asleep curled in the backseat. Hankins and Callicoon looked like sawmill towns quiet in the night. 17B was the way into the Catskill resorts near Monticello. Cars littered the two lane road.

Dawn found David wide eyed in the VW and Kady too drowsy to grapple with the sight of humanity rolling on the hillsides. Then came the musical wake up call. John Sebastian sang light and happy. Crosby, Stills, and Nash wove harmonies beautiful beyond belief. Hendrix played his apocalyptic Star Spangled Banner. They ate sandwiches made another morning in Cleveland and drank from a large bottle of vin rose. They walked to the fields and slept in the grass and sun. Only later in the day did they chance upon John Lonigan and his Mexican girlfriend, Angelina, both ragged-looking, spaced out, and happy. John hugged Kady and said it was fiesta time in America.

"Wow, you guys. You missed some great music and some bad shit for weather."

John smiled like a long-haired Texas ranger.

"John, you bring Angelina to Millbrook for a few days."

John's girlfriend with black hair to her waist, said, "Thank you for the invitation."

"No. Tell Aunt Katherine, college starts next week and I got meetings."

John and Angelina led them to the congregation of all their stoned friends. Rainclouds hung in the sky. Angelina remarked how much Kady looked like John, except her eyebrows were like Kurt Kallini's. Kady shook her head at the resemblance. Kady recognized Joshua Steen with his girl named Dierdre Hartford. Her soft eyes, flighty blond hair, and perfect teeth gave her a beautiful smile, but dressed in rolled overalls and clunker boots, she looked like a guy. Josh liked her, anyone could tell. And Kurt was glad they were on hand for the celebration.

"Hey David, long time no see."

Early Hayze had on his muddy fatigues and a very intense glare, muted by his shaded specs.

"You break out, Early?"

"No, released for the time being. Unfit for service. I'd have told the Green Machine, hey I'm a nut, if they asked. Saved us both a lot of digging."

Early smirked at Peter Bergman who laughed.

"Yea, Early's special duty was digging a hill of sand and moving it twenty yards. Never worked so hard, right Early? Then the cracker sergeant asks you po-lite as pie to please return the hill where it belongs."

"Cracked me up," Early admitted.

Kurt Kallini and Bill Cougar came back from Monticello sharing dinner and a joke. Kallini told Kady her mom was fine, and her father and him worked out their differences. No revelation surprised Kady any more, nor David.

"Say Kurt," David asked, "talk Bill into coming to our French commune."

Kallini gave him a look from his dark eyebrows. "I told Bill to join the exodus for months of love, peace, and music. Wily Bill wouldn't have it."

Bill looked huge, like the lineman he played at San Diego State. His black hair was like straw and thicker than Kallini's, and his turquoise eyes had none of Kallini's intensity. His were calm and blue. No rage with his lot in life or with the world at large.

"Mi compadres, you all come to Pacific Beach, find work, and we'll live the real life. You know you'll never catch Kallini, the Roadrunner. His dream is like the illusion of water on desert. Run faster and it disappears."

"We in The Brotherhood take our chances, you take yours."

"Let's drink to our elders and betters," Early said.

He was way up high on acid, far out, way too far out for his own good.

David passed Early the half gallon of vin rose. Sunday service at Woodstock. The rain started falling again. By now the half million folks used to showers moved to tents and tarps, or onto cars and vans for the journey out of there. The rain fell heavy. It was time to say goodbyes. Everywhere was sound and celebration. One last hurrah. One look backward on America. There was no one to stop the war in Asia, and no one to stop the rain.

77
Bontecott Comes Clean

"Bring your wine glass into the livingroom."
Katherine agreed with Bontecott. It was her one nicely decorated room. Her plush, understated New England. What Yankee style meant to her at age 20. An easy comfort, restrained only to refine character. Not that she lost this illusion. But this style applied to her detached Texas self and no one else. Puritan New England by restraint meant madly pursued success to prove one's special election, restrained by guilt and regret, if others saw the shortcuts taken and errors pursued long after one was aware of them, until the errors were cherished as much as the success. Her private illusion pleased the New England magazines for home decorating.
"Katherine, I hoped to talk with you before Kady arrives home."
"We should talk more."
"We should."
"You're busy with Bontecott Stones. Your work worries me."
Katherine heard him shout out of character, "Get that hoodlum out of my house." Bontecott told her why he got upset. She took the revelation in stride, and asked her husband to trust Kurt Kallini, as she did.
"How do you like the nurse, the maid, and the cook?"
"It's nice to have a prepared dinner and time to sit together. Kady may think her services are superfluous and stay away."
"I don't think so. She may come and go, without all the chores to do. As Grannie Lonigan said, you have a daughter and a friend."
"Less fuss then. All the people coming and going doesn't bother you?"
"I had to be fair. On the farm there's as much coming and going. Why not as many service people inside? Bridget can clean when I confer with the foreman."

"Why the time in your study then these past weeks?"

She'd noticed his left eye twitch and how his eyes blinked as if sun spilled in a window.

"I set my affairs in order."

"For Kurt's sake?"

"And Kady's too. I'm sorry to be shut away from you."

"It's nothing unusual."

Katherine lost her Texas drawl soon as she mastered an accent, acceptably New England, but never lost her directness. She never copied Yankee convolutions of meaning by what was said, not said, their thinking, expecting, regretting, until what was meant was far removed from spoken statement. In New England the convolutions passed for wit, understatement, irony, and religion. Taciturnity and the unspoken word was its final expression, further downeast. Katherine was direct, and cut off from New Haven society, by word and later deed, she remained so.

"The usual is also regrettable. Let me make up for years I neglected the care your love deserves. Years you have not been happy."

"How could I be, with illness and all?"

Katherine crossed her legs and the patterned skirt of her own making.

"But I pursued business at the expense of our time together. To prove to my New Haven brothers how much better I ran the show, especially after father, with their consent, sent me on the road like a regular salesman."

"Where we met, Bontecott."

"True, and the one happiness of my life, along with Kady. One happiness, among many errors. I have another one to confess if you care to listen."

Katherine recrossed her legs, and they were long and beautiful. She was amused by this regret in sackcloth and ashes. It was common to his brothers and their sons. They apologized for poor sales, failing grades, faux pas made in the social graces, the errors made among the Bontecotts, when she was young and part of the clan.

After her cancer and Evander ran Bontecott Stone in New Haven and then New York, off on travels whenever he got away from hospital and wife and daughter affairs, she lost touch with this Bontecott habit of guilt and public confession. Amused because the admissions were innocuous, as if they hid horrible sins.

"What other error have you made I can forgive, Bontecott?"

He saw her ingenuous smile, her Miss Dalhart 1940 smile which impressed all the boys in town, and her simplicity which soothed his jaded heart of a salesman on the road.

"An Irish girl in the office. I was young. Nothing happened, except so much was made of the incident."

"The one who threatened the court suit for seduction?" she asked.

"You know?"

"Your brother Jonathan told me of the maid who wrecked havoc on the family. And money, lots of it was offered her. It wasn't important."

"Mary Conlin never had a child."

"Jonathan said the family gave her money to fly to Ireland, or find an abortion if she wished."

"She seduced me. She was 15 going on 30. Father never believed me. He sent me on the road to sink or swim, just what he said."

"It doesn't matter, Bontecott. Make a mistake, correct it, and live on. That's Grannie Lonigan talking."

"She is direct."

"You done anything else I should know?"

"I've cut corners in business."

"What your brothers implied. And made the business profitable too. They're envious. You know ten times what they know about business."

"Too true."

His left eye twitched. He swore to be upright and moral as possible the rest of his life. Which affirmation brought him peace. Truth on the table.

"I asked Kurt Kallini to clean up the business with me. Why he comes to the house this evening. I will trust his business sense as you trust his sympathy."

"You two will work together to whitewash Bontecott Stone?"

"That's right, Katherine."

"Right as rain."

"Yes, no more cutting corners."

"Oh Kady called, speaking of rain, from Monticello, to say she'd be home sometime after 7PM. First she'd drop off her boyfriend in Hudson Park."

"We should meet the boyfriend."

"We should, Bontecott. But first things first."

"How is Kady?"

"Okay. She wants to tubsoak for a week. How I feel when I'm in Texas. She impressed Grannie Lonigan, who wants her to live on the farm. I told her Kady's free to do as she pleases. Like me."

"Let me tell her about the servants and her part of the business I sold off. Then she can make decisions."

78
The Whitewash

Kurt Kallini rang the doorbell to the Millbrook mansion punctually at 7PM. He rented the black El Dorado from three weeks ago. He recalled his exit with ill will. Carlo regretted it because it worked to their disadvantage. Kurt now knew what Carlo knew and planned how to use Bontecott Stone.

Bontecott called Carlo a week later to apologize for his behavior. He had been rash and suffered a slight stroke. They spoke congenially of everything concerning Kurt Kallini, though Bontecott avoided the subject of shared business.

Kallini entered, dressed in a Brooks Brothers suit, cool and collected, even after the chaotic crowds at Woodstock.

"Hello Kurt," Katherine said. "Pour some wine and let us talk as we did years ago. You are always in my prayers."

"Thank you Katherine. It's good to see you in good health."

"Healthy as a horse. What doctors in two hospitals say."

Bontecott interrupted the amenities for the sake of business.

"Let me apologize, Kurt, as I did to your Uncle Carlo for my rude behavior."

"Surprise caused your shock. Me too."

Kallini poured wine for himself and Katherine, when Kady barged through the door. She dragged her huge canvas bag across the flagstone design, toward the rug and an empty chair. Unlike Kurt, she was bushed. Six thousand miles traveled across the country and a rainy Woodstock Sunday beat her down. And seated before her was Kurt Kallini. The hoodlum back like the prodigal son in her father's home.

"I hope everyone's on speaking terms this time. You're gussied up for cocktails and I smell of the ten states crossed in haste. Should I shower and dress first, or wasn't I invited?"

"Kurt and I work together on Bontecott Stone."

Kady gave her father the Grannie Lonigan look to say, you expect me to believe this. Kady got herself a cup of coffee she knew would corrode her stomach.

"You can trust Kurt, as I have since my illness, Kady."

"Thank you mom."

"And I apologized to Kurt for the evening three weeks ago."

Kady recalled the evening dressed in her skimpy tennis skirt, and her father shouting at the hoodlum. She felt some sympathy for Kurt Kallini. As she assumed Kurt helped Bontecott with business and her mom with her illness and looked after her. If her parents were at ease with Kurt Kallini, then her too. She had other troubles.

Her father told Kurt. "I'll share the business and do what's best."

Kurt appreciated family talk, a bit ambiguous, to let Bontecott's wife and daughter assume the best. Then in private trust him to expand the business pipeline and profits, which he intended to do. What Kurt wanted was their working relationship, only closer, better, because more trusted and the endeavor shared. It was Carlo and family. And the Mayflower magic of the New Haven Bontecotts. Catholicism and The Brotherhood too. It was a personal and shared connection. It was his religion of spiritus mundi, whereby the individual soul senses convergence with the whole world of things and people coming into being. He'd put profits to work in the GI Resistance too.

Katherine helped Kady meet the cook and put away her things. She filled in the details. Bontecott took Kallini's arm to explain what he meant by shared business, as they entered his study.

"I sold all aspects of Bontecott Stone back to my brothers and their sons, who are lawyers and accountants, able to handle the complications."

Kurt stared in amazement. The momentary brilliance of a supernova passed him by. The blowout of stadium lights left blindness and sour darkness behind.

"You understand for both our benefit, we had to disconnect the legal from the illegal. No more cutting corners for Bontecott Stone. We will whitewash the business and name."

"You have cut me out," Kurt said, distinctly, tasting the first flush of a virulent passion.

"Let all be legal. Help me put an end any illegal business. I blame my deals and my living a lie of a private life. Let all be above board. Let's do what's right. Once I did what's right I don't fear a serious illness coming on."

"You mean give up the business?"

"I don't want you, Kurt, to pursue success with the same obsession I did. It's not only illegal, it's wrong. I pulled the plug. I did my duty. Now do yours, you understand?"

"No I don't," Kurt Kallini shouted.

Bontecott's zeal cut him out. His soul like a filled vacuum leaked meaning into the void. He groped for air and found none.

"Let me out of here. This facade of respectability is a trap."

He walked into the livingroom and its vaulted ceiling like a domed mosque, now empty of the spiritus mundi. Katherine and Kady stood halfway up the spiral staircase, looking at him, knowing him.

"Trust me Kurt, it's for the best."

Kallini knew the failure of polio and back pain and seeking metaphysical solace discovered nothing but the void. The whitewash. That's what it was. He controlled his voice. It was decided. Let the soap opera pass. He shared in the selling of Bontecott Stone and he turned his back to the wall of being. The smug satisfaction it fostered. The whitewash was a trap. There was no return. Only him going on. He would take over all Bontecott Stone when he had the where-with-all. Diamonds and dust would come in from Europe. He would trap the brothers in a deal to bankrupt them. He would have it all.

"Katherine, we are friends. Words regretted are spoken. I will help Evander with the business and its execution. Trust me to do the right thing. And Kady, if you need my help, I'm there for you too."

In his dress suit Kallini made the grand exit, and drove off in a limousine. Money meant less to him. His deeper feelings needed a deeper satisfaction.

X
Vichy Commune

79
Sanctuary

Morpheys had his one last look at America. Leave it and take his love with him. Off to Vichy to make a life all their own. Not a life of metro, boulot, and dodo, but one with transcendence, a life worth living. Aurora was the dawn. As stormy weather and turmoil blew past them. They were invulnerable. They made the moment their own. There a month, and Vichy for the fall, and Paris for years, if necessary. Bernard said Vichy sat beside a beautiful lake, no different than Lake Cayuga.

He trusted Bernard of the Basque country. Another foreigner sharing the wayward warmth of Paris, city of civilized folks around the world. Warring factions palavered over the shape of the peace table. Exiles found sanctuary. Algerians served cous-cous and discussed incendiary devices, like strategies of sport teams. It was his place to find peace away from home. In Dalhart, Texas David liked his guest status. There for Kady when they returned. San Diego offered sanctuary and western beaches. Someday to return to dry spaces and wide oceans when the war was over. Someday soon.

It wasn't his draft notice, only his warning. Poughkeepsie draft board wrote, "We received the summer waiver from Hamilton College and expect a graduation notice before fall commencement. Please be advised we begin processing draft notices for numbers 1-100 the first of September. Yours will be included."

Peter Bergman called from Westchester. He and the Hayze were ready to leave. Peter's dad worked to get him into law school. The Hayze looked better. He needed rest. Their families helped them. Look at the Hayze who had no family. He never got beyond basic training. Not to mention, Vietnam. It was up to them, Peter and David, to help the Hayze. Like Early took them away from the Hill, where they'd never have gone without him. Their guru to the road, which David called the journey east. Time to leave. Time to lend the Hayze what help he needed.

Time to call Kady too. She said her mom needed another week. David took Kady at her word. She needed another week to recover from their cross-country trip. A week then.

"David, I'll meet you there."

"Vichy will work for the both of us. Let's give it time."

"I miss you."

"I miss you any day we're apart."

"You're right. I need a week to recuperate."

"See one of your mom's doctors. Check with Kallini to see if Bill Cougar and Janey Tower stayed on."

"They didn't."

Kurt told her of their departure west. He had them to dinner at Joey Gallo's restaurant. Kady missed Janey Tower's advice, even if she didn't believe anything was easy. Least for her.

"Get well then, and hurry over to Paris. We'll have a Vichy commune like theirs. Bernard and Marie Montfort are good people. Let me get to work for us. Turn our back on America because it's come to this. To Paris. Hope you're ready for an extended stay together."

"Ready as I'll ever be. Traveling gets to me, so let's settle in, okay?"

"Certainly. We got it coming. Time apart this year makes our time together, now on, all the more special."

"Bye David. Say hello to Peter for me."

"A week then."

80
Local Control

For Morpheys crossing the Atlantic was a breeze. He said goodbye to America. Paris was warm with memories. Tourists teamed the city streets as Parisians were away on August vacation. Early Hayze visited the Gobelin Hospital for an infection. Kallini took him in.

David showed Peter the people at Lenoir, where Christian, happy to see them, enlisted their help for Vichy. They needed to leave immediately. Vichy was understaffed. David rode the bus, reluctant to leave with thirty viellards, and no Kady. Bernard promised to bring her. He was detained for a week.

It was a nice ride. Down the Loire into the south of France, the river valley ran green beside the deep waters. Off the Loire ran the Allier tributary to the watering hole of Vichy. White hotel on the boulevard along the lake stood four stories high with verandas and shutters at every window and a mansard roof from the past century. It looked the restored mansion of America's deep South with its cool white exterior and stone step entrance. Walkover to the lake led to a park of pathways and tall shade trees. Vichy was a resort on the lake, with its spring for health waters nearby.

They arrived early afternoon. Capable manager of the hotel, Mme Olachon, made ready the Alsace menu of sausage, sauerkraut, and watery beer the French brew. There was little kitchen cleanup with the meal. Old folks needed rest after dinner and the trip. Peter and David were free to view the city on the lake. Mile of park was great for walking. Breeze blew off rippling waters under shade trees to mitigate the August heat. Sails way out there swooped in the sun, white and gracefully clothed in canvas. Hundreds of white triangles veered in wind, like butterflies between the waters and horizon of cloudless sky.

"Going to be good times. Wish Cheryl came and it'd be perfect. But NYU starts early for law school, and she's lucky to get in."

"You hear anything?"

For David it was an academic question, and school was no longer his concern. He was gone.

"Got two weeks, else it's grad work in poli-sci."

"Good luck."

"And you?"

"I'm here for good."

Peter gave him a mild-eyed look from his full beard. This summer his brown beard turned auburn.

"You worried being stuck here?"

"Not particularly. I promised my dad to finish the paper and college. But when I left, he didn't bother to say, "Listen, these are the best years of your life." The shakes kill him. He's got Parkinsons. He doesn't care what I do, or can't care. He has his concerns, and figures I have mine."

Coming back, they crossed the walkway into the parallel lanes and town squares of the city. South was downtown to small shops and bars and residential housing. Peter wanted cuisine Algerienne for a bowl of cous-cous and shots of desert thunder. White robed patron never heard of "desert thunder" so they settled for two beers. No German steins. French beers ruined the heat of cous-cous. No fuel to the fire.

"Roof of my mouth is scorched," Peter complained. "Kallini would know better."

"He knows more than he tells you."

Getting back they had to quicken pace through the crowded streets. Peter threw out his legs trucking, to forge ahead. The race was on. French never rush in the swelter of August heat. People regarded them as tourists.

Hotel des Freres bustled with dinner prep. Mme Olachon told them, don't be late. Kallini and Early Hayze arrived in a sleek Citroen. Kallini came into cash.

"Hey Early, sorry we're late."

Sweat beaded Peter's forehead and matted beard, and Mme Olachon scowled at him. Local cook from a Vichy restaurant and his son went to work without looking up again. She returned to the dining area, where Christian, with ivory pipe, made polite conversation over the dinner of lake trout. She adored him. Her neat smile like a bowtie on a child's Sunday suit looked absurd with the lack of fanfare in her aging face. Her double cheeks, round chin, and short curly hair stuck Shirley Temple style around her eyes, small and sharp in her pudgy face.

Somehow the crowd of them late for dinner annoyed her. A working woman past forty with a provincial scorn for Parisian elegance, and foreigners. She worked hard. She expected them to work harder. Except Christian, whom she coddled with care. Her dress offered little but covering for her large, strong body. Her heavy shoes were serviceable, what a man might wear. David saw her, contrasted to Parisian women, with their cosmetics and grace.

Christian came in the kitchen. Its track walled by stoves around an oaken slab of a preparation table. Early raised an eyebrow when Christian lightly shook his hand. He led them out into the courtyard with its cafe tables and polished wood floors, canopied by a transparent roof up four stories. Rooms tiered up from the courtyard open to the air and sun. Place for Sunday dances.

"Mme Olachon likes all the frères to be punctual," Christian told them.

"We got stuck downtown, and Early arrived from Paris."

"But the locals follow the example we set, d'accord?"

"Oui, d'accord."

"It's different here, okay. Not like Lenoir."

"Where's Marie Montfort?"

"She's not coming, and neither is Bernard. The locals want local control, and they want the Paris equipes to stay in Paris."

"For every chateau?"

"No, Vichy and others south."

"Thanks for the lowdown, Christian, we'll toe the mark, as you will."

"What did Christian say?"

Peter had little French to follow the dialogue, Early none.

Kallini had gone on his own.

"He means this Mme. Olachon runs a tight ship. She's in charge and we're servants to the old folks."

"So it's not our idea of the commune, with a little work and a lot of freedom."

David shook his head. Work was work, and he'd be back in Paris in a month. The provinces like Vichy in revolt against Parisian interference. Bernard and Marie Montfort were out. Mme. Olachon was in charge. Toe the line.

They walked the old folks in the park and watched French TV, which rarely entertained. By nine the folks went to bed. Kallini took Early Hayze out on the town in his Citroen. Peter took the alternative to TV, sleep. Good night.

David practiced his German. Without Kady's arrival, time hung heavy on him. The Vichy set-up disturbed him, its plush ambience and rigorous authority. To escape this timelock he worked on his senior thesis. Promise to his dad to finish school. Reread Mann's Magic Mountain. He'd have to return to Germany in winter. For Kafka too. He read himself into the metaphysics and read himself asleep. No sign of Kallini and the Hayze, no noise from the slick Citroen.

Mme Olachon bolted the double doors.

"A chambre, monsieur."

Upstairs about two AM he heard knocking, then pounding on the front doors of the hotel. He was up reading again. In a few minutes he saw a bedraggled Early Hayze headed toward the fourth floor on Kallini's arm. Kallini muttered to the Hayze, who was completely out of it.

"Somebody ought to stick a sombitchen knife in that cochon. Local Algerians would do it gladly."

81

Lost Vision

David closed his door and got some troubled sleep before the 5:30 alarm. The service of cafe and toast to each viellard took time. Old folks were grateful for small courtesies. Pleasing them was pleasant. Seeing them open to charity, nice to one another, gave David a good feeling. A few complained their rooms were small. Or they wished for a single like Mme. Mariveau, the elegant vielle dame, but these were complaints of a second or third vacance. They knew Mme. Olachon had her favorites.

In mid-morning David saw Early Hayze in the hallway. No shades and his bulging eyes bloodshot, his skin pale, a bloodless gray color that alarmed David.

"No way I'm going to rise and shine this morning. Try me noontime, or sometime tomorrow, Sergeant Morpheys."

"Sure thing, Early. Sleep it off."

He saw haze all round Early's brain and forearm marks among his frosty sores of psoriasis. This was serious, and Peter called, there was a meeting in Mme. Olachon's office.

She sat behind her big office desk, a dull dress showing her flabby upper arms. Her cheeks and double chin added nothing to her nondescript, sharp eyes. Gone was the ridiculous bowtie of a smile she wore for the old folks. Kurt sat next to the window, staring into the street. He wasn't there. Peter shifted his feet uneasy. In French she asked Kallini where his friend was, and he said Early was sick.

"Sick! He is bourru. Il est un ivrogne."

Olachon screwed up her flat nose with her closed hand, one of many French gestures.

"Yes, he is a drunk."

Kurt reported frankly, what Olachon surmised. She then issued an ultimatum, and David stretched to hear the peremptory tones.

"You volunteers have a choice. Either wait upon the viellards here at the hotel and make them feel special. Or leave for Paris. That's the job of Freres volunteers. No wandering off to fill your time with foolishness. If you need to parade off to town, then return to Paris and do it there, not here."

David heard the constant shuffling from Peter's sneaks. Kurt Kallini stared out the window. Only his wild eyebrows contracted. David saw the rage glow in Kallini's stare and expected he'd throttle Olachon.

"I expect you young men to conduct yourselves in a Christian manner. Show respect for the viellards and attend to their needs. Talk to them, humor them, and make their stay satisfactory. They have little life to find joy. You have forever."

David watched Kallini turn, stare into her eyes, and see him explode.

"Is that all, rien de plus?"

Olachon turned to David and Peter to ask if she were clear, and David answered oui. He thought about the decision part, whether he should be back in Paris for Kady's arrival. He was surprised Kallini stayed calm, like his robed companions in Gobelin. Peter was confused. David took him upstairs to talk with Early Hayze, and saw Kallini walk out the front door. From Early's room they saw him put bags in the trunk and drive off in his Citroen, not to return till the end of the week. His decision. This takeover of the Vichy vacance excluded him. He was back to Paris.

Early was incoherent. His and Kallini's room had a strange smell, a musty smell heavier than the fourth floor heat. Early got up at noon, but didn't eat. He went on the zoo trip, where African animals caged in the dusty August of south France. Early put on a hilarious show, like his old self. He was a riot with the old folks. He gestured to each chimp, cowered before the tiger, and played his best Cyrano, the gallant gentleman, for the ladies.

After dinner Early sat with them in the courtyard, like college roommates telling tales. He repeated how the army broke him.

"I shoveled a twenty foot pile of Jersey sand and carted it twenty yards. Easy shovels sapped every last onze of strength. Shoveling

I became the Sandman, the sleepwalker in the dark, the ghost of my effort sitting like a spectator on watch. I don't know how I finished, but I couldn't sleep until I did. No sleep a-tall the cracker sergeant said. I finished and slept like the dead. Next morning the sergeant said shoveling sand was my daily bread. Move the pile back where it belongs. I couldn't do it. I cried. I begged the sergeant, forgive me. They broke me. They broke me and never put me back together. Friends of Kallini removed me from the barrack hospital. So I owe Kallini and he collects."

"Meaning what, Early?" David asked.

"Kallini collects. I went with him to an army PX in Munich and bought cases of cigarettes. Cheap smokes, electronics, other gadgets. We met these Turkish dudes by the rail station. Not turbaned or weird looking. Simply a black market deal. Kallini says The Brotherhood takes bargains as they come. Kallini's into revolution on a world scale. The GI Resistance causes a big stir in the States, he says, and it's only part of the picture. The army's in revolt in Vietnam."

"Early, you better come back home with me," Peter told him.

"You guys are good to me, but I have no home. My dad's long dead. My mom remarried. Brother at Cornell thinks I'm crazy. Dad told me a handful of tales about the aborigines in New Zealand and Borneo. My memories of him. He did some bureaucratic bullshit for the Brits, taking census, checking the logging companies. I've told you guys about him."

"Tell me," David said. "The tree god of your chapel climb."

Peter chuckled and Early rolled his Topps tobacco.

"Aborines have their tree god, Aki. They believe we all have our niche on the tree. Well guys, I'm off the tree. I lost my niche and special vision. I can't find a way home. It's like millions of mosquitoes. They buzz thick as ants on every tip of skin, and there's nothing inside me, nothing but sand. And now the Sandman's calling. You guys are buddies, and my home's with you. College was cool and we shared some cool times. But Kallini's not my buddy. He collects his due. I know him and he knows me."

"Hang in there, Early. It will pass."

He shook Peter's hand, and said thanks, before he said goodnight.

Early Hayze was his hilarious self one more day. The next night he left the hotel when TV got boring. "Going for a stroll," he told Peter. He didn't return. Olachon locked him out on the streets. David stayed up till late reading German. Early was gone, and Olachon said good riddance to the "ivrogne." Early was gone, Kallini was gone, and Kady was coming.

82
Kady's Call

Kady listened to her mom. Something subtle changed in her Millbrook house. Her parents exerted less pressure on her. Her dad settled into routines without business. He took care of her mom. Good for Kady. She took her Janey Tower approach and told the truth. She returned to work in Paris with her boyfriend. And Janey said to forget the tests for cancer. Forget that guilt. Having a baby or an abortion in France was a worse case scenario. Two sick parents and one screaming infant. What else wouldn't they blame on her?

"You made your mind up?" Her mom asked.
"The work teaches me more French than anything else."
"Then teach at Bennet School next term."
"Me and David need a chance to make our own decisions."
"And when to return?"
"Christmas at the latest. Sooner or later, I don't know. Kurt Kallini's in constant contact with dad. You'll know my every move."
"Trust Kurt Kallini. You can do that, trust him."

Kady waited a week. She needed the rest and used her mom as an excuse. Like her mom returned from hospital tests, she recuperated. No more halfway measures. She planned on Paris. Tell David. Make a decision. Get help from Kallini if she had to. He knew how to get things done. Janey Tower or Bill told him. Grannie Lonigan would tell in no time. This was Kady's call to make a life worth living. If she failed miserably, she failed. Time to do what had to be done. Time she was her own person.

At least she didn't throw up on the plane. She collected her satchel stained red with wines, carried and spilled. David had her big canvas bag in Paris. Orly Airport crowded with Parisians returning from vacation. September was come. She looked for David Morpheys. At the airport she saw Kurt Kallini reading Le Monde. Her parents set her up. It was part of her world.

"Hello Kurt, and thanks for meeting me. I know dad asked you to."

"He did."

"You okay?"

"Fine as can be expected. And everyone in Vichy?"

"They're put off by the lady in charge. Marie Montfort handled that vacation, and the local woman handled the kitchen staff. The politics change. Sorry I suggested the Vichy vacation. She's like a petty dictator and the guys hate her."

"That bad?"

"Two more weeks and it's over. We Catholics do our duty. Some priests are inspired and some not, but the word remains the same."

Kady tried to follow Kurt. Her stomach tightened. The nausea she knew all month. It wore on her. She didn't really believe it was pregnancy, how could she."

"Excuse me Kurt, while I use the bathroom."

She returned, her forehead beaded with sweat, her skin without color. Kurt stared when her knees trembled and she sat quickly beside him.

"What's the matter?"

"Sicker than a dog. It's the up and down of the plane and not eating. I didn't want to throw up on the plane."

Kurt drove her to Hopital de Gobelins for a complete check up. For the cancer too. Kady told him the situation. He called Antoine with the wiry hair and van full of albums and he arrived in Paris to counsel Kady. Kurt sure had a network of friends. An extended family, with her father included. She wished Janey Tower was here.

Antoine told her soon was better for a DNC. He couldn't believe in any cancer. Two weeks would make no difference. If she decided to carry to term, she was perfectly healthy. Kurt listened while Antoine explained the procedure. Kurt wasn't as shocked as she thought he'd be. He made matters easy for her.

Everyone told her, examine your options and make a decision. Physically she felt pressed for time. Antoine was on hand, and unlike

Janey Tower, who talked of women's day all over the world, he talked of the procedure. A few days and life begins over. Fall in the air. Everyone returns to Paris. Let David finish the work at Vichy, and they start anew. If it didn't work out for them, she'd return to Millbrook, tutor French, with an eventual job at the Bennet School. What she planned all along.

Her body said baby, and she hesitated. Antoine was ready. It was neither too soon or too late. Make her decision. It was hard to be direct, even with herself.

Kurt drove her in the Citroen toward the Loire Valley.

"Nice car."

She made small talk.

"Yes, your father's generosity."

"So Kurt, give me your advice. Should I have the baby?"

"Have the DNC. You're too young and David drifts across Europe until the war is over. Neither of you is ready."

Silence except for the smooth tread of tires and air conditioning inside the luxury car. The sun shone through the tinted windows and the trees stood luxuriously green along the Loire Valley. She waited for Kurt to give other reasons. He was direct too. She knew growing up on his own took a toll on him. He spoke from more experience than she had.

"What about the church ban on abortions?"

"You asked for my opinion, not the Pope's word. See David without adoring eyes. You know he's drifting too. A child needs two parents. My opinion. See for yourself, though."

Kady heard Kallini's air of certainty. His direct advice left her confused. More she thought over the matter, more she was scared. Her body said baby. Her mind said make a decision. Always the fear of something worse too. The car carried them along the Loire to Vichy.

83
Sign on the Wall

Advising Kady to have an abortion. Kallini hated his advice. His faith furnished sacred walls around mother and child, like his own mother Marie and him until he was fifteen. Advise Kady, you're on your own. Kallini made it on his own with Uncle Carlo, his father all along, and he meant to take over the business of Bontecott Stone. No whitewash for him. He meant to dispossess Bontecott and make the business his own. Then use the proceeds for GI Resistance.

That work consumed his anger, and anger occupied this time of life. He saw Kady and Morpheys with a son. The happy family. Bontecott wanted his grandson. No more failure and fault. No more mirror on his obsessive need to succeed, whatever the means. Need born of need. No whitewash. Kallini wouldn't let Bontecott off the hook.

From Kady's son the new time, and him outside the wall, with no way in. David Morpheys ends his drift. Morpheys married with a pregnant wife finds reprieve with the local draft board, especially with a brother and an uncle gone overseas. A year reprieve to find work teaching. Tutor and teach like Kady. Bontecott, the impulsive grandpa, sees Kallini as intruder, the one who urged him to cut corners. Morpheys takes Kallini's place, slips into his spot silent as the first snowfall, all which Kallini reads like a sign on the wall.

All consuming anger answered need in his nature. Ruin what lay in his steps, if the gift wasn't his. Contented nature never satisfied him. He would take over Bontecott Stone.

WIth Uncle Carlo's help he'd bring a great volume of stones through Hasidic cutters and finance this import with Turkish drugs. Africaner diamonds came north through Antwerp, and back into Paris through frères and Algerians. He had Early Hayze buy all kinds of PX cigarettes and hi-tech equipment to send back to the States. Little at a time Turkish product worked its way into NYC and financed the diamond cutting. Finance revolution on a worldwide scale, the Brotherhood, and in America the GI Resistance. Do more than Quinn and Joshua and Dier. Do more than Burn and her Weathermen because he was not naive what made a revolution. Money, and more money.

By Christmas when US Customs floods with incoming gifts all the product finds its tried and tested route, and the one found best carries Africaner stones, diamonds and dust, for a new year killing. Kallini would become Bontecott Stone. Kallini would fund GI Resistance because connected to global revolution. Kallini's time, this sad, sorry end to the Sixties.

He watched over Kady. Let her make the logical decision. Vichy was no vacation. He knew the Freres: the faggot Christian and that fat old putain, Mme. Olachon. He knew how they worked.

Early Hayze too. He traveled back to German army bases, with his PX card, and sent off cigarettes and equipment to Gobelins in Paris. There Akim, his son, and other Algerians packaged product for overseas, sending to Freres in Montreal for safety's sake. Montreal south to NYC he saw as his best bet, through well paid customs officials, specially well paid and tested these coming months.

Trouble with Early Hayze was his drug intake. As courier he was useless. He did okay at the army bases. His gift for gab got him in and out of the PX unquestioned. In the Vichy Hotel des Freres he slacked off. He didn't meet the demands of rising to serve meals, and Kallini made plans to house him at an Algerian bar in town. If drugs used up Early Hayze, Kallini needed another soldier of fortune to buy gift supplies. He had use of Early Hayze's PX card till the end of the year.

The military base he wanted for the big product move was Istanbul Air Force Base in Turkey. There he knew soldiers inside the PX itself and product moved from there. He modified and made perfectly safe the route across Europe. He removed any surprise from CIA-FBI who locked onto used routes. Drug shipments were expendable. The one big shipment needed a special route new to normal business. Only Kallini knew how this one went.

84
Face Down and Drowned

They parked on the Vichy sidestreet the Hotel des Freres fronted. Kady was glad to see David and Peter "slaving away in the scullery", as they called preparing meals.

"We scullions must keep busy," Peter said. "No time for pleasantries. Work on we must and will until the job is done. Caviar for the viellards and scraps for the kitchen slaves."

Kady smiled and kissed Peter too.

"Where's you pal, Early Hayze?"

"He's not with you and Kallini?" David asked. "We hoped he returned to Paris and you guys would tell us he's fine."

Peter exploded. "I knew that bastard Kallini didn't give a good goddamn about him. I told you we should go to the gendarmes or search the city ourselves. We're a couple of idiots."

Peter threw down his apron and stormed past Mme. Olachon coming into the kitchen.

"Pardon, Monsieur."

"Go to hell."

Kady didn't know what to think. She cried for no reason. Mme. Olachon bustled past them and took soup to the tables herself.

"It's a bad scene. Sorry you came, Kady."

David held her close, and said not to worry.

"Pas d'embrasser ici," Mme. Olachon told her.

"Pardonnez-moi, madame. Qu'est-ce vous voulez?"

Olachon told Kady, as she told the messieurs, they were here to serve the veillards and not to serve themselves. The old folks were guests at the hotel, pas vous Americains, vous comprenez?"

Kady said "oui" and let go David's clenched hand. It was all strange. She couldn't follow David's feverish explanation. She should go with him and travel into Germany. He saw a Bertolt Brecht film called Baal and Germany was the place to go. The four of them could travel all the way to Berlin and back. It was absurd, Kady thought, and David's idea too. He said Olachon told them to decide to stay or go. David waited for her arrival to say let's go. Kady arrived and David wanted to run off.

"Kurt said we volunteered for the three weeks. We have promises to keep."

"Kallini's an asshole. He took off and left us and Early Hayze, who we haven't seen for three days."

"He came to pick me up. Lay off Kurt, would you."

David gave her a look and told her he had to see Kallini. Kady was all torn up. It was clear Kurt and David were not best of friends, what could she do?

Kady followed David through the dining room. Christian with his ivory pipe smoking introduced himself. He told her Kurt Kallini went to find Early with Algerian friends downtown. Everything was all right. He got the beef Bourguignon dish from the kitchen.

Outside the hotel she heard Peter shouting, "Where the hell is he?"

She excused herself to Mme Olachon, and went outside too.

"Early is all right," Kallini said. "He's at that restaurant you went your first afternoon. Be cool."

"He better be all right. Let's go see."

"Go after dinner. He wasn't there today, but slept there last night. He comes there after closing time. Be cool, finish the dinner service."

After dinner there was a concert in town. Chopin and Schubert and Mendelssohn the program read. Kurt took Peter to search for Early Hayze, while she and David escorted the viellards. David kept talking of Germany, homeland of his imagination. This music has soul. And we got to be free of this bad scene.

"Best for everybody," he whispered to her.

Light piano cascaded notes of Chopin, sad and somber notes of the Nocturne. She couldn't believe David. He'd leave the old folks unattended. If something goes wrong, he takes off. He wasn't responsible. They promised to do this vacance. She stared back at him, when he repeated, "best for everybody." She didn't know him anymore and she knew him too well.

"You mean, best for yourself."

He was silent a long time, and then said he was sorry. Why not stay? With her here, any work was bearable. Kady was relieved.

The concert finished with a Polonaise, light piano lead with a moan of the entire orchestra. David smiled and said German music had a heartful of soul. They ought to go. To Munich, if not Berlin. Of course, after the vacation. She couldn't tell if he were joking or serious, never could.

He was worried about his friend. Early Hayze at Woodstock was completely out of it. Covered with mud in those army fatigues, Early's crewcut splattered with dirt and his eyes glittered. "Zonked," he said to her. She never saw anyone so spaced out. Kurt implied Early shot up, which was why he had Early stay with Algerian friends. He shouldn't be at the Hotel des Freres.

Mme. Olachon told them all to go to bed. She asked Kady if she felt better after the long trip. The woman wasn't so bad. David asked to stay up until his friend Peter returned. He explained his reasons and Mme Olachon said, "An hour more and the doors must be shut."

David walked Kady to the second floor and held her uncomfortably tight, then let go. He said he'd come see her in an hour.

"Not tonight, David. We have a lot to talk over. Not tonight, okay, I'm too tired."

"Fine. The madame expects us all up bright and early."

His face winced when he said "early".

David confused her. Nice, then irresponsible. As she got into bed the darkness suffused with lamps from the street. Her father confided he remembered David's dad, George Morpheys. Hard worker, with a terrible temper. Foreman told a story of his taking a monkey wrench to a tractor when it stopped cold during harvest. Then a fight with the foreman's son. The old foreman said Morpheys wasn't the responsible person to put in charge of a whole farm. Better his own son. Morpheys said give me the job or I'm going, and Kady's father gave him five hundred dollar bills and wished him luck. George Morpheys took his son and pregnant wife and left the same day. Hard worker, with a terrible temper. The story scared Kady.

She got up when she heard the car park on the street below. It sounded like the new Citroen of Kurt's. David came out the door and down to the car. She heard it all, even if she couldn't see clearly in the lamplight.

David came to the car window.

"Where the hell are they, Kallini?"

Kurt she couldn't hear, but he must have said, "Overdosed."

David shook Kurt and shouted, "You son-of-a-bitch, you bastard, you never gave a shit for nobody."

Then the car door swung open and David sprawled backwards. Christian, the older guy with the pipe, came into the street and asked them to quiet down. David rammed full force into Kurt and threw him up against the Citroen. It was terrible. She didn't see Kurt get up at all. Kady dressed quickly and ran down the stairway and out.

David was enraged. Christian's mouth was bleeding. Kurt was all right, but groggy.

"Vous Americains," Mme Olachon said, "Allez vous en. Foutes le camp."

David entered the hotel, he said, to get his and Peter's bags. He told Kady to get hers too. She couldn't look at him. Kurt said he was all right and managed to lean on her and walk the stairs.

David saw her and Kurt go into the livingroom.

"I see what's up now, I see it's you and Kallini."

David left Vichy.

Only later did Kady learn Early Hayze overdosed and police found him face down and drowned in the waters of Vichy. The gendarmes allowed Peter to fly the body back to the States. David returned to Paris, and left on a train to Berlin.

XI
Berlin Walls

85
Go Underground

David sat alone in the train station. Gare St. Lazare stays alive in the darkness of Paris. Trains tunnel in directions all over Europe. High overhead lights flood the concrete forms, which border dozens of tracks. A ticket to ride. David was ready as he'd ever be. St. Lazare never dies in darkness, never wakes to light. The trains come and go. They journey out and return. The lonely power of the underground drew David in. A second home, away from the heated streets teaming with cars and the crowded faces of humanity, ticket to ride and be free, ticket to eternity if time stands still in the hollow light, if night knows not darkness, to know and say no, the underground, home away from home. Welcome St. Lazare.

He was witness, the body was Early Hayze. Gendarmes at Vichy needed David as second witness, official business, before they allowed the body to fly to the States. Not St. Peter offering wings. The dead letter of the Code. They saw no more than the mishap, an American bursting his heart. The needle shoots a drug like bottled helium into the ballooning body, enough to float enough to fly, over years of no family and Vietnam training to break the spirit and move mountains of sand twenty feet and back again, and enough to float out the sunrise and strange faces and failed dreams and sunset to the tick of time. Enough was enough. Trouble and he shot too much. The drug like helium burst his heart like a balloon. Over in the moment was the internal war, a bomb leaving little sign of its he-he-he-he-ahhHHHH… WIPE-OUT!

Early fell face down in the tainted waters of Vichy, but he didn't drown. Whatever last breath hollowed his body, which the waters filled, and his face bloated yellow and green, pale gray too. The filmy orbs truly looked like fish eyes. No cover of shades except those of eternal darkness, too cool and too cold.

Peter said, once over the tears, "I called my dad and he'll meet me in DC. He says Early's mom is only mildly interested. You knew Early's dad died of leukemia. Early always talked of his bad blood. Remember his older brother at Cornell. He said put the druggie in the ground. God, was he one cold character."

"So what's the plan?"

Peter lightened some. He realized David wasn't going home. Everyone goes his own way now. Mr. Bergman told Peter he was accepted to Brooklyn Law School. Good news, bad news.

"Dad says we'll bury Early near his father. No national cemetery. Early's father trained for World War II. Dad said Early fought his own war too, which was nice of him to say. I'm starting to like the old man."

"I like him too."

"So we'll bury him in DC. My dad made arrangements with the power of attorney he got from Early's mom. I'll write and tell you what happens. Be sure to send me an address from Berlin, if you stay there."

"Sure will. Say hello to your dad and Cheryl when you get back to the City. Keep me posted."

"One other thing. It's none of my business. You know there's nothing between Kallini and Kady. Though I don't trust that creep, I trust Kady. Make up with her, if not now, then soon."

"Is this pro bono advice?" David joked, wishing he kept quiet.

Peter smiled. Always the good nature to think the best of a person. Then he went "trucking off" toward the plane, his front legs thrown forward, back straight, get the job done. David respected Peter. He wished him luck. Peter's life got under way. Bury your friend and face up to the future. Why the hell not?

86
Speak Anglish, Mr. America

Time, nine o'clock in Paris. David journeyed from Gare St. Lazare six hundred miles to Berlin, en route the Germans used twice to lay waste France and the low countries. He saw nothing out the dark windows of Liege and Koln and fertile north Europe. On this north European plain his ancestors farmed: tillers of the soil, tanners of hides, restless roving barbarians of the forest and boar culture. Morpheys failed to find foothold in the City and Hudson Valley of New York. Grandpa's breath pumped into the shell of his body. Decomposed stench delayed by life prolonging apparatus. The machinery of night.

His dad hopped the St. Vitus dance of Parkinson's with his unnerved machinery. Timing so far off no dopamine tamed the shakes. Dad loved life on the farm. Up at dawn, work hard, eat well. Childish fantasy of the Depression. Morpheys sold the farm to Bontecott. Foothold in America sold to pay a mortgage. As a precision toolmaker dad worked for IBM and farmed his quarter acre in the housing development.

David left Early Hayze dead in the compromised waters of Vichy. He journeyed east to find reason for his failed family and face his own failure too. He had made his choices, Sartre's existentialism. There were iron laws of production, Marxism. Surplus value marks the worker's share expropriated, as Grandpa lost the farm and dad his farming dream. Let Bontecott hear the knell for private property sound. Let the expropriators be expropriated.

He journeyed east further into darkness on a crowded train. Grandpa gave him the photo of the German family farm. Another doubtful image to pay homage. All seats taken, David sat on the carpetbag Kady left him. He'd packed everything for the long haul. Reach Berlin and find work. Then find passage through Poland into Prussia and journey further into the Dostoyevsky dark side of American fears.

No seats available, and when a young girl moved his backpack

David said, "Verzeihung bitte". New words and a new world. Girl with brown hair the color of his own called Huli. She started conversation in German, shifted to French, and discovered he was an American from New York City. Huli was a teenager. She graduated from the gymnasium and visited Paris with her friend, Veronica. The two of them went onto the university. Veronica returned with word there were seats in a back compartment.

Huli introduced David from NYC and he was a world traveler. The family in the half-filled compartment spoke Spanish. Bits and pieces of language glinted like smiles among them.

"Ya, this is David, and this is Veronica," said Huli of the high cheekbones and darting brown eyes of her first time away from home.

"Ya, das bin ich, ich kann nicht anders.

David thought he'd be Baal of Bertolt Brecht with these young girls.

"Speak Anglish for us," said blond Veronica. "We need to practice to go New York next summer. Come visit you Mr. America."

David smiled with a sense of the ridiculous. Mr. America, ya. Baal, ya. Das kann ich tun.

"You come to Hoffsprung with us, to the university. Visit. Be roommates for a few days. University like hostel, good place to meet people."

"Ya, du habst recht, mein Huli."

These girls offered new days of a journey east. Another time and place. An evening side by side, a warm compartment shared across Germany to the border, and pleasant goodbyes. As if his ticket stamped, not for das spiel, bound for the Berlin Wall.

The girls, Huli and Veronica, bubbled over about museums and cafes, and David told them of his travels. They listened and helped with his German. Huli leaned her head on his shoulder. David put his arm around the younger girl. She kissed him and lay her brown hair on his chest. The swaying train rocked them asleep.

They startled awake at three in the morning. The girls heard the conductor say their border town. Huli asked David to please, please stay with them at the university. David smiled, "danke schon." Spontaneous attachment made on a crowded train. He'd like to, another time, if he wasn't headed for Berlin. Iron law of his plans precluded stops on this journey. They exchanged addresses. David lost connection, except the hint of Huli's high cheekbones and mild eyes. The whole watching world with fewer places to visit, fewer stops worth the wait.

87
The Bombed Black Ruins

The girls left and the train was empty, all cold upholstered metal. Border guards checked his passport. Another train replaced the West German one. Armed guards patrolled stops of gray concrete, breaths smoking in the chilly spotlight. It wasn't till late afternoon the train breached the final checkpoint before Berlin. The station, towered like Grand Central, had stairs down three stories to the street pavement.

Center of town smoldered the bombed black ruins of the Marienkirche. Grim reminder of Allied revenge and Teutonic failure. Jagged blocks charred by fire kept a grotesque dignity. Like Notre Dame collapsed on Isle de France as war wreckage, vaulted roof down, flying buttresses down, stained glass shattered, down to bombed black rubble.

Around the church in mockery lofted highrise stores of modern shopping and tenement life. A west side of New York perched like skyscrapers. Ultra modern statues without a whole lot of soul. The Marienkirche smoldered like a spirit in hell. Too old like Grandpa and his dad, all fitted to black failure and death.

David rented a room and prices were high, the exchange rate poor. The drowning dream off the Mid-Hudson Bridge and he sank too exhausted below the surface. Down like Early Hayze, and he woke to four dark walls, with windows open to the gray city, and a fall breeze bit into the air.

Berliner Zeitung offered no cheap rooms. He lugged Kady's carpetbag and hoisted his heavy pack. His funds failed him. Acute housing shortage. The Wall squeezed Berlin tight. Dead end streets, an island of high priced apartments, and prostitutes with hard features, faceless in leather dresses. Morpheys assailed the IBM offices with their hanging panels of glass twenty stories high. His dad worked as tool and die maker at IBM. No openings available. No future for David Morpheys.

To save cash he located the hostel. It allowed the traveler a single night. The dorm packed with Americans on tour, all talking of Bavaria and Octoberfest. David talked an hour with a teacher from San Francisco named Ted Westerbrook. Ted reminded him of Harry Heinz, Early's friend. Imagine Harry with grannie glasses and bellbottoms teaching thirty kids like himself. A leap of imagination.

Otherwise, David steered clear of tourists until bedtime when they packed together in bunks thirty to a room. His dreams were all confused. High speed joyrides, cop chases, skids off the bridge, then into a lake at Grandpa's Long Pond camp. He caught a snapping turtle and getting Grandpa's help the old man was skintight to wires and his eyes were the fisheyes of Early Hayze. God, what a scream!

Morning came wished for. He searched for lodging, then gave up. No room and no work. He faded from the crowded streets into the Kaiser Museum. Chinese and Rococo art, the far east fantasy of Watteau and Fragonard. The fall sun cast shadows east toward the Brandenburg Gate. The Wall was that way.

By nightfall David found his dreary way to the train station. Vagrants bused to the Bahnhofs Mission at ten PM. Any bed was better than nothing. Men entered the second floor dorm and the wooden slab with its thin mattress afforded no soft fall. The pillow starched like army shirts of his brother on drill team. Rancid air rattled with drunken snores, hacking coughs, and a dreadful melange of German, Italian, and Slavic languages. He hit the wall and sought solace of a night's sleep. Like Robinson Crusoe washed up in a strange land, he returned to the sea for his belongings. Shipwrecked with a sea of troubles, in the Bahnhof's Mission David dreamed of home .

With sleep he dreamed of Grandpa's camp and David was ten that summer. Fog hung like darkness at dawn over Long Pond. From the screened porch where they slept, he sensed bullheads and eels twisting on the dock pylons driven deep in the soft muck. Squirrels and chipmunks scurried along the branches.

He tied up tennis sneaks and slipped catlike past Grandpa who snored like a beached walrus. The screen squeaked a slight whine.

Sneaks soaked in the grass clammy against the soles of his sockless feet. Fog billowed like smoke off waters warmer than the air. Voices of fishermen echoed like TV talk, like Grandpa watched late into the night, filament line woven into David's dreams.

Setlines baited at dusk on cuts of sunfish sank an open handed hook into the underwater night. He tread on the rickety slats of the dock and undid the first stick from the pylon. Out of the cloudy muck came a bullhead, feelers curled aside his squat head.

David carried the bullhead to the stump, took the spike, and drove it mercilessly in the skullpan. As Grandpa taught him to do. He pulled the sleeve of skin, broke the backbone, gutted the intestines, and washed the meat clean in the lake. He wrapped the meat in newspaper for Grandpa to fillet for dinner.

Next station for the setlines was the point stake of the property. Lake currents kept the rocky bottom clean. He saw the line taut to where mist vapored the lilypads. The slant line contrasted with the serene fog. He pulled, and the water thrashed with a finned eel, its black gullet like a pickerel. It snaked through the wet grass, until he dragged it in the sandy pitcher's mound and skinned the eel like the bullhead.

The final station loomed around the bend, past where the current kept the bottom clean, into the cove near the swamp. Low roofed camp there belonged to a musician from the New York Philharmonic. Rabinski rarely rode the eighty miles from the City and left the sagging camp in disrepair. He was Jewish. Grandpa objected to Rabinski driving across Morpheys' property. Hatred of ancient origin. Rabinski came from Poland and Grandpa from Germany, bad neighbors then and now.

Rabinski wore a carefully trimmed beard and played cello. One rainy morning Rabinski arrived and asked David why he fished in the cove. Gloomy rain the entire day. Low roofed camp groaned with the inarticulate sorrow of the cello. Rabinski left in the night. It was music David heard at the Wells concert. It haunted him.

David tugged on his last line lodged tight where muck met the foggy air. He hauled in an unseen weight. Like a braided fuse attached taut to an explosive. It came toward him like an unstarted car. It came hard and then easy. Mossy, the lidsize of a manhole cover, it reared its head like an anaconda. Its beaked overbite hissed its tiny viperous tongue. Its beaded eyes replaced by a darker sense. Grandpa had to see this. Come off the machines and help me.

Grandpa snored, his skull slanted with the menace of a torpedo. Jaw jutting out, big nose and meaty ears, cranium like the carapace of a turtle, Grandpa was an armored animal. Only his blue eyes looked human. He woke with a hacking cough. He sat up his heavy torso and lit a Pall Mall.

David followed him to the lake. He lumbered his Major Hoople body with a massive torso over skinny legs. He looped in the string, motoring shell to the surface, yanking the spitter jaws and viperous tongue. Snapping turtle riled. Grandpa strung out its live end and grasped its tail, bumped with armor like a stegosaurus.

"Come with me to the Kasbah," he told the turtle, his voice calm as an executioner. He talked like a loving predator marveling at his prey. Grandpa culled his Kasbah mantra from a late night movie. The traveler lured by his greed or lust or just his idle curiosity enters the Kasbah den of iniquity, from whose luxurious gloom no soul returned.

The tail gripped, Grandpa hoisted the reptile and hobbled along. His forearm suspended the turtle. Its jaws perilously close to his leg. Man and reptile transfixed in time: executioner and predator, hand to tail to jaws.

The operation began in earnest. Grandpa drilled twin holes behind the turtle's shell, wired it to a stake, and let neighbors glory in its rage. David's brother Robby, home from hellraising late that night, used a broomstick to crank vicegrip jaws open to say "AHH". The turtle's hissing and mad lunges diminished in the July sun.

Grandpa came with his sharpened machete. From his mom's deli in the City he cut and sliced as his father butchered animals on the German farm. Robby pulled the hook and unraveled the neck. Grandpa pulled the armored tail and hacked at the neck, gushing blood and gaping flesh. No need of bold words. No Sir Walter Raleigh gallant to the bitter end.

It was not over. Turtle, shell, and carcass Grandpa covered with a steel milk casement. The turtle's body on stumpy legs lifted David and trod with him standing on the casement toward the lake. The reptile refused to acknowledge death, its failure and finality. It crawled toward the murky depths, its Kasbah of iniquity. David feared for his life and Grandpa caught him falling. The snapper danced out its nervous tremors in the afternoon sun.

At dusk Grandpa butchered the snapper and made soup. He shared it with old Mr. Lenington, the neighbor taxidermist, who mounted the hoary head upon a board. Grandpa buried the shell in the swamp. A month later he dug it up. The carapace bleached clean in the sun.

Grandpa suffered a stroke and spent time strapped to hospital machines. It was time. Grandpa deserved burial with due ceremony too.

He woke with the sun streaming through the church windows. The rancid air lifted in a multitude of foreign voices. The whole worshiping world. He got his rest. For Grandpa he wished an early death and delivery to his Kasbah of luxurious gloom. Turtle dreams floated his compromised world. Roots here and further east were long ago destroyed. He returned to the Kaisermuseum and gazed on layers of paint. That evening he returned to Paris. The Wall and its realpolitik were in his way.

Among the homeless multitudes swarming this island, David waited for the train. At a table he worked on his senior thesis. Title was Prodigal Time. Or was it a journal of his journey east? Up the marble stairs roared the westward trains. No way through the Wall. No way to break through to the other side.

First year teacher from the hostel, Ted Westerbrook, sat beside him. Ted had the long reddish hair of a San Francisco hippie.

"You leaving town too?"

"Yes, other side of the world. Any luck finding a room, David?"

"None, you back to teaching?"

"Right. Labor Day, and then a wall of seventh graders I bang my head against for 180 days. The Wall was such a depressing sight."

"I never got there. Witness to the Wall and I never saw it. Why teaching?"

"It's frustrating as hell, but it's a living. It's not teaching kids the books that spaced me out. I keep the semblance of order. It's so hard. I finished a year and blew my savings, seeing Europe."

"Funny, I never pictured you as a teacher when we met at the hostel. With long hair and wire rims, you're my image of San Francisco, you know, Haight Ashbury and all."

"The Haight's a slum. It's the end of the Sixties. Time I cut my hair and made teaching easier. Kids think you're one of them and don't hear a word you say. I'm from the suburbs anyway. Ever hear of Marin Country?"

"No, ever hear of Hudson Park? Doesn't matter. We're all from the suburbs, don't tell a soul."

"Got a plan, David?"

"No idea. Back to Paris and loose ends there."

"Luck then."

"You too."

"I dread facing kids again, but I guess work is what an adult does."

They got on the train to Paris. Company shortened the ride. No more Bahnhoff's Mission. No more street walking days and sleepwalking nights. See Kady Bontecott. See what they could salvage.

Train left Berlin at 7PM. David wanted the window seat. See the two rivers Berlin connected, for the family farm. It was there before nightfall. Tall three story barn living above the farm animals. Grandpa's dad at the table got the piece of meat, others the cabbage. Morpheys left for NYC, deli and butcher work.

Grandpa told how his dad returned after 1900 with enough NYC cash to purchase a bar, but regulations in the Deutsches bureaucracy told who to serve and who not to. When Herr Morpheys served the town drunk, his bar lost its license for six months. He packed his family and baggage and his Herr status for Manhattan and hard work. His Frau cooked good food and the deli prospered. Money saved bought a farm in Millbrook. Farm sold then to pay a mortgage. Bontecott bought the farm and raised horses to race in Goschen and Yonkers. Herr status for Bontecott, the life of a country gentleman. America is ripe and rotten. America is mobility up and down.

"So Ted, what to do with our San Franciscan nights?"

"Keep order in a seventh grade class. Keep the boys busy and the girls interested. Work them so they don't work on me. Cut my hair, wear a suit and tie, and prepare diligently. Take the advice told me last year."

David heard the realpolitik of junior high.

"You're not saying kids shouldn't read Salinger and Steinbeck, only they need to be seated and off your case before they can learn."

"In a nutshell."

"Why not go to grad school, if the parents will pay?"

The train pulled into a station. Guards with guns looked very Gestapo, very communist.

"I'm prepared to teach now. Things happened and I'm no good in college."

"It means something to you?"

"School's the working world, and kids got to learn something of literature. College is too spaced out for me. You got to know yourself. That old Socrates cliche. I'd go on smoking dope at Berkeley, reading more Vonnegut, and never make a difference in anybody's life, or my own."

"I dig what you say."

"And things are rotten on campus. I was friends with this beautiful blond. She came west in a VW van with an educated black guy from Cornell. He wasn't interested in her, so I took her to ballgames. She liked doing anything. I loved her and knew she'd been with twenty guys before me. Well shit, she'd been with the Panthers and she was there the night police raided the pad and shot up everybody. What a crying shame! I had to get away from the college scene. It got weird. I had to do something with my life, anything, it can be over so soon. It's not my parents' wish. My dad's a hotshot lawyer in Marin County. But teaching makes a difference."

"I think you do, Ted."

"I got a high draft number, unlike yours. So it's a choice."

"So what do you write in the notebook?"

"It started as a literary diary in England, but I'm not literary."

He handed the binder to David. I was filled with plans for teaching each book: the quiz materials, plotlines, essay topics.

"You been planning school all summer vacation."

"Yes, enjoying here and planning for there, so I'm ready next year."

They left East Germany deep in the night, and the stations filled with passengers again. Koln came in the sunlit grandeur of morning across Belgium. David was eager to reach Paris by evening to see Kady and sift through the wreckage of Vichy. Or had she gone with Kallini for good? He'd work then.

Ted slept until late morning. David adjusted east and west again. Europe was less vast than the States, but every mile marked another dutchy with a 1000 year history peculiar to its walled-in entity. What if David started over in America, where every new idea can be Utopia, an idea realized, if one works hard enough.

At Gare St. Lazare David said goodbye to Ted Westerbrook, got his Berkley address, and wrote him regularly from Paris, Munich, and from New York when he too became a teacher,

"Good luck with the kids, Ted, and sorry about the girl."

"No day passes I don't say a prayer for Barb Kelly."

"Oh shit, I know Barb Kelly. Oh Jesus, god damn, I know her."

Barb Kelly gone and the world was empty. Her name repeated like a lost phone number. Pick up Kady's huge canvas bag and go see her. How to tell her the bad news?

88
Like Mother, Like Daughter

Kady returned to Paris. She despaired of David, sorry Kurt fractured an arm, and figured she'd meet David there. Kurt said she should have the abortion. It's a simple procedure. Antoine set Kurt's arm and slotted her time at Gobelin for a DNC. What if David barged into Gobelin? She'd have to tell him everything. Why didn't she tell him? Why wasn't he responsible? Why did it all depend on her?

Kallini told her David was gone. On the police report for Early Hayze, David wrote Berlin as his next residence. The news shocked Kady. Sure she knew David took Early's death hard and slamming Kallini against the car was what guys in a fight do. Kady thought David went to Paris. He'd be nearby and they'd talk. Like the soap operas her mom watched. One big scene and all works out. Vichy was no soap opera. Here she was alone.

It was irrational. She blamed David for running off. Why had everything and everybody gone crazy? Day of the operation she had cold feet. This wasn't her. Kurt Kallini whispered in her ear and her little world blew apart. Antoine was efficient. It was a simple procedure. Whatever anesthesia used, Kady came out groggy, then empty. She didn't want food, only sleep. Empty. Her body said baby, and now her baby was dead. Not aborted, but dead, and she committed the worst sin of her life.

Kallini left during the operation. Whispered in her ear and left. He'd been cold as hell since Vichy she realized. He didn't want to see her after what she'd done. Kady was left with her sad self. She hurt after the vacuuming out, but that was the least of the pain.

She sat sipping a chipped cup of Chamomile tea in Kallini's sixth floor garret. The sliding glass opened to the September breeze. She saw most all of Paris from the Gobelin hills, and it was a sad sight indeed. Evening wind twinkled the Montmartre gaiety of a Monday night off from festivities. Putains of Pigalle washed their linen in brightly lit laundries.

Kady sat alone. Kallini was gone. Antoine had done his doctor business, told her the baby had been an "enfant garcon", and called for her taxi up the Gobelin hill. Already by four in the afternoon the caftaned Algerians walked the hallways. They stared as if she invaded their sanctum, as if she should be in Purim, veiled, or streetwalking. Ghosts of her gangrene conscience, her mauvais honte, paraded like angels on judgment day.

Radio KADY reported this is the end of the Sixties. Our souls have been touched, hands laid on, our souls found wanting. San Diego sun, west Texas wind, not even the liberated streets of Paris belong to us, you and me, David Morpheys. Once they did. No more. City which beckoned to us, which bridged our hands like a bridal bower, dropped, parted, never to return. Sad city of September despair.

Kallini's garret offered no phone to call her mom. Kady went nowhere. The halls patrolled by white robes deterred her. Sore from the horrible ordeal in body and soul, she let emptiness seep into her memories like anesthesia, like darkness settling over the city, so that each constellation of lights signaled her undoing. She had damned herself. Kallini had damned himself. David left her in the lurch. All alone. Bring the tab. All alone. Which Kady deserved, worthless, even to herself.

Her Dunhill cigarette burned to ash and sipping the barely warm tea she lit another. Tears of temptation riveted the sallow fright her freckles made of her face. She knew this nightmare of the soul lasted as long as staring over Paris left a light on. Sleep was out of the question. She tired. No way to lay down and forget it all. A full pack of Dunhills she bought in the hospital tabac. Kallini had a hot plate and tea and somebody left his cheap Gaulois. The breeze cooled off. No escape: smoke, tea, and grievances no reasoning mind resolved. No way to unweave her fate and fashion another destiny.

Here was no Janey Tower to take her hand, and say, you did the only thing possible. Kady had come to her mom's condition. To sit wishing upon the soaps of TV and cynically laugh how incense and stardust sent her so far away from home. KADY radio played on the airwaves of her fate. Out there scintillate the stars. In here all burns to smoke and ash. Diamonds and dust. Not that mom's Amarillo radio swing or her Beautiful Day played lies and delusion. There were lives worth living. Like Janey Tower and her sisterhood of San Diego. Like Marie Montfort across the street at the Freres foyer, closed. Back over the rainbow with Grannie Lonigan and her dead husband John. This life no longer delighted her. End of the Sixties in Paris, France. Like mother, like daughter.

Darkness clarified the layout of Paris. Kady tracked over places she found pleasure: the Tour Eiffel, Rue de Rivoli along the Seine, and the church on the far hill, Sacre Coeur. She traveled a long way from Millbrook and wished she were there now. Why didn't she play the part she was meant to play? Pain, heartbreak, desolation were words for a sore absence Kady no longer identified in the smoke and ash. Her despair was her own making.

Her mom's too.

Name her dream KADY and make a life with the Bontecotts of New Haven, then Old Saybrook and Millbrook, and weave this dream into tapestry of homes beautifully decorated. She was delivered to long distance where she was what she saw. She stood back straight in a plaid dress beautifully etched in a photo with Amarillo radio playing raucous swing on the dusty streets of Dalhart, Texas. Like mother, daughter lived no better life. Like mom in Millbrook, daughter cursed this end to the Sixties. Flow on waters of the Seine, never to return. Kady slept when the last lights of Paris extinguished.

She gave birth to her baby boy in Amarillo and despite the pain it was all worthwhile. No one knew David in the city or state. New York knew he worked in Paris and they came back from Paris before Christmas. "A spring baby is born with good luck," Grannie said to bolster her confidence. Her mom had come from Millbrook. With two months of Texas sun her arthritic pains ceased to be of grave concern. Back to her embroidery Kady knit and upholstered chairs and made the Dalhart farm more comfortable. David worked hard dawn to dusk with help from young John after his university hours at WTSU. They tractored a crop of wheat and corn on land the Depression winds laid waste. David wrote good poetry, read a while by her side, and rubbed her back until she found a soft spot to fall asleep.

They married under civil law in Paris before coming to Texas. Bernard of the Basque nation and Marie Montfort arranged a nice service and little party. Until Christmas the two earned a salary, which saved, covered expenses coming home, the doctor and the delivery. Wedding gift from her father made their lives in hiding more secure. Kady was never more happy with Grannic, mom, and several aunts catering to her needs, offering wisdom in small doses, sharing housework.

Never more happy with David, especially. All he needed: settle down and go to work. Soon as the war was over he'd retrace his steps to Paris and JFK Airport and enter America without legal hassle. Her father arranged matters with the Poughkeepsie draft board, where his brother and an uncle had gone to war. They were welcome in Texas, in California with Janey Tower and Bill Cougar, even back in New York. A world opened wide to David Morpheys and Kady, and their baby boy, _____.

Kady could not for the life of her recall her baby's name. Had she never named her baby boy? Was the end of happiness forsaken for want of a name? Name this time this space this extension of them. She couldn't wake without a name for her "enfant garcon". Kurt Kallini had seen to her shame.

Kady couldn't wake from ennui, this lassitude ten times worse than the scream of consciousness staring into Antoine's shortened physique, like a normal torso runted on midget legs. "Kady, you'll be perfectly okay. Any time for children you are perfectly healthy."

Kady recalled his medical manner, equal to life or death, another male doctor stuck standing in a white room without a soul. She woke on Kallini's couch in the same clothes, feeling dirty, needing a shower, her stomach yawning for a cup of coffee. Her body said baby with physical force. Her baby floundered as refuse in the Gobelin outtake.

That sin was her undoing.

A lit cigarette let her believe she breathed. A shower of water turned cold. The mirror stared at her incredibly pert breasts, poised with sustenance, at her flabby stomach, at her bleeding. She hated herself. Kady pulled over her the same paisley dress she wore in June, so proud to leave Paris for the States, and wore a faded jean jacket for the morning breeze.

Akim had coal for eyes seeing her come downstairs into the bar and sit at a table. He said nothing to her request for "cafe", and shook his head no to her two francs. She wasn't wanted. She walked into the street, and God only knew what a walk downhill would do to her. What if a hemorrhage split her wide open? Fair is fair, she thought to herself. A cold wind blew her off course. She hugged her jean jacket around her and backed to the door to stop her cotton dress pleating up her legs. The streetwalker look served her well. In a shop window she saw the spitting image, Katherine Lonigan and KADY, very lost in Paris and a long way from home.

89
Convalescence

"Allo jeune fille, allo Kady."

A girlish voice called her from the closed Freres across the street. Upstairs she saw Marie Montfort, her head thrust from the window above the foyer.

"Bonjour Marie."

"Come up and speak to me, please Kady."

Kady offered a half smile, unsure why this capable director of the Gobelin Equipe wished to see her. Marie exhorted her in an English Kady saw caused her difficulty.

"Okay, I'm coming. Je viens, merci."

Thank you she repeated to herself. She stood against the door as not to collapse. Her knees were weak and she hobbled across the cobblestone pavement. Faint blackout spots in her vision. She saw herself falling against the hard stones. What she deserved.

Marie met her at the Freres foyer and helped her upstairs. Kady saw her tiny upturned nose and eyes looking at her. Marie sat her down at the kitchen table, poured her coffee, cut and buttered bread from a fresh baguette, and importuned her with her tiny blue eyes to stay.

"Kady, you stay with me. I know Kallini has gone to Turkey. What's the matter with you?"

"Non-non-non I can't stay."

Kady couldn't look into Marie's clear blue eyes without feeling ashamed.

Marie asked in broken English.

"Where is votre ami, David Morpheys? I met him at Richard Lenoir. He was so gentille with the viellards. He had compassion for them and treated them like personal friends. He is a good person too, like you."

Kady began to cry softly, seeing she had not trusted David Morpheys. She recalled how he liked Grannie Lonigan, how he hustled her across Europe sick as a dog to go home and see her mom. He loved traveling with her, excited for the both of them, and listened to her whims and weary fatigue. David loved her, it occurred to Kady Bontecott.

Then she cried hard. Why hadn't she confided in him, instead of Kallini? David would never say, "abort my baby". It wasn't his nature. Compassion for all living things was his nature. He'd be a proud father, loving her, loving their son, and stop his wandering. Her dream last night.

"A baby is a blessing." Grannie Lonigan said that to her. "Your mom was my pride and joy, my last baby, a perfect piece of God's whole, holy world, and Him watching over the piece as over the whole world." Jesus, was Kady sorry.

Marie met Kady's non-non-non with her own intense wish to help.

"Please stay with me. Make me happy with your bon compagnie."

Kady agreed. She had no will to resist really. After her cup of coffee and a good cry, her eyelids drooped. Marie noticed and smiled at her. Marie hugged her and Kady sobbed like a little girl. Her knees were weak and gave way. Marie helped her to bed in the only other room.

Likely as not Marie knew all Kady could tell her. Why then was she concerned for Kady's welfare? Tears released her from the spell of yesterday. Marie helped her, into a single bed all neatly made, with too clean sheets for her. Sheets smelled of lavender and breezy September. Marie sat beside her, stroking her hair for an hour, until Kady fell asleep. The words repeated softly. "It's okay, c'est bien jeune fille, c'est bien, dormez, dormez bien."

Marie waited until Kady slept soundly to cross over to Akim's, who refused her the stairwell to Kallini's room, where Kady's things were. Marie had a will of her own. Her piety had working class sympathies and she knew next to nothing of the Islamic Crusade. She knew nothing of Algeria and Morocco and French imperialism in North Africa. Her Catholic piety was indigenous to the Parisian poor. It made her determined.

"Je vais, Je vais," she said twice and flashed Kallini's key as testimony. Only a few caftans crossed her path and stared at her to no avail. In fact, Marie made a second trip to retrieve all Kady's belongings. The cook and his helper managed to bring up from the cellar a mattress, springs, a frame, and move Marie's meager furnishings aside. The commotion stirred Kady to go to the bathroom, bleeding profusely, and return to bed in a feverish sweat.

Marie sat by her side. She applied cold compresses to cool her fever and called Gobelin for another Freres doctor, who told her fever and infection were fairly normal following a DNC. She had the pharmacy send medicine, which by evening took effect. Kady got up for soup and rolls and a slice of meat with small potatoes the chef made for dinner. A cigarette and two cups of coffee on a full stomach delivered Kady back to the land of the living.

"Merci, Marie. I feel better now. I can go to a hotel."

Marie wouldn't hear of it. She pleaded for Kady to stay a week at least, knowing Kallini was gone for months. Kallini told Marie not to help Kady, "because she had done a horror to an unborn child," which suggested any crime from murder to abortion. Marie knew Kallini abandoned the poor girl. She urged Kady to call home. Though she had never been on a plane, she planned to fly with her to America. She planned to help Kady get back home.

"Please call your mom this evening."

"I don't want to be a burden to you."

"Call your mom, j'insiste."

Kady called at 4PM New York time. Her mom heard her voice and knew she was unwell. Her mom was nervous Kady wasn't telling her what happened.

"What's really the matter with you? Kady, you sound terrible."

"Mom, I committed a bad sin. I was pregnant by David Morpheys and aborted the baby boy two days ago. I am so sorry. I can't stop crying and want to kill myself."

"Kady, you get hold of yourself. That changes my opinion of your boyfriend entirely. He told you to get rid of the baby, get rid of him. You listen."

"Mom, David could never be so heartless. It wasn't him. I never told him I was pregnant."

"Then who?"

"It was Kurt Kallini who told me to abort the baby. And I trusted him."

"It's Kurt then, who has done wrong. My opinion of him has changed. Come home Kady. We won't deal with Kurt Kallini again."

"I want to see David. Maybe go on another vacation with Marie Montfort, the girl I'm staying with. She's taking care of me."

"Have you told her about the abortion?"

"No. She never asked. She's such a beautifully Christian person I didn't dare. I'd be a wreck if I came home now. I got to talk to David. Forget that remark about killing myself. It was the first thing that popped into my head. You know the maudlin soaps we watch. I didn't mean it. And thanks for listening mom. I'm better now."

"You call me back every night."

"I can't mom."

"Then give me the number and I'll call you."

"Okay. I'll tell Marie, in case I'm out."

"You be there at 9PM. And don't go near Kurt Kallini. He's done a terrible thing, and he did it on purpose. He doesn't cherish life the way we do. Bontecott called him a hoodlum and maybe that's what he is. He intended to hurt you and Bontecott and me too. You leave him alone."

"Mom, he left the day of the DNC operation. He went to Istanbul, Turkey for God knows what reason."

"And where's David?"

"He went to Berlin, after his friend Early overdosed in Vichy. I explained it to you. He thought Kurt was responsible and broke his arm in a fight. I should have trusted him more, and told him. He'd never tell me to get an abortion. I know that now."

"Well, you stay close to Marie, and I don't know about Morpheys either."

"David will return. I really believe that."

"Well Grannie liked him, and she's a pretty good judge of character.

I want you to come home where you belong."

Coffee, a couple cigarettes, and a cool breeze started her morning. She opened the window to clear the smoke. September's breeze stirred her. Somewhere leaves turn color, burn brown, cranberry red, and the weird orange of Halloween. The city disconnects the season and sad ennui becomes its color. Marie Montfort woke her at nine o'clock to say she was leaving for downstairs. There was a new pot of coffee, towels for the shower, and laundry in the basement. Nice of her, Kady thought, and asked how she'd ever return Marie's kindness.

Physically she felt better. Her bleeding needed no more white towels to staunch the overflow. Like an abnormal period this morning. She could take care of herself. A shower and then she washed what red stain she could from towels and garments. The basement shelves stocked with wine and foodstuffs delivered to veillards who couldn't come to the Freres foyer.

David liked those errands. He wrote her of walking the arondissement, up flights of stairs to lonely women, overaged and useless to any social scheme but charity. The work of washing, drying, and carting upstairs appeased her angry beehive of a brain. It stilled the noise, and Kady breathed a sigh of relief. Clean laundry, unclean conscience. Up and down stairs from one task to the next, whose sequence she didn't question for significance.

Kady tried to help Marie serving dinner to half a hundred old folks for whom this meal was their one for the day. She labeled the food shepherd's pie with its biscuit, chicken, and vegetables. As she passed out plates and measured greetings, everybody asked who the gentille jeune fille was. Toothless mouths and whiskered jawbones grappled for nutriment. The sight made her sorely aware of suffering humanity. Her piddling concerns were merely personal. How could she punctuate her life with an exclamation point when so many hungered for one good meal served with a kind word?

Marie saw her blanched face, and chary of her good cheer escorted Kady back to bed again. Later that afternoon Marie came to chat, sitting beside the bed Kady occupied.

"How is my gentille assistant?"

"Better back in bed. Sorry I fell faint. I wanted to do my part and all I do is distract you from yours."

"You were helping, Kady. All the old folks said how gentille you were. Your new face brightened up their entire day. Think how lonely they are, and the only faces they see are Chef Thomas and my poor excuse for youthful beauty."

"Marie, you are modest. Your personality is beautiful. Your smile lights up their lives and mine."

"You are kind to say so, Kady. We are both jeune filles and like sisters care for one another. Our beauty is the sympathy we offer one another, our parents, and old folks without anyone else to care for them. Kallini and Akim aside, we have only ourselves as sisters."

"Tu as raison. You are beautiful beyond my meager belief. Especially your faith in common humanity. You have great heart, Marie, and we jeune filles need to be sympathique with one another."

Tea and bread and cheese graced their meal together. The fall temperatures once cool with an inkling of winter surged again with September heat. Marie visited her parents in a working class bainlieu outside the city. She asked Kady to accompany her, but Kady stayed for her mom's call.

Kady smoked fewer cigarettes that evening. The heat urged her to unshutter the kitchen windows and sit sideways looking down to the Seine. City lights twinkled like the starry heavens. She wished to walk to Sacre Coeur and sit on the steps like one June night she and David surveyed their chances. A time that would not come again.

90
Truth Be Told

David returned to the Freres at Richard Lenoir. First he apologized to Christian for the scene at Vichy. There was no excuse. Next he washed dishes as spindle-leg Germaine cooked the cuisine. Andre, the rouged secretary with bird eyes, alerted him to the number of old ladies in need of food and visits. Walking the neighborhood was routine. Work took time. Work took his mind off problems.

Kady wasn't there waiting for him. Wishful thinking. He'd travel clear across Europe and return to the open arms of his girlfriend, Kady Bontecott. He prepared an apology to her.

Bernard told David there was a slight salary for him. For Kady too. She was at Gobelin. David delivered hot lunch tins and pondered what to do. Kady was with Kurt Kallini. Should he tell Kady about her best friend, Barb Kelly? Did Ted Westerbrook have the facts straight? A bomb exploded in the Black Panther building. He may not see Kady for weeks. Do his work was the adult thing to do.

Upon his return he saw Kady waiting for him. Her freckled face, without color, sat beside Andre with her rouged face. Kady kissed him on the cheek and said she missed him. During lunch with everyone acquainted, David saw the pallor of her face, her freckles barely visible, hair pulled off her forehead, a serious glint hardened in her green eyes. She was considerably thinner.

"Take off the afternoon," Bernard suggested.

Kady thanked him. David went along with her to the metro, en route to Rue de Rivoli and the Jeu de Paumes. Few travelers on Thursday. Gone were the summer tourists. Paris was theirs for the asking. They could well be French. Kady held his hand, and David was happy with her company. She looked sad. Gone were the flair and the fun. On the metro she said she had a plane ticket for November. Her mom went for an operation in Boston.

"How serious?"

"Not too bad. A hysterectomy to help with menopause and arthritic pain. Male doctors are smug. Mom's resigned to whatever comes. At least she has her faith."

David was startled by the faith remark because Kady said it seriously. He suggested they order espressos and not go to the Jeu de Paumes.

"I'm not in the mood for a lot of Renoirs."

Kady understood he was different too. The light swirl of colors sang of a happier time. Now was time for the truth. She rehearsed what to say all week. She had an abortion and she was sorry for herself, for David, and most of all for the unborn child. She got talking.

"Kurt Kallini is the bastard you knew he was."

"Yes he is. For what he did to Early Hayze."

"I'm sorry I listened to him."

"But he fascinates a person. He knows what you want and steals it from you."

"I should have told you I was pregnant. Time we tell the truth and be responsible. Both of us."

David never guessed. But it made perfect sense. Kady threw up on the road west, but she was sick on the journey east too. Now he knew. Now he'd do the right thing. Whatever Kady wanted, he'd do.

"I'm sorry I never told you. I was wrong. Faith tells one what to do, not for the sake of any rules or law, but because a person can do nothing else and be Catholic."

Kady didn't pause for a reply. She wiped her eyes dry and lit a Dunhill cigarette.

"We could be parents, Kady, here in Paris. We have an income. Bernard said both of us."

Kady looked at him, green eyes glassy and sad.

"You don't understand, do you David? You just don't understand. I had an abortion. I went to Hopital des Gobelins and there is no more baby. Every morning I wake up pregnant. Then face the reality of my life. No more baby. No more faith. And no more happiness for you and me."

David was blown away by the news. Again he never guessed. He put his hand over hers. His mind was elsewhere. Kady blew out smoke, relieved. She told him. Later she'd explain the rest. They walked past the boutiques of Rue de Rivoli and took the metro back to Richard Lenoir. Christian wanted them to see the latest comedy with Fernandel. They went to be polite. Slapstick comedy, it made no sense. They had to know more language to appreciate the jokes. David cared less. Nothing was funny anymore. He and Kady shared the room above the Lenoir Equipe, and with two beds they slept apart. Kady was sore and figured David accommodated her.

But there were problems sleep couldn't solve for David Morpheys. The next morning David didn't know what to do. Germaine and Andre said "dommage" about Kady having an abortion. Why blame her and not Kallini who took her to Hopital des Gobelins? Word got around. Andre with her bird eyes and Germaine with his five foot shuffle knew more than David. And he knew nothing.

He did deliveries without Kady and never returned. He went to the fantastic darkness of the Muse de Cinema and watched film. Goddard's A Bout de Souffle, his idea of revenge on Kurt Kallini a bad gangster copy, like Belmondo copying Bogart playing a thick-lipped gangster.

Go and confront Kallini. He had a kitchen knife in his suit pocket. Germaine wouldn't miss it. Find out what's between him and Kady. Why did Kallini get her an abortion? Idea bit like a bee sting. It wasn't his baby; it was Kallini's. That time before he came in June. The letters Kallini kept from him. It didn't make sense and it all fit together. The truth hurt. In fact, the truth terrified him.

Kid named O'Neil tried to punch him out in fifth grade. O'Neil blamed him for breaking a kid's arm in a science fair fight. Bigger kid caught him coming off the bus. David got away and grabbed a knife from home to scare him. The knife scared David and made him act silly. Scared to use it and silly if he didn't.

David arrived at Gobelin after the dinner hour. Le beau garcon sat in his white caftan at an outside table. He smoked a cigarette. David recalled the kid groping him. Kid's face was a blank.

Le beau garcon took a blade from his caftan. He pointed the blade at David and laughed.

"Vous voulez, Monsieur?"

Beside David the restaurant door opened and Akim with his jet black eyes asked in English.

"What do you want here? My son does not like you. I told him to stay away from Lenoir."

"I need to see Kallini."

"Kallini traveled to Turkey. You broke his arm. He would not want to see you, except to take revenge."

David held the kitchen knife stuck up from his fist. Beau garcon dandled his blade in an open palm.

"I need to see Kallini. Settle things. I'm going to his room."

The boy got up from his chair. David stood between the boy and Akim, the Algerian terrorist, and waved his fist at one, then the other. Someone grabbed his suit coat from the back.

"Leave David Morpheys alone."

He swung his head scared to see no one. Marie Montfort was five foot two and fearless. She took David's hand and put the kitchen knife on the table, along side her keys to Kallini's room.

"I told him Kallini was gone," Akim said.

"It's true," Marie said. "Kallini's gone. He left Kady crying in his room and she stayed with me. Let's leave David."

He did, backing away, startled, scared, and exhilarated too. His eyes riveted on the boy and Akim, but they looked blank. Nothing happened. Nothing was settled. And he still knew nothing.

Marie made chamomile tea in the Freres kitchen. She asked about Kady.

"She's with me at Lenoir. You may not know. Kady had an abortion. Everyone knows Kallini took her to the hospital at Gobelins. I blame Kallini."

"She blames herself. She didn't tell me, but I know. It took a week for her to recover and now she needs your help."

"I know. It's easier to blame Kallini. Kady and me, we made a mess of our lives together. I blame myself too."

"Go talk with her."

"Thanks Marie, for everything."

As night fell he was totally exhausted. He walked Gobelin to the Bastille over the Pont Mirabeau. So much water under the bridge. If he couldn't get his mind straight, why hold it against Kady? It was late when he returned to their room. Kady was sound asleep. He undressed and slid in bed beside her. Kady screamed, "Jesus", as she bolted out of bed. Silence settled in the dark room, reverberating off the walls.

Kady's skin scratched and her elbow ached with arthritis. Cool air blew in the window.

"How the hell can you get into bed with a person you hate so much?"

"Let's talk Kady."

"You been gone all day."

"To see Kallini, I had to."

Good an answer as any.

"To see Kallini? You're gone the worst week of my life, and leave again when I come for your help. How can you do it?"

"I hate Kallini and had to confront him. But he's gone and you probably knew."

"Of course I knew."

"We got to talk."

"I should have told you everything at once."

"What else is there to tell? The baby belonged to Kurt Kallini?"

Kady stared at him like he had his kitchen knife in hand. If she had a place to go, she'd have gone.

"Of course not."

"Then why let him take you to the hospital? Why tell him anything you didn't tell me?"

Why didn't Kady tell David Morpheys? She had no answer. No good answer for him now, other than to tell him everything. Then see what David would do.

"The connection him to me, it's complicated."

"He was your boyfriend then?"
"Never."
"Not boyfriend, but somebody you trusted more than me."
"Yes, no."
"Tell me. You told me nothing about the baby."
"Kurt Kallini is my father's bastard son."
David didn't understand. The words, yes. What they meant, no.
"Listen David, my father left the Bontecott farm to Kurt Kallini in his will, gave him money and a car, and let him in his house. But he hates Kurt Kallini."
"Bastard son?"
"He didn't know. My father or Kallini. And I didn't know."
"What's your dad up to? What's Kallini up to?"
"Listen David, my father had an affair, you understand. Too long ago to matter, to him or even to my mom. But it matters to Kurt. And it did matter to me. Kurt is my half brother."
"What?"
"My dad is Kallini's father and neither of them knew. He treated me like a brother after Woodstock, with advice and all, and I trusted him, and I felt sorry for him. My father hated having him around, but I felt sorry for the way he'd been treated. Then I took his advice about the abortion. I'm sorry about our baby, David, but it's over. I did it, and you can hate Kurt Kallini and you can hate me too."
"Kallini's your half brother? Jesus, the resemblance."
"David, don't hate me. I need you now ."
"For Christ's sake, I don't hate you. But I'm having trouble with this half-brother idea."
"You got to help me, who else can?"
David saw tears in Kady's eyes, her arms crossed, shivering. David hated how he was acting. He wanted to reach out and comfort her. It wasn't Kady at all, it was Kurt Kallini.
"Half my brother, my father's son. And I never want to see him again. With you gone all day I went to Sacre Coeur. I couldn't confess my sin. I couldn't sit inside and say prayers. It did help to sit on the steps. I watched the children and the families stroll in the sun. I may

never pray again, but sitting there eased my pain."

She turned and took up a blanket and sat on the bed. Breeze blew in the courtyard windows. The metro burrowed floors below, and shook the building. They sat knee to knee, naked.

David got a grip on himself, her there, things explained.

"Kallini haunts me in the streets of Paris, like one of his Gobelin friends in white caftans. I blame him for Early's death and he stands between us. I know he's not in town, but he haunts me."

"Let Kurt Kallini go. He's a soul damned in hell. Kurt is my half brother, and my dad, mom, and me will never see him again."

David got up quickly to pace, suddenly hot and cold, and numb, not knowing what to say.

"He's your brother, that's it, I should have known, damn't I should have known. The resemblance. You should have told me."

"Don't be dense, David, please."

"I know I know."

She got up too. Both naked now and cold. Her elbow like a toothache.

"I know, I know now. A bastard brother, not your companion and not your friend. Kallini makes sense to me. At last. Just some dude who fascinates the hell out of people, because they never know him."

Kady watched him, shivered, and cried.

"I'm sorry Kady, I should have known. About the baby too."

"I should have told you."

"Yes. Tell everything."

"That's how it is, and it's late."

"Sorry I wasn't here for you. Marie told me how bad a time you had."

"Marie's a saint. It's over."

"Yes."

"We know the worst. What we do now is up to us."

"Tell everything."

"Nobody to blame from now on."

Kady smiled and the sad smile lit her freckles.

"It's not over, Kady."

"Not between us?"

"Of course not. Only it's not over, telling everything. Let me tell you."

Kady wrapped in her blanket and stared at him.

"My friend Early Hayze, your friend Barb Kelly, there's more."

"I haven't heard from Barb in months."

"Guy who knew her at Berkley. Guy I rode back with on the train."

"She okay?"

"Ted Westerbrook told me she died in a police break-in of a Panther building in Oakland. A bomb went off. Ted liked her a lot and I believed him. Kady, I think it's true, sorry as hell for her and you."

Kady collapsed to the bed. David wrapped the blanket around her. Tears for her friend, Barb Kelly, who never hurt a soul. The carefree years were over. A life worth living was a bad joke. Time to be an adult. And a baby she'd never see again, a girlfriend she'd never see again, all because of a brother she never wanted to see again. It was too much for Kady Bontecott.

David walked around the room. He shouldn't have told her. One more thing was too much. Much too much. He paced and she caught him. He turned and held her in the blanket. She shook all over. What to do? Not draw away, not resist, it was too much for the two of them. All was done. All was said. As if all effort on their part wasn't worth a thing.

They held each other. Nothing stopped them and nothing helped. How to forgive when so much happened? They were nobody special. They were scared, hurt, and lonely people, once so much in love, and losing so much they blamed themselves. Only together in the world this one time round.

The metro roared inexorably every quarter hour. They had no easy words like I love you to say. Or saying the words had no effect. Kady let her blanket fall, not magically like the walls of Jericho for Claudette Colbert and Clark Gable, but purposely to ease the pain. Warm arms and legs eased them into bed. They slept together, like spoons, like half moon bright and dark moon half seen, come full circle, waxing complete and waning to go. Both were glad all was said and done. They slept, both glad it was over.

XII
Munich

91
Train and Tram

Near Christmas, David left from Gare St. Lazare for Munich. Train cut a path across France into southern Germany. With Kady gone a few weeks earlier, Paris had too many memories. Try someplace else to finish his thesis. Let cold winter cleanse his soul and silence his jangled nerves.

David tried to sleep on the night train. The cars deserted. A few passengers huddled in December overcoats, lumpy like hills on a rolling Ohio landscape. He stretched his legs and lay sideways, a steely cold hollowing out the train.

Memories of Kady flagged in the warm winds of his dream. White bird veered in breezes between ocean and land. But time wasn't intimate with la mer melee au soleil, with eternity at their fingertips. Farewells were pleasant. Last weeks they acted like tourists seeing the sights, as if they wouldn't pass this way again.

Late the last evening they drank champagne and closed the foyer curtains. They danced tête-à-tête to accordion tunes true to the moment, shorn of past separation and future plans: perfect, but like a perfect tense in language, a completed action and final. They spoke of David returning at Christmas or Kady coming back with the new year. Nice to talk that way.

They never coped with what happened. Too much happened. Kallini didn't come back to blame. Or if he did, he stayed at Gobelin among the caftaned Algerians. Blame was on them too.

"Mein Herr, die lege auf dem fussboden."

Conductor spoke to David about his legs sprawled on the opposite seat. Stern countenance asserted rule and regulation, different from the laissez-faire of Paris. David sat up, head heavy from his lapse into memory. The car was empty.

"Fahrkarte, bitte schon."

He surrendered his ticket to the conductor."

"Danke."

The car lit with an overfull moon magnified the grandeur of the Barvarian Alps. The Black Forest at four in the morning. Like Grimm Brother's marchen. But it took more to captivate him. Too much happened.

Train docked at an hour of business rush. He lugged his belongings. Kady gave him her big canvas bag. He'd need it more than her. Bernard lent him the Freres radio. Heavy stuff filled the bag, but no longer a cornucopia. It was stuff. Books for his thesis, radio to connect with the world, and clothes to wear in winter.

He put all but his carpetbag in a train locker. He exchanged three hundred dollars of Freres salary into marks, two to the dollar, a bad rate. He parsed his way into a crowd of foreigners. Newstand hawked familiar Time and Penthouse magazines emblazoned with Teutonic script. Turbaned attendant glowered at David with his dark, creamy complexion, with his jet black eyebrows and sharp eyes.

"Verzeihung, Zeitung bitte."

David negotiated a Munich paper. The section renting apartments yielded two possibilities. This was a better start than Berlin. One rented for 75 marks a month up Grabenstrasse. Close to the train station, it said.

A fresh coffee and smoke launched him into the chill December morning, skies a tense gray, unsettled before their winter cast of steel. Following the tram tracks up six blocks, he located the number. The brick buildings leaned over the tram tracks both sides of the pavement. Across the street the neon and glass Schwartzkatz advertised tables for two. A long mahogany bar muted lights in a kinky dive. David weighed proximity to the station against the noisy distractions. His books needed a room to finish his thesis. Graduation promise to his dad. Tie up the loose ends. With the New Year encourage Kady to return to Paris.

At the threshhold he met an elderly woman, brisk and diligent, replying she had a room. Her man sat stiff legged in the parlor, retired from all activity. David shared a bathroom with other boarders, two girls from Radcliff, off skiing in the Barvarian Alps. His single room had a sink and oil stove, for which he supplied the fuel. The bed was freshly made with a goose down comforter. Warm in bed without fuel. The deal consummated he paid for the month and sent Les Freres a letter to forward his mail.

He sat at the desk with his thesis. Godawful shaking up and down, the room, the building, earth and sky. He rushed to the second floor window. The tram cranked its heavy metal cars on electric hangers. A quarter minute it roared like Lowenbrau lions. David stared in fascinated horror at speed and power close up. An impersonal wall of sound surged like floodwaters up Grabenstrasse. The apartment tipped like a riverbank about to washout.

Ride the rails top speed full out totally destroyed at the turn up ahead. The transcendent moment in modern lit rock-and-rolled. From Blake's tiger in the forests of night the moment of vision harnessed to an industrial revolution. Invention and advance light speed progress up and away and down down to hell and the underground. David's paper burned in flashes of brilliance. Brief glow of braincells burned up fuel.

The tram passed, David saw furred woman and gentlemen enter the Schwartkatz Bar for noontime drinks. Fashionable hideaway with dance floor and cozy tables. Playtime for easy money. He unlocked his bag of belongings. The lugging of Kady's bag up Grabenstrasse wore him out. He was in terrible shape. With his worldly possessions he holed up for winter. Books stacked like battlements on the desk. There'd be no slacking off.

Everything in place, he emptied his pockets to count cash, front pocket for expenses and wallet for his stash of savings. The wallet was gone. Grandpa's story of a bump and slash in Grand Central. By chance Grandpa saw the slasher. He felt nothing losing his wallet. Shouting out thief was the furthest thing from his mind because a pickpocket sticks the knife in your belly. They're gone and so are you. Keep a hand on your wallet and your mouth shut.

In the Munich station among hordes of Italians and Turks, Slavs and Pakistanis he suspected nothing and felt nothing. Now he was lost.

Most of his cash was gone. All his identification gone. Just a passport and pocket cash. About a hundred left, a train ticket to Paris and a plane ticket home. Life lines to the glorious world gone. Imagine the worst that could happen, and it had. Too much happened.

92

Diamonds and Dust

They met nearby the army base in Trenton, New Jersey at the Harass the Brass Bar. Dix was near enough to Trenton and Philadelphia to avoid the army brass, and their reach outside the base. Kurt Kallini asked Josh Steen and Dierdre Hartford to come along to meet and deal with Mike Emmett and his wife Julia. It was a good occasion to clear the air. He arrived from Montreal to Philadelphia and took a limo to Trenton.

He wasn't early, nor meant to be. Mike wanted things from him. Why he made the meeting with Mike last minute with both flying in. They shook hands, got a pitcher of beer, and relaxed among the enlisted men at their hangout. It wasn't crowded and they didn't look like MP's, officers, or army brass.

"We need to discuss funding," Mike said, not willing to play the amenities.

"Who do you want at the table?"

"You and you alone, Kurt. This is a full blown bar, not a cafe. Somebody got a liquor license and somebody's making money. Ft. Killeen, Texas, Hood in Oregon, San Diego Navy base, South Carolina, and the Bay Area, that's where things are happening, not here."

"Well, keep Josh in the loop because he's doing dispersals."

"You mind Julia, Dier? It's finances and you don't want to be involved, you know, legally if the shit hits the fan."

"Me and Julie got lots to say, and maybe we can find a few servicemen who want to dance."

Julie smiled, her whispy strands of dark hair, loose and unmanaged. Dier had her hair clipped short a week ago, for the Days of Rage in Chicago.

"You guys break in for a dance anytime," Julie smiled, "but be sure you mean romance and not a lot of lollygagging around. We're two hot chicks among an army of real men."

Mike seemed to bulge out at the shoulders and he pressed his two fists together. Kurt Kallini leaned back and his browbeating eyes hid behind shades. He took to wearing shades like Francois Searcy, his partner in transporting cargo across and ocean. People didn't see the person, they saw themselves reflected in the shades.

"So give us news from the GI front. What's happening to slack the army's ability to wage war? Tell me and tell Josh how those extra funds will serve the revolution within the armed forces."

"Josh needs to hear the nitty gritty?"

"He does because he's my courier with the cash."

Kurt Kallini wasn't sure it was the right play, but what he needed now more than anything was a way to clean his money and clean his stash with the jewelry business. Else his money stuck in Swiss bank accounts for years until the furor over his making a killing blew over.

"Well what's happening, it's been happening pretty fierce for a while now. The fragging of officers like the colonel who led Hamburger Hill with all its casualties, there's a bounty on him. Any hotshot second louie who leads his men into trouble, frag him. That says to the brass, beware. At Killeen they resisted going to Vietnam, at Hood it's all long hair, drugs, and revolt. On ships like the US Corral Sea there's an actual mutiny planned. This is out of San Diego where Julie and I live. It's the underground papers collecting the sentiment and it's not all draftees. Enlisted guys are even more pissed off. They had expectations the draftees did not, and enlistees got treated like shit too. It's 65,000 deserters last year, it's 30,000 combat troops on smack, and it's a thousand sailors who dared sign a Fed Up petition."

"Things are happening I didn't know about," Kallini admitted. "My mind was elsewhere."

"Money and organization will make things happen quicker. Harlan Clay wants to get involved with the Hollywood types and go where the drab green rebels make noise, and then salute the troops in revolt."

"I'm not your organizer Mike and I'm not sure that's what Josh signed up for. But let Josh know where money will make a difference and he'll be there. What else is happening?"

"Over in Vietnam with the fraggings, it's 3 day pot parties on patrol, what they call search and avoid missions. Nobody wants to be the last soldier killed in Nam. Nixon has to withdraw troops because it's an army on the verge of collapse. Now the main way to stop the war waits on the Navy and Air Force recruits, none of them drafted. They need to take over the ships and stop the bombing missions. Sabotage the equipment, strike the San Diego docksides, kill the main gear shafts, SOS, and Stop the Ship. Get the air force servicemen not to service planes because Nixon wants an Air War with its executive freedom to call the shots, and it's not going to happen. We Are Everywhere, sit-down strikes on ships, air field with disservice to planes, and FTA, Free the Army. It frag, drug, mutiny, and sabotage to end the war as soon as possible."

"Great doings in many places, but mostly West Coast, Honolulu and Subic Bay, and all over South Vietnam. Then let Josh Steen be your cash cow. Whenever you need him, give him a call, let him hop a plane, tell him what you need. If it's fifty thousand dollars, just say a fifty. Keep it simple whatever you say on the phone because don't think for moment there's not FBI, CIA, and DIA closely tracking one and all involved in the GI Movement."

"I'm tracked, but my dad's in the Pentagon and he told me. What about you?"

"I'm doubly tracked because of the finances and how it goes places across Canada, Europe, and the Middle East. And Europe's where I'll be, if not Montreal. Josh and Josh alone knows how to keep in contact. So you contact Josh. I'll have money, Mike, and it will keep on coming."

Mike liked the pep talk to his exposition on GI Movement success. He was all business back in his IBM days, and he still computed life in terms of success, Kallini now too. They shook hands, nodded to Josh, and let matters rest.

"Well Kurt, I'll put my mind at rest. Tag Josh's pocket with a fifty and we'll fund a US Corral Sea mutiny and a San Diego dock strike. I know there was an AWOL rebellion at Ft. Dix back in June of 69', but the goddamn Weather plan to bomb Ft. Dix at an officer's dance, that news gave Agnew dinner talk for a year. We want both moral and material support for the GI Movement, but we don't want to incite violence. We want simply resistance, mutiny, and non-obedience. We want that good vibe of the early civil rights days of non-violence. We want to end the war by the refusal to fight or aid the planes who bomb the countryside. Every GI refuses to fight, the war is called off."

"Good publicity if possible then, Josh. We're good then Mike?"

Mike nodded.

Antoine arrived at Kallini's hotel room overlooking the Munich tracks. He came with a chemistry test for analysis of the Turkish dust. It was the best ever. A shipment of fifty pounds at once no one dared do before. Kallini meant to make a killing. Win the worldwide revolution. Already the Weathermen raging the streets of Chicago in Octoberfest collected felonies and fines enough to send them into hiding. Especially Josh in the Greenwich townhouse. Kallini should save the Movement. Kallini should revenge what his father had done, and take over Bontecott Stone.

Each bag of dust hid as many as fifty Afrikaner diamonds. A one time bonanza, a last time, forever. Enough diamonds and dust to seed the spiritus mundi and free Uncle Carlo from mundane connections. Enough to put Kallini in control of his own destiny. Enough to solve his problems and save him any further shame.

Antoine nodded to Kallini.

"The dust is pure as driven snow?" Kallini asked.

"Yes. Have you talked David Morpheys into carrying the canvas bag through customs?"

"No. I don't intend to. Too risky to involve him directly. I got a girl in Paris to carry it through customs. Her passport and her look match Kady Bontecott. A blond hippie chick coming back from a Christmas ski trip and tour of Paris."

"Morpheys is not reliable?"

"Thinks too much. I don't trust him. Involve him in a guilt trip, so it looks like he has the perfect motive and no possible connection at all."

Antoine stood, washed his hands, and looked over the Munich tracks. The turbaned attendant at the newstand glanced up and saw the shortened torso in the hotel window.

"Why involve him at all?"

"In case agents investigate there should be leads and deadends. Also we need Kady's canvas bag. Morpheys keeps it till the last moment. With all Kady's markings on it I want Evander Bontecott to know who bought out his family business and how. Best he knows Kurt Kallini pays his debts, of money and honor."

"Don't overstep yourself."

Antoine dried his hands and waited for the turbaned attendant to give him a sign.

"If you're caught, all you do, Kurt, means nothing."

"Exactly. The import needs to look perfectly natural. Agents will investigate. Kady innocent and Morpheys has the perfect motive."

"The quantity of dust and diamonds will flood the market?"

"All agreed on. Hasidic jewelers wait. As do the dust peddlers. Bontecott's brothers don't expect any qualified offer when they float the New Haven stock. Jews in NYC gain a distribution network from New Haven to Dalhart, Texas. Jews get the jewelry and Bontecotts lose out. Until I buy the firm back at a suitable time."

"Fund the worldwide revolution, Kurt."

"We will do our part."

"The Brotherhood will thank you."

Antoine straightened his tie and Attaturk let him know his train was called.

"A long time planning?"

"Anything worth the wait takes a lifetime of planning and patience to pay off. The mystery of spiritus mundi. The Brotherhood benefits, as we do."

Antoine packed his chemistry set for the trip back to Dijon.

"Let me know what happens. I'd like to see San Diego again."

"After the dust settles and the diamonds sparkle we'll go en vacance, and see Bill Cougar too."

9.3
Memory Makes the Man

Gone was the day's euphoria of a warm room in winter. Morpheys needed sleep. But he told his landlady, Frau Huber, days for her to clean he'd be at school. He lodged his money inside the cumbersome poetry of Paradise Lost. Which fit the bill.

He trudged up Grabenstrasse to the twin lions of the Lowenbrau Brewery, dating to 1400. The tram swung left on erected steel across the intersection. David turned toward Hitler's copy of the Brandenburg Gate. Within a few blocks he found the university's warm library of German books. Here he would work on his paper until he finished. By the new year write his thesis on Prodigal Time.

That afternoon near Christmas David slept in a brown leather chair. Sunlight streamed through the window and the shadow of another student stirred him to look up.

"You sleep like the dead."

David concentrated to see the dark-bearded face of Kurt Kallini.

"How the hell did you find me? You're an amazing dude, you know. I wanted to slash you in Paris. You wreck people's lives and go about your business. And goddamn return when they least expect you, or want to see you."

"I saw you in the train station. You're wasting your time here."

"You're in my light."

"Time for the truth. I don't like you and I know you don't like me. So what? We start to know one another. All the world's a Poughkeepsie."

David wanted out of his leather chair.

"Stay, hear me out. You and me got screwed by Bontecott. He's my father you know, and he's the man who fired your dad."

"That's way beyond me. Before I was born. Time you forgot the guy too. He's one cold character."

"So am I."

David nodded in recognition.

"Memory makes the man. Hear me out. Bontecott always had money, so he did as he pleased. I scraped by, best I could. Bontecott sells out a business which should belong to me. It's a whitewash. But his will gives me the Bontecott farm. Get it Morpheys, the farm, which belonged to your family."

'It stinks you get it, Kallini."

"So you think?"

"It's the past."

"Memory makes the man. A long memory."

David shook his head.

"Morpheys, how would you like that farm?"

"You're an amazing dude, Kallini?"

"I mean it. Do me a few favors, and it's yours."

"Really, who do I have to murder?"

"Nobody. Just a deal to benefit The Brotherhood, and yourself."

"Early Hayze sucked up water doing a deal for you."

"I'm sorry for him. But he overdosed. Hear me, Morpheys, I'm willing to overlook our little squabble."

"And Barb Kelly?

Kallini stared down.

"You sent Barb Kelly west to her death."

Kallini nodded.

"You know."

Morpheys played the game and improved his mind.

"Her death grieved me. And the death of Lionel Dubois, a black brother at Cornell, who returned to the Panthers. We shared the revolution. These are dangerous times. The pigs wipe out the Panthers. First the Blacks, then the Weathermen. The time of repression has come. Why the Brotherhood needs your help."

"I suppose you got an excuse for Kady's abortion. It grieves you terribly."

"No, I got no excuse. You broke my arm. I could have the Turk knife you in the train station. That's revenge. But I got no excuse. And I don't grieve much. We're even."

"I don't think so."

"Get this Morpheys. Somehow in the scheme of things we are meant to do business. I don't like you. Your Nana in Poughkeepsie helped me and my mom. She's no more than your fat grandma."

"We were never close, like Grandpa. He's on the machines in Vassar Hospital. Nana looked after Nana. She ignored us kids."

"Or you ignored her."

"We did."

"That's the way life is. I help you for a relative you care nothing about."

"You don't care for no one. You're a cold character like your dad."

"And you're a failure like your dad."

David tried to get up and leave the stacks, where Kallini blocked the tunnel of books.

"Hear my offer. I need someone to buy boxes of cigarettes and tech stuff from an army PX. You look enough like Early Hayze to use his card. Buy the goods and there's a thousand dollars each time. I'm sorry about Early and Barb and Kady too. She's my sister. Her and her mom I dearly miss, but Bontecott cut me out."

"What goes around, comes around."

"Agreed. Only you do a few favors for The Brotherhood, and we'll make an arrangement. The Bontecott farm will be yours. Who knows, maybe you and Kady, with some backing, can make a go of it."

David hated Kallini, but he listened. He couldn't help himself. Do one deal and he'd be free and easy. Kady was gone. That ship sailed. He had no money, no job, and winter came early."

"Listen Morpheys, think it over. I enlist your help for The Brotherhood. And one's got to live too. We got much in common, and you know it. I got Turkish friends on hold till the new year. The holidays are a window of opportunity. Afterwards closed. Little black market transaction, that's all. Help us and help yourself. Here's the number. Hell, we don't have to like each other to do business."

94

Beer Hall Putsch

Kallini was gone. David couldn't work anymore. Thinking what to do, he walked to the museum. Late afternoon wandering the lit corridors of the AltPinoctek. His mind soared with the apocalyptic paint of Albrecht Durer's Four Horsemen. The same fauvist paints the Impressionists used David saw in Mathias Grunewald's cruel colors of crucifixion. The German masters of the Renaissance unnerved him.

On special exhibition was a Norwegian painter, Edvard Munch. One painting called the Scream stuck in his mind. Ladies in white with flowing dresses and silken parasols. They cross the bridge. Away from view in a far corner of the perspective, a slump shouldered man up tight in his gentleman's suit. His close-up face whorls in worry. His form crucified with turn of the century angst. The Scream crossing the bridge. An image engraved in fresh ink on the woodcut of David's mind. His inner tableau was too impressionable. This was no Pont Mirabeau.

To finish his paper, David returned to his chamber to capture the transcendent moment of the Scream. In the hallway he met Dawn and Judy, the other boarders, come home to dress for an evening at the Lowenbrau and steins of beer. He spoke to them once in passing. With them was Jesse from Wells College. Jesse stayed with her brother from Chase, which had business in Europe. They were all on a ski trip to Bavaria.

"David's your name, right? Frau Huber said you're here for school."

The girl asking had shaved brows above her soft, unsettling eyes. Crossed eyes made her delighted smile a bit crooked. Jesse had to go see her brother for the evening. She hugged David and said maybe she'd see him at The Lowenbrau.

"I hope so, Jesse."

"Go home. Kady needs you."

Jesse left with that advice.

"So what are you really doing here?" The cross eyed girl asked him, then smiled. "Jesse says her brother works for a group called Cointelpro. Not bank work but intelligence."

"Me too. I'm working intelligence. And finishing my senior thesis. And staying warm and far away from the war in Asia. I'm here because the Draft's back there. Excuse me, you must be Dawn."

"I am, and she's Judy."

"I'm Jude Becket. Listen, I heard Nixon intends to end the Draft with the New Year? Volunteer if you want, but it's over."

"The Draft's over, Jesus? I'm drifting. Good news then."

Jude was a waif with black hair clipped close to her ears. She didn't smile and her green eyes pecked holes in one's confidence. Astounding news, if true about the Draft.

"Come with us to the Lowenbrau and celebrate," Dawn said.

"Why not celebrate? Ding dong, the goddamn draft is dead."

He didn't believe the news, but it was possible. Tall girl Jude had reasons in her look why he shouldn't come with them. Difficult to read the Radcliff type. In his denim and workshirt he wished he had a thousand bucks.

The three of them paraded the streets toward the refurbished oldtown of two level stores. Second floors, red-shuttered, jutted out like Tudor homes. Allied bombers leveled Munich like Berlin, and the Barvarians rebuilt the oldtown in 16th century style. No bombed black Marienkirche. No modern high rises of steel and glass, cold and cost conscious, like Prussia's military gone modern. All was Bavarian hospitality. Moonlit flurries offered a Christmas charm.

"To the beer halls then, Dawn. Let's quaff a few steins to your ski trip."

"Come skiing with us, David."

Dawn gave him a sly look from her crossed eyes. He liked her. Much as he distrusted the Radcliff girl. Clipped hair of a hippie chick, and none of the naiveté. He told Dawn he had no money for a ski trip and he couldn't ski.

"Try it. The cold, the speed, the views are out of sight. You'd love it."

"I would. But I got a paper to write and little money. When I go broke, I return to my Paris job."

"Why not quit dodging the draft and go home?"

Like Jesse advised. He looked at Jude and she at him. Something told him she was a real debutant. They took their huge steins of beer to a table with two guys, who knew them. Part of their group. The guy looked familiar with his blond hair and blue eyes, like a California surfer, bleached hair from the sun. It was Hamilton's Stephen Hancock, the quarterback who took the position from him without a tryout. Now he was on the European tour, working for Jesse's brother, onto a career in high finance. David realized he was Jude's boyfriend.

Other guy Dawn introduced from Boston College and he played football as a defensive tackle. He sat with squared shoulders and bottled forearms grasping his stein. He was the size of Bill Cougar, but all cocksure and arrogant. Unlike them, he'd been a football star.

David was odd man out. He drank his dark stein of beer, all of it. Dawn was with the damn football jock. David had to buy a round of beers since they bought for him. Then take off. Huge steins of dark beer.

Football jerk talked to the girls about the price of oil going up and gas lines. There were delays for them on the ski trip. Things didn't run smooth and they complained. Ugly Americans.

"Hey, until the Arabs open up the oil business we should bomb them like the Gooks in Nam."

Their remarks directed at David with his long hair. Jude told Mr. Football about the draft. And David learned Boy Wonder's parents were in the military. Steve never told him. David didn't use the oil in his room. Frau Huber said older people made sacrifices. So these were students for Nixon. Insiders who found jobs open to them. David decided after a few remarks he'd stir up critical thinking.

"Bombing the Arabs, you got to be kidding. We Americans got half a million troops in Vietnam, our CIA in Chile, Cointelpro tracking down the Weathermen, and now bomb the Arabs. We deserve a wake up call. Like the boycotting of buses in Montgomery woke up the Southern crackers. How many imperialistic messes do we have overseas before we wake up? Learn the lesson we can't control our small world after all. Learn to see matters in a global perspective. We people in the United States should be good citizens of the one world we share. Spiritus mundi."

David got their attention with Kallini's term. Talking up lightened his load. Dawn's crossed eyes mystified him. The football star Don, looked at David and back at Dawn.

"Where'd you girls pick up this jerk? What do you say Steve to this bullshit?"

"He's a jerk who quit the football team."

"Because coach picked you and you did shit to deserve his choice."

"Now you're dodging a volunteer draft. What kind of asshole, are you Morpheys?"

"Not an asshole who has everything given him. Like taking that cool chick Jesse to bed in the same room where Douglas slept. You know he tried to kill himself. You know he ended up killing your frat friend, Walter?"

"Don't talk shit about Walter. And that loony's where he belongs, in an asylum."

"You helped put him there."

"Bullshit."

"And how did you get Jesse into bed when she slapped you the first time."

"Her brother straightened her out. We work for Chase in the City. And she's with him on the ski trip so you can ask her."

"I should."

"Hey don't be so cool and radical. We know you're just another hippie asshole."

David had the idea he'd been gone from the States too long. Or not long enough. Time's change. Where were these guys coming from? They made him look small. He looked into Don's eyes, opposite on the line of scrimmage. And Boy Wonder from Groton, the quarterback who stole his position.

"Say, you two jerks come here for Christmas skiing, and a little inconvenience at the airport bothers you. Anything money can't buy or muscles can't bend to suit you, pisses you off. Do me a favor and don't blame me. Blame Nixon who you elected and blame your goddamn country."

Don spoke to Boy Wonder, and didn't even look at David.

"You are right, he's an asshole."

"You dumb jock, you're the asshole."

Don pushed up his shoulders with his forearms and glared at David.

"You get your ass out of here before I put you through a wall."

Months invisible in foreign eyes and magnified in his own got to David. This was America making his life hell. All American Boy Wonder whose life was made because his father made a lot of money. Good enough. David tossed his beer into Don's face. In return, David got hit with a fist on his forehead and blacked out.

95
Take Kallini's Offer

David came to. Snow fell in the tram-filled streets. He walked out the heavy doors, aware his wits were gone. The ski trippers got kicked out too, and left him alone. He got a concussion in freshman football, same thing. He saw everything, nothing made sense, and he heard nothing at all. He woke to the sound of a car roaring past him like a snorting animal. He sat on the steps of the Alt Pinoctek and let the large flakes of snow melt cool on his forehead. Snow flurries fell eerie in the moonlight. Beer ate like acid into his convulsed stomach. He hadn't eaten since breakfast.

He felt the bulge above his eye. He saw himself disfigured. The stone steps turned cold. It must be late. He couldn't tell. His watch was gone. Only when he walked the six blocks back to his apartment and got under the goose down comforter did he start shivering. He shook a long time. He woke to each shake, rattle, and roll of the tram screaming past his window. It was close enough to reach out and touch.

Early morning he regarded himself in the mirror. He saw a gash on his forehead and blue around the blistering wound caked with blood. His eyes were clear, untarnished. Glad tidings, to see and not be seen. The landlady wanted to clean his room at ten. He told her of his late night in the beerhall. The girls, Frau Huber said, were up and gone. She wasn't pleased.

At three in the afternoon he went to the student restaurant for a sausage, roll, and beer. He was better and somewhat worse. His stomach turned queasy, like food lodged below his throat. The girls really were gone. Just as well. How stupid his beerhall putsch. No reason for the brawl. With Kallini, he had reason. What fight? He got punched out. He lost the better part of his sanity. Why spend Christmas in Munich? Finish the paper. Spend his money. Make a decision.

Take Kallini's offer. Why it would be like getting on with his life.

Why drift any longer without a draft? Kallini's offer would be a first real job. Like an adult job where one cashes in his idealism and takes the money on the table. Maybe it's not right, but it's what an adult does. Put away his college thesis with all its foolish ideas. Like Jesse sleeping with Steve Hancock. For a brother at Chase and Cointelpro connected with Steve's family in the military. Kallini offered a place at the table for David Morpheys. Or better, Kallini offered a chance to blow up the whole house. Disturb the peace of Kallini's spiritus mundi. At Christmas, no less.

That evening with the Freres radio playing concert music, he sat writing Kady. He said why he left for Berlin and why Munich, and why none of his travels made sense. He imagined their raising a child. She should have told him. As cold settled into his room, his head throbbed.

David felt more and more foolish. He watched men and women enter the couples bar across the street. Shades drawn, he stared at the wall and saw a cool congress of ghosts doubting his intentions. Chamber music played a cello piece, melancholy Bach, long strings groaning low. Rabinski's music. The tram rumbled, shook it up, the street and the houses, shouted holy hell, every half hour. Leave the consolatory letter until tomorrow. Get out of this place. The letter confused matters.

Low on money, David liked the idea of a couple beers at the Schwartkatz. Money gone was good reason to get rich or go home. Easier to face than a failure of the will, a crippling of the conscience.

"Ein Bier, bitte."

His small table stood by the window, well lighted by the streetlamp, warm and cozy compared to the steady drone of snow blanketing the tramway. Now the letter to Kady got easier to think about. All the devious twists their love took were mistakes made. Transcendent moments, shared journeys, and a situation or two tinged with tragedy. His letter had scope and perspective, unlike snow covering their tracks, from dawn to dawn, when night was falling in a foreign land. Return and make things right. Have another glass of dark beer and see things as he'd like to see them. Hope dwells eternal.

"Guten Abend, mein Herr. Auch ein Bier fur mich?"

A big blond woman sat down, crossed her legs in her black miniskirt, and made conversation.

"Ya, warum nicht. Zwei Bier und wir konnen Deutsch sprechen."

She rose v-necked with a braless bosom, heavy sodden breasts pink-tipped and smeared with a coin of mud. How could he not gaze on her? She returned with two steins of beer and sat next to him. Her legs uncrossed close to his own. Her hair colored the cornsilk blond like Kady's, only roughened by the harsh light. Her face had a photograph's beauty, the lines drawn neatly with lipstick and eyeshadow. But the lines didn't move. She really didn't smile since nothing was amusing.

Christmas was business as usual. The bones of her high cheeks and flat chin hardened. The cleavage of her breasts, and the crossing and uncrossing of her legs invited him. He looked on her and drank his beer. She stroked him under the table, getting a rise from him, then no response. Her hardness disarmed him. He made a mistake looking for solace in a garish bar and blond ambience.

"Ich kann du nicht interessieren?"

Her tone was formal as a clerk in a store.

"Nein, aber danke, und gute nacht."

Twenty marks for the time left him nearly broke. He deftly left the Schwartkatz, cold in his decrepit suede jacket. He walked Grabenstrasse to the train station. The swan's down of snow disguised the seedy section of town. As he watched the streets fill up with snow he recalled Robert Frost, old man at once calm and remote from him. He longed for home where they have to take you in.

The station crowded with Turks in headdress and cream-colored darkness. All wisemen and cutthroats drawn to the glowing warmth of this starless night. Bent toward Bethlehem. The moviehouse played Kung Fu films. Mongol hordes, oil rising in price, and Christmas crucified in the Middle East. Attaturk stood against his backdrop of world news.

"You with the long hair. Kallini needs to know if you help us with army supplies. He needs to know soon. Tomorrow at the latest."

David shook his head, opened his palms, and gave no answer. He went back to a cold crypt of a room, mindful of two bottles of beer on the window ledge. He drank them and fell asleep under the goose down comforter. One last night of sound sleep, like the dead.

96
Christmas Eve

Next morning he saw the blue aerogramme, wafer thin, beneath his door. Kady's latter precluded sending his own. He piled up the desk of books barricading his withdrawal. It was a neatly printed type from the Bennet School, almost business-like, very formal. It covered only part of a page. Flee to the Alt Pinoctek and read it there, but one look entranced him. Closure on a type-printed page.

"The last thing I want to do is write you at Christmas, but I must set my life in order and let you worry about you own. I never told you I was pregnant. You never offered a reason to tell you. Your life centers around travel and books, not me. You have a life, but you also have mine.
   You are too self-involved. I believed Kurt cared for me like a brother. He told me to abort the baby. What's done is done. It was a terrible thing to do, but life has to go on. As you always said, every man is his own minister. Make your amends too. Then go on with your life.
   My Grannie Lonigan died in Dalhart. She liked you and maybe if we settled down on her Texas farm we'd have made a good couple. She was a nice old lady raising eight children and living to eighty. I needed you here when she died and you weren't. I asked you to return and you didn't. Now don't. Or don't return for my sake.
   I set my life in order and do what's right. At the Bennet School where I tutor French, I met a nice teacher. He's older and responsible and he loves me. We are going to be married, so again, don't come back to America on my account. Return for your own reasons. I wish you luck, get on with your life, and say goodbye for good."

David read the letter a second and a third time and with each reading came the sense of finality. All the good times and their memory lost meaning. They haunted him the moment they were over. A part her, a part him, and no part us.

Leave the room in search of answers. For years he gazed into eyes with questions, a inquisition of humanity, and no reply. Now his gaze burrowed out and in, twice insistent, brief candle burning at both ends. So many people: corner salesmen, last minute shoppers, parents lingering over children, old people bundled against the cold, foreigners turbaned and foreigners like him, drawn like magnetism to the crowds, sizzling like sparklers in the vortexes of his brain, clutching at his heart for sympathy. His gaze lit into the eyes of a kindred spirit, held on tight, and she spoke to him.

"Everything all right, mein Herr? You are distressed."

"Distressed as the next person, schone madchen. Why speak to me in English, here on a Munich street?"

The telepathy surprised David.

"I guessed you are American. You asked for help. No words mattered. My name is Gretchen and I belong to a Christian group. Come tonight at seven. Several English speakers come regularly. Please come, will you?"

Gretchen handed him a business size card with the address printed. Then she was gone. David promised to join their meeting. It was Gretchen's face moving him. Her braided brown hair and eyes soft as lakewater, very blue and transparent, not listless. A plain face, save for the eyes and braids, and the radiance. She left him like a messenger. She had the Jesus high. She caught him at the right time, that was all.

He searched out the street and located the two story residence up above Munich, a half mile from the oldtown. No sign said Christian fellowship, and he saw no connection between Gretchen and this home. The search took a couple hours of the afternoon. Sun set with blood red brilliance.

David returned through a factory section of town. In a tiny park he watched ratty kids garbling in Italian. A harried old grosmutter sat on a bench. Thick stocking legs like his Nana. When an urchin stole her knit cap, she shouted curses on them, and they scampered off. She ran after one with her cap, and another pushed her sprawling on the pavement. She begged for her woolen cap. The four mongrels laughed. She cursed them and swung her pocketbook. One got smacked and he came in punching. It was a horrible scene.

David watched too long, ashamed. He came to help this grosmutter. Ten year old kids spread out, except the one punching. David grabbed the kid, but she swung the pocketbook at his sore head. He snatched away the pocketbook and chased back another urchin, who gave him four fingers off his chin, ah fungoo.

He gave the grosmutter her pocketbook, but she cursed him too in German. He set it down and walked off. What else could he do? More verbal warfare and she sat back on the bench, exhausted. Two blocks away David saw the kids tracking him. Not until he reached the crowds of oldtown did they leave him alone. The street bustle exhausted him too. It got cold with sunset. But in his room he found the oil heater stirring waves of warmth and on his desk a tray of fresh cookies. His landlady Frau Huber came in.

"So, Herr Morpheys, Gute Christus Tag. Konnen Sie zu Kirche heute abend mit uns, wenn ich bitten darf?"

"Danke. Aber ich gehe zu sehen eine Freunde."

"Gehe zu Kirche, Herr Morpheys."

"Ya. Danke fur die kuche. Zehr gut. Danke Frau Huber."

"Gute Abend, denn."

Her face filled with Christian goodness. She didn't understand his solitude, especially on Christmas Eve. He sat listening to an army station nearby. Why not go and buy what Kallini wanted? A farm for family pride. A thousand dollars for material needs. Kallini knew what a person wanted. It doesn't take much. Life isn't worth much. He dozed on the bed listening to Christmas music. He awoke to a dark deserted house. His heart was empty, a dead lump. Weariness was all around.

Silence broke with the seven o'clock roar of the tram below his window, always on time. David was free of the ties that bind. Despite the warmth it was an empty room. He sought escape from his captivity, to elude the turmoil of his soul. Wrongdoing for which he'd never atone. Time hung heavy. Radio program turned to static, books to closed passages, and writing he had nothing to say.

He stared in shame at the Schwartkatz Bar with its own Christmas cheer. He walked the streets for the holiday fanfare and solemn churches. His heart ached for Kady. He found the Catholic church of Frau Huber. The stained glass glittered in glory with its scenes of shepherds and still waters. The up and downs of the church service confused him. He sat with unquiet thoughts. He saw Frau Huber and she saw him leave.

David tramped the decorated town, up the poorly lit hill streets to the residence listed on the card. The sky was without moon or stars, blackness overall. The home possessed a small lamp above the cellar entrance. The sign said Wilkommen. He wanted to turn and leave, but go where? His room waited. He entered. Converts sat around a large table, or aimlessly in chairs. Head of the table sat a young man about his age, with a black head of hair and beard, carefully cut, who spoke with a fellow turned away from David.

"Gruss Gott, mein Herr."

"Gruss Gott. Ein Gretchen…"

Then he couldn't recall the word for "invited".

Black haired youth with his riveting eyes and an easy manner spoke in English.

"Gretchen left for home after the seven o'clock service. Please stay and talk."

He listened as Heinrich counseled the bent over person, back turned to David. His eyes accustomed to the low lights and he understood most of the German.

"Listen," Heinrich said. "We all undergo trials of the spirit, depression so deep only Jesus helps us ascend the abyss. Call on Jesus and He will calm your nerves. You will be of service to Him as He to you."

Heinrich ate deliberately from a bowl of grapes, as the listener slumped further into his chair. Others in the room passed upstairs with only four in the basement. A red-haired person with bad acne talked across the table like an inquiring attorney.

"You wish to come to Jesus, do you not?"

"Yes, but I can't find the strength."

"You must make an effort. Lift your eyes to see. Lift your spirit to find Him."

"Yes, I try."

Heinrich had a fervent look eating grapes, listening to the boy's complaint. He was like a doctor with a crowded waiting room. The more people converted to Jesus increased his practice. But his skill lacked challenge with the poor soul slumped in the chair. Heinrich's eyes bore into the boy.

"Listen Johann. You need a task to do, some task to take your mind from its selfish concerns. Go to the Bahnhoff. Look into faces with the same look as your own. You will see faces, I assure you, which look as worried as you are. See yourself as you are seen. Then I want you to stop that person and ask to be of assistance. You will find solace in the knowledge others suffer as yourself. Such is the condition of man, until he opens his heart to God and seeks salvation in Jesus, our Lord. You will benefit from this task. Go now."

David tensed up as Heinrich finished. It was time David made his confession. Then ask for atonement. Johann slumped over. Heinrich got up and spoke to Gottfried.

"Continue with Johann. I go upstairs for dinner."

Heinrich reminded him of Kurt Kallini, taking charge of human souls and letting them go. He was too good. The teacher gone, David chose obscurity. No trial by confession. He left quickly and night turned coal black and bitter cold. Winter sky hung low over the hill. Go see Kallini.

97
The Bottom

The half hour walk across town wearied him. A swollen face from a fight with Mr. Football. A queasy stomach from Frau Huber's plateful of cookies. See the turk at the station newsstand. Do the simple job. He went for a paper and saw Kallini sitting beside the turbaned clerk.

"Good to see you. I didn't want to come up Grabenstrasse."

Kallini's eyes surged with their dark enthusiasm. He was the salesman and the ghost that haunted his dreams.

"Kurt, I could sure use the money, that's clear."

Why did he start that way, as if he meant to refuse Kallini's offer. It was Kallini so intent on him saying yes. But he said no. A slipknot of incalculable chance, and he said no. Maybe the project became too real. To use Early's ID card. To enter a PX like the one at Ft. Dix where David visited his brother Robby. To purchase a shitload of cigarettes and hi-tech equipment and look innocent of all pretext. Hell, he couldn't do it. Early couldn't do it after the one time.

"Truthfully Kurt, I'm not your man."

"You're kidding me. You make me wait around this ice cold city until Christmas and tell me you can't do it. Okay, let me be straight with you. The Brotherhood needs it done. I'll give you five thousand bucks and afterward you take the money and run. Think about it. Enough to live a year, write your thesis, and live free and easy."

"I thought about it too long."

"You're like your father, Morpheys. Bontecott fired your father because he didn't make the grade. You will always want what you can't have, and you can't have it because you're too f____ afraid to do what needs doing."

David got mad. And he knew that was Kallini's intent.

"And you're a bastard to talk that way about my dad. You're like

∞ 424 ∞

your father, Bontccott. I saw him tall and thin in his white Cadillac. His sophisticated manner, his cynical tone of voice. Christ, you too deserve each other."

"And Kady wrote you a Christmas letter with hugs and kisses."

David stared. "Damn you, damn you."

"Yes Morpheys. But I'm a worse bastard than my old man because I'm willing to do what needs to be done. Better and worse than his lily white business of cutting corners. The whitewash. And you, Morpheys, are so much less than your old man because you do nothing. Cross the line. Do what needs to be done."

David wanted to hit Kallini, like Vichy, like Paris after Kady told him of the abortion. He wanted the big money too. But he shook his head, much as it hurt.

"I can't decide tonight."

"Make the damn decision. After Christmas there's no reasonable way to walk into a PX and purchase what we want. My connections are on hold. Time's up. What do you say?"

"For Christ's sake I'm not doing it. For my family's sake, and for my own sake too, I won't. I won't do it because I don't dare do it. There's a wall one cannot climb over and live with oneself. Call it conscience, but it's nothing so high and mighty. I'm just not your man."

David turned and walked away. Kallini yelled after him. David passed Johann. He knew like Gretchen he looked for a lost soul as troubled as himself. David ignored his salutation, to go with God.

"You're going to do it, anyway, and make something of yourself."

David walked faster, not out of fear, not from indecision, but simply to go the route he'd chosen. Up the empty street, snow fell like cold confetti along Grabenstrasse. The club Schwartkatz shouted in high spirits. Hollow inside his soul, he ignored the shivering which quaked his stomach. His room awaited him.

Frau Huber and husband were in bed. His room had no heat. Either the oil used up or the Frau turned it off. Kady's letter was nowhere to be found. Like her. David shivered among the debris of his baggage. Ten o'clock and the tram hurled its passengers below the window and shook the house to its foundation. It was coming. Coming for us all.

David stared down to the tram tracks, longingly. Here was his imposing moment. He screamed without a voice.

There was irresistible pull downward to the tracks. His will unstrung. He opened the window, shivered, then stopped. Nothing snapped, but some fixed strength let go, like the banks along a raging stream, which floodwaters take away. David saw he lifted the window. Falling twenty feet down to the tracks, the train finished the job. He saw the action as possible, not willed or chosen, but compelled by spiritual collapse. He saw how terrible the fall. Perfect tense, as if an action completed.

Kady had a doctor's prescription for darvon. A Gobelin doctor gave them to her, and Kady left them in her big canvas bag. He took them, not too many, but enough to make him sleep the night. He could not do what Kallini wanted done. He could not be Early Hayze. He could not do wrong to be rich. He could not leap into the night nor lose his soul. He was not a great man or a good man. And what he could not do, he didn't do. Hier stande ich. Ich kann nicht anders. Tomorrow began his journey home.

For years David Morpheys sought the bottom. That's what his search for knowledge was about. He used his time and used it up. Down to the bottom like a stepdown of bass notes on a rock song. Heaven reaching guitar, the base burrowing underground. Guitar in the sunshine, base in the shadows.

David found the bottom he sought. He crossed a border into uncharted territory, too personal for the mint of public maps, and too personal for the world of human endeavor: the bottom. It's unfair the bottom falls out, but a fact. From the bottom, glory be to God in the highest.

98
Carpetbag

David woke Christmas morning. Had he overdosed like Early Hayze? The tram shook him up. He lit a cigarette and watched the smoke. His conscious mind out there, and his physical self in tow.

He packed and said goodbye to Frau Huber. She regretted his departure, but it's best to be home for the holidays. Lugging baggage caused him to sweat and his swollen forehead hurt. The train to Paris didn't leave till evening. The turbaned Turk saw him from the newsstand. If Kallini wanted him, let Kallini find him. He parked his bags in a locker. He paid his way into the movie to avoid Johann lurking in the station.

In the dark his eyes bulged red like a rodent at night. He wanted to get lost in the flickering cascade of gallant forms. The film was a Kung fu phantasm. Orientals vaulted twenty feet to deliver blows. Such leaps of faith defied gravity and David's power to suspend disbelief. He watched anyway, knowing he wouldn't sleep until he got home, far away, across countries and continents.

After the movies he spent time eating brotchen and dark beer, drank coffee, smoked a Dunhill. Luxurious smoke, thick and scented like the alluring entrance to the Kasbar den of iniquity. David sat with the Balkan populace, refugees headed home after a stay in Munich, their Mecca of employment. In this dark, brooding poverty he strained to keep his wits, not Aryan superiority, just humble sanity. The Turk sold papers and Kallini wasn't around.

The Teutonic loudspeaker announced "das Zug nach Paris auf Bahn ein und zwanzig." David hoisted the burden of his backpack on his shoulders. He lugged his carpetbag of luxuries, books and radio, clothes and blues records. The train on track 21, he loaded his pack on the wall bars and returned to the concrete for his carpetbag. The compressor doors slid irrevocably shut.

He looked through the smudged dust of the door window. Clench fisted he hammered the door and ransacked his brain for language: my Kaste, warten bitte, Achtung, Halt! What worth are words? Ringing of hysterical silence echoed in his soul. The stern steel bounds of this moment closed.

Down on the platform his bag carried his worldly belongings: ticket, cash, passport, the last vestiges of his identity. He pounded the doors, but controls resided in the distant engine. German efficiency gripped him in tow. Pleading to other passengers, he saw to his horror the same Ellis Islanders he sat among in the waiting room. The Slavic languages spoke full of K's and guttural slurs.

"Woher gehen wir, Woher, Woher?"

"Nach Budapest," answered an elderly man. Hell opened its gates, with no escape on the journey east.

He looked back to the station concrete, and his carpetbag was gone. His fate to travel the wrong direction till he leapt from the train. He had no strength to protest. Inexorable ride on laid rails of a journey east, away from home. Filament line of his sanity stretched taut, as if hooked onto a hoary snapping turtle, jaws open, viperous tongue alive in a deep dark hole. David heard a scream humming inside the tolling bell of his brain, and no voice. The Turk selling papers walked to the train door and put a Munchen Zeitung on the concrete step. Then went back to his business.

Time passed as David stared down. The air-compressed doors hushed him. He breathed and they opened. The train into the Balkans had been early. The paper contained ticket, cash, and passport. Nothing more. David heard the train nach Paris across the platform. Danke, mein Gott. He left his worldly belongings. Kady's carpetbag was gone. The cornucopia of good things zippered shut. He was beaten. Get to Paris and fly home.

In Paris impeccably dressed Christian drove him to Orly Airport. He was late. David arrived seconds to take off and ran with his backpack up an endless corridor. He ran anxious not to miss the plane. Somehow he made it. The flight took forever and no time at all. Imposing moments had staunched his flow of time.

99
US Customs

He waited in the US customs line. He saw Kady and her mom coming in on a domestic flight. A coincidence like first they met. She didn't want to see him. Her letter made that clear. Her mom needed to sit down. Kady saw David and came over to him. On opposite sides of customs.

"So you decide to come home. I wish you came a month ago. I needed you when Grannie Lonigan was dying. Now she's dead. I wanted you with me, not my mom."

"But your letter made it clear it's over between us."

"I never wrote. I'm bad with letters, sorry."

"Your letter said Grannie was dying and you're engaged to a Bennet teacher."

"All true Morpheys, but I never wrote you. Never write bad news at Christmas. It wouldn't be right. Sounds like something Grannie would say. Or Marie Montfort acting upon right and wrong."

"You're set then?"

"Yes, I'm set. Time to teach French, get married, and raise a family. Like Grannie Lonigan, a life worth living. The Bennet teacher loves me. Responsible man and we want to raise a family. The time is right. Old person dies and a baby is born."

"You're okay then?"

"Yes Morpheys, I'm okay, you're okay. Buy the book."

"Luck to you, Kady Bontecott."

"Luck to you, David Morpheys."

"Kallini's typed letter, you think?"

"Him again. Bye David. Under different circumstances."

Kady held open her palms and tried to smile. Her mom needed her.

100
Father in a Fallen Land

Good to see her one last time. Time it took for US Customs to search through his backpack, suede coat, suitjacket, and up and down the shame-ridden limbs of his body and soul, Kady was gone. She escorted her mom outside JFK and took a taxi to the Hilton. David wished her well.

It was late afternoon, nearly dark with the dying year and winter's first snowstorm. He signaled for a taxi to Grand Central. One was already full and sped past him. A door swung open and out slid his carpetbag, Kady's carryall. Flattened canvas. Nothing in it, but a deed signed over to him for the Bontecott farm.

David Morpheys sat in the last train out of NYC north to Poughkeepsie. It was a bad snowstorm. He listened to his lungs gasp and lit another Dunhill. He sat with Kady's carpetbag beside him. All he had of her. And the deed to the Bontecott farm. Kallini delivered. All this rigamarole of imposing moments fixed in his mind. Moments explode all proportions. Since the moment he stared from his Grabenstrasse window with uncontrollable longing at the street concrete and steel track of the approaching tram. Munich tracks carried him home.

He sat aware of staring. Like years, tall tenements of the Bronx departed by vertical corridors in time to the rankle of track and train. Two story homes lined the plateau along the steel fenced ridge, their backs turned to the tracks and their doorsteps to communities of Yonkers. Snow and the winter curtain of sundown slept monotonously on the land. Over was the war for him.

Morpheys stared at a worker standing up front. His sinewed fist, like a snapping turtle's head, gripped the lusterless chrome of the control bar. Metro, boulot, dodo. The worker like David's dad looked over the cheap colors of the Daily News. His jowls bristled with two day's growth. His lips were askew. His jaw lacked molars. His eyes were keen and his stare stubborn. Father in a fallen land, I've come home.

The next day he sent Kady her big canvas bag with the deed inside, and looked for work.

Hidden TRAX

1

It was twenty years ago today. Twenty years, David looked around and they were gone. He moved from New York to Maine to be near his two sons. The woman he married moved there. He loved his two sons as his dad loved him. His dad he remembered fall evenings winging a football with an underarm toss, which spiraled into his hands as he cut a distant down and out. His dad the farmhand, precision toolmaker, tall man with a spade manicuring his backyard garden. Tall man whose good humor and hard work invested in his son's better days.

George Morpheys died after his son's return from France of the Parkinson's disease. The shakes racked his six foot six frame with the St. Vitus dance, which he stilled with El Dopo and alchohol and died of a massive heart attack. A season in hell and then the stillness of death. The empty room filled with David's two sons.

He loved them with the abandonment of self his dad gave him. But the ties came undone and his wife moved them to Maine. David left his job teaching at Greenhaven Prison and found a job teaching in Caribou and lived in an old farmhouse nearby. Winter was his companion when he completed his End of the Sixties story, which rewrote his college thesis.

The commune of Sixties idealism failed and he and Kady Bontecott went their own way. He asked Peter Bergman why. Time was a few years afterward. Peter married Cheryl and David visited them in Westchester, forty miles from the prison he worked. The Seventies like fog settled in. Peter slouched in a worn chair, cigarette smoking, as he scratched his heavy brown beard. Peter put youth in perspective. He pointed the cigarette like Early Hayze, the red tips tying knots in smoke rings, murky bubbles of thought curling to the ceiling. David listened as Peter tried to make sense of what happened.

"The whole scene was a bad one, especially after Early Hayze overdosed and crashed in those health waters of Vichy. What the hell were we doing in Vichy, France? Kurt Kallini's the guy Cheryl blames. She never liked his piercing eyes, the way they bore into a person. How old was Kallini anyway? Over thirty at least. We never trusted anyone over thirty, with good reason too. Kallini made Early's drug connections and he's to blame. Kallini was much too heavy a dude for Early Hayze, for us all."

"Maybe if we hung together," David suggested.

He tried to see reason through the smoke silken like a parachute below the apartment ceiling.

"Early Hayze needed our help, and Kady needed mine. If only we hung together. We blew it."

"No David, we never had a chance. Blame it on the war. Blame it on Kallini. Hell, Early Hayze can't be blameless. Remember when Early won the Treasure of the Sierra Madre. I said the what? The Towers, my man. He won the room lottery. Best rooms on campus belonged to us senior year. Early won the draft lottery too with a number ten."

"It was the war, always the war."

"Yes, but we lucked out with the Towers. Paradise the way we blasted the campus with music. Paradise, we were high and above it all. Then by spring Early dropped out for bad grades and joined the army. He said no draft forced him into the army. If one's car skids in snow, turn in the direction of the skid. Same idea he had to beat the draft and join the army."

"He got used by Kallini and used up."

"You're telling me. That idea of resistance from within the army, all Kallini. Then that sale of black market cigarettes, Kallini too."

"We knew what was happening, Peter. We knew Kallini and the Hayze got stoned every night in the Towers. In Vichy we could have helped. I could have helped Kady too. Time sped by so fast, and then the good times were gone. Used up."

"Forget it, we tried. We tried like hell. Kallini was much too heavy a dude for Early Hayze, too heavy for us all."

Next time David visited Westchester, Peter and Cheryl were young lawyers. Peter had no beard and wore a trimmed mustache. Furniture with deep cushions graced their fashionable brownstone in

White Plains. A thousand dollar turntable offered Crosby, Stills, and Nash in concert sound. Woodstock captured live in their apartment. No rain or mud, nor a million kindred souls.

Peter's cavernous eyes kept the same twinkle, but the ardent look was gone. Now he labeled Vichy a lame idea. Cheryl served Bordeaux wine in fine crystal. She asked him how he liked teaching in prison.

"It's a job, and no more."

It was a job with coils of razor wire scintillating along fences and lights so white they weighed heavier than the darkness. It was East Germany on his journey to Berlin. A job teaching Blacks and Puerto Ricans basic English. No more.

Peter's cavernous eyes were uneasy. Maybe it was David's presence. The Seventies wore out everything radical about the Sixties until it was just decadence. His law firm dealt in lucrative land deals sold to mall enterprises. They liked short breaks to the Bahamas and Aruba. Cheryl pushed him to this uneasy success and they split up. David married in the Seventies and his first son opened his heart.

2

When David returned home from Munich, he took the teaching job at Greenhaven Prison. He sent Kady her flattened canvas bag with the deed inside. The prison was no more than ten miles from Millbrook and the Bennet School, but he never bothered Kady Bontecott. As if a time warp displaced him, he watched time pass by like the fields out a train window. Work was heavy security, as his mind continued to wander. The intellectual vagaries of the Sixties were space exploration, without a soft landing on the moon.

Once David skipped work on a May morning and traveled by train to the city. At the Met he gazed on Renoirs and Monets and recalled the swaying green grass of the sculptured Luxembourg Garden. Noon he sat on the sunny steps and ate pretzels with a coke. Across the street he saw Kady Bontecott in a cotton dress, her straw blond hair blowing in the warm breeze. David stared, and waved to say hello. Kady squinted into the sun, started to wave, and stopped. Older guy was her husband and they filed their students onto the bus. He wasn't convinced it was Kady, but wished to believe so.

Another time after he was married, when paychecks and bills bothered him, David rode to JFK to pick up his brother returning from a business trip. As he parked by Eastern's doors, hoping his brother's flight arrived on time, Kady walked out holding the arm of her infirm mom. She wore a fashionable coat and her hair pulled back and bobbed in a knot. She looked different. Her freckles disappeared and there was no softness in her green eyes, no smile of delight.

She looked in David's car, looking for a cab he supposed, and it was definitely Kady. In the clear Christmas cold he knew it was her, but didn't wish to believe so. His picture of Kady was a dauntless girl unafraid when both tires of her VW blew out near Joplin, Missouri, the girl with the excited freckles and strings of straw hair in her eyes, the girl hitching a ride with him over the Alps, and the girl waking to

Sunday service at Woodstock. He liked to remember her that way.

Chance encounters failed to fit his fantasy of youth. Memory fired brief candles. Ghosts of former selves cast shadows on our lives. His end of the Sixties was like a St. Peppers tape of songs he played beginning to end, over and again.

3

Twenty years ago his weird collection of poems and lunatic writings made up his senior thesis. His professors nodded their approval, and he got on with the rest of his life. In a Maine winter he began writing. Aroostook snows recalled the white winters of western New York and Wells College. He wrote three chapters to recall Kady Bontecott. Far was near and dear in memory. From his hill across the valleys he saw south to the twin peaks of Mars Hill. East was British red in New Brunswick and north was Quebec, radio francais, and hockey night in Canada. Steam fluked from the Ft. Fairfield potato factory. Ten miles lit the city lights of Caribou, the dazzle in the darkness. There was Loring Air Force Base, its watchtower tracking 747's along his south-north axis road for soft landing. Otherwise he was alone.

He recalled Kady Bontecott. The sky full of stars mirrored her straw blond hair and face full of freckles. His star map tuned to the music of the spheres. In winter Orion the warrior strode the skies above his barn, and the dipper emptied snow into the valley. Was Kady out there, at her Millbrook address? Did she stay there like the stars stayed in their ancient patterns. He sent her a letter with chapters of their story, and there was no reply to appease the rigor of his heart. Then he sent chapters to Peter Bergman, to an address in the Hamilton register. Peter replied, come to the twenty year reunion. Peter liked the story and said to send him more.

David wrote all winter. Winds whirled the snow, and words drifted memories, snow forms like waves on a white ocean beneath a full moon. Before David wrote to the story's end he witnessed the double vision of times changing again. The bombed black ruins of the Marienkirche told of his Berlin, while Berliners looking like him then, made merry on the Wall. Telling the past released him from the turmoil of the past.

He wrote Peter about finding peace in the whirlwind, in the whiteout at fifty miles per hour. Prodigal son, he found peace in the western world gone wrong. The cult of reason honed on the fine edge of the guillotine split hairs of aristocrats, while the science of fission spoke of final solution to the suicidal welter of tribes whirled off the Russian steppes to conquer and settle and be conquered again.

One Aryan language created the pax Romanis surrendered to the Huns and Mongol hoards until Eurasia one world under the battle ax to break the frozen seas within us. All the same race. Caucasian memory of fiery sky gods and they chased the wild boar through primeval German forests to the edge in Greece and Rome and France and England, and over the edge, sea power on which the sun never sets, an ocean frontier like space in the Twentieth Century.

Science and the splitting of the atom over the edge to ultimate destruction. Half civilized in science, the Aryans turned east to pillage and plunder in the name of the white man's burden. The old world fired awake, sleepy in their Confucian and Hindu lethargy. Sword of Islam sheathed. Aryans turned east to prosper and burn. They learned no bureaucracy to combine Ming and Manchu. The learned no Hindu conglomerate of race and religion. Aryan purity a myth that cut aggressor and his conquest. Twentieth Century like a medieval hundred years war. Learn before too late the mystery of global peace before cold war turned hot, before whiteout blew worldwide.

Prodigal son came home from the sty of racial hatred, Hun and Italian, Turk and Pakistani, home from Munich on the edge of the Balkans. He was crazy with the millennium of tribal hatred, cults of reason and cults irrational. Hitler sacrificed Europe to the image of Tamerlane the Magnificent ruling the entire land mass. David came home to the States for what else could he do, father in a foreign land, fighting wars of containment a world away with the weapons of napalm and failed regimes.

Twenty years ago then, but today the world was a better place. America mortgaged to a world in debt, wars of containment and the economy wrecked, but a new world. Russia surrendered her fear of foreign conquest, economy wrecked, and opened her steppes again.

They like empires of France and England prey to overage.

As winter waned with sudden storms and thaws, David saw the new world of the Nineties, age old dream of the world at large. One year he'd cross the Atlantic and with the Aryan word follow the Berlin road through the wall. He'd go through to the other side and travel those lands of southern Russia, to trans-Caucasian lands Jason sailed to meet Medea and Samarkand to view Tamerlane on his single slab of green jade. Tamerlane whose casket open brought a greater conqueror than he, opened the next day and Hitler invaded Russia.

David planned to travel like the Venetian, Marco Polo, through the black sands of Turkistan whose storms are the polar extreme of whiteout in Aroostook County. Onto Mongolia and break on through the Great Wall into the fertile plains of the Yangtze. Or perhaps down through Islam into Kabul and the Khyber Pass, the Aryan way in the Punjab of the Indus, all the way to the Mogul minarets and splendor of Delhi, Agra, and the Taj Mahal. Come with me to the Kasbar, like his grandfather dreamed. His own dream of the journey east.

Is it all a magic dream? The commune of the Sixties idealism failed and he and Kady gone their ways. Andy with his book of Rajah India says, "Pluck your magic twanger, Froggy." And all will close half a world away. Are these times prelude to global peace, the New Millennium, or a few light years in the black sands of a hundred years war, the whiteout before the dark ages? Is the book open or the book closed on our Prodigal Time?

4

David was eager for winter to end. Return to Hamilton College for the reunion and see his good friend Peter Bergman. The photos showed his new wife Carol with a baby girl. He had a three year old on a Little Tykes racing car. David's sons were four and ten. He hoped Peter had time to enjoy his kids. He knew legal life took many nights for planning board meetings. Peter sent him a cassette instead of a letter.

"Hey Bro. Finished the final chapter on the Woodstock Generation and it brought back some good memories, and some bad ones too. I'm in NYC interviewing prospective lawyers for the firm. They're a bunch of greedy assholes coming out of school. Not one of them has a sense of humor.

I remember Early Hayze and the Treasure of the Sierra Madres, like gold dust held up to the high winds of senior year. Remember Early, our freshman guru of the open road. You and I never far from our hometowns, and here's the Hayze with tales of hitching down South for spring break. Then his stories of New Zealand. I recall his father in the British foreign service, and the Hayze telling of Borneo and Ceylon. I never bothered to separate fact from fiction. It was all the Hayze, mishandled and barbered in a Georgia jail for hitchhiking. Maybe the Hayze ran out of stories, or people who listened.

I remember clearly the time of the Hamcoll church tower, the foggy night without the foggiest idea what was happening. Just for kicks. To be above it all. I was never so scared in all my life, exhilarated but scared. He went down the lightning rod in air thick as a rain cloud. Higher than I ever been before. He went down and I followed our guru of the high life. Like acrobats in a high wire act, we were above it all.

It all made sense. The Hayze met the meaning of existence in a cloud of smoke. Nonsense these twenty years, but as I talk to these hotshots fresh from law school I think time lost with the Hayze of more value than their time is money, make it before you're thirty mentality. Some truths sought are better than BMW Beamers.

Vietnam was a sorry scene, but we fought racism by changing people's minds. There was Robert Kennedy and Eugene McCarthy, if one of them saved the day. The good died young. Our beautiful balloon burst on the jagged-edged hypocrisy of Nixon. We were close to getting it right. Or least getting at what was right and wrong. I don't know anymore …"

The tape clicked into airy silence. Then the voice returned, with a different tone.

"Hey Bro, I'm back again the next morning. Sorry I had too many beers last night and got sentimental. To be truthful, your book depresses me. I don't know. Life goes by so fast. Twenty years. They're gone. I don't know. I'm real happy and that bothers me. Carol, my new wife, is a lawyer with the firm. She's a little young for the Sixties, but she loves the music. She's off a year with the baby. She's a good mother. The boy's in nursery school. I wonder where all his energy comes from. So I'm happy, and your book depresses me.

Come to our 20th reunion, will you. We'll get good and drunk. Who knows, maybe we'll climb the chapel tower and slide down the lightning rod. I miss Early Hayze. He was an okay guy, our guru of the open road."

David liked the cassette. The fast forward and reverse put the ramblings of Peter in perspective. Once written, David's book of the Sixties reeled like a cassette for him, a number of songs, when all was said and done.

5

June, the weekend after Memorial Day, David packed a bag into his far eastern compact for a trip down Route 95. Out of the rolling hills and valleys of Aroostook, route 95 tunneled through the pine palisades of Maine into New England. An overfull moon hung heavy in the Berkshires, and west he went on the Mass Pike and the Thruway to Fran and Ollie's Utica Club. Reunion Central supplied him a college room on Kirkland's campus, and he slept until noon.

It was a windy clear day. High skies on the Hill. The old library turned art gallery called him. David stared at the painting of cloaked Ezra Pound, his hair wind-whirled and disheveled gray, his eyes hollow and Medusa dead. Old Ezra at graduation ceremonies, the old man seeking peace on the Hill. His journey east took him on a European tour, which a war made permanent. Home to die on the Hill.

Fourth floor library was David's garret apartment. He sat there twenty years ago among the steel shelves, winter cold with cracks in the window casement. He read Plato and cut tomes of Schopenhauer and Nietzsche, fourth floor of philosophy and the high life of ideas. Young dreams gave fancy to the boldest statement and the driest logic of unlived life. Then he lived a life on his journey east. He lost most all of it to Prodigal Time, all but the scenery of Paris and Berlin and Munich. All but the kind, excitable eyes of Kady Bontecott. The casement window looked out on snowy fields and fraudulent rage of foreign war. For this place in time and his good friend, Peter Bergman, he returned.

David spoke with a few acquaintances. All through college he withdrew, from the football team into the quiet rooms and catacombs of the library, into books and into himself, and withdrew altogether into the journey east. He ran though Root Glen and back through the forest preserve behind Kirkland. A good run vanquished the hazy doldrums of the overnight drive, and he slept a few hours more.

Morpheys came late to miss polite conversation over dinner. Tom Acker was late too. He cruised to McEwen in a limousine all duded up in a tuxedo. He worked for Chase Manhattan, and privately he eased channels for companies going to Japan.

"So Morpheys, you're a teacher. You guys sure got a job to do."

"And you on the inside of Japan. With their zen and samurai as businessmen."

"It's all pretty interesting, let me tell you."

"How's it go?'

"I develop connections for companies to follow. It's always the flow of influence and who you know."

"You learn the language?"

"No. Everybody speaks English, why bother?"

The alumnae president came down to check on stragglers, old Bill Henly, bald, red-faced, and corpulent.

"Morpheys, my old roomie."

"Henley, my man."

They'd been roommates in Dunham four to a cubicle freshman year and thus bonded for life. From Plattsburg, New York Henley studied local history under Chalmers.

"From Caribou, Maine then?"

David was certain that would end conversation with Henley, but no.

"I toured Maine from Bangor to Canada. Caribou is not the end of the world, Morpheys."

Then he smiled, as if speaking at a business luncheon.

"Not the end of the world, but you can see it from there."

6

David liked the sociable Henley, or anyone who eased him into conversation. In McEwen the rock hung by a chain from the second floor dining hall. A heavy merry-go-round suspended around a massive boulder, both free to swing two floors hung up on high, like the earth in orbit, and like the soul a heavy stone inside the wheel of rebirth. Karma come late to take David to dinner. Past lives play havoc with a person. McEwen was all cast foundation with waffled ceiling and red carpet over concrete floor.

Off to face the music of a reunion dinner. David saw dressed up alumnae over a dinner of chicken cordon blue and asparagus hearts. He caught sight of Peter's hand palm up, the gaunt face still mustached. The blond haired woman beside him David assumed was Peter's wife. Her long blond hair frizzed and disheveled, all yellow like cornsilk, her shoulders bare and tanned, the black gown provocative like the night. She must be beautiful. She turned, green eyes and shy smile, Kady Bontecott, lightyears away, like a comet returned. Kady laughed with Peter, as David tried to contain a multitude of emotions.

"Surprised to see you Kady. Glad too."

"Not surprised to see you Morpheys. I knew you were coming."

She held Peter's blue jacket and nudged him.

"Me and Peter got this special relationship. I'm learning life's complications, and he's my mentor to secrets of the high society."

David had no idea what Kady meant. She wasn't married to Peter, was she?

"What Kady means," Peter said, shaking off Kady's good-humored grip. "She means to say I'm her visiting professor in law school, teaching her how to do closings in real estate. The first course I teach and there sits Kady, way in the back row scribbling out contracts. I looked as goddamned surprised as you. Well almost."

"Yes Morpheys, talk about mouth gaping."

"Didn't expect to see you."

"I'm back in school again. Out of the French business and into the law."

"Good for you."

"So Morpheys, you aren't all broke up with your divorce? If you waited another year, I'd handle your case and close your estate."

As the waitress set dinner before him, David saw Kady's freckles for the first time. With age they vanished. But her face flushed and they showed up. It was the tense meeting. He reached for Kady's clenched fist.

"How are you doing?"

She smiled and covered David's hand with her own. It was a game of one-up. Kady said in a low voice that put her flightiness on hold.

"I wanted to see you guys."

Then she covered up her sentiment.

"How come you guys got such young kids? Trying to make a mark on the world before you settle down. Want my eighteen year old girl to babysit the kids? Sorry she has no time, that is, no time between dates. And she's off to Vassar next year."

Again she paused and tried smiling. She was uncomfortable.

"So how's your lovelife, Morpheys?"

"And yours, Mrs.___

David left the name blank, perturbed he'd make a mistake.

"Miss Bontecott again. Looks like we all got one strike, right Peter?"

"Yes Kady, and another chance too. David, I told Kady she should come up from her Wells reunion and see us. I met Kady at the summer session. Why I didn't tell you."

"Why, you think Morpheys' been waiting twenty years with baited breath to see me again?"

David nodded. He drank the white wine, more composed, and Kady reached over to cut off pieces of his chicken. David gave her the plate.

"So where's your wife, Peter," David asked. "Your baby okay?"

"Carol's with the baby. My father said he'd help out too."

"Like to meet her and your dad."

"Tomorrow. Say, why don't we go somewhere else, like the Inn downtown?"

"Let me finish eating Morpheys' dinner."

"You already ate the better part of mine."

"Well I was hungry. What do you guys want, to starve me. Okay I'm stuffed. Let's go drinking."

They slipped away from ceremony. Kady took the front seat in David's Nissan, her black gown wrapped too tight for her. Down the Hill they traveled into the college town. Kady drank vodkas at the Inn, and said let's go to the Rock and shoot pool. Places she recalled from David's letters. In the crowd of townies and college kids left on campus, Kady got loaded. It was fun, but Peter had to return to the hotel. No one touched on twenty years ago. Let the past alone. Let the ghosts lie easy. Now had to be enough for shadows of those warmer bodies. He didn't know why the distance in Kady. Why expect any more from her? Party and return to the lives they led. It must be him thinking too much of her too long ago.

"Peter, I got to see this chapel Early Hayze and you climbed."

"You're kidding Kady. The Hill, the Rock, and now the Chapel."

"I asked for the grand tour. Come on, if crazy then, why not crazy now?"

Kady wanted to talk about the past, but couldn't. Her daughter's choice to stay with Donald at the Bennet School betrayed her. Her daughter grew beautiful and Donald in his fifties grew fatherly, until he deferred all affection to Cathy. His crowning achievement, her admission to Vassar.

Cathy had none of her mom's sense of duty. In fact, she ignored Kady the older she got, and more beautiful, the boys treating her like some jewel of the Bennet School. Divorced from Donald, Kady stayed for a time with father at his horse farm, but he was cold as ever, moreso after Kady's mom died of osteoporosis and a bad fall. When Donald and Cathy left her, Kady felt nothing. Even for her Catholic faith. Donald's Episcopalian manner found it distasteful, and her daughter cared little for religion. Kady studied law to make something out of herself, from nothing at all.

They left the Rock, rode up the Hill to the campus, and parked behind Bristol.

"Ah Kady, you need to know the weird reasoning why we climbed the chapel. Early's father told him about aborigines in Borneo. They worship the tall trees in the forest."

"Peter, shut up. Save the lecture until we get to the chapel. Really professor, let's go."

The frontlighted chapel stood solemn in the warm night. The Commons muffled the midnight band, where alumnae of more recent years rocked out. Peter pointed to the tower above the roof's apex and said there the circular stairs come up the back balcony.

"Come on, prof, let's go inside."

"Probably bolted tight until Sunday," David said.

"Churches stay open, you atheist creep."

The sarcasm stung him. Why did Kady come to the Hill, to get back at him?

Sure enough, the doors opened wide. It was pitch black inside. Peter reached for her hand, and Kady said, "Hold on, Morpheys, Peter's taking us to his leader."

"Quiet, you infidels," Peter joked. "The Hayze told me his father journeyed into the Borneo outback with natives, some bureaucratic census job to do. The mosquitoes swarmed so thick he couldn't think straight. His father gave up and simply followed the aborigines tracking high into the humped back mountains of the island. Hours went by him all buzzing with pain until they reached lean-to's carved in the mountain forest. Streams surged on high all deafening sound."

"Tell us more, Professor."

"The mass of mosquitoes vacated the high lands, and the Hayze said his father had vision and greater hearing, even though all bitten raw and sore from the climb. Afterwards, a half native employed by the lumber company told Mr. Hayze how aborigines have hunter visions of wild monkeys, forest pythons, or mountain deer, how they become one with the forest, one with the tree of life, Aki, tree god of Indonesia. His father told Early of his vision. Early said it blew his mind. That the climb blew his mind too."

"Come on Peter, find the door to the tower," Kady whispered. "What's this story got to do with your flight into the night?"

"Peace, perturbed spirit," David said, and Kady squeezed his hand hard.

The door to the tower was locked from the other side.

"That's impossible. Locked from the other side. How did Early open it?" Kady demanded.

"He kicked it hard."

"Kick it hard."

It sprung open and up they climbed. No light at all.

"The Hayze said the tower was the tree of the chapel, up the trunk to the highest branch."

The top of the tower brought with it vertigo, a weird elevation, with no data of light and sound. Like they locked in a tomb.

"Where are we, and where's the lightning rod?" Kady asked.

Peter said the space was shuttered. Then he found the shutter locks, where the Hayze found them. The window opened to a moon rising overfull east of the Hill. The Common's band echoed. Distant and near. The drums kept beat. The lightning rod crossed the moon, a vertical plane, metal in the moonlight.

"The Hayze said the foggy night held him if the rod gave way. I followed him like a zombie."

"Early jumpstarted his soul from the doldrums of Kallini's drugs," David said. "But it lasted such a short time."

"Don't think, David," Kady said in a chanted whisper. "Just go, David. Damn you, David. For the love of God, for what we were to one another, just go."

And David, lulled by the illusion of twenty years ago, saw the tree branches bleached white by the chapel spots, and the full moon split by the rod of lightning. He saw it all. For Kady he grabbed the guide wire and metal cable and suspended in the summer breeze slid down like the aborigine monkey, to lower life, down the cycle of rebirth.

Kady came next, and Peter, each with a soul journey and a life to squander. Selves on the line of a high wire landing, all together now. Back on solid earth, Kady hugged David, her bare arms trembling around his neck. Hands raw and cut, she held him tight. Tears welled up in her eyes. She hugged them both, together in the warm summer night. June in Paris.

"I miss the excitement, really."

Her voice quavered, her arms on the two of them trembled.

"Thank you guys for the lift."

Peter smiled, shaking his head, dazed with Kady Bontecott, as he was with Early Hayze.

"If crazy then, then crazy now...I mean crazy."

"You got to go yet, professor?"

"Yes, get back to the baby. Funny how a little walk across the sky gets the blood flowing."

"Bye dude," David said, with a power handshake and a football hug.

"See you back in school, professor."

"See ya."

"I won't tell the class you're crazy. Like hell I won't."

Kady waved at him crossing the campus. She hugged David again, and they kissed, unlike other kisses, with a soulful sense of lost time.

"Take me somewhere quiet, David. I'm in no shape to drive home."

"Further up the Hill, what do you say?"

"We have an unfinished journey then, Morpheys?"

"You could say that."

7

It was warm after midnight with time before the dawn. Magnificent maple trees towered in the overfull moon: the lunar downside, the wet lawns new mowed, all the dark green foliage casting shadows on the pavement. Big canvas bag like a cornucopia, open again. Walking hand in hand after the fall, their tense exuberance mellowed in the endless night. Trees, grassy meadows, and dark blue sky. The motorless road belonged to them. At the reservoir surrounded by canyon walls and plantations of pine trees, David said let's go for a swim. Kady's antagonism was gone. The flight through the midnight air blew her cool.

"David, wherever you go, I'm with you." Kady paused. "For one night only."

"Till the dawn?"

"The unfinished journey."

Her feet in her black flats ached. Moonlight hid her raw palms and skinned ankles blistered in the descent. Kady became calm. Old friends like Peter and David eased her loss of faith. She was insecure with law school too. These guys bolstered her confidence. On the banks of the wide reservoir with the moon a silver mirror over the surface, they dangled their feet in the warm waters.

"My feet feel good, but my hands hurt. Tell me never to get crazy again."

"Never."

David took her hands and washed them in the water.

"Kady, I'm sorry the way I lost you. The way I mistreated you."

"Shut up David. It's too long ago to matter. I got an eighteen year old daughter who makes her own mistakes. Who knows what's right and wrong when you're young? We shared growing up and we had a time. Forget it."

"What's to remember then? Why do we hurt the person we love?"

"Too many questions, Morpheys, without answers. Why I wanted to ride the lightning rod. To forget and begin anew."

"Well it was a cool ride, and so was twenty years ago. If I didn't have my boys we'd take off tomorrow for the coast."

"And begin anew the journey."

"What about Kurt Kallini?"

"I should forgive him too. But I never knew Kurt well enough to forgive him."

"You never heard from him then?"

"New Years, he sent back my canvas bag with a deed signed by him to the horsefarm. Dad was happy to have the farm back, and mad when Bontecotts lost the jewelry business. At least Kallini's out of our lives for good, he said."

"Nothing else?"

"A diamond and the smell of moldy flour inside my big canvas bag. Dad was mum about that stuff. I think Kallini made a killing. Everything pointed to him and no one caught him. Dad said he had to stay out of the country. Among the caftans of Gobelin, I guess."

"He got what he wanted."

"Did you get what you wanted, David?"

"No, I wanted you. And the whole world too."

"Well we had a prodigal time." Kady paused. "I read your story and wrote return to sender. Thanks for thinking of me."

"Really. I'm always thinking of you."

"I know. Kallini never cared. He touched no one and no one touched him. You cared, David, I know that now. I think a person has to care."

"Yes, Kady. Compassion and taking care of the ones you love."

"Yes, David."

"You know, when Huey Newton got gunned down a year ago. Some bad drug deal, face down in his own blood, I thought of Kallini and felt sorry for him. The picture of an angry radical was just his front. Huey Newton's end fit the picture of Kurt Kallini."

"I guess, David."

"But I hope not."

"Me too. Whatever faith I have is one of caring and forgiveness."

"Forgive me my journey east, Kady. So many places I wanted to go. So many lives I wanted to live. There's only the one life, and I'm sad we lost it."

David sought penitence, which Kady no longer believed of value.

"Please forget it, David. You're my friend, but the past is gone. I need you now."

Kady saw the pained look in his eyes linger and subside.

"Come on, I'm going for a swim."

David helped Kady unzip her black dress, the tanned skin warm to the touch, and he held her in the moonlight. Terrible, how long desire lives on, how long he wanted her and not the mere memory. He kissed her neck where the blond hair grew soft and rubbed her shoulders and arms and held her tight.

Kady broke free and dove into the reservoir without much splash. She swam way out and yelled for him to "cool off". Out of his clothes he swam after her and she eluded him by diving under the dark water and swimming deep. Down deep underwater where darkness and death by drowning wait for a person.

"David, enough," she yelled, surfacing out of breath. "Let's go back to the shore."

The grass warm with dew sustained them, friends and lovers and two ghosts in the night, passing this time together. Make love, make love, make love. Bridge Mirabeau and toujours la joie venez apres la peine. Joy comes after sorrow.

"Thank you Kady. Like the Upanishads say. The embrace of one's soul with the oversoul, c'est l'eternite."

"Be quiet David. Be still. Your mind turns on a merry-go-round of ideas. You got a restless soul Grannie Lonigan said. Somehow the world you want is different from mine. No big deal, the difference. I take friends as they are, especially you, Morpheys."

They dressed and walked back to the road. It was lighter toward morning. Aurora was the dawn. Up the road was the high ridge of the Hill. Up there they saw light coming in the east, while the overfull moon settled down west toward Syracuse and the Great Lakes. Distant hills rolled onward like ocean waves on a calm morning in San Diego.

David recalled Bill Cougar and his community of friends. Out there survives the Sixties commune, where hills rolled like waves toward the Pacific. Beyond there the home of Early Hayze and Aki, tree god of Indonesia. The whole world is watching, the whole world is watching, more than a body can bear.

More Extra TRAX

✥

Interrogation

CODA: Prodigal Time, the 1970's.

1
A Shroud of Snow

Snow fell over western New York to wipe out radical dreams and write plans for the end of the world. Quinn took to homemade bombs. Lionel left with Barb Kelly for sanctuary with the Black Panthers. Kallini walked a winding route into Wells College to see them off. Kady came from Millbrook late and missed her best friend Barb's departure. David Morpheys arrived at Wells with decisions for the draft and what to do about it. Snow covered their tracks as time took their lapses into account. It was early in the year and late in the decade. Only time left for a requiem on what the Sixties failed to do.

What happened in this prodigal time to lose such a precious commodity? I don't know and at the time I didn't care about the drift, the doubts, and the darkness. Revolution had been in the air earlier seasons. Spring in the Sixties sang sweet songs of John F. Kennedy, a Port Huron Statement, and lunch counter sit-ins by the SNCC kids. Summers sang of freedom, love, and groovin' on a Sunday afternoon. Fall songs urged all free birds of passage to fly away before Kennedy waved, King studied, and another Kennedy shook hands, assassination, war, and hope, no more. Winter came much too early in the day, end of the decade. Storms came on without capitulation. Sturm and Drang bedraggled the youthful souls to find refuge, violent revolution, and the end to days of rage.

A Cointelpro agent questioned David Morpheys about the carpetbag he passed through customs. Nice enough guy. David worked in Downstate Prison teaching college writing courses for Marist, nights. Days it was the GED curriculum.

"We know, you personally, did nothing wrong."

"Really," David answered.

"You didn't know the contents."

"I didn't. And it didn't come with me through customs."

"No? You sent it to Kady Bontecott a few days later, then got this prison employment."

"I did. Hey, believe this or not. I waved to a cab outside Kennedy, which didn't stop. Bag flung over the taxi up a ways, I saw what it was, and took it with me home."

"Why were you solicitous of the bag?"

"It belonged to Kady. I knew that, and I got separated from my stuff back on the Munich tracks. I was glad it came back, without my clothes and stuff. Hell all that stuff, records and books and souvenirs, it weighed a ton. Now it weighed nothing. Just a bag Kady left with me when she left late in the fall. I sent it to her, it was hers, and we had lives which didn't mesh anymore. She got married. I got a job. You got concerns over an empty bag. I understand."

"But we don't understand how you lost the bag in Munich, how you found the bag in Kennedy, and what happened to your stuff and whatever stuff took your stuff's place."

"Ask Kurt Kallini. He knows everything."

"We don't have him for questioning. Last report, he's in Europe working for the Brotherhood."

"You got me without Kallini. The guy goes places you guys go. And you guys don't know what he's doing?"

"We got you sending a bag to Kady Bontecott. We got the bag with a dusting of remains, diamonds and dust, and suspect this carpetbag carried through customs the motherload of heroin and diamonds, worth well over a hundred million dollars."

"Again, you got me. I'll tell you everything I can recall."

"Take your time. We have maximum security, for the duration."

"Do I get to teach my GED and writing classes?"

"You do because I have reports to make and other cases."

"I'm staying here?"

"We have a room on this floor two doors down from interrogation. Make yourself at home."

"I don't know where to start."

"Start at the beginning."

Agent Smith clicked his recorder and it was showtime.

I simply can't recall properly that prodigal time. I recall it like yesterday, yes. Like it was twenty years ago, today. But the bliss and beauty beyond belief, the veritable heavens above our heads, that's gone. A shroud of snow whites out the sheer ecstasy like darkest night. I was young and now I'm not. All that happened I can picture down to the dearest detail. I simply can't touch those prodigal times when we had forever to live, when we took chances and made outrageous decisions, only to change our minds and do the direct opposite. Why not drift, why not dawdle? What's the difference we change our minds because there's always tomorrow? Hey, I had an Etch-a-sketch and now I don't. No more shaking the sands of time for another look, another chance, another life as lit up as it once was. That's gone. Now it's like a time graved in stone. It's like yesterday with a Berlin Wall masoned up over night. I see all the places I used to go, but I can't go there, anymore.

"What are you on drugs!"

It's not as simple as one pill or another. It was a Sixties of rabbit holes and Platonic caves. It was sunshine on the beaches baking bodies tan with surfboarders cutting the waves, East Coast and West. East Coast kept an eye on media. West Coast led lives sunbaked as hallucinations. The Sixties like America moved from East Coast to West and comprised everything in between. It was Sunbelt and Chicago, Boston and Michigan, and every bastion of the South capable of letting sunshine into the American dream. Wait a moment there. I may have stumbled on something a bit more significant than who won. May prodigal time be the American dream?

May time be as prodigal as the expansive nature of America? This place is big enough for the both of us. It's a win-win combination of the two. All created equal can mean blacks and Indians and Hispanic too. It can mean every immigrant from every part of the world, to us all, Thomas Paine's rights of man apply. You're welcome. Come over here. Make the most of your God-given talents and if you merit an extra helping, great wealth, or invention, take your fair share, as will I. In boom times prodigal waste matches prodigal progress for everything in life that matters. Didn't we have boom times, you and me, all of us this postwar generation?

All of us didn't know Depression and total war and a crippled man leading a crippled nation out of hard times, leading a nation through total war on two oceans and four continents, and like Lincoln failing to see like Moses and Martin the promised land. How could we know? It was America in the sunshine and the rest of the world in the dark. It was a world divided between superpowers, US and USSR, mirror images never seeing nothing but reflections in fear what the other might do. It was MAD. It was mutually assured destruction. Yet it was boom times too. As prodigal as proved to be the American dream of equal opportunity, coast to coast and everywhere in between, it should very well last forever. But it didn't. Winter arrived, a shroud of snow covered the land, and it's over, except for the single year, 1969.

"We don't need so much introduction."

"Humor me."

"Just the facts, Morpheys."

"Ha. Me and TV grew up together, you too."

"Get to Kurt Kallini and how you met him. Like it was."

"I got it. Tell it like it is, I mean, was, a year ago, or so."

"Continue. Another click of the recorder. Another drink of coffee from a Styrofoam cup."

Here's how it was. I came to Wells College for winter study. Okay, you know it's a girl's college on Cayuga Lake not far from Cornell. It wasn't for the girls I came to Wells. It was a French House where everybody spoke French. Least that was the concept. So I would learn French well enough to skip over the line to Canada when the draft call came. Get out of college in June, and that's the time the draft call would come. Be prepared like boy scouts, like the marines, like me. Speak French along with a house full of girls. It's like two birds with one stone.

That's what I mean. I can't really recall the desertion and existential nature of making a decision on which one's whole life turns. Go to Vietnam like a brother, who never really lived it down. Go to Canada and maybe never return to the States. Who knows really what to do? It wasn't like my dad wanted me to go Vietnam. My brother went. I went to college. Go to Canada if I had to go, well maybe that's okay too. He was a farmer married to my mom working for Bontecotts during WWII. He was exempted. His younger brother and my mom's brother too, served in action. One was a bombardier over Europe. The other convoyed supply ships to Britain until his ship went down. Dad didn't object to anything else except dropping out of Hamilton College with six months to go.

Fair enough for a father. Only he didn't know I was used up. I don't know why the end of the Sixties a young kid who played football three years of college, who studied like somebody late to academic discipline, who learned a whole lot in one hell of a hurry got used up. I wanted to learn it all. I mean Sartre and Camus, Shakespeare and Dostoyevsky, the history of the world and a language or two, its literature too. Only I came late to the party, made up for lost time, and after midnight I was pretty much used up. Take a breath, take a break, and take a semester off.

Of course, do that and dad says you never return. Do that, and I knew the draft may very well come calling. What I mean. There was plenty of "Splaining to do" like Lucy, but the crux of the problem I didn't know what to do. How do you explain to a dad who lived and died with his interest in sports I played and the college I attended and the son who would succeed where my brother didn't. I just couldn't go on, this way. And what way was that? Not his question for sure, but mine. This snowbound route to Wells along Lake Cayuga wasn't the way I was going. It was different. Snow fell like all the dark stars from heaven. The car took a skid trying to miss Kurt Kallini walking like a madman in the whiteout of Sunday noon. Wells was somewhere new. I got well over the month there. Things sorted out. Good and bad things happened, and I was better by month's end. It wasn't the end of the world. I was left alone with the off chance of seeing her again, someday soon.

Who am I talking about now? I've been talking the blues. Now I'm talking blue skies on a snowy day. Now I'm talking, mesmerized by her green eyes, hair the color of cornfields for a thousand miles west, and get me now, freckles like a smart aleck, sitcom kid across her cheeks and nose. I'm talking the first time I saw Kady Bonticott. Come to my room crabbing it was her room and saying in French so fast I couldn't follow, she was wrong and I was right, sue me, before she rushed out again. She bolted to say goodbye to Barb Kelly who was already gone. Lionel, the black dude, was already gone. Kallini stayed on to see if Cornell RYM blew up with black protest, to see if Quinn the Eskimo blew up himself and others too.

Oh yea, Kurt Kallini in long black coat, like a raven saying nevermore to travelers come to Wells, he's the dude my dad almost killed. We spun out and around. Close call, him or us, and time down the road I sort of wished it was him and him alone. You never knew exactly where you stood with Kurt Kallini. He had connections in crime, in revolutions, in the movement too. What was left of the Movement in 1969. The Brotherhood was big with him too. Run him over before he runs over you. That was a vagrant idea which came to me later. To hear him play bass guitar and sing in the cellar of the Aurora Inn. His music was like Joey Gallo's. Then he said to me, why not learn a little guitar and fill in for the drunken buffoon who left the band. His offer for a spot in the band, that was special to me. Like football had been. I'd have served my time in Nam to play in a band and Kallini knew what made people stand up and beg for a chance at destiny. He knew. He knew everything. Except something didn't register at the heart of Kurt Kallini, and I'm talking for a friend, Kady too.

Kady returned from her rush to the Townhouse, pissed Kurt didn't keep his promise to her and Barb. He waited an hour he said. So Kady returned with bags of records and a player verboten at the French House. When I tried to carry that cornucopia of all good things, her frustration pinned a nasty look on me. I played the part of suitor and bellboy, neither part she liked, and she left in a rush. The heavy bag weighed a ton. It carried all good things like her car did when it ran like it should. It was the bag she carried to Wells that Sunday shrouded in snow and it was that bag which subsumed everything in her room, empty as heartbreak and empty as eternity, when she left.

No, she didn't leave that day to follow Barb Kelly west to Oakland, California. She wanted to, but she knew Barb chose Lionel. Her journey as a misbegotten daughter of a St. Louis missionary was to show off her body and her art and make a home in some fabled San Franciscan night. It wasn't on the Haight but some hole in Oakland. She was among the Panthers hoping to hold off the pigs, the courts, and FBI's own Cointelpro for as long as possible. Barb was pregnant so her prodigal time had a due date. She knew her due date. The rest of us only guessed at ours.

Roommates, sure. Guy roommates, the fool and the clown. Doug Bryant was wrapped too tight and Walter Rink was wrapped too loose. Doug with pipe in mouth to protect from foot in mouth, brought along a Playboy book of one line invitations. His dad gifted him with a binding code of business protocol, straight arrow in the extreme, and then aboard a Pan Am flight go for the stewardess. At the convention buzz handshakes and wink, drink, and dream about the nude girl providing entertainment. It was harmless and outdated protocol, like a Babbitt came alive in the Sixties to good fellowship, but never to return to his family, his business, and his small town. Bankers wear beards now.

Walter with his overweight and nimble flair wowed us with a Deer-killed-my-car story. It actually did. A deer crashed his GTO and ruptured a radiator, bent fenders, and stopped dead in his tracks, deer and car dead, but not Walter Ring. He was born entertainer, as Doug's role was primary audience, secondary sidekick, and lastly target of pointed barbs. Walter wielded a group like a DJ come to spin records at a hop, or Catskill jokester to tame the overfed ethnics. He came from Colgate, us from Hamilton College, and played to a Wells table of girls back of the dining hall. There we met Trixsie and Deb, roommates as freshman, roommates for the Paris semester, and friends for life, just as Kady and Barb expected to be. I could see Walter and Doug, odd a couple as one could imagine, the fool and the clown, together at the table. See Laurel and Hardy, with a Laurel as the straight-arrow with a few lines to contrast Walter's magnificence to his lesser star. How can Walter shine if he has no shadow? And Doug if he never sees the light?

"The first day had a night?"

"It did."

"Press on, please. I got a Poughkeepsie appointment."

"I got a night class on Narrative, for fun and profit."

"Inmates got stories, I bet."

"And you would win."

"Tell about the night you met Kurt Kallini."

"Sure thing. The first day had its night, just as every day has its dawn."

"I've made inquiries and it's true."

"Nice of you to make inquiries. It's your business I guess."

See now, Kady Bontecott hated me for interrupting her. She missed Barb Kelly. Her records were like a stash a Narc would just love to discover. Hey that's the carpetbag ahead of its time on trial. Just as I am on trial like the Kafka novel. You don't know the book. No big deal. It's a hard read and really goes nowhere, slowly. It's like Kady hated me for simply showing up, for carrying her carpetbag, and for breaking into her room that night. Got your attention, good.

Kurt Kallini was sitting there in a chair like the Buddha playing old Robert Johnson blues. Record he got and gifted to Kady Bontecott. I figured this dude must be Kady's boyfriend. My elder and better told me tales of Robert Johnson, a Silvio story of a hacked head, and how Mike Bloomfield was a kid compared to Muddy Waters. Guitarist for Electric Flag, Bloomfield. You got to listen to more music, read more books, if you want to understand the milieu of the counterculture. Music is the message. I don't mean somebody's going to uncover the motherload of diamonds and dust, but you never know unless you listen. Kallini baffled me almost as much as Kady. She hated my presence on the second floor and Kallini treated me with disdain.

Well Kallini was off to the Aurora Inn where he worked wonders with the ragtag band practicing Sunday night. He got them a gig, a place to practice, and a frontman like himself. Then he motivated Kady to think in terms of a violin concerto with her and him singing Marrying Maiden, the David and Linda Laflame Whitebird. Got to listen to the music, my man. When he had her motivated too, along comes Joshua Steen saying the shit hit the fan down the road at Cornell. Quinn the Eskimo with all his drug money turned to bombs and the Movement's turned against Kallini. Quinn's coming for Kallini and Kallini better have reason for sending Lionel, the black dude, to work with Black Panthers in Oakland. You got to understand all the fissures inside the Movement.

Oh you do. Probably ten times better than me. I'm just a naive kid thinking I'd learn French, go to Canada, and wait for hell to freeze over before I ever come back home. Of course, you're not as concerned with a potential draft dodger as you are with a drug deal worth 100 million, terrorists lighting bombs, and Panthers talking revolution with guns in their hands. Kallini had some "splaining to do". We all do. Come Kady home I hear her slip into her room, play White Bird, and sing along with the tune. Her crystal clear voice sang like the angels do. Bathrooms connect along the pipes. Romantic means to speak to a girl, and I tell her, that was nice. Sort of spooked her. One more reason for her to hate having me on the same floor. I left a note telling her of Kallini and me sharing her new record. Hatred, disdain, and naiveté, that's me.

"Did Kallini go see this drug dealer named Quinn the Eskimo?"
"Yea, later that week he took off to Cornell."
"You see him?"
"Kady told me."
"You get to know her?"
"She knew him and he stayed at the Aurora Inn. Whenever he was gone, the band played without him."
"Did you find out the relationship between those two?"
"They weren't boyfriend/girlfriend I knew for sure."
"And Kady, you get to know her?"

In classes every day for a week there was a vibe. I did annoy her by my presence, I guess. Classes were a stage beyond my comprehension. These girls going to Paris took French since seventh grade, and me I had a few years in college. Again the team of Deb and Trixsie played little games, like Walter with Doug's routine. They knew the exercises and the patterns, the country tour and the city swing, I liked them. They were approachable in a way Kady wasn't. She sat reading this great poet Apollinaire. Greatest poem, The Bridge Mirabeau. I asked Kady to read it in class. Again, the angels sang in the heavens.

Whitebird and water passing like time past the bridge. Time's fleeting. The Sixties took a day, then came the night. Those days won't come again. Kady and me won't cross paths unless you make us.

It was fun first meeting her. She sang, she recited poetry, and she did yoga. I got her friend Jesse Latimore to the bookshop, got to have a card, for my copy of Apollinaire. Kady accused me of stealing hers and reading at table with greasy fingers turning the pages. I didn't steal hers and told her, nicely. I learned the Mirabeau poem to placate the Mamselle asking me too many question in lab. Line for line, repeated. Then Kady did yoga on stage back from the gym. We had a pick up game, Deb played. You play too. Pick up game with the guards, yes, for good behavior. Well I scared her sweating like mad dog. She called me the Abominable Snowman when I walked in on a call to her mom. Her mom's had cancer and she's got a daughter who cares for her. Share Kady with another guy, not Kallini, but her mom, that's another story. Some girls got a heart and some don't.

So I spent time walking and working on a poem for her. Sort of impress her if I may. She went to a concert and they played a Bach piece that floored me two ways at once. It was in a Bergman film and it was one the Jew who lived next to Grandpa's camp played when I walked by, twelve years old. Grandpa had prejudices, the Jew had culture, and I was simply a kid pulling bullheads, eels, and snapping turtles from a muddy pond. Grandpa showed me how.

"You're off on a tangent."

"Holden Caulfield said they're the best parts."

"I read the Catcher."

"You know TV and you know JD Salinger. Kady cultured me a slice or two and maybe I can suggest things to read, music with a message, and a movie for you. Bergman is all snow and sadness and musical sorrow. Dark as Danish winters."

"Kallini stay all week in Ithaca?"

"He went Thursday and came back Friday and then returned when Kady went home to see her mom. Weekends with her mom I guess was a pattern. I had a day with her. I didn't complain again. The Sixties were such a glorious day and then night fell, over everything."

"Tell about Kallini gone and returned and gone again."

Kallini worked wonders. He had everybody against him for letting Lionel go west. But he got at the meeting, he said, and simply said Nixon and Cointelpro invaded their privacy. Look to the person next to you. He or she, they're telling the government all you do. Use fear to his advantage. Then play to their exalted opinion how they can party, how they can smoke dope, drop acid, like no federal agent who infiltrated the RYM or PLP could ever do. Kallini had them going, fear and desire, wedding one and all, east and west, black and white, SDS of Ann Arbor and Lawrence, Kansas with all its prairie power. Josh Steen, he said, saw which way the wind blew and played off him. Who could rap most radical won. Luther Rene, Quinn, went to the cellar to suitcase another bomb, by now an obsession. After all, most radical, most corporate, Dow Chem. and DuPont all in one, Quinn the Eskimo, turned night into dynamite, whiting out one and all within the sound of his call.

What I heard a year later when Kallini came with a proposition for me. That's was your first and last question. Don't let me jump the gun. You simply want to know what relation the Weathermen had with Kurt Kallini. Far as I can see, none. They won the most radical contest, which was raging against cops, breaking glass, and landing in jail back in Chicago. Kallini was conservative by their standards. Far out is the bomb which explodes when a fool crosses the wrong wires emulsifying brick and plaster and wood with anything flesh and blood too. Far out is over and out. Kallini worked the margins, worked the extremes against one another, but he had an agenda of his own. I saw how he was a master manipulator from day one. Least I liked to believe so. Of course, you would like to see how he manipulated me, bag and bagman, him and me.

Like I said, the Sixties lasted a day like the meltdown of winter one Friday the first weekend. What a day. Not simply sunny to wing a Frisbee in the backyard and walk the beach and explore the forest above Wells College, but to dream of punching a hole through the gray, suburban skies to eternity. To where the mer melee au soleil, where the sea and sky meet with eternal beauty, and a life worth living. You see me now doing my day to day once the Sixties are over and done: the Metro-boulot-dodo routine. Get up and out to work, teach classes, and sleep the sound sleep, only to do it all over again. It's a routine seen from a break-through to the other side. I'd like to think I've seen a single day when Kady and me knew we were meant for each other, two for the road, across Europe, across the States, and hopefully home again, though we never came home together. A slight delinquency from a life worth living. Worth it if only for a day, only for a year, it was never the "only" that mattered. I'd like to think so.

We went everywhere for a day, spoke out our deepest plans, connected on a personal level only couples in love do, and then let the good times roll, long as travels took us where we wanted to go. Of course, happiness has no common denominator. Tolstoy says happy couples are happy the same. True as long as their happiness is the love and marriage and live together forever. Ours over the long haul was not to be. Ours was for a day and for a year. Barb Kelly called from Oakland, distraught the Panthers meant to kill the pigs and be killed themselves, pregnant as she was, Lionel a black preppie as he was. Her call sent Kady like a guided message to tell Kallini, who already sent Barb to Berkley and classes, along with Lionel, who was not meant for the revolution neither in Oakland nor at Cornell. Kady pulled Kallini off the stage and made him drop his bass bang to the floor. He told her it's fixed, go see your mom who needs you.

Kallini worked wonders but he knew strings to pull across the continent and right there in Kady's heart. I saw him do it, fix matters 3000 miles away and fix matters 3 feet away too. I stared, Kady left for home, and Kallini put me and a guitar in the band, fixing matters for me. He showed disdain, cold hearted detachment, even cruelty, but when he wanted you, he knew what you most wanted, and said here it's yours. Heart's desire, see how it helps or hurts you overall. Kady went home without saying a word to me. Her mom and her, two fingers close, mother and daughter, together. Barb Kelly called and I answered. She was so cool. If I was with Kady I was in her heart too. I wish I got to meet Barb Kelly, I really do. Let her be at Berkley as if the confines of a college campus kept her safe and secure. I had two girls in mind, Kady and her roommate 3000 miles away, neither with me that weekend.

2
Preps Got it Easy

Kallini got called away to meet with the Movement and try to bridge the gap of black and white at Cornell. It would never work. It had gone to guns and bombs and shows of force. Just the things Cointelpro, the FBI, and Nixon's kids willing to do the dirty tricks waited to go to the culture wars. Preppies against the radicals they hated like communists. Bring on the preppies that used to lord it over anybody except the jocks. Most of them wished to be athletes and they were what they wished. Only my roomies, Doug and Walter, didn't make the grade. And I long left the flock to play a Squire guitar in tune with the Townies of Wells College.

"Anything happen on a Wells weekend with both Kurt Kallini and Kady Bontecott gone?"

"The usual roll of guys from mostly male schools to girls' colleges. Steve Hancock came to town. My nemesis in football who started quarterback because Groton guys lead and scholarship boys don't."

"Let me understand. You played football on scholarship, didn't get to play quarterback due to favoritism by the coach, so you quit?"

"I should get over it. Kady said it was all resentment."

"Rich kids get all the breaks."

"Now you're talking turkey, Agent Smith."

"Same in all the agencies. A few of us come from humble backgrounds like President Nixon. We work our way up by merit and talent and longer hours than the Ivy league patrician, whose family are diplomats, career politicians, and scions of secrecy in the CIA."

"Now you're talking gospel. You and me, we pull ourselves up by our bootstraps. We suffer hardships. We know the power of determination, hard work, long hours, dedication to goals, and when success seems within our grasp, like quarterback of a college team, coach chooses the Groton kid with blond hair, the AD frat boy, the kid who can make the throws in practice but not in the game."

"So you want back at the Steve Hancocks of the world?"

"Yea, damn certain I do."

"Tell me how you handled this prep invasion to the place you believed belonged to you."

David gave Agent Smith a quizzical look. Jimmy Smith for the first time tipped the interrogation. It was like Jimmy Sullivan and Jerry Seagram become narcs on Lower Main in Poughkeepsie, tipping the scales, old police to young investigators, ready to make their names, which they did. A number of David's high school buddies suffered from one set of drug salesmen screwed by another set of law enforcement. Like Poughkeepsie DA, G. Gordon Liddy writing a mag article on his bust of Timothy Leery's hideaway out in Millbrook. How would that elitist Millbrook crowd like Alduous Huxley tripping their brains like a bag of heroin delivered from the train station, from crime central, Lower Main, Poughkeepsie? David saw Flash Gordon tripping up and falling to the up and comers. Poughkeepsie's DA had gone to the White House staff. Good ole G. Gordon."

"Know him, Agent Smith?"

"I do."

I didn't like the preppies come rolling into the Aurora Inn. I liked the girls like Deb and Trixsie and Jesse Latimore. I shared a week of classes with them. I played ball with Deb. I got escorted by Jesse to the store for Alcools and on stage through a yoga session. Kady gave me a one day tour of the campus from Cayuga shores, to the Fargo above the gas pumps with its lakeview, riding with Deb's Townie and my drummer Don, power handshake and rock music shared, and out through the fields, forests, and streams rushing with the meltdown, what a day. It was the essence of the Sixties I told you. Then with the night Kallini left for Cornell, Kady left for Millbrook, and I strummed Lloyd's backup Strat to the juker tunes. Count the beats to chord changes. Let Lloyd fill in a few leads. I was his backup. Don't f__ up was all I tried to do.

I watched the boatdocker guy and Steve with his shock of short blond hair make their plays for Trixsie and Jesse. I'd made my play for Dana Dupont and Candy by the juker, under the same setup. For some reason I was implicated, whereas my roommate Doug Bryant was not. Doug voiced his righteous indignation. I did not. What if it was Kady with a guy like Steve pawing her, preying on her, making her feel small. Only then would I fight the SOB preppie. Steve did all these things to Jesse. She told him to get lost. An arm around her shoulder copped a feel of her delightful pert breast. It turned me on as much as it made me mad. So Jesse fisted Steve Hancock in the face. Bright welt and bulge along his cheekbone. He yelled, "Lesbian bitch" when Doug stepped between boatdocker and quarterback to say, "Treat the girls with a little more courtesy."

Preppies took off to upstairs tables, with Trixsie introducing them to debutants, where girls expected to be wined and dined before they took somebody of their class for a one night stand. Follow the courtesies as Doug said. But he had no idea how the sex game played. He only knew the etiquette and the stupid one-liners he'd never use. Girls in class least treated him as one of the guys, then on, not as some straight arrow freak, who never moved a step beyond his dad's accountant techniques.

Oh the girls joked me about Kady and her mom, saying how home with mom was a pattern. They got used to Kady copping out most every weekend and vacation, sometimes for a week missing school she could well make up. Sure her mom was sick and sure Kady was the caring daughter. Only the girls joked me into knowing I had to deal with this close connection, however close I got to her. I said, sure I understood, but I really didn't. Anytime I deviated from that one special day the Sixties came and she went home that night, I knew if I messed up, she would go home. I knew, but I didn't really understand the deal. She went home with the Sixties all the same. Her mom and Kady traveled to NYC, saw another male doctor who didn't help her mom, and spent a day on the town. It was a week before I saw her again. Talk about a cooling off period of time. Walk the beach, compose a poem, memorize French like a good boy should, and play guitar in a band, which was about as much fun as football.

"Listen David, we do have tabs on the Weathermen and their antics with bombs. We had a chemist inside Quinn's lab reporting to us. We knew the bombs went to the Panthers on the coast. We knew case-bombs went out to NYC, Boston, DC, and Chicago."

"Who's your snitch?"

"A Layton Hayze shared information to us for his own immunity. Now he works for Dow Chem and he's a happy camper to be out of Quinn's lab and into the parent corporation."

"So let me snitch and you can get me a job with IBM?"

"I don't like the word snitch or informant."

"Do my patriotic duty then?"

"Okay. Job with IBM, done."

It was the last week of winter before Kady and Kurt Kallini got back to town. Kady didn't need the French. Kallini didn't need to play in a townie band. They liked Aurora, the Inn, and the Fargo too. College towns are nice, especially if they connect with the campus. At Hamilton, the town of Clinton takes a mile ride downhill to the Rock and five miles out toward the Thruway exit for the Route 5 place. The Inn and the Fargo were downhill from the Townhouse and a short walk from the French House. Campus was a longer walk than the town.

Kallini came back and Kady came back. The band with me timing chords played at the Inn. Kady shared a couple cassis and her Dunhills with me. It was nice upstairs at the bar with its dining room windows in view of all Lake Cayuga. There was a living room with armchairs, plush carpet, and a chandelier. Hotels are nice if a person has money. Downstairs in the cellar the floor and ceiling above began to pulsate sound. I told Kady it was time for my first gig. She said, keep an eye on her, she'd be my number one fan. It was so cool. Dark ambience filled with sound. Kallini came alive on House of the Rising Sun. Boy he could sing a song and he could make the bass pop and boom and climb the cellar stairs. Kady got a little unnerved knowing I slept with the Janis Joplin slut who played ball and chain. That was freshman year. It wasn't anything to be proud. Kady talked with Candy, it happened, but Candy vouched I wasn't one of those snooty preps. Kady let it go, I believe.

We drove out to the park on a Saturday, listened to Sixties pop, and I told her in a different time we be like Paul and Paula. She wanted to tell me none of that mattered anymore. I know it didn't. She then believed she wasn't as sophisticated as Dana DuPont with her faux pas, nor sexy as Candy riveted to her Jukebox Janis. I told her what she was. She was beautiful. She was unique. She had integrity. That didn't endear me to her. But it was true. She was pretty normal, nice to her mom, and told a person who loved her and persons who didn't give a damn, the truth. A certain integrity comes to a girl who deals with different people. Either she's a chameleon like Trixsie, Kallini too, on a darker side, or she's honest as the day is bright and the night is long.

These were gray winter days. I called my two buddies doing winter study in DC and met Kady at the Fargo. Turns out my asshole competition for quarterback pinched her butt and she kicked him into the table splashing the beer. I got there as she was coming out. Let's go back and kick the crap out of him. She liked the idea, but decided, why bother. We spent time making out at the Townhouse, sitting on a couch with snowfall funneling the lamplight. Deb said I should come to Paris when Hamilton finished. I said sure. Graduate, work a month for airfare, and be there in June. I said it with sarcasm. Then I said it with decision. I could do it if I said I could do it. Kady and I let it slide. We listened to music, shared a last evening in touch, and left after midnight in the silently falling snow. French House light made the downstairs empty and cold. We walked the stairs to my room.

Open the door and there's Steve Hancock humping Jesse Latimore in Walter's bed. It blew my mind. Doug sat up in the opposite bed bug-eyed and ambivalent. I yelled at Steve, but the couple of assholes were too drunk to care. Why bother. Kady said I should come to her room and share the extra bed. Once there she asked me to share her bed and I did. It was a wonderful night. Bright is a Friday the snow melted down and temps rose to 70 degrees, like magic in the wintertime. Honest as the day is bright that Saturday night and Sunday morning, time lasted just as long. Only I wished it lasted forever. "O Claire de lune, O Prodigal Time!" Poem I wrote for her. Kady collected all good things, dumped them into her carpetbag, and told me to stay as she left my life. Let me tell you, Jimmy Smith, as much as that carpetbag was worth full of diamonds and dust, Kady and its cornucopia of all good things were worth millions to me. Kady packed her carpetbag and took the Sixties with her.

"You did get over to Paris."

"It was no easy thing to do."

"Tell me what you think Kallini was doing this month you remember too well."

"Biding his time."

"To what end."

"To the end of the Sixties. The Movement literally blew itself up. He saved a few and sacrificed a few, who once considered him a friend. Maybe he waited since the fall moratorium to bring May flowers, a great March on Washington, but nobody knew what Nixon would do. Not even Nixon I bet."

"I'm not so sure you should collect your bet."

"He wanted to win the war, but maybe the Movement had one more grand time to shine, like it did earlier turning public opinion against the war."

"And equally against the movement."

"Yea, damn hippy freaks. Cut their hair, wash them up, send them to Cuba."

"Like you David. Only to Downstate Prison."

"Just visiting."

"We'll see."

David did give Jimmy Smith the look, see if he were serious about David's stay in prison.

"Kallini had alternative plans, I'm sure of that."

"Plans for the Brotherhood?"

"Over in Europe, sure, and right here at home with his mafioso family. Maybe his Uncle Carlo was always his top priority and the Movement meant a place to do business. He was a drug dealer, once or twice removed. He was an arms dealer if it leant him credibility. He was a brother in the Marist seminary, never forget that fact. I'm sure hospitals and Freres to the poor and even reform of America connected to his spiritual ideal of the whole worshipping world."

"I'll go with drug dealer and arms merchant. They carry incarceration penalties, and here we are hoping Kurt Kallini comes to see us."

"Biding his time at Wells College, and once Kady was gone I had a Sunday to wait for friends, Peter Bergman and Early Hayze to arrive from DC."

"What did you do? Have a fancy dinner at the Aurora Inn?"

Kallini dined with the owner, Mr. Jacobs. After that we were all spectators on what Kallini called Fate accompli. I knew a little bit about the badgering Doug took from Walter and the AD crowd from Hamilton and Colgate. He wasn't such a bad guy until he went nuts. He took Walter for a final tour of the town. One last ride in his Thunderbird to match any ride Walter expected for the duration from his GTO a deer killed. Doug sped through town unchecked by cops, down a plowed path to Lake Cayuga, and sped on the ice far out as the eye could see. He spun back around and came back to the Aurora Inn. I wonder what Walter said on the dusky lake with a full moon already cascading down light. The Thunderbird aimed for the Inn.

Kallini said he saw fate come to terms with final things. At some speed Walter must have known Doug wasn't for a joyride to take a bump and back to the road through town. Maybe he screamed, maybe he pleaded, and just maybe he grabbed for the wheel. To no success it seems. The car did bumb on the land, run the slope, but veer into the Cellar of Sound where I played in the band. Smash into the sliding glass doors and smash to a stop against the wall. Walter got his head sheered off in the collision, Doug was barely touched. Walter got taken to the morgue, Doug to the insane asylum, let's say for the rest of his days. Who knows?

"I did read the report. It had nothing to do with Kallini."

"Nothing at all. Blame the preppies. Blame the badgering, the bullying, and Doug's prurient attitude toward sex. I don't know many straight arrows as tight in their moral code as Doug, or as Doug's father. But there was a definite smash-up, and Walter rode shotgun into a cellar blast."

"Kallini went with you back to Hamilton College?"

"Yes, with his bass guitar of Acapulco gold."

"Talk about the time with Kallini at Hamilton College. For the record may have a few layers of what I know and what you know, and what we piece together between us."

"Okay Jimmy. Like I have a choice to say skip this, and go home."

"To a single room apartment near Vassar Hospital. Better digs right here on the second floor of Downstate."

"Into the prison there's an absence of security. I could take a ride with Walter and Doug any time. Coming in is careful security for one and all. This second floor is no man's land. I've waited here hours during a shutdown and I suppose I can wait days here for interrogation."

"Go ahead, teach classes, I got a good start and it all has to be typed to paper."

"Give me a week, while you translate audio to visual?"

I could do that and David, I'll check if we can give you a break as long as you're cooperating with us."

"Time off for good behavior?"

"Let's call it that. You be here for classes and you go home."

"Check to see who's following me?"

"You can check but you don't go anywhere, we already checked."

"Metro-boulot-dodo. I ain't got a life, except dreams of might have been."

"Well you got a friendly audience for the year with Kurt Kallini, a year of living large."

"I like that."

"You're writing in that apartment you have and you can write here too."

"For prying eyes?"

"For your eyes only."

3
Introductions

Carol Hunter came to speak with Kady Bontecott. Kady was married and planning to have a baby. Teaching at the Bennet School and married to a mature English teacher, Edward Butler, her life took on the normal progression from daughter, to wife, to mother she hoped pretty soon. The request for an interview from a Chicago attorney surprised Kady. She thought surprises took a backseat in her life. She thought travels here and there ended when she came home from Europe. With the new year she was with her mom at the airport and David Morpheys returned home. She wrote him no letters after she came home, but she told David there and then. Don't call me. I'm married, happy, and settled into a life. She got her carpetbag back from him a few days later with the deed to her father's estate. Bottom of the bag was all dusty sequins and an odd smell. Police came for the bag and that was that.

Carol Hunter wanted to know more about the bag and how she and Kurt Kallini connected over the past year. Carol had a transcript of what David told Jimmy Smith and debated whether to show its romantic narrative to this woman married and planning to have a baby. She saved it until she had a better read. Kady asked who she was, she knew Chicago attorney, but what did that mean? Carol gave her a brief synopsis of her mom's lineage in the black community, how she didn't support the Daley Machine, though she sent Charlene to Northwestern and Chicago Law. She wasn't that much older than Kady Bontecott, but she had a job with Nixon's anti-terrorism unit and she worked with the FBI extension called Cointelpro.

"I got French classes to teach."

"Already we let your husband, teacher and headmaster, find a replacement for a few days."

"Didn't he object?"

"He was impressed with Justice Division and Cointelpro and President Nixon. I mean this isn't the local Millbrook beadle inquiring about an unregistered car. This is the United States government."

"What do you want?"

"We want to know all you can tell us about Kurt Kallini, and all you can tell us about the carpetbag sent to you by David Morpheys shortly after the new year, which the police picked up for us and put on file as evidence?"

"I left the carpetbag with David when I came home and he stayed. He had stuff to carry and I had none. It was all over for him and me, but he asked me for the carpetbag, calling it the cornucopia of all good things. It was a sweet, last night, and I left it with him. He took it to Munich and he brought it home, I think.

"You don't know?"

"My mom and me happened to return from Grannie Lonigan's funeral in Dalhart, Texas, a Christmas till New Year's visit. Chance has it David returned from Europe the same time. He came through customs and came over to say hello. I said hello, this is my mom, but he didn't give me any bag then. Maybe it was still coming through customs. We spoke for a few minutes, said goodbye for good, and I told him, don't keep in touch. I told him I was married. I wasn't, but was going to be. He said, congratulations, he had to go. He went outside for a taxi to Grand Central. I haven't seen him since, nor do I want to."

"Then he sent you the carpetbag because it was yours and not his."

"Yes." Kady didn't want to say a thing about the deed, belonging to Kallini, but left blank for whoever signed. David didn't want it, but her dad damned well did.

"Was there anything in the carpetbag like a diamond or a bag of heroin dust?"

"No. It was empty. I think it was empty for David too."

"Do you know over 100 million in heroin and diamonds came through customs in that bag. Police found traces of both and the market for heroin and diamonds had been saturated ever since."

"I knew none of that. David sent me the bag and the police took the bag from me. It's of no value whatsoever to me."

"Let's say we believe your testimony and we believe David Morpheys too. Then someone in Munich took the carpetbag, all full, brought it over and came through customs about the same time, emptied the bag of 100 million dollars in heroin and diamonds and had the bag tossed back to David at Kennedy."

"That's David's testimony?"

"He said the bag got stolen in Munich when he got on a train to Budapest by mistake and when the doors shut someone took the bag from the concrete platform."

"He was off to Munich when I left."

"The man was a Turk who took the bag, but left David's passport, his wallet, and other identification."

"It could well have happened."

"It's a pretty far-fetched story to me."

"If you know David, you know with him, there's a can't cross line of things he can't do and live with himself. I don't see him doing something like that for Kurt Kallini."

"You left him."

"He left me first to see Berlin after a friend died, Early Hayze, where we worked in Vichy, France. Tough time for him, tougher time for me."

"You have to tell me all about it."

"I'd rather not."

"You'd rather not, but if you want to stay put in your prep school, you should tell me and Cointelpro and the Justice Department all you know. We have a million other things to do."

"You have your work cut out for you."

"It's what I signed up for. It's what I always wanted. My folks only had influence in the black community, but I want influence in the city, state, and national community. You help me here to find out Kurt Kallini and how he got his motherload of drugs and diamonds into America, maybe Cointelpro can make sure it never happens again. I see the war on drugs just as important as the war in Vietnam. In fact, most drugs come back with the troops from Indochina."

"Then stop the war."

"You too, Kady Bontecott?"

"And everyone else with any sense at all."

"Well you have the right to your opinions as I have mine. But you have no rights to be accomplice to 100 million in drugs coming into the black community and wrecking so many lives."

"I don't do drugs, for some time."

"I believe you, but let's get all you know about Kurt Kallini recorded and put on transcripts."

"I'm ready when you are."

The recorder clicked on, although another mike picked up everything Kady had said.

"Tell me everything about Kurt Kallini from the first time you met him."

4
Kady's Testimony

Kurt Kallini came to Wells College from Cornell. It was like he wanted to escape the turmoil of the Movement. That's what my roommate, Barb Kelly, told me and she liked him. She liked everybody who paid the least attention to her. She like Lionel Dubois, the black guy from Cornell, and she liked the Jewish guy, Joshua Steen too. They both had manners and made a big deal about Barb's painting. They shared good grass with her and other girls and townies that had girlfriends at the Townhouse. We shared a room there and walked downhill to either the Inn or the Fargo about every night. There's not too much to do in Aurora.

Sure there's studying, but I've taken French since seventh grade and knew what could be known till I left for the French semester that winter. It must have been late fall, before Thanksgiving, Barb got infatuated with the trio from Cornell. I tagged along. We played bridge and gin rummy, drank long neck beers, and yes smoked a little dope. Kallini took an interest in me. I liked listening to music and he tried out records by these black bluesmen. He tried jazz, but that was beyond me. Sometimes he played a little guitar, oddball stuff like classical, or sit at the Aurora Inn piano and play Dave Brubeck Take Five. That had a racy tempo. Other jazz was bebop, birth of the cool, and John Coltrane.

He said bass was his instrument, but he needed a band. The townies like Don and Lloyd, Eddie and Tim Burt had a rock band, but they weren't very good till Kallini decided they had possibilities. Like I said, he escaped whatever bad stuff went down at Cornell and relaxed with us at Wells College. We never bugged him. He sort of entertained us, like a mentor for music, what was happening in the news, what the Movement meant against the war. We weren't political, none of us girls at the Townhouse, but it didn't concern him. He knew plenty of politicos. Like he got into radical fistfights with RYM, SDS, PLP, and the Black Student Union. He made fun of the initialing. He was at a point in his politics where he could take it or leave it. Only it seemed they couldn't take or leave him, anymore.

The political scene must have gotten worse over the holidays because him and Barb Kelly were close and then they weren't a couple at all. It was Lionel Dubois and Barb who took a van west. Lionel was supposed to join up with the Black Panthers in Oakland. Kallini told me he'd delay them until I got back from home, but it was a monster storm and I was late and they were gone. Sad I couldn't see Barb off. I took our records, and her free form painting from the Fargo. It was a nude with her big boobs sprawled on a red and white tablecloth, like they have at the Fargo. It's not too classy there and Kallini laughed at the tablecloths because the dumb hicks at the gas station didn't know the linen sold to guinea ristorantes. Barb posed then in a trashy pose for all the dumb hicks who wanna be Italians.

Don't take Barb for a slut because she slept around with Kallini and other guys. She just liked guys who liked her. She didn't see why if she liked sex she shouldn't show off her body in an artful way. She wasn't like me, who stayed a virgin because no guy wanted any more than a quick lay. Only Morpheys was different. He looked through a person, much as Kallini did, but he was less critical, less driven, and full of enthusiasm. Kallini could be cold. Anyway I was attracted to David Morpheys. He upset me from the start.

"Tell me about you and Morpheys. I don't mean the romantic subtext and how that played out. Just what was your relationship?" Carol Hunter wanted to ascertain if Kady would lie to protect David Morpheys. If she did, would she tell anything very truthful about Kurt Kallini. She had checks from other transcripts. Truth was a priority.

"Me and Morpheys after the new year, 1969 or after the new year, 1970?"

"Start at the beginning."

Kady recalled she hated him at the beginning. Tall, slumped, and bespeckled guy with a Racine mustache and manners less refined than a prep and more refined than a townie. A work in progress. He spun her dials as she rushed to see Barb. She missed Barb and dropped off her stuff. He wanted to carry her carpetbag filled with records and player forbidden at the French House. He wanted a conversation with her when all she wanted was to get out, go see Jesse Latimore, and bemoan the departure of her roommate. None of her impatience was rational. She acted like a ticked off bitch with him, and didn't care one bit.

I liked him, not at the beginning, but that was me. What Kallini did with my best friend Barb, sending her to Oakland, under pretense people on the West Coast would appreciate her painting, pissed me off. He wanted Lionel out of the cauldron at Cornell and he sweetened the deal by sending Barb too. It burned me up, and Morpheys simply touched the hot stove with it all red and raw. Then he kept on. He came to my room with Kallini there and me gone, to discuss a Robert Johnson record and black blues. Kallini found somebody impassioned with the blues, like him, but like me a neophite checking out Electric Flag for the Chicago blues and Taj Mahal for a acoustic twang. We were blues volunteers and Kallini the commander barking orders to try Son House, try Herbert Sumlin, as least listen to Buddy Guy. David left a note detailing his discussion. Who leaves notes? It's like the Saybrook matrons leaving their cards for my newly arrived mom till they decided she wasn't worthy of their attention.

I liked him, but he irritated me. Girls at Wells have 3-4 year friendships with other girls they had little in common. Barb simply grew on me. She was Episcopalian from a dad's mission in St. Louis, reaching out to people with her friendship, with her sex, and with her desire to share God's love. I was a hard-boiled Catholic like my mom. The kind of Catholic in her West Texas town of Dalhart who's literally one of a kind. The only Irish Catholics in town. Lonigan and McCreery in a town of Scotch Irish and southerner and Tex-Mex. I'm singing a Marrying Maiden song at 3AM above the Whitebird record and I hear this tap on the bathroom pipes, "very nice."

Jesus, I jumped out of my sox till I understood it was Morpheys in the can complimenting my voice. Then in class he complimented my reading an Apollinaire poem "Le Pont Mirabeau" which collection he bought at the bookstore, memorized at lunch, and lined during exercises with Mamselle. I accused him of stealing my copy. I accused him of having no manners reading at lunch. I accused him of slobbery with his french fries, greasy fingers on my stolen copy of Alcools. He was guiltless. I was a horrible hoyden. Again I didn't care one bit.

I liked him more when I learned from Jesse he liked me. I saw him play basketball with Deb and the few girl athletes, professor's son, and another winter study guy. David wasn't much for manners, wasn't much musically on guitar, but as an athlete he was a boy to behold. Like it all came natural to him. He'd say sports came to him when he got told he'd never walk again after a car accident. Instead he ran and performed every sport there was, every hour of the day, if he could. Then he lands next to me and Jesse doing our yoga, said he tried it, but it gave him nightmares. Back to basketball and Jesse told me of him and Dana DuPont freshman year, like penpals, like brother and sister, unlike the concern for me, unlike the rapt glare in his eyes and eagerness in his voice, for everything about me. He was just a crazy boy smitten, as my mom would say, by me. That never occurred before. And I sort of liked him.

I liked him and then he disappeared to return with poems written for me. I mean he spent time at a Bergman film, in the library, in the gym, in classes across from me, and a few days later, all these lines and rhymes, for me. It amazed me a guy could be so corny. Write a poem to impress a girl. He wanted to write and he wanted to impress me with his writing, I guess. But it was so outlandish, so corny, so endearing in a naive, ninth grade way. Well I was never courted in ninth grade, new girl at the same Bennet School I hated then and work for now. I was never woo'd in high school like countless other chicks who soon assumed to be debutants. I ran track and 330 high hurdles and studied and took care of my mom, who had cancer and whose recovery counted on me. Sad, all of it. My whining over school as an adolescent girl and my lack of attention. I grew not to need anybody but myself, my Catholic faith in God, and my mom's recovery from cancer.

"Did Morpheys write poems complimenting your beauty? You

know cheeks like cherries, teeth like ivory, your eyes your smile like the sun coming up at dawn?"

"No, none of that sonnet crap."

"No. Then he pictured in words the nude, attractive babe like you told me in Barb's self-portrait?"

"No, none of that sexy stuff either. They were poems trying like hell to repeat Rimbaud and Baudelaire, or like the Doors to break on through to the other side, to find a psychedelic synesthesia like a Hendrix solo, to see God, source of all human endeavor, and put the break through into poetry. He'd work at this Rimbaud stuff all the time we traveled together, like a Journey to the East, a Journey to the West, to Woodstock, and way back home to the source of it all."

"Doesn't sound very personal."

"No, but it was for me. It was him in love with me, almost completely. Like if one or two people might punch a hole through the bourgeois ceiling above and in our heads, then they might live in paradise, know heaven, if for nothing more than to marry, have kids, and settle down. Discover what a life means, free one's mind, and find a life worth living."

"So you fell in love with a dream of some life better than the one you were living."

"No he did. And I was the effective cause. One of Aristotle's teleological arguments, he said. Christ I got Kurt Kallini speaking of Catholicism as the universal religion, summa theologica, the whole worshipping world as one. And I got David Morpheys dedicating poems to me. Pretty heady times for a girl with little she determined to do, than spend her last semester abroad, teach back at Bennet School, and take care of her ailing mom."

"So Morpheys threw off the plans you made for yourself?"

"I don't think so. We did the journey east and the journey to Texas and west to the coast and lived together in province and Paris. That was pretty special. It turned dark later in the year, but it was a sunny life for a good long time. Like if you live a life beyond what you imagined, and afterwards, come home to teach school, take care of my mom, and raise a family. It's a life worth living in the context of an imagined life lived fully and ultimately found lacking. All life is metro-boulot-dodo. Plain and simple routine, over and over again. David teaches GED and writing courses. I teach French. Neither of us does anything special, but it's a life worth living in the context of one year living beyond the pale."

"He got to you."

"Marlon Brando in the Wild Ones. We spent too many afternoons in the Muse de Cinema. I still watch films and read Rimbaud, but like cassis and Dunhills, there the little pleasures in a larger life."

"So none of that you're so beautiful and you're so sexy crap, him to you?"

"Not so much at the start. Get this, the last Saturday he's relating us to a Paul and Paula pop song. Like we'd be married end of high school, say five, ten years earlier. Or married after a month of romance at Wells College. I'm still pissed because he slept with Candy the campus slut back as a freshman and because he ran around with Dana DuPont, one of the debutants with a family background where faux pas count. Why not me, sexy? Why not me, sophisticated? He'd say, sure you are, but what makes you special, you have a normal character among all the neurotic hippies and careful conformity. You're simply yourself. You got integrity."

"Integrity?"

"Probably, you got it too, Carol Hunter of Chicago Law, the Justice Department, and FBI's Cointelpro. And you're deserving to have integrity of character."

"My mom says I have integrity of character."

"See Carol, your mom. I thought a compliment on my integrity was less than expected, in the context of Paul and Paula type romance and marriage. I wanted whitebirds flying away to a better place, a better time, for all time. It was the last Saturday we would have together. I was gone on Sunday, piling everything in my carpetbag worth one incredible time a 100 million dollars, worth to David Morpheys the Cornucopia of all good things, worth nothing to me now. You got my carryall and it's worth nothing to nobody. To me, to David Morpheys, and I venture to say in terms of spiritus mundi nothing at all to Kurt Kallini."

"You still connected to Morpheys and Kurt Kallini, tell me."

"What they meant to me, yes."

"But you got clear of both of them. You spent a last semester in Paris, traveling Europe, spreading your wings like the whitebird once trapped in a cage."

"It wasn't as special as one month with Morpheys, the time missing him."

"I see, Kady."

5
Carol and Jimmy

Carol Hunter took the tapes to a Poughkeepsie office Cointelpro shared with local police. She wanted Jimmy Smith's advice on the case. They were both Republican types, Black and Hispanic. Their moms were ethnic. Hers high class, the talented tenth of a small Chicago enclave, his a wetback maid in LA for an Irish family. They both had brains and moms who encouraged them to succeed. They were totally driven through college and law school. For poorer ethnics it was the army where one's merit secured a future. For ethnics who made it through university, it was the government. Nixon, unlike Kennedy, was an outsider to fortune who fought for everything he got. Sometimes he fought dirty. They did too. There was Vietnam and there were the culture wars in America. It was the rich kids of liberal parents destroying an America where Carol and Jimmy wanted to earn their way to success.

Jimmy prepared to denigrate the Pentagon Papers by showing how Ellsberg was in psychiatric care. Carol was hard at work preparing an interrogation of the Chicago 7 and how they were linked in treason, terrorism, and revolution against a Middle Class America who worked hard, lived family, and belonged to a church. It looked like they would work together in the next years on any number of projects. The Nixon team liked young, bright lawyers to do the legwork. Do everything they could and see a career take shape first in the departments and then in a recognized law firm who would pay their expertise.

"I wanted to know, Jimmy. What if the two of them did connect to Kurt Kallini?"

"You met Kady Bontecott, what do you think?"

"She still likes David Morpheys and she never wants to see him again."

"Well she's married, planning to have a child, so what's past is past, right Carol?"

"Right, for her mother's sake."

"She and her mom are close?"

"Like you to yours and me to mine. Moms gave us everything to carry us into good careers with the government. Only Kady's mom got sick, caught cancer, and never fully recovered all the years Kady grew up from adolescence to children of her own. The push got reversed. With her mom it's a pull back home. To stay with her mom till the day her mom dies. It's nothing weird. It's a warm world of mother and daughter and now she's married to this older headmaster, English teacher, she and her mom are together more than ever."

"How's her husband react to such tight relations?"

"Edward Butler doesn't interfere. He's a 35 year old preppie turned professor in a private school of girls who adore him. He takes good care of Kady, but he doesn't need her adoration, her passion, nothing. Just a happy home, a settled life, and someday a daughter or son of his own. He doesn't rush her. He's in no rush at all. Like he's where he planned to be in the conformist Fifties and where he plans to be forever."

"Well, we're going places, he ain't."

"I can't believe she wants this life, which is like watching paint dry."

"Some people do."

"But I get a distinct feeling the year she spent with David Morpheys and in some personal way too, with Kurt Kallini, comes alive in memory the more she settles into a Bennet School existence, encased like insects in amber."

"No ambition at all?"

"Him, her 35 year old husband, no. You tell that the moment you meet him. He's safe, she's secure with him, it's a Fifties life for someone like us, Black or Hispanic, who never knew how to be white, respectable, and happy doing nothing. I mean he's in charge of a girls' school and she teaches French, but it will be the same, twenty years from now."

"Why did she choose such a life, Carol? In fact, why did Morpheys choose a similar life teaching GED and writing courses for Marist, and not much else. It's like they put both their lives on hold. Live life to the utmost for a year and then live the same life for twenty years afterward. I see what you're saying."

"Do you, Jimmy?"

"They planned with Kurt Kallini to slip 100 million worth of diamonds and dust through customs, only to slip into the least offensive lives possible. Then live inconspicuous lives for five, ten, twenty years, long as it takes, for the motherload of millions to come to them."

Carol got up to walk around the Poughkeepsie office, stare down to the market square and up to a Bardovon Theatre. She stared the other direction to one of those FDR Depression era post offices. She stared and shook her head looking back at Jimmy Smith.

"I heard you say it, what squirrels through my own suspicions, and I can't believe it to be true."

"Nobody can do it."

"Nobody."

Jimmy gave voice to a shared thought everybody in law enforcement knows. They know human nature.

"Nobody can live a inconspicuous life with millions hanging over their heads. Nobody can wait till whenever the skies clear and the sun shines its normal day."

"Jimmy, I agree with everything you say, and yet."

"We're nuts, they're normal. Interrogated, they should be paranoid beyond belief. They're not. They're enraptured by a month's romance and a year's journey, but happy to be home for a life of Metro-boulot-dodo."

"Jimmy, we got to crack them, we got to open them up to the month, the year, and the lifetime they put on hold. Else, we're some sad-sack investigators not worth our salt, our salary, and our education."

"Carol, I can crack the kid if you can crack the girl."

"Age 22, they don't seem like kids anymore."

"No, they're like an older man and woman, secure they lived a life in the limited time available to them. Now they can wait patiently at normal jobs for the millennium."

"Edward Butler lives. Lives of a conformist Fifties with a secret life kept in close memory like a vestal flame ever burning in the temple, until Jesus returns with the happy days."

"Jimmy, is that your mom talking?"

"About bliss for the blessed, yes."

"In the Chicago neighborhood, we marked people like them living quiet lives. We marked them when the FBI uncovered their double lives. They were communists living more than normal lives, working for the party."

"Waiting for how long?"

"What does it matter Jimmy, communists, Jesus freaks, or simply con-artists after the big heist waiting to capitalize on 100 million dollars from Kurt Kallini. We need to know more about Kurt Kallini. If he could indoctrinate a couple to come through customs with 100 million, come home separately, and live lives no one suspects. He's the brains."

"We don't have Kurt Kallini. We hear he's in Paris. We hear he's in Turkey in the heroin trade. We hear he's in Nassar's Egypt working with The Brotherhood."

"We got them, David and Kady, and they know Kurt Kallini."

"And we're paid to suspect the inconspicuous, Carol, it's our training."

"Go to work on my cassettes and let me have a go on David Morpheys."

"I gave him a few days home to see his parents, his friends, anyone he wanted."

"What the hell for?"

"Local police here, Sullivan and Seagram, guided our agents where he goes. That may give us a heads up."

"Well get him back, will you?"

"He teaches GED classes Monday. Same boring work with convicts all with ten years. He's settled in as they are."

"Exactly."

6
Contretemps

Carol Hunter sat across from David Morpheys on a Monday morning. He looked at her. She crossed her legs and smiled like a black Cleopatra floating in silks down the Nile. David opened his hands in prayer to say, what's up. He planned to teach classes at 10 AM, but they called to say, come at eight.

"You want coffee, David?"

"A cup would be nice."

"You want to know why I'm here and not Jimmy?"

David nodded. Carol thought him a bit lethargic, or simply patient.

"I spoke with Kady Butler and she still loves you."

"A year ago I liked to think so. But the flame died out."

"You should hear her recall the romantic days and hours and moments of your shared month at Wells College."

"Yes it was nice."

"Why did you give up on her?"

"Mind if I ask who you are?"

"Another agent in the justice department, like Jimmy. Law school in Chicago. I didn't need affirmative action because I worked hard to get where I am."

"Nothing wrong with affirmative action. Better world if a woman like you makes it and a man like Jimmy too. This prison wouldn't be 80% black and Hispanic, if 20% of the population had equal opportunity to make it in America."

"Why doesn't a smart kid like you from Suburbia with a dad working IBM want to make it? Go to law school?"

"I did say I wanted to be a lawyer when I won a football scholarship to Hamilton College."

"What happened to your plans?"

"Maybe next year. Or maybe grad school in comparative literature.

Or maybe I can write something."

"You're biding your time?"

"I'm stuck in an interrogation over a bag once full of diamonds and dust, but not when I got it back."

"You zipped it open, outside JFK Airport?"

"On the train ride out of Grand Central. There was a deed to the Bontecott place with a blank space for me to sign."

Carol leaned forward, uncrossing her legs, listening more carefully. "Whose deed?"

"Mine if I signed it."

"Who was it from?"

"Kurt Kallini I assume. He offered me the Bontecott Estate, where my father worked during the war and afterward and where he got fired for complaining the foreman hired his son and not my dad. Dad has a temper. And a sense of fairness. But Bontecott came to him, gave him $500 dollars for his good work, and told him he had to back up his foreman. Dad got a job at IBM. He got a better life, THINK."

"How did Kurt Kallini get a deed for somebody's signature?"

"Bought it I guess and Bontecott Stone too. His Uncle Carlo wanted entry into the jewelry business."

"Why leave the deed with you?"

"Kallini offered me the deed back in Munich if I brought the package through US customs?"

"What did you say to the offer?"

"Sorry, I can't cross that line."

"Simple as that, no?"

"My dad didn't cry over one dismissal. I didn't have any grand schemes for revenge, for winning a big payday, for being rich if it meant crossing a moral line I couldn't cross and still live with myself."

"You said no, and Kurt Kallini had a Turk assistant take the carpetbag from you."

"I was on the wrong way train with half my stuff, nach Budapest, and the iron doors fell shut. The bag was on the platform. The Turk took it and five minutes later another Turk deposited a Munich paper on the concrete. Another minute or two, the iron train door opened, the train was delayed, I was free to go to Paris."

"What was inside the newpaper left?"

"My passport, other identification, stuff like that. What an American in Munich and Paris needs to get home."

"So that was that. You didn't see Kady's bag again, till Kennedy?"

"Till after customs, till outside, and like the Munich platform, taxi car didn't stop for me, but tossed me Kady's bag twenty feet from me. Take it, it's yours."

"And the deed was yours for doing what?"

"Nothing. For other things I don't know. For the trouble I'm having now."

"Why send the bag and the unsigned deed back to Kady Bontecott?"

"It belonged to her, not me. I wish I simply dumped the empty carpetbag, the cornucopia of all good things, once a year before, now nothing. It was a gesture, damn't."

"What kind of gesture?"

"To say we're quits. It's the deed to your dad's estate and I don't want it. Why one holds on to memories of only yesterday because the bag carried everything we had as we crossed Europe, as we crossed the States, and when we had an opportunity to live and stay in Paris, if only I kept us together like I should have, and didn't complain. Listen Carol Hunter, I'm just confusing you. It's a story, a year in a life, start to finish."

Carol had a key. It was the deed to the Bontecott estate, about which Kady didn't say a word."

"Then start again. Start after you and Kady parted from Wells winter study, and your friends took Kurt Kallini with you to Hamilton College. Start with Kurt Kallini and tell what he did at Hamilton."

"Okay."

Kurt Kallini is the man who works political miracles. At Cornell he managed to work between the Black Union, White radicals, professors, and administration. Black dude he sent to the Panthers in Oakland returned, and it's his picture in all the papers, Lionel Dubois, leading them out of the Straight, a battalion of Blacks with guns. You know more of who was responsible and who was irresponsible. I read a newspaper and I heard from Early Hayze what Kallini pulled off. My pal, Early Hayze, was biased toward Kurt Kallini, taking his word as gospel. From the time he got with my roommates and shared some Acapulco gold with us, Early took The Man at his word. Kallini stayed with Early Hayze in the Hamilton Towers, where we roomed.

Early Hayze with his gift of gab and line of bullshit lived out his welcome at Hamilton College. He failed classes, smoked dope, and languished with his senior thesis. Both of us had been at rope's end before winter study. I returned from Wells to write my paper on the transcendent moment in modern literature, which I entitled Prodigal Time, and Early Hayze did not. Winter at Wells motivated me to finish college and graduate, earn money for planefare, and meet Kady in Paris. It was a whitebird of the imagination, both projects, thesis and trip to Paris, and I tried like a suburban fool up on The Hill to see a solution, take resolve to reach two goals, and bridge here to there like The Pont Mirabeau. The Hayze fell under Kurt Kallini's sway.

See The Hayze all anemic white skin and puddly eyes, thick lenses, long fingers rolling his Topps tobacco into thin cigarettes by day and thick joints by night. He sat in his Tower room beneath a parachute ceiling he got skydiving on another venture. With him were Kallini's freshman contingent of Mark from Valley Stream and Lester from a Queen's redlined neighborhood, but roommates like The Hayze and Peter Bergman, liberal lawyer's son from Westchester. Kallini pushed his product through Mark and Lester and Kallini lit up The Hayze with heroism. The Hayze about to crash off the road of his college career decided to turn into the direction of his skid and sign up for the military. Kallini turned his random idea into the revolution from within the military, when the guys with guns say no to the Establishment fools who say fight. The French and the Russian revolutions begin when the armies switch sides and lead the people.

I heard Kallini's rhetoric enough at Chapel and the March on Washington to know how persuasive he can be. He's a master manipulator. He takes your deepest fear or desire and transforms a vague anxiety or a persistent itch into a grandiloquent gesture for Early Hayze to lead the revolution from within. You want to know who

Kallini planned to slip 100 million in diamonds and dust through US customs, say Early Hayze in military uniform and you'd have the culprit caught at Kennedy. Of course, Early Hayze never made it into the army overseas, never made it out of basic training, never survived to lead the revolution from within or the Treasure of the Sierra Madre through customs.

Early Hayze climbed the Chapel tower to the top of its tip, where the lightning rod falls like cable to the ground. Peter Bergman was with him on a foggy midnight climb. Peter who's pretty normal to Early's pretty abnormal, with his New Zealand to DC heritage and tales of his Brit dad climbing the Tree of Aki in some Borneo jungle to find one's niche on the Tree of Life. Early said he lost his niche on Aki's Tree and by sliding from the Chapel's tip down the chain of evolution renewed his animal nature. No, he didn't leap to his death. Neither did my liberal friend, Peter Bergman. One after the other they slid down the lightning rod of existence of a foggy night and renewed a faith in being.

I saw The Hayze resurrect his commitment to a military revolution and Peter Bergman, my good friend, further ready to pursue his liberal dream of a color-blind nation, where all men and women are equal in opportunity for the good American life. I simply tried to make it through the long winter, writing letters to Kady Bontecott she never returned, writing my paper on Prodigal Time I never finished, and waiting for word, if I worked through to graduation I could connect a month in January with a month in June, back with Kady. It was the most absurd winter on record.

"Want me to tell you what Kurt Kallini did at Cornell?"

"From a Cointelpro perspective? Tell me, Carol Hunter"

"He was the voice of moderation. Along with Joshua Steen, Kallini stopped a wild rush into the night of 10,000 students into the teeth of a police force frightened enough to shoot into crowds. Lionel Dubois spoke for armed rebellion. Weathermen like Quinn spoke for rushing en masse to occupy all the buildings on campus, especially Day Hall. Kurt Kallini kept the peace and Josh Steen kept the 10,000 where they were in Barton Hall. If Cornell erupted in racial, radical violence and police and the people there shot each other, it would have been chaos. Cornell will never be the same great university. A number of their name professors transferred to University of Chicago after the months and years of administrative liberalism. Only solution for radical revolution is a combined Cointelpro subversion from within: local, state, and military order, and a legal retribution to prosecute the perpetrators of revolution to the full extent of the law."

"If Kurt Kallini was ever the voice of reason, you, Carol Hunter, are not."

"How would you solve the culture wars in America?"

"First end the war in Vietnam, finally."

"Then what?"

"Care for the casualties: soldiers, students, silent majority."

"As Nixon said, bring the people together?"

"As Nixon promised and never did. Never meant to do. He meant to create divisions among the people, right and left, hardhat and hippie, sunbelt South and rustbelt North. Nixon divided to conquer, as he's always done."

"Then this nation can return to a land of opportunity and enterprise and hard work?"

"Or a nation moving so far to the right we will view the Fifties conformity with nostalgia as a lost paradise."

"It was."

"In any black community without a select few, the talented tenth like you and yours, Carol Hunter, it was the worst of times until Brown, Rosa Parks, Martin Luther King, integrated rock-n-roll, the Little Rock teens, Sit-ins by SNCC, Freedom Summer, voter drives, LBJ's Civil Right's bill and Voting Rights act, Malcolm X and Black Muslims, affirmative action, immigration reform, soul music, MOtown, Black Panther breakfast programs, and so on.

"Morpheys, all the liberal programs, that Great Society BS, it led to Watts, Newark, and Detroit burning down. It led from reform to riot to revolution. Law and order, that's what's needed now."

"Over an empty bag this conversation is meaningless. In prison with least 80% of the inmates Black and Hispanic, we're having the wrong conversation. You and Jimmy are on the wrong side of history."

"What kind of communist infiltrator are you, David Morpheys? What kind of criminal of drugs and diamonds are you? What kind of future are you waiting for, doing next to nothing, teaching criminal trash, their ABC's."

"It's work, it's a job, it's not nothing."

"Morpheys, talking to you drives me nuts."

Carol Hunter pressed stop to the cassette recorder and figured to send him to classes.

"I see how you drove Kady Bontecott up a wall with all this radical, liberal, political, transcendental BS. You're one of those suburban white boys who get a little education and they think they can think."

"It takes one to know one."

"How low do we go, trading childish insults, it takes one to know one."

"I agree, a little learning is a dangerous thing."

"Jesus!"

7
Resentment

Carol Hunter wanted no part of David Morpheys' interrogation, then on. She returned to Millbrook and the Bennet School, like one she attended near Chicago, for bright, young, prosperous children till she attended Northwestern and Chicago Law. Kady Bontecott was more her style, where black and white didn't matter, a little class did.

"I see now why you ditched David Morpheys. I never been more frustrated by any black militant talking revolution than him, with his righteous routine every liberal holds to."

"He got more radical over the year I knew him. It was an intellectual and cultural journey for him."

"When's it going to sink in, all that is BS for a middle class boy from Suburbia."

"He wasn't as talkative at Wells. He was shy and unsure of himself, among the girls, among the preppies and debutants, among the courses and ideas we took for granted. It was all new to him. Like the black blues. Like the existentialists, like symbolist poetry and Russian novelists, like the life of ideas having any relevance at all. He's a jock, basically. It's all athletic grace and competition and fairness by the rules. Sport's the great meritocracy."

"Just a jock, Kady?"

"Without a thought on his mind till he believed the coach picked an AD prep over him at quarterback, not for merit, but because the kid's Groton class gave him leadership skills. He played three seasons, did well at another position, got a concussion, a broken ankle, and the resentment of college organizations closed to merit and talent. He broke through with football and he wanted to break through with his intelligence, if it took years, if it took a lifetime. All resentment."

"Damn't Kady, he resented me, a black girl with class."

"And, Carol, that's what got you pissed off with him."

∞ 500 ∞

"You too?"

"I guess I got over it. No, I guess I never did. When we shared a journey, going places we would never see again, doing things we never did before, sharing a bed, an attitude, a romantic sense of the possibilities of life, it was more blissful than enervating. Finally I couldn't take the travels, the daily sense of so much more we could and should be doing. It never stopped with him. The ambition to be somebody he wasn't. He was simply a small town boy a long way from home, fearing he never could go home again. Or that was all he'd do."

"That's why he resented me because my black family has class and his doesn't?"

"Something like that."

"Why should he?"

"You let him know you were better than him?"

"I am, Kady. I'm a Chicago lawyer working for the justice department and he's a GED teacher in a maximum security prison."

"You got under his skin."

"He got under mine. And I thought I was a pretty tough-skinned black girl."

"I think you are too."

"I had to be."

"Him too. The resentment with him it's a way not to be hurt. And he's relentless in that pursuit to prove himself as good as you are. An intellectual competition. All the arguments, all the rhetoric, all the ideas, they're all weapons to defend a small town boy competing out of his league, with the likes of you."

"I'll keep the competition to a minimum. Just the facts, mam, as Jimmy Smith, my Hispanic colleague, tells me."

"What facts do you want to question in this session?"

"What did you do in Europe?"

"In Paris take a few courses at the Sorbonne. Stay with a family who treated me like a daughter, you know, be home at night, study, take care not to shame the family, and if I had a soiree with the group be home by ten. I saw a little of Europe with Jesse Latimore whose brother's at Chase Bank, and looks after her like my French family."

"Where in Europe did you go?"

"Some of France, some of Switzerland, and to Rome to get a papal blessing for my mom."

"That's all you did in Europe, study and travel some, and wait for David to come get you."

"He wrote long letters about all the ideas which put off a person like you, about his thesis on romantic literature, and what was happening on the college campus, till they closed down."

"And you wrote back?"

"Little blurbs on postcards, a note here and there, but none of it resulted in communication. It was as if he wrote at length and I wrote short blurbs, and we didn't connect. I pretty much gave up. Later he told me Early Hayze took my letters for Kurt Kallini and dumped them in a closet. From what I saw of Early Hayze, a drug crazed lunatic in Vichy, it's possible but not probable. I trusted whatever he said till then, and afterward, I didn't take him at his word."

"Why was that? He told lies?"

"He took off for Berlin. We're a little ahead of ourselves."

"Except he says in the carpetbag with its traces of diamonds and dust, there was a deed to your dad's farm. Is he telling a lie?"

"No."

"Why are you withholding information then, in a federal investigation? Do you know the penalties involved?"

"It was a deed to my dad's farm. It didn't belong to David Morpheys."

"Who did it belong to then?"

"My dad, of course."

"David said it came from Kurt Kallini. Is he lying?"

"It's possible, but not probable."

"Kady Bontecott, I'm about to send twenty accountants to see your dad's connections to Bontecott Stone. I'll be curious to find out, just the facts, mam."

"Do what you're obliged to do."

"Of other matters then. It doesn't seem you engaged much with the adventure of a semester abroad."

"And what significant journeys have you taken, Miss Hunter."

"Blacks can't travel with any security across America."

"I guess that's the case, down south."

"All over. And white girl, you don't know how it is for a black girl."

"Oh I see, a little color."

"Don't give me that bleached black girl crap, I don't like it."

"You don't have to. I simply replied to your assumption I did nothing with my French semester."

"Did you, Mrs. Butler?"

"I did as a French daughter would do. I learned the language, did my studies, and prepared for a career teaching French at the Bennet School. It wasn't much different than a semester at Wells College. It was well protected, well monitored, and not well spent."

"I know what you mean, and I apologize for the color. I spent countless semesters at Northwestern and Chicago Law and seminars in DC, NYC, and Boston doing nothing but studies and sucking up to professors who wanted a black girl for a protégé. Everything for a career, nothing in the least foolish."

"You never ventured forth in the cities, saw a little music, drank a few beers, tested the waters?"

"I had a few nights out. I had a few flames. No, it wasn't much. I was well protected and monitored too. More by my own sense of never shaming my family and always sacrificing fun for ambitions to be a lawyer, have a career, be somebody no woman in my family could, a person to be reckoned with."

"More power to you."

"You've ruined this recording."

"I have?"

"No Kady, I apologize, it's my fault."

"What was the intent of that line of questioning, what I did or didn't do with my semester abroad?"

"The intent, I don't know. The result, girls don't do a hell of a lot on the way to their wedding."

"You're not married?"

"No I'm not. Far from it. I'm a career woman. It looks like it's a choice, career or family."

"David and me, we did plenty. I got memories of good and bad times, but we didn't waste a day together, and when we did, I think we were apart."

"I believe you girl. Again, sorry."

"No apologies. Like life living with girls over four years at Wells, it's water under the dam."

"Let me fix the tape. Do some editing if I can, or start over next time."

"I got a class to teach verb tenses to."

"Do you like the girls?"

"They're so naive."

"Weren't we all?"

8
She's Justice; I'm FBI

"Jimmy Smith, good to see you. Carol Hunter and me got off to a rocky start. I don't know why."

"She's justice department. She's used to taking depositions, but also digging, tripping a suspect up, getting a little on a witnesses' nerves."

"It just seemed we didn't click, my ideas and hers."

"Her view, you're a liberal, a radical, maybe a Marxist, and all your ideas are wrong."

"You don't butt in, as I ramble on about romance, poetry, movies, philosophy, and all that jazz. Why not?"

"Carol's justice, I'm FBI."

"What's the difference?"

"As I said, she takes depositions like a lawyer, FBI simply listens. To your phone, to your classes, to your times out to see Joey Gallo and Thomas Gordon."

"That's the difference. I was going to say good cop/bad cop like my buddies Jimmy Sullivan and Jerry Seagram."

"You know the local police?"

"We grew up together in Hudson Park. With Jimmy I went to jail for 4th of July firecrackers and played on Rotary little league with Jerry. Don't worry, the bonds are broken. But I know them on sight. Or Flash, Tommy Gordon, knew their undercover car."

"Well, I let you out to see what extracurriculars you did. Not a whole hell of a lot. I see it's spy/counterspy everywhere we go, Cointelpro I mean."

"Sign of the times."

"But you're happy to teach GED inmates and a writing course two nights a week?"

"As I told Carol Hunter, it's honest work, it pays for an apartment, and teaching's what I do."

"Carol asked if you talked with communists on your stay in Berlin?"

"On my way to Russia to catch visions of Dostoyevsky, Tolstoy, and Eisenstein's cinema, no. It looked mighty Gestapo or KGB from west to east, and Berlin with its bombed black Marienkirche, surrounded by towers of business, even IBM, it all seemed surreal, as if it were a fake city framed by walls all around. Walk a quarter mile here, come to a wall. Walk a half mile there, and nowhere to go but back to the hostel or onto the bum beds in Bahnhof's Mission. It cured me quickly. A week later I returned to Kady, whom I left behind to travel into what darkness we fear: the Iron Curtain, communist control, and the red tide. It was dreary all right. It was a long way by train, okay. It was no pleasure trip, so I wouldn't do it again."

"And no business trip, no?"

"I don't get Carol like I don't get preps whether they be black or white. Are there any preps who are Hispanic?"

"None I know. There are old Spanish families in the states from Florida to Oregon, but they have no say."

"Tell Carol I can't be a small-town upstart from Suburbia and a commie agent at the same time. To be an authentic college boy as my non-college buds call me, I'm damned if I do and damned if I don't."

"They don't like me anymore in the barrio."

"Yea, the way it is."

"Talk about the March on Washington and how involved Kurt Kallini was with the Movement."

"Okay, back to our business. Whether Kady's carpetbag was half-full or half-empty."

News broke Nixon sent the armies to invade Cambodia and spread the war over Indochina. A thousand college campuses came alive and ours at Hamilton was no exception. Kallini led the charge. He spoke in chapel as a delegate from Cornell and Oakland, California. He told us Nixon made his big mistake, thinking he would expand the war to end the war. Action and reaction, news came in and crowds of kids from all over the country converged on the Capital. I took off on a snowy night with white on white in the chapel glow. The campus was double lit and universities were on fire. It was as if all Kallini's half-hearted plans took shape over night and transferred half a million protesters from quiet campus life to a Capital alive with politics.

Somehow it was a Second Awakening. You know American history speaks of first and second awakenings and pre and post millennial spirit of the times. Well the Zeitgeist spoke that night for nights afterward of revolution, whether it be Weathermen, revolution from within the military, Panthers, SDS, PLP, SNCC, any number of acronyms and fringe groups of kids come for politics and good time rolls, like the oldtime revivals of the Evangelical Front. For me football was gospel, and Kady Bontecott with our month of romance at Wells College, that was a first awakening. But this political madness was something more like a madness of the masses, in a good way, a second awakening.

In Peter Bergman's Pimpmobile, as Early Hayze dubbed the big car the Grannie of Peter gave him, we rocketed into that snowy night, reached Valley Forge with a cold but clear morning, revolution in the air, then by late afternoon arrived to DC with its magnolia blossoms the first of May. We left winter and chapel protest and arrived Mayday in the Capital with summer coming in. It was magic, it was miracle, it was magnificent fun. That night there were bands and speeches by David Dellinger and Rene Davis, bands like Rhinoceros, and Phil Oakes singing I ain't a marching anymore. I think it was Judy Collins too with her sweet clear voice and Washington's Monument taking a poke at a Jimi Hendrix, excuse me while I kiss the sky.

Night to night, what a day. Next morning it was Peter Bergman dragging me to the Capital to speak with my congressman. I said yes, but opted for no, since I was dressed in jeans, suede jacket, and moccasins. Hey Hamilton Fish, what do you say, end the war. Peter had his congressman give us tickets to the gallery and we heard little debate except for Mississippi Stennis say all this invasion was justified by presidential power. If the speakers and singers put on a variety show, it wasn't much less of a hoot in the Capitol building. We stayed in Georgetown and roomed with Early's bud, Harry Heintz, who took Peter's Pimpmobile and christened it the Revolutionary Taxi, which he drove everywhere.

Early Hayze had this date with destiny. He was signing up for the military. He was to travel out to Fort Dix on a bus of soldiers to start a revolution from within. Protest at the bus station performed by the hallowed peaceniks, and they prepared to sit down in the buses' path until they got dragged away. I met a man who'd done this peaceful protest several times and I sat down with him. Came the cry, the buses are coming, prepare for mass arrests. All I worked for. All I did to get ahead. And I was going to jail to stop Early Hayze from going to Vietnam, where my brother had gone. We shared a cigarette, elder peacenik and me, athlete and college boy, braced ourselves for non-violent protest, and then learned the buses took off from another exit. So much for our shared conviction.

Early Hayze was off to Ft. Dix and his bud, Harry Heintz, followed the bus in the Revolutionary Taxi in case Early and others actually did break loose and needed a getaway car. Early was off to basic training, rather badly bruised by the MP's who knew what was up, more than Early Hayze. Friend Peter Bergman lost his ride and then the next morning he saw the light, how Nixon tipped a stone in the China Sea and Cambodian waves caused a equal and opposite reaction. Out on the horizon DC filled up with protesters, filled to the brim with bus after bus, and out there too Peter saw his Pimpmobile come back from Ft. Dix. Harry Heinz got out, came toward the dorm room where we surveyed all DC, to tell us, Early got the crap beat out of him. He was definitely in the army now.

"You blame Kallini's using Early Hayze for his revolution within the military?"

"Who else is to blame?"

"The RYM and the Weatherman who took care to give Kallini a jackboot to his twisted spine. We had insiders at the meeting and he wasn't wanted after what he did to Quinn the Eskimo, supplier of drugs, pipe bombs, and terrorism."

"You think again Kallini was a moderating force?"

"Least he wasn't a zombie following the Redbook code of combat."

"Good to think he was persona non grata, where he once was The Man of the movement."

"You don't like him very much?"

"It's a longer story."

"Can't be because he asked you to carry Kady's bag through customs, you refused, and he still gave you a deed to the Bontecott Farm where your dad worked."

"Again it's a long story. He's a master manipulator, that I know."

"Didn't he find you a place in Paris with The Brotherhood?"

"No, it was the Freres providing charity to old folks called vieillards, and yes he helped. Especially with Peter Bergman getting a place at the American Church. I was set up in Paris if I ever managed to get there."

"Get a job?"

"Go home, get a job, and this and that happened. Hudson Park is no place for a month's work, easy money made, and a take-off into the wild blue yonder. It was home turf, like your barrio, that downed anyone who tried to fly away. Especially me, the College Boy."

"How come, you and Joey Gallo, along with Flash Gordon, still seem pretty close?"

"You're close in ninth grade and so there's a bond ever afterward, like it or not."

"You go to Joey's Ristorante to buy drugs or sell drugs?"

"Neither then, nor this weekend. Don't do drugs."

"Well tell them it's no news to local police Joey pushes $20 bags over the counter, more bags than fancy dinners. Also tell your friend, Flash Gordon, his pushing drugs from his Marist loft is a known quantity too."

"Why give me information I can't use?"

"Why not?"

"I'd have to tell them my good bud, Jimmy Smith, a Cointelpro agent let me know."

"Oh. No trade off like you warn them, then let us know where Kallini may be. After all, it's Joey's cousin and his Uncle Carlo too."

"You don't think I carried a bag of diamonds and dust through customs?"

"Not me. You're the college boy disconnected from his hometown.

You could be. Carol's not convinced you're not, but I don't see you waiting five or ten years to be rich. None of Kallini's 100 million is going anywhere soon. He may be smarter than anybody knows. Maybe the cash launders as we speak, but no cash shows up. Maybe he's funding Brotherhood operations in Egypt, Turkey, and Marseilles, but we have no word. I think he's sitting tight and knows, he overreached himself, and the next five or ten years he's SOL, shit out of luck."

"Well, then we're all stuck."

"Then where is he? Give us a clue."

"Gobelins, protected by Aki and the Algerians. His own room in the compound, it oversees all Paris from the Hills of Gobelins, southwest of the Seine. There's another Freres station across the street. I worked Richard Lenoir near the Bastille, but Kurt Kallini liked the safety of Gobelins."

"Well thanks. Tell Flash and Joey to cool it because Jerry and Jimmy are hot to trot, hoping to make a mark with the incoming grass at the train station."

"Buds look after buds, Cointelpro too?"

"We play all sides, FBI is bigtime politics."

"I'm smalltime GED. If I have nothing to do with a bag of drugs, Kady has even less."

"Carol's checking out the estate and the business, which belongs to the Bontecotts. This is third generation jewelry business with connections to all the Hasid jewelers on 54th Street in NYC."

"Connections have nothing to do with Kady."

"Nothing at all. It's WASP and Yale and New Haven business, and it's untouchable, as I told Carol. Even the diamond business in the City and Antwerp and South Africa, it's untouchable, probably moreso. There's a connection between South African diamonds, nuclear materials, and the Israeli state. Talk about levels above my pay grade, Carol's too."

"Why tell me anything?"

"You got some smarts. I thought you, knowing Kurt Kallini, might fill in a connection or two. After all, an agent like me has to know where to take an investigation and where it crosses a line. This is sticky business for two neophytes, and just maybe, you and Kady Bontecott, know a shade more than we do. I let you know your buds should step lightly, you and Kady fill in the picture on Kurt Kallini. You don't have a 100 million dollars, he does. Only we don't have him, we have you."

"Keep us talking, something may come up?"

"How was getting home after college and DC's second awakening?"

"It was sleepy time time. Truth, time lapsed. All time is prodigal time until it lapses."

"Home town with nothing happening, at all?"

"Things happened. Only it was all the same stuff, as when I went off to college. You can come home, but you can't leave town, like the Roach Motel."

"Get a job."

"I got a job at Payless gas station, only I didn't keep it. I got a job at Hudson Printing, third shift from time to go out till the wee hours of the morning. Only I got hammered through the back of my hand with a book sorter. Broke their safety record, like I didn't snap to at the Payless. College Boy, what are you doing that shit work for, Flash was eager to ask. After a stint at my local church and condemnation of both me and my parents for my long hair, I did drop a tab of acid with Joey Gallo. That was a trip I'll never forget. No friend of nature, no hand for football or horseshoe, no stomach for DQ Deluxes, no heart for Carnival rides at the Staatsburg Fair. It was a riot. I was disconnected from my hometown vibe, that was crystal clear.

We made a round of all the bars, here there and everywhere till four in the morning when I met my brother at Highland's Circle Inn. "Pitiful drinker, you are, little brother." He was off to Saratoga to bet the ponies, eat a fancy dinner, and lose what money he made selling insurance for Met Life. Joey drives us home scraping his wreak of a car off metal of the Mid-Hudson Bridge. Full moon fell hollow and empty when I made it home to the housing development. That was that, full circle, until Kady's dad came for me at four in the afternoon, still asleep, with a letter from Paris, Kady telling me, come see her. Dad gave me a graduation present, the planeride over. So I wasn't rolling in dough over the ocean. I needed work with Les Freres and Kallini assisted me.

"That's it for me, College Boy. Once over the ocean you're out of Cointelpro's and the FBI's jurisdiction."

"Really?"

"No, the CIA keeps tabs on dissidents overseas."

"They do?"

"Only you're not over the ocean, you're in prison under our interrogation."

"I think you have a sense of humor, but I'm not sure."

"More than Carol Hunter who wants to have another go. Tell her that Kallini stuff about how he's hold up at Gobelins with twenty Algerian terrorists prepared to lay down their lives against any and all intruders."

"Okay. Your prisoner of Chillon, moldering for thirty years in captivity, will say anything."

"I just said it would take Kallini five or ten years to free up his cash, for his closest friends, you and Kady Bontecott."

9
Kallini has a History

"Tell me Kady," Carol Hunter asked, their last session tapes edited to her liking, "how you first heard Kurt Kallini related to your family."

"You mean my mom's call?"

"Let's say yes, and get started there."

"Mom told me when she was sick with cancer Kurt came to the Vassar Brothers Hospital to simply talk to her of life and death."

"Why the concern?"

"He was a Marist brother in the Seminary and that's what he did."

"Before he was a hip honcho with the Movement, with SDS and the Panthers and all the crazies collected in fringe groups by the end of the Sixties."

"Way back to 1960. It disposed me differently towards him."

"And if you knew that Jesse Latimore's family are investment bankers, brother and father, heavily invested in the diamond trade in Antwerp and South Africa, including nuclear projects the Israelis fund through a Jewish network in NYC?"

"I knew Jesse's brother was way too controlling of a sweet girl like her."

"Playing upon her sympathies or telling her what to do?"

"Both. It was his doing she slept with Steve Hancock when she didn't like him, when she doesn't like boys, at all."

"She's a lesbian?"

"At a girl's school it's the perfect blind for a girl like Jesse."

"And you?"

"No, I liked her as a friend. Jesse always cared for a girl like me and like Barb, whether it was a mutual feeling, or just friends."

"But you traveled over Europe with her?"

"For a couple weeks, yes."

"So she knew her way around, trains, planes, and customs?"

"You don't trust anyone, do you, Carol Hunter?"

"Only if they're trustworthy. And Steve Hancock has relatives in CIA connected to the Israelis, and fresh out of college he's being used for specific tasks."

"What's Kurt Kallini got to do with any of these people?"

"I don't know, do you?"

"No."

"Tell me how Kurt Kallini changed. Not from seminarian in 1960 to movement guru later on in the decade, but over this year you shared blues records, and he sent off your best friend, Barb Kelly to the coast."

"He came to Paris as seminarian, not from Marist College, but for The Petites Freres des Pauvres"

"You mean The Brotherhood?"

"What's that, Carol?"

"An organization of religious zealots across North Africa and the Middle East."

"He lived with the Algerians at a restaurant that served cous cous. He seemed at home. He dressed differently too. He wasn't in revolutionary black, as with the Movement. He dressed Parisian, acted suave and sophisticated, and came off like it was as much his town as Aurora, New York."

"Did he ever discuss his religious views with you?"

"As a Catholic, yes. He believed it was the one true religion to unite all the countries once belonging to the Roman reach of Constantine. That Europe and the Middle East had to come back to the true church, to become the whole worshipping world. He had a Latin phrase I don't remember. The more religious each culture became, an awakening of the fundamental tenets of their faith, unification of the whole worshiping world would be not only possible but inevitable. The center was Rome and Constantinople and within that arc of Eurasia the one true church would reign supreme, immortal, and divine."

"What did you think of his Catholicism?"

"As crazy as his concept of the Movement in America. It was ideology run amuck. I listened to his discussions of religion with the same fervor as he talked of Robert Johnson's blues and Charley Parker's jazz. It was another of his acts of faith that kept his twisted back and shorter leg, he had polio as a kid, from plaguing him with a pain that compromised his spirit."

"You understood him as a crippled, Christian martyr to the faith?"

"No, of course not. His faith defined his character and helped him deal with his pain."

"You sympathized with him?"

"As I did with my mom in her pain. I got arthritis which acts up with wet weather too."

"How are you with winter coming on?"

"Fine, thank you."

"Did David Morpheys know you were seeing Kallini in Paris?"

"Kurt was seeing me. He showed up outside the Sorbonne, gave me news David was coming over, and that his friend Early Hayze was doing better half way through basic training. I didn't know Early Hayze till later, but when I met Peter Bergman, really nice guy, I assumed his roommate was much like him. College must search for the most impossible combinations, put together opposites, to see what happens. They're Nazis experimenting on vulnerable teenage kids, crippled in mind and spirit for life. You know I'm kidding?"

"I got a sense of humor, girl."

"I'm not so sure."

"Simply believe we're roommates and whatever happens, we'll do our best to get along."

"So be it, soul sister."

Carol smiled with Kady's comment. It was a positive point to stop for classes, a trip to the CIA office in the City, to see if the names of Hancock and Latimore and Bontecott too, were either taboo, or open to interrogation.

"What's on the menu for your French classes?"

"The pluperfect tense."

"Give it to them good."

10
Romantic in a Way

Carol Hunter wanted another go at David Morpheys. She wanted to listen to see if he told the truth about mixing with Kurt Kallini in Paris and how close their collusion was. She tried to trip him up, frustrate his narrative, and get a rise out of him. This time she played the romantic, in nice black dress, big brown eyes, and rapt fascination.

"Tell me about your trip to Paris. I've lived nearby a city like Chicago, but I never got to go to Paris, nowhere near. It must have been different for a guy from a small town. I mean, romantic in a way I'll never know. Make it come alive for me."

David gaged she was half in and half out. It didn't matter. Paris had been what Chicago was to her, only in another language, another continent, another time in his life, entirely. He'd tell it straight to better understand what it meant to him, then and now. It was more than culture shock. It was distortion, elation, and raised consciousness which elevated the patterns of Paris to symbolic importance.

You land at Orly, bus to Concorde, and find an apartment in St. Antoine where the Defarges of Tale of Two Cities take revenge on aristocrats who believe they're heads above all people. Among Dicken's classics of resentment and revolution the Defarges have a townie like me beat by a mile. I'm waiting at the Metro stop for Kady to rise from the Metro like Eurydice so I can stare at her before she stares at me. It's her, it's us, it's the imposing moment of time then and time now, side by side. I'm so nervous and her too, that when I touch her shoulder from behind she about leaps out of her skin. Too long waiting not knowing missed letters, difficult time working for airfare, and then, we're together, me and her and good friend Peter Bergman on the hilly street near Montmartre.

Then Kallini arrives. He has a black cape and news of our buddy Early Hayze in and out of basic training. We half believe him. He has a job for me at Gobelin, and offers to treat us to cous cous at Akim's Algerian place cross town and cross the Seine, in Gobelin where he's living his Parisian life, doing whatever he planned doing since day one. My dad and I nearly hit him on a winter road, nearly ran off the road to avoid hitting him, and joined our destiny at Wells and Hamilton and DC and Paris with his. Meeting him upset a tentative reunion between Kady and me. At Gobelin after we ate dinner, I checked out The Freres job across the street, while Peter took a tour with Kallini to his sixth floor pad in view of all Paris. I got to hold Kady, check again to see it was truly her and me, more than memory, in the moment when I asked her to come with me to my morning interview, translate for me, because work would make it possible to remain in Paris.

She did, the next morning after an exam. We met Marie Montfort and she wanted the two of us to travel to Biarritz on a Freres vacance helping the old folk, and their wretched age shocked Kady, so like her mom and so not like her. I saw Kallini planned for my month away from Kady and her return home, but when Kady withdrew crying and I made plans for a month from now at Richard Lenoir, away from Kallini, we managed to stay together, move in together with Peter, and Kady after our tour of the town up to Sacre Coeur agreed to travel France and Europe together. She agreed to a Journey East, meeting whatever magic travel entailed, order to live a life worth living. She broke with Kurt Kallini and her Dad's demand she come home, and her mom's pressing need, all to give us the prodigal time to be together over space and time, across Europe, together 24 hours a day.

It was made real by her decision to simply steal away because Kallini was in communication with her dad and she was supposed to call her mom, but she didn't. A night we slept side by side in St. Antoine and the next morning we hitched out of Paris to Fontainebleau, with castle walls and Versailles parks and little town cafes with rooms upstairs. Out in the woods lounging in the summer grass, a military excursion saw us and apologized. Later we met their captain, a Francois Searcy, tall, upper class gallant who planned to North American diplomacy in Quebec after his one year in military and communal service with all his countrymen. We agreed this wasn't the worst thing. That service to one's country and sharing with one's countrymen was a positive duty, unless the military be in Indochina, Algeria, or America since 1965 in Vietnam. We shared the elevated debate on duty and responsibility, Francois, Kady, and I before we let him suggest a route for our journey east, across the heartland of France, Troyes to Dijon and into Switzerland. Then we retired to bed, me and Kady, to celebrate the shadows of night.

Next day it was no easy ride to Troyes, further on than Paris to Fontainebleau, but by late afternoon and several rides we made it to the factory town and out to its hostelry, whose double doors labeled the porte magic, like Hesse in Steppenwolf, for madmen only. We had a meal. We learned there was a party coming for music, for Midsummer's Eve, for celebration in a lean-to of a rock band. It was magical, the fires of night, the rocking music, the coincidence of a party and us being there. Then we saw the bass player, Kurt Kallini, and the coincidence took us one step too far.

Ask how he got there and what he had to say about a summer bash, he said Early was out and added a few precious digs at Kady deserting her mom. We didn't sleep on top of the world. A single sleeping bag was simply close quarters. But in the morning the revelers left the hostel and we got a breakfast, a shower, and I got to play a Gibson on a Marshall stack. Cream's sunshine lit up Troy and set the city on flames. No magic doorway, no madmen only, just the walk to the highway and long hitches over the golden wheatfields on two or three trucks to Dijon. We dropped off at a bus station when a French doctor who'd been to San Diego offered to ride us to the hostel at the university and take us to Switzerland the next day, Sunday at 4PM in the afternoon. We took him up and liked the university for a good dinner, a good night's sleep together, and a trip into Dijon.

Kady turned sour on a Sunday in Dijon, with the monument of a church and grey skies empty overhead. So began her guilt trip. I offered to attend church, but she couldn't go and not have called her mom for a week. Antoine, our ride and guide, took us to the Alps, showed up a religious celebration like Kallini showed us the midsummer revelry. We talked of San Diego and Hawaii, all the California bands, serving people as a doctor, and actually stopped at a rural church ritual. He asked us to forego Geneva and travel with him into Italy to his parents place in Genoa. I saw the shocked look on Kady's face, her No No No a thousand times No, and I passed up Antoine offer for rain, high Alps, and an uncertain night journey to Geneva. Loose of Antoine she told of his records in the van's backseat, several with the KK on the cover like her Robert Johnson blues. Kallini was with us again.

We lost him in the rain and the Alps. A truck took us miles and miles to a summit above the entire world, above the Rhone River, above the clouds, above time itself transfixed at the heights. Then down we came into driving rain, dropped off on the highway outside Geneva, walking into the outskirts, picked up by a kind woman who directed us to the hostel before it closed at ten. Kady was up at dawn to wash clothes, put her apparel and self in order, and try to quell the guilt and gag reflex, with its taste of metal in her mouth. We washed up, swam in the public beach to Lake Geneva, and ate a sitdown dinner with a waiter far too sophisticated for the likes of me. We relaxed in neutral Switzerland with no sighting of Kurt Kallini.

We climbed sunny mountains into German speaking Bern. We saw museums and zoos and enjoyed the ease of moving back and forth underground. Over another range of Alps to Zurich and we arrived at a seven story hostel with swans on the lake. Later a old man biking beyond us showed his map into Austria en route to Vienna. I got excited and talked Kady into another journey east more ambitious than what we had undertaken, something to tell our grandkids when we grew old as the gnarled fingers of our ancient biker.

Off by morning and soon riding in a convertible sports car across the triangle borders of three countries with travelers to Vienna and us with them. When Kady asked out, our journey came to an abrupt halt. She threw up and said she packed it in. I got her to Inverness, where she called her mom and promised to be home. It was the 24 hour flu and meantime I got us by train back to Stuttgart and Strasburg and all the way returned to Paris, come full circle. It was a two week journey east, we got to say goodbye, and it seemed like a goodbye for good. She was going home. I was going to work. Two weeks and we were an ocean apart, a second time, for who knew how long.

"Tell me Carol Hunter, what did I do wrong? You listened, thank you, but I lost her and really don't know where or how."

"Blame Kurt Kallini."

"He was in contact with her parents. I think so too. His meeting us at Troyes around midsummer night was no coincidence. Yet we had our space and time away from him, away from her parents, away from a faith that sustains her."

"You had yourself a time, in your retelling, more than two weeks it seems."

"It was a life worth living for sure. All we saw, all we did, all we saw and did together twenty four hours a day. It was all new. It was total freedom which wears on a person."

"I think, David, it wore on her and two weeks was all she could take. I bet it wore on you as well."

"Time expanded like an endless day without sleep, in bed, above the Alps, above Paris, the long hitches, seeing everything new, for once and done, museums, monuments, Nature, new people, food, drink, ideas, visions, two languages, a thousand miles, and back to Paris to see it all alone, as if her leaving for a time, she'd come to share it all again."

"I'm not sure time expands, unless it seems so to you."

"Of course it expands, it levitates, until gravity proves the greater force, for then heavy is the word. I took my baskets of food to the old people, I sat in the Muse de Cinema through three and four movies a day, I toured every nook and cranny of the streets of Paris, but I could lift the burden without Kady there. The old ladies got sad and ones I liked died in the hot, endless summer without end. Kallini and his Algerian friends got to Peter and people I worked for. It was a season in hell after Parisian dreams lighter than air, bouquet brighter than a French wine, poetry of a Rimbaud like alchemy of sights and visions and the mix of everything else."

"Kallini again in your life?"

"Never out of it. With Peter to let him know about Early Hayze. With Early to let him know what to do when the army broke him down. With Kady connecting her back to her mom so her dad wouldn't do his duty to his wife. With the Algerians and the Freres and whatever else he was planning between Europe and diamonds and dust raison d'etre of our conversation."

"How much did you know of the diamonds and dust?"

"Nothing of the diamonds. Peter told of the potent hashish in his apartment, and I knew of the grass he sold at Wells and the Acapulco gold he brought in his guitar case to Hamilton College. There were drug dealers and Movement gurus, often the same persons, but the plans you tell about dwarf the little dope he shared. You're talking 100 million dollars worth and he didn't seem so involved in that business as he was involved in our lives for whatever he planned to do."

"In some way was he sick as Kady's mom?"

"Good question. He wasn't well, especially during that summer inferno. He had polio as a young kid in the Forties and a touch of epilepsy too. He never simply had his health. His back was twisted, a leg shorter, and something a bit off toward people, as if control, manipulation, and cunning were key to what he did. If he wasn't too much in the life of me and my friends, especially Kady, I'd blame myself for picking on a cripple, wouldn't you Carol?"

"He's a very clever cripple and a very well off sick person. It's all part of his profile I'm trying to build, as it pertains to Bontecott Stone and The Brotherhood, not to forget the one prevailing connection to his Uncle Carlo's mafia."

"Well I wish I could tell you more, that I knew more. Wait, I got called home by Joey Gallo to his wedding to Sue Gordon, and Kallini said he couldn't go, what with local problems in Poughkeepsie. You might check with Jerry and Jimmy, the local police, because he shows up soon afterwards, like it was no matter, his coming home, like me and like Kady."

"Who are Jerry and Jimmy?"

"Ask Agent Smith. He had them giving me and Flash Gordon a lookover when he let me go."

"I will David. Let me talk with Kady, see if her tour of Europe and her return home agrees with your narrative."

"Say hello."

"You still love her?"

"We don't mesh anymore, it's a sad thing. But a hello isn't much different now than a goodbye, once we said goodbye for good."

11
A Life worth Living

"So did you and David go at it in round two?"

"No, I listened like a demure black girl eager to impress an employer with my professionalism."

"Did that get him to spill the beans?"

"You mean, Kady Bontecott, to tell the truth."

"Yes I do."

"I believe so. Of course you may contradict or collaborate his testimony."

"Would you like me to tell the truth to the best of my knowledge?"

"A clean record would be nice. Enough with his visions of time expanding and contracting, of an imposing moment, touches of eternity, heaven and hell, time then and time now, and a life worth living. It's like listening to my minister at Chicago's Black Baptist on psychedelic drugs."

"Religious mysticism, philosophical ideas, and Rimbaud's poetic visions. I had my fill too."

"Of course the meeting again and Paris and the travels across Europe, I thought some of it was romantic."

"You do?"

"Of course, if you didn't … "

"I did. It was a month at Wells and a month in Paris I'll never forget. So intense, so carefree at times, so close to another human soul, yet such heartbreak you can't imagine."

"Try me, but keep Kurt Kallini in mind and how he's involved. Recall, he's the target of our investigation."

"Wells was a one time thing. Live a life with all the emotional intensity, then leave that boy-girl stuff behind. I had my semester abroad, then return home to tutor French, and take care of my mom."

"Just what you've done."

"I know, but heartbroken."

"Was the month in June like the month at Wells?"

"Wells was good, Paris was better. The time wore on me, though. I'm not built for the long haul, you know, cheap hotels and hostels, hitching roads, over mountains and rain and rough ways, it's not me. I'm a train to Rome with Jesse Latimore. I'm for the little luxuries like cassis and Dunhills, not nursing work with geriatric women. I'm a spoiled rich girl, even it I haven't one bit of the debutant."

"I see you in a routine, tutor, take care of a mom, take care of Edward Butler, with no one taking care of you."

Kady smiled at herself, and Carol Hunter, who didn't try to be mean.

"You see me in a routine life, but you didn't see me in the rousing adventure of a lifetime. I said it wore on me, it roused me too from my routine slumber. I saw Paris, I saw Europe, I saw the States, and I saw it all through the eyes of love. It was wonderful."

"You don't complain of Morpheys?"

"Plenty. Sure his talk wore on me too. How did a Journey East of imposing moments, traveling at the speed of time, and time together crossing times zones make a life worth living? David came alive on the trip. David's mind caught up with his physical being, and it was lovely to share the excitement with him. He came alive, I came alive, we came alive. It's what he meant if one once breaks through the routine, like a Cape Canaveral rocket, like Alps through the heavens, like Jimi Hendrix kissing the sky, a return to routine isn't only a comedown, but it's also a savoring of a life worth living. Only we never came down, to pause, find a Dalhart opportunity to settle down, and live that life. My fault too. I don't make myself clear, nor does he. I rush back to take care of my mom, and it's an excuse as much as a duty."

"But Morpheys wrote down this crackpot stuff for a senior thesis to graduate college?"

"I guess he did. He hadn't finished when we parted for good. Probably he finished what he had, graduated, got his prison work and writes into the imposing night. What do you think, you see him?"

"Maybe he does. It's all on his mind, more than any question of what Kallini did then and does now."

"Kurt Kallini kept tabs on me for my dad's sake."

"Not your mom's sake?"

"He needed me to nurse her because he's a person sick persons make sick."

"So he had Kallini monitor you like he listened to your mom as a Marist brother, way back when?"

"I think so from day one, say his first time come to Wells. Then catching up to me in Paris after the Movement fell apart and the crazies took over. Then what got to me, he was the tail on our comet crossing Europe on our journey east causing like physics our comet to return to Paris. Really I can see him hearing from the soldier diplomat, Francois Searcy, traveling to Troyes to oversee us at a city Francois sent us, then having Antoine meet us in Dijon and take us to his parents' place over the Alps."

"But you lost Kallini's tracker. You got out in the rain, topped the Alps, and raced into Geneva just barely for the Hostel's closing time. Yes, an adventure, and like Morpheys, a stolen time to be together without Kallini's interference for another week."

"An adventure, Carol. A time off the beaten track, in the neutral territory of Switzerland. How romantic? If only we could spend cash at fancy hotels and eat lavish dinners like jet setters do, like some James Bond couple."

"It wouldn't have been the same, Kady. It would be on vacation, and hardly worth the memory. David said traveling is travail and when it's difficult, tricky, interminable, it's then the breaking through, churns into the sweet ice cream of memory."

Carol heard none of the words or ideas from Morpheys. They were from a few business trips with Agent Smith whose adventures stirred the blood and rippled like waves into her store of memories.

"Yes, that sounds like Morpheys. Some new idea come from the trip at the time, long afterward."

"How was Switzerland away from Kurt Kallini's monitoring?"

"He didn't need be there. After Dijon and not calling my mom for a week, the guilt trip wore on me, then on. We still moved over the heights, across Alps from Geneva to Bern to Zurich, with stops to enjoy the museum or restaurant or the sights of the city. It was nice, as David claimed any time in between. It was earned income from the travails of the road. When David flashed on a vast journey east to Munich and Vienna and through the Iron Curtain to Istanbul and India, we were off once more on his Orient Express of the imagination. I broke down in a sports car convertible half way there. I got out, threw up, and broke down with the twenty four hour flu. David had me call my mom. He got me on the train back to Paris from Wiesbaden to Stuttgart to Strasburg, all the way back, our comet returned. He worked very efficiently, on this end to the journey east. We made love in a Pigalle hotel I don't want to describe or recall. We ate with an elegant waiter bringing us drinks at Concord. And we parted, me for America, my life of routine, and he stayed to make pay a life of social work with the Petite Freres."

"He told me."

"The month he spent without me in Paris?"

"It wasn't much. It was work. It was Kallini with Peter Bergman, a Christian, a Bernard, and Algerians from Akim's place in Gobelins. You think Kurt Kallini may be hold up in Gobelin, while we speak?"

"While we speak, President Nixon may be hold up in the White House, but how the hell do I know?"

"Point taken."

"Yes, he's there."

12
Complications with Kurt Kallini

Agent Smith returned from New Haven and Boston. Jerry and Jimmy, the locals, had nothing on David Morpheys, except he lit a desk and appeared to be writing every night he didn't teach writing. Writing, maybe Morpheys, had more about Kurt Kallini. After a weekend, Smith interviewed Morpheys in the interim between GED and writing classes that evening.

"So did you give the skinny to Carol or did she have to jack you against a wall and pull toenails?"

"She'd do that for me?"

"Or have someone 6' 10" dude from the slammer do it for her."

"Good to know. I'll keep my story straight."

"Ask me how my time off was?"

"Okay. Meet any interesting people? See any sights one doesn't often see? Learn a revelation to make your life worth living?"

"Met some CIA agents who say it's a nasty business abroad just like home."

"The crazies in the underground acting up again?"

"An occasional bomb blows up a statue or a toilet in Congress, but mostly they blow themselves up. Just seems a lot of dirty work goes on as we move toward elections. I told my buddy, and he says it's the same all over. Since we don't have friends across the Middle East, Israel is our default friend to replace Nassar, Quadafi, and Saddam. We got the Shah in Iran, but he's power mad to run everything. The Saudi family want new airplanes and weapons, everything the Shah gets, they get too. The Israelis take better care of military hardware since they took over chunks of Egypt and Syria in the Six Day War."

"So it's US and Israel in the Middle East. Trouble is the Arabs all see Israel as another colonizer in Palestine."

"That's the case. The Israelis are as Semitic as the Arabs, but they're seen as European and supported by the Americans in NYC."

"They are."

"So we're not liked because of them."

"We're not liked in Indochina. We're not liked in Chile. Hell, we're not much liked in Europe anymore. How soon they forget the David Morpheys, American social worker, came to save France in both WWI and WWII, as if he personally liberated Paris along with Hemingway."

"No kidding. I got to read your press clippings. Or whatever you're writing in that apartment down from Vassar, every night."

"Jerry and Jimi acting as your eyes and ears?"

"They're the locals."

"I'll have to invite them up for a beer, or blow some dope."

"Let me negative the second option. So what are you writing?"

"Our shared interrogation stirs me to write about the year Kady and me lived a life."

"Kallini play a active role?"

"He has his part to play."

"Tell me. Do you see Kallini connecting with South African diamonds?"

"He may well be, or may have been."

"May he be a conduit of funds from the CIA to fund Israeli settlements on the West Bank?"

"No, I don't believe so. Do you?"

"I'm not so sure after my conversation with a buddy of mine."

"You said Kurt Kallini most certainly connected with funds in excess of a 100 million."

"A low ball estimate. If he can pull in heroin from Turkey to Marseilles, and he can pull South African diamonds into Antwerp, and find a market for both in NYC with couriers crossing through Kennedy or coming down the NYS Thruway from Montreal, what can't he pull in for cash?"

"Money never seemed to be a prime mover with him. It was more a question of power, manipulation, control over forces beyond his control, and himself. Recall he's not so far from crippled. His health is often a hell for him."

"But understand me, David. A clever criminal we can commandeer police and detection to ferret him out. But if the French and the Italians and the Turks have a stake in his business, we may too. We may want to keep our connection with Israel, with South Africa, with the French in Europe, at the expense of simply raiding his sanctuary at his Gobelin place you visited."

"So Kallini is an operator who may have lost his come and go to the Poughkeepsie streets, but may find sanctuary in Paris?"

"You see it's not only Israel and France in play here, it's his connection to the Brotherhood. They are not liked by the military men in Egypt, Syria, Iraq, and Libya, but the Brotherhood has a powerful sway with the people in those countries."

"So Kallini plays both ends against the middle and maybe all means to all ends. He's a manipulator, for sure, what do you say, Agent Smith?"

"I say yes he is. What he did wrong was buy up Bontecott Stone at the expense of that family. He can't come and go to America, so his deed to Bontecott's estate and his massive payment for the Bontecott business, all's up in the air and in the courts, what with our charge of him for importing diamonds and dust. Again, there's a war on drugs going on."

"And a war in Vietnam too."

"Yes there is."

"I don't think your interrogation of Kady and me goes as planned."

"It's certainly more complicated."

13

A Surprise Meeting

    Kady bulked her navy coat to her exposed neck and pulled down a French wool cap over her ears. It was a harsh November wind whooshing the path between her and Edward's faculty house and the campus building. Just as bundled as her coming from the girls' dorm she saw what looked like Jesse Latimore in a purple hood, like the Bennet school colors. Kady stopped dead in her tracks, so did Jesse.

"It is you."

"It's me, older and wiser."

"You here to see me, why not call?"

"Do we have to carry on a what's up talk in the freezing cold?"

"Come to my classroom on the second floor."

"Come to my classroom number 313, if you don't mind showing me where it's located."

"You're lost."

"Your husband says, in dire need of somebody to teach maths to your honors calculus and trig, I'm found."

"313, damn, you're directly above me, with nice views of faculty lane."

"Show me, Kady Bontecott."

"Nope, wrong name."

"What's Edward's name, let me see, ah, Butler. The Butler did it. Married to the headmaster, there's no further step to the top, you're there. Demand the moon and expect sunshine and blue skies."

    They pulled open the double door back entrance, touched lightly on the worn, stone stairs, one floor, two floors, three. Jesse's room was a small cubicle on a corner with windows right and left, and her desk at the apex triangle. Books for trig and calculus piled on a mahogany table, and the slate boards filled with white chalk. Somebody went to trouble to make the third floor garret a pleasing place. Edward would have senior girls desperate for game theory and nuclear numbers make the new teacher welcome. They had college applications on the line, to Yale and Harvard and Brown, and Jesse Latimore was fresh from grad school programs at Yale, a math whiz.

"Why break off grad school prior to the holidays?'

"I got too many promoters back of my brother, Janson, and he wants too much of his sister."

"He expects you to jump and only ask how far?"

"Like your mom."

"No, like my dad. But nobody should pull strings like him."

"Speak of your dad, speak of the devil, and the manipulator of all puppets, Kurt Kallini. Speak of my brother and speak of your curator of cosmic effects."

"You haven't seen him at Yale?"

Neither the God of Bill Buckley, nor Kurt Kallini. Which doesn't mean I haven't felt the effects of his machinations."

Jesse Latimore arranged numbers of books to the number of girls in her honor classes. It added up, her here, Kady here, her brother Janson in NYC at Chase, and Kurt Kallini in Paris. There was a certain symmetry in the arrangement.

"You want help from me, or my husband?"

"I do. Since we'll be seeing plenty of each other, let's let class times fill in the gaps. Right at nine all the pretty darlings should be on their way. You and me back at an all girls' school. Does it suit you as much as it suits me, tell the truth?"

Kady didn't know what to say. Jesse cute as a Goldie Hawn had let her hair grow long, thick, and blond. It was no longer clipped short, butch style. Jesse Latimore was more beautiful than all the girls Kady had seen, and it was a beauty tres amere, tres froid, like the first harsh effect of November winds.

14
East, West, and Woodstock

"Okay, Morpheys, a short talk for Christ's sake, then a ride up to Joey's ristorante to see what he knows of Kurt Kallini."

"Why do you need to bother Joey Gallo? He doesn't know a thing about Kallini."

"You asked him what he knows?"

"No, I leave him alone."

"Hasn't his marriage to Flash Gordon's sister worked out for the best?"

"Sue's pregnant, Flash sells drugs, and Joey can't keep the ristorante a going concern."

"Without selling over the counter to keep afloat. Hey it's not the best of times for anyone."

"And my girlfriend from high school came home from Florida, where she goes to law school, with a mono which ended a semester of law she'll never make up."

"So you don't want to go into a hornet's nest, especially with me, Jimmy Smith. Jeez, I thought Thursday night, you'd want to show your pal a good time, pay for beers, and try to make me forget the investigation."

"Just what I'd like to do."

"Then get through this coming home stuff from Paris, the wedding, the trip to Texas and San Diego, and the road back to Woodstock. I mean really, you said, it wasn't much different from the journey east, only west."

Lorraine, the girl home with mono, paid the air fare along with Joey, so I could be at the wedding. As I told you about coming home from college to work for airfare getting there, this wasn't easy to take the money. But it was their wedding. They were all best friends from high school, they expected me to be there. Then when I got there, all time entombed from flying into day and it still being day when I arrived, I was strung out. Lorraine thought we'd get back together again, I didn't. But it was always part of a group dynamic, Joey and Sue, Flash and Lisa, me and Lorraine.

Only this time it wasn't going to work. Flash was always first to go for the juggler. Hey College boy, why do you think you're better than us. Not better, just different. Lorraine was drinking daiquiris like shots. She saw us all as inbred in some weird way. Did I love this Kady Bontecott, this girl with tennis courts and horse stables? Flash knew her and Dhalia Richards. It was weird, all us in the wedding party, all us in a car to the Holiday Inn, prepared to fly to Orlando for Disneyworld. I had to get out. The next morning I hitchhiked in my tux to Vassar Brothers and saw my grandpa hooked like a corpse to machines, half alive and half dead. It was horrible, it was sad, wedding and funeral, none of it made sense.

Then I got reprieved. I got away with Kady Bontecott in her red VW bound for her grandpa's funeral in Dalhart, Texas. It was wonderful at first, just the travel into the Monday morning, summer sun, but Kady wasn't entirely well. She had the throw ups like she did on the journey east. So I drove after rain into Ohio. Curvature of the earth created time. Cornfields crowded the super highways west. The sky leaped out of sight and the land lay flat as far as the eye could see. I drove and I drove, while Kady slept, all the way to St. Louis and the Archway to the West.

It was good sleeping with Kady again. I told her she got inside the way I think and the way I feel. We were two for the road. Car broke down in the Missouri breaks, but it was okay, time for it to be fixed. We got across Oklahoma on Route 40, across the Panhandle of Texas, and up to Dalhart to see her Gram, what a woman. Kady and her went to the funeral. Young John Lonigan, who did peace corps in South America, showed me the farm as if I were to buy it. If I wasn't so dense, I'd have known Kady wanted to stay with Gram and with me working on the farm. Let the threat of the Draft pass me by. We'd stay there and live there and be together for as long as time lasted.

Gram told of old John's trip to San Diego to see the ocean before he died of cancer. So bee-u-tiful. And I wanted to see the Pacific, to see the Coast too. In my pocket I had a card from Antoine in Dijon of a Bill Cougar on Pacific Beach, go see him, go see California. God, any American determined to drift to Europe the rest of his days, had to see the West Coast. So we did. Across the desert and the canyons, Phoenix rising in the sun, over the Sierra Madre, and seeing the ocean, getting there, welcomed by Bill Cougar, Janey Tower, and their band of crazy communers. We ate Thursday night specials from Tubb's Tavern: taquitos, refried beans and hot sauce, salad and blue cheese dressing, and Olympia beers. We saw the sun take its leisurely drop into the Pacific out to Hawaii and over to Nam, where I did not want to go. Drawn, drifting, and doomed. Paradise was there and it wasn't for us. Kady got to see Bill and Janey who were doctors, and get her problem straightened out, while I played beach football for all I was worth. The way it was supposed to be played. No rules, no coaches, no favoritism for the Groton kid, Steve Hancock, and played bee-u-tifully with an ocean sideline.

Then we were off on a gypsy caravan, the road back to Woodstock. We picked up young John Lonigan in Dalhart with Angelina, we pushed far as Kady's VW would travel, but again it needed repairs. We waited a day, traveled on Route 90 into downtown Cleveland, across Route 17 of western NY state, the Thruway was closed man, and got there late Saturday night. Sunday morning Hendrix played his star-spangled banner for wake up call. It was the last look at America, it was the congregation of all our stoned friends, it was Early Hayze far f___ out of it with Peter Bergman, and all of us pledged to meet in Vichy, France for the August commune, like Bill and his gypsy band had their Pacific Beach. The rain took up again, full force, Sunday, and there was no one to stop the rain. Kady took me home and when she went home, Kurt Kallini who visited in July with his Uncle Carlo to meet Evander Bontecott was back before her, same black Cadillac, same expensive suit, same reason to oversee the Bontecott business. Something went terribly wrong Kady later told me, but that's her part to tell, not mine.

15
Just Tell Him

"You know Jesse Latimore's teaching maths to the honor students?"

"We wanted her here, Kady, and no longer there. Don't go telling anyone. As soon as keep it secret, she's no longer at Yale grad school."

"Why may I ask?"

"She's had more recent information on Kurt Kallini. Her brother Janson Latimore works with Chase in Europe, and he's closely connected with Steve Hancock's family in the CIA."

"What did she tell you?"

"I would rather let that be part of our side of the investigation."

"I mean about us."

"That she's a lesbian?"

"That doesn't matter to you?"

"No. I don't see how it affects her math skills or her relay of information or her distrust of her brother's handling of her in the past."

"You surprise me, Carol Hunter. You're a Republican in the justice department with strictures on how people should live their lives, and yet when it comes to somebody important in your investigation, things don't matter at all."

"That pretty much sums up my view of the matter."

"You want me to tell you all about Jesse Latimore."

"We pretty much know all you know. So go on with what David called the Journey West."

It was pretty much a bust. I wanted company to travel to my Grandpa John's funeral in Dalhart, Texas and David wanted to come along. It was a tough trip on me. I missed my period and my second one was approaching. Grannie Lonigan seemed to know first thing. A body dies and a baby's born. I had young John show David around the farm. I wanted him to stop drifting because of the Draft and say, yes, let's stay here till the end of the war, you and me. Grannie needed our help. Young John taught Spanish at university. David could do what me and Grannie could not."

"You tell him you were pregnant?"

"I wasn't sure. Mom's got cancer, grandpa John died of cancer, I figured I got it too."

"You didn't tell him?"

"No, and next thing I know we're en route to San Diego to see Bill Cougar and Janey Tower, doctors at a free clinic, from some card given us by Kallini's friend, Antoine, way back in Dijon. It was all nice at Pacific Beach, and Janey Tower made sure I was pregnant and not sick with some incurable disease. Also she let me know about DNC's and women's groups, and how her dad divorced her mom age 40 for a younger model. I saw David drifting and complaining about favoritism in football and I didn't know if I could trust him."

"Do you know now?"

"Now it's too late."

"Just trying to keep your rocky romance in perspective. Go on and get to Kurt Kallini at your home."

"Well everyone got into a gypsy caravan to Woodstock. I wanted to stay in San Diego and decide about my baby. I wanted to get back to Dalhart and have the baby with Grannie Lonigan to take care of me. But we were on a magical carpet ride to what everyone talked about then and now, Woodstock. We got there late on a Sunday morning and saw Hendrix and I got to see David's friend from the army, Early Hayze, and he was so stoned I didn't believe it. It scared me, this friend of his, and Peter Bergman saw it too. I dropped David off at home and when I got home, Kurt Kallini was there in suit and Cadillac car all ready to deal for Bontecott Stone's business. He'd been there with his Uncle Carlo in July, the mafioso, and it seemed to go okay until my dad blew up. He shouted, get that hoodlum out of my home. Now he wanted Kurt, that hoodlum, back in his home and in his business and whatever else I didn't know at the time."

"So you knew Carlo Kallini was mafia?"

"Kurt had told me in terms that said pretty much that. Seeing his Uncle Carlo, he seemed like a nice old Italian gentleman, with the best of manners, good as my father's, and the two were there for business."

"You knew that your dad wanted to either do business with Uncle Carlo or sell out Bontecott Stone?"

"I didn't have a clear conception at the time what was going on. I simply had the impression, neither time did the business go well, first time with my father, shouting, hoodlum in his home, the second time with Kurt leaving without any sign of satisfaction."

"But the deed to your father's estate coming in a canvas bag from David didn't make it clear something had gone wrong?"

"By that time I knew everything had gone wrong. But it was the deed to my dad's estate, where I was living, and I figured it belonged to us, not to Kurt Kallini."

"You never mentioned the deed first we talked."

"No. I never knew it needed to be mentioned to the law, especially since it was up to my dad, and not to me. I gave it to him and he said, about time it returned. He believed Kurt Kallini returned him the deed because it was my dad's property."

"A last question cause I got a date with Jimmy Smith. We're going to Joey Gallo's place and have dinner. Did you ever tell Morpheys you were having his baby."

"No I never did. I never knew I could trust him to be a responsible father. There's quite a difference between the man with whom you go to bed and the man you marry. I didn't say that right. I acted irresponsibly, but I didn't know if David would ever be responsible."

"Well me and Jimmy will discuss your moral dilemma over pasta and veal."

16
Message to Kallini

Jimmy and Carol dressed up nicely to have dinner. Joey's place situated in the Italian section of Poughkeepsie above the train station. It wasn't a dive. It served pretty good food because Joey learned to cook from his dad. Only there were too few paisanos left to support a ristorante. Everyone moved to the suburbs with the better times in the Fifties and Sixties. Now there were fewer paisanos and not so good times.

Sue, Joey's wife, came to take their order. She had a beautifully chiseled face and slate gray eyes like cats do, but she was well along in her pregnancy. The waitress apron flagged over least six months along and pregnancy weighed on her. She sweat a little from heated kitchen to bring food to tables. Friday was a busy night, as it had been a busy lunch. There was a pallor to her drawn face that told her troubles.

"What can I bring you two?"

"We heard from the locals you make a great veal and pasta," Jimmy said. He had a smile which pleased people, and Carol Hunter was on her best behavior.

"Joey makes a nice veal and pasta. Both of you?"

"Yes, please," Carol replied.

Sue gave her best smile and returned to the kitchen. Really her eyes were knockout eyes, her cheekbones chiseled like a model's, even if all else weighed down with her pregnancy. Joey came from the kitchen to see how they liked their veal. He believed he'd seen the guy with Jerry Seagram come for a beer. Jimmy Smith told Joey to keep it to the tender side. Joey set down salads with an antipasto all vegetables and meats together and hoped they liked it. Told to bring a nice wine, he had some paisan vino his dad kept for special occasions. Carol said it was the best she ever tasted. Jimmy didn't know wines and asked for a beer with dinner. The veal and pasta was excellent and they enjoyed their meal.

"Come sit with us," Jimmy asked when Joey brought them Neapolitan ice cream.

"You came with Jerry. Now you come with questions."

"Your wife go home?"

"She went upstairs to get off her feet. Her cousin Lorraine came by."

"David Morpheys said the cousin was in law school, but had to drop out a semester."

"Yes and she seems better."

Joey Gallo with his broad shoulders and longer hair took a seat. He took off his apron when he delivered ice cream.

"You know David, you know Lorraine, you must know Tommy Gordon."

"It's not them we're interested in. This is Carol, she's justice department, and I'm FBI."

"I wondered if you were internal revenue doing an audit. We not turning much profit."

"What do you hear of Kurt Kallini?"

"Not much. His Uncle Carlo keeps in touch with my dad. He lets him know Kurt is okay, but under surveillance and I expected somebody to come by. The locals, Jerry and Jimmy, have other concerns."

"What does Uncle Carlo think of what Kurt did."

"That doesn't come down to me, nor even to my dad. I only know Kurt should be vacationing in Paris a good long time. He's sort of a cooked goose."

"By such a phrase you mean he's in deep trouble?" Carol added.

"He made a mistake, that's what I mean."

"Every crime is a mistake."

"I mean he overreached. Instead of taking a slice he took the whole pie."

"That he did," Jimmy Smith let Joey know they knew.

"You could use a Kurt Kallini investment."

"I suppose I could. Sue's having a baby. It doesn't take the FBI to see that. The ristorante has seen better times, mostly when my dad ran it. And I can't make ends meet with gigs playing music. There's no longer a scene in smalltime venues. Music's moved to the big arenas."

"You play the piano?" Carol asked. I used to please my mom no end, when I took lessons."

"Go play, it's on the house."

Carol looked around and the tables were empty. There were people at the bar, but not a crowd. Joey came over to turn on the piano, rather than the Hammond organ. Carol ran through a Mozart piece, a slight concerto of Shubert, and then the light round of Debussy. It had been too long since she sat down. It was such a true instrument too, a concert quality piano, like the one in her mom's Chicago home.

"Thank you Joey Gallo, I liked that."

"Somebody at the bar sent in beers for the two of you."

Carol smiled with accomplishment.

"I'm a piano player who got paid."

Jimmy smiled to see Carol Hunter so happy.

"You play too, Joey?"

As the bar empties I drink a few beers and reminisce.

"Play something," Carol asked.

Joey played Procul Harem for Lorraine Shanessey upstairs. All the fandango, drums, and cartwheels cross the floor weren't much anymore. Everything in Joey's life turned "a lighter shade of pale." Life was sort of washed out for everyone.

He returned to table. Carol was wide eyed with his playing and his voice. Jimmy paid his bill and added a hefty tip for the evening's entertainment. Carol complimented Joey Gallo.

"You're a professional, the kind of talent that fills arenas and sells records."

"I never lasted on the tours. With show after show, I was too wasted for the next trip, the next gig. But for a time our band TRAX made good music."

Neither of them knew the band TRAX, but asking around they did certify it was a still playing without Joey Gallo. That was a shame, but Joey knew it wasn't for lack of talent he didn't play on stage.

"Real reason we wanted to meet you, Joey. Make an offer. If you communicate to Uncle Carlo and Kurt Kallini, that justice may be looking to make a deal, if not now, then later there may be an opportunity. Okay?"

"Kurt overreached, and I suppose he regrets the length of his vacation in Paris, France, much as I regret my absence from the music scene."

"Both you and Kurt have regrets," Jimmy Smith suggested, with no air of criticism.

"We do what we do and regret what we've done."

"Good luck with the baby on the way, and if I had the time I'd be by for lessons."

"As I would teach you Rascal music and learn a few classical tunes myself."

"Bye Joey Gallo."

"Bye Carol and Jimmy."

"Great meal too."

17
Things Don't Work Out

"We met your buddy, Joey Gallo."

"Thanks for not taking me along. You take Carol Hunter?"

"We enjoyed the meal. Joey's cuisine was excellent and his music superb. He impressed Carol no end on piano since she played too."

"He has talent in music and Sue was a whiz at photography. Together I thought their restaurant would make it, but it's hard times."

"I'll send all my FBI buds there regularly."

"I know you will."

"Joey said Lorraine came by to see Sue, and she seems better."

"Good to know."

"You go see her?"

"I haven't decided. We go way back, but we don't go way forward. As Lorraine said, we're all inbred, us Townies, in some weird way. We're not suited for smalltown, anymore, and we're not suited for the wide world either."

"Carol listened to Kady tell of her dad and Kurt Kallini getting down to business, after the Woodstock celebration."

"They did and they didn't. What put Kallini on the course he took?"

Same thing that put us all on the course we took. The Vichy Commune turned out to be less than expected. It was work with this local, Mme Olachon, lording it over us Americans. She didn't like us, nor Paris, and we didn't like her. Early Hayze came with Kallini a couple days later and didn't fit in. Kallini had him stay with Algerians in town. We didn't know where he was, but Kallini said he was okay. Early Hayze got broke down by the military, zonked by the Woodstock party, and used up by Kurt Kallini. We worked, me and Peter, at the Freres job, and I read German, saw a Brecht film, and dreamed of Germany. Where my Grandpa, Jakim Morpheys, stuck on hospital machines, came from. You got roots too Jimmy Smith.

Kady arrived a week later. Kallini returned and picked her up. I distrusted her with Kallini, and when she arrived I told her it was shit work here, no commune of true believers. I said, we ought to take off to Germany. She didn't want to hear of any more journeys east. Guess she about wore out with the trips we took. In fact, she called me irresponsible and wondered what I meant to do. Again, I had a sneaking suspicion something was up with her and Kurt Kallini. There was, but not in the way I suspected. You never know, I suppose. It's all a matter of trust. You and Carol Hunter cool?

Anyway, word comes the Hayze was in trouble and Peter runs to the Algerian place with Kallini to find he's overdosed and face down in the tainted waters of Vichy. Returned in Kallini's Citroen, I go nuts with Kurt Kallini and he yells at me. Big fight and I push him against the car, breaking his arm. No big deal. But Kady comes out crying for him and I see how it is. It's Kady and Kurt Kallini, with me, the odd man out. With Peter I had to identify the body, get it shipped to Paris, where Peter and I parted ways. He took Early Hayze back to the States, and with his dad's help, bigtime lawyer, got Early a proper burial and got Peter into Brooklyn Law School. I took off for Berlin where grandpa came from. It was a pretty desperate attempt to leave it all behind.

It was a trainride, meeting a couple younger girls, Huli and Veronica, who called me Mr. America and invited me to university. In another time ripe with opportunity I would have taken them up. But I made my existential decision to travel to Berlin. I made my Marxian analysis too. My family, who came to America, worked in NYC and made money to buy a Millbrook farm, shouldn't have lost it in the Depression to somebody like Evander Bontecott. Talk about resentment, Kady. You got it. I resented her dad firing my dad and buying up a mortgaged farm belonging to Grandpa's brother out in Millbrook. The expropriators will be expropriated. That's Marx at the end of Das Kapital. I was ready to see grandpa's home, come back to him on hospital machines, and swear to work a life to expropriate the farm estate from Bontecott.

"And Kurt Kallini later offered you the opportunity."

"And I didn't take it because there's a moral line you can't cross and still live with yourself. I know now."

"But you didn't know then?"

"A lot of water over the dam and under the Pont Mirabeau."

"What was Berlin like? What was a life behind the Iron Curtain like?"

Cross the border leaving the younger girls behind, and it was Gestapo, it was KGB, it was darkness, cold, and barbwire on the way to Berlin. Once there it was three floors down to the street to see the bombed black ruins of the Marienkirche lorded over like Central Park by soul-less skyscrapers. Berlin was one crowded piece of real estate with nothing cheap to rent, no jobs to be had at IBM, and not much to do without running into the wall. I tried the expensive room for a night, I tried the hostel for a night, and finally ended up in the Bahnhoff's Mission for a night among the drunks, druggies, and guest workers from Italy and Turkey, smelling badly and speaking foreign language.

Only point I recall with pride, a meeting and ride back to Paris with Ted Westerbrook. He taught kids in 7th grade as a hippie, took his savings for a tour of Europe, and returned with all lesson plans to suit up and sit down the kids to listen to him. It was the world of work after the Berkeley world of fun. It was the end of the Haight, now a slum, and dawn of the realization, we're all from the suburbs, Marin County and Hudson Park. When we go back home, we go to work, take responsibility, and do our job. Ted was a good guy with a pregnant girl who came to Berkeley ditched by a black dude, and Ted took her to A's games and treated her nicely. Like Ted, I wanted to do better than I'd done.

Returning to Paris I hoped to see Kady at Richard Lenoir where I did my Freres work again. She was at Gobelin with Kurt Kallini I guessed. She came to see me. We didn't tour the Tuilleries nor shop Rue de Rivoli, but sat down to talk our problems through. Finally she told me she'd been pregnant. I should have known. God, I should have known. She should have told me. First I thought she was pregnant now. She disabused me of that notion. I saw she didn't trust me. Was it really my baby then, or Kallini's? She rocketed out of her seat. How could I accuse her of such perfidy? She saw I could.

We returned to Lenoir, slept in separate beds since she just had an abortion, and I left in the morning to confront Kurt Kallini. Not to break his arm but to break his head open. He wasn't there, but the beau enfant was. He waved a knife at me and really I'd taken a kitchen knife along. Come, let's go at it. Pulling at my suitjacket, it was Marie Montfort who'd helped Kady though the time after her operation. I'd had enough. I wandered the streets of Paris, saw hours of film, and came home late as I could. I got into bed with Kady and she leaped out of her skin. Did I hate her? How could I hate her so much, to leave her alone, at Vichy, now all day today, how could I believe anything between her and Kurt Kallini? How could I treat her with such distrust? How could she ever trust me?

Truth be told, all of it. Kurt Kallini was her father's bastard son, and she never knew it. Kurt was her half brother looking after her. How could I never know it? They looked alike, dark and light. There was always a bond. David, she told me, I trusted Kurt because my parents after Woodstock took him in and trusted him. He advised an abortion. He said you drifted irresponsibly. You were not to be trusted. He got the abortion done by Antoine. He whispered in my ear, an enfant garcon, while I still was half under. He left me alone and left for Istanbul. I was left for shame, bleeding, wasted away, and among the Algerians. Only Marie Montfort took me in and cared. Only she saved my life. So you can say and do, whatever you want, now you know everything. Any more you want to tell me. Any more truth to be told?

I told her I met a Ted Westerbrook on the train, Berlin to Paris. He told me of a pregnant girl he cared for at Berkeley and took her to the ballgames. He told me he loved her, and her baby, black or white. Girl returned to the Panther headquarters with a black dude, father to her child, and the police or the Panthers set a bomb to explode, while she was there. Lionel Dubois and Barb Kelly are two more casualties of the revolution, along with Early Hayze, and people like Kurt Kallini don't care if they live or die.

It was a sad scene that night, truth be told. I should have left the last revelation for another time. Kady took it badly. We did work for the Freres a couple months more, but Kady Bontecott was on her way home. I was on my way to Munich for a winter of work to finish my college thesis. We danced a final night in the Freres office to tunes full of accordion music, but it was over for us. The Sixties were over for us. Prodigal time was over too.

18
Over for Us

"I heard what happened when you got back to Paris, you know the scene in Vichy, the abortion and how Kurt Kallini left you for shame, how David treated you badly, and yet how the two of you parted in December of 1969 with a little hope left of love again."

"No, it was over for us, just as the Sixties of our lives were over for us. Only it took a month back home, knowing David was not coming, for the cold fact, it was over, to sink in."

"Was it so bad?

"It was worse. I lost my faith in everything. A good Catholic girl can't have an abortion and simply say that's that. What Kurt Kallini did was horrible. No matter how mad he was at my dad for abandoning him, nothing excuses him. And David broke my heart. If I didn't tell him, he didn't help much when I did tell him. Too much truth shared in one night and too little trust between us. It was over. I stayed on, and we sorted out the pieces, while we did Freres work for Bernard and Marie Montfort, good people, but I had a plane ticket home for my mom's hysterectomy in Boston. And when I left and he didn't come home raving I love you more than you ever know, it pretty much dawned on me, he didn't. I got my job tutoring at Bennet and met Edward Butler who helped me settle in, and a more settled world took the place of the heartbroken world I left.

"Was it so bad as that, or so good to be home? I don't mean to rephrase the question, but there seems more there and less here."

"Too much there and enough here. I stared out Kurt Kallini's sixth floor apartment night of my abortion, sun sinking over a Paris of possibilities I knew and none of it mattered. I smoked cigarettes and stared over Paris until the last light scintillated out and till a pack of Dunhill and a pack of Gaulois filled an ashtray, diamonds and dust. No one in the whole building of caftaned Arabs wanted to see me. Akim refused to serve me. I walked out into the windy street and nearly died. Marie Montfort saw me and took me in. I slept in her room, ate her food, she was a sister to me. I tried to repay her working for the Freres and never did. Why I stayed the extra months. I was abandoned as I abandoned my baby boy. Kallini had whispered in my ear, an enfant garcon.

Horrible dream of having the baby. Grannie Lonigan was in Texas and David working the farm and us together sharing a family, waking up to none of these dreamed possibilities in the least true. I lost my faith. I lost my youth. I lost everything worth caring about. That's what heartbreak is. You can never go back. You can hardly go forward. It's all over. That's about all I have to tell you. The truth all told. Barb Kelly dead. My baby dead. Peter's friend, Early Hayze dead too. Only me and Morpheys alive like ghosts of our former selves trying to live a life, which is not worth living."

19
This is the End

David didn't stir for a week because Munich was a nightmare and he didn't want to relive the bad experience. For almost two years he tried to live down the month he spent there. It was the end of the journey east. He left Kady in Paris and she went home. It was a lost time, like a car crash every ten minutes on Rue de Roosevelt, splintered glass spilling over onto the streets. Or like Douglas taking his Thunderbird to the outer limits of Lake Cayuga before he returned to earth and crashed into the Aurora Hotel bandroom, splattering the windshield with Walter's remains. It was a tram roaring up Grabenstrasse every thirty minutes whose timetable swept all matter into its soundstream, including him, one Christmas eve on the journey east. He returned to America, but part of him stayed in that Grabenstrasse apartment. Part of him leapt from his window to the tram tracks below.

This was the end. He dared not step over a can't cross line, but some better part of him, some deep-seated enthusiasm for life, some way he'd never be again, stayed in Munich. Leave your heart in San Francisco, but leave your soul in Munich. Edvard Munch's Scream had been on tour at the museum. Kurt Kallini had come to town to work his magic, offering the world and all that's in it to possess, and David had nothing left to possess when he said no. He met girls who invited him to Lowenbrau's, asked him skiing in the Black Mountains, Jesse Latimore was with them. Their boyfriends at the bar let him know Nixon ended the draft, it was a volunteer army, and when he told Steven Hancock and some football jock from Boston College what to do with their patriotism, he got hit upside the head. He deserved the punch because he tossed a beer into the jock's face.

Christmas eve David tried Catholic church for his landlady's sake. He followed a Gretchen to her evangelical friends luring young souls to proselytize other young souls. Both were good long-term offers.

He saw their recruit Jonathan looking for lost souls at the train station. Kallini made his final offer to lure David into using Early Hayze's ill-fated military ID. Simply buy electronics at a PX to ship back to the States. David didn't know why he refused. His refusal simply came to him like another start of a journey east, or west, or to Woodstock, a last journey into adulthood and a land of limited means, opportunities, and people to be. Work for his car and apartment and whatever things he buys. Teach GED and writing class. Live a life whether it's worth living, or not. He believed it was worth living about two years later, but it had been an uphill battle to see a bright side to days, which once knew no night.

David sat in the interrogation room, come early after a two week break, for Jimmy and Carol Hunter to collect their thoughts, follow the money wherever it may go, and prepare for a prosecution. It was Christmas come again, and like the last one and the one before he wasn't terribly enthused. Lorraine Shanessey was home, but he didn't say boo to her. Kady Bontecott was married and didn't say boo to him. She testified about the same things he talked about. But the nightmare of Munich didn't belong to her, it belonged to him alone. Except for a letter telling him, don't come home for her, she wasn't there for him anymore. Perhaps Kallini sent him the typed note. Kady said no, she'd been to Grannie Lonigan's funeral in Texas with her mom, but yes she was to be married and told him no, don't come see her. He didn't. He honored her refusal, just as he refused to do things for Kallini.

This was the end. When an empty carpetbag got tossed to him outside Kennedy. Take back an empty bag which once filled to the brim with all good things, a cornucopia of a life worth living. Don't do any Dustin Hoffman breaches of the wedding ritual, no cross barricading the church doors, no taking a bus on a journey east, or simply to nowhere. What did we do that for? It was a brave act of defiance of all Fifties conformity, which acts of defiance, come the end of the Sixties, were a dime a dozen. Blow yourself up, oh Mighty Quinn, and take a couple of good people with you. Put your head down in the tainted waters of Vichy, Early Hayze. Go into the Panther's Den, Barb Kelly, pregnant with child, to show them, Lionel Dubois shall return to Oakland. Blow up the whole world with the Cold War. Now waiting for that apocalypse, what do the lives of a couple more travelers in Paris mean in terms of the whole wide world, no longer watching?

David got up for another cup of coffee. He ran into Kady Bontecott coming upstairs from Check-in at Downstate Correctional Facility. First time in, it was a scary place.

"I'm sorry they hauled you into my workplace?"

"Morpheys, not as much as me. It's time to get lawyers, when this interrogation takes us to prison."

"I don't blame you. Me, I got no money, for baggage handlers."

"It's no joke."

"No. Want a cup of coffee?"

"You bet I do."

Jimmy Smith and Carol Hunter came upstairs behind Kady. They talked about the Committee to re-elect the President, Creep, and how they got called in, briefed about what they should and shouldn't do, and what it meant to them. David returned with two Styrofoam cups for him and Kady.

"Can I get two more coffees?"

They shook their heads no and sat across from David and Kady.

"Of course Nixon gets reelected, but whoever helps him make good gets rewarded."

Jimmy said, "It's all the dirty tricks again, don't get involved."

"I'm involved, you're involved, above our heads, whatever we do, or don't do."

"Don't mind us, you two, it's politics, which has nothing to do with justice."

David glanced at Kady drinking her coffee black, hair tangles falling one two three over her gorgeous green eyes, narrow nose, and freckles dotting the pallor of her face. She wore a bulky beige turtleneck, bangles on her ears and wrists, and her cornblond hair with an uncombed look. She was beautiful, like the first time he saw her. Two years out of tune with this girl he met at Wells. Aurora was the dawn and there was no new beginning these days. He didn't want to tell her the Munich stuff. It didn't shed a favorable light on him. Nor did Vichy,

Berlin, or the last months in Paris, but he told those times to Jimmy Smith with no great concern or interruption. This was different. This changed everything.

"So should we get started?"

"I won't say a word about Munich with Kady here."

"Sure, until Santa comes for Christmas."

"No Jimmy, really. This changes things."

"Morpheys, we don't want you to say anything, we're done."

"Good then. Kady too?"

"You told us everything, Kady, didn't you?"

Carol turned to Kady to make sure and Kady shook her head. David looked at her again. She didn't look good. The cup of coffee sat on the veneer counter, half drunk, and she had that look mornings with the taste of metal in her mouth, upset stomach, turning down the day. It was the look of a gilded guilt trip. David didn't know her at all.

Knock on the door. Another girl in the glass looking like Kady's sister. Jimmy waved her in. It was somebody David knew. It was Jesse Latimore with her blond hair hanging thick and long, not clipped short. She wasn't the same perky girl David knew at Wells College sophomore year, nor the month of January with Kady Bontecott. This girl was grown up, she meant business, and Jesse arrived late for the sake of an entrance. David stared, while Kady looked the more disturbed with the new girl in the room.

"David, meet Jesse Latimore. She works at Bennet School the past month or so."

"I know her Jimmy. We were friends of a friend, with Dana Dupont and Kady, and met again in Munich."

"You're still not talking about Munich, a couple years ago, Morpheys?"

"No Carol, I'm done, and you said we're done."

"Then listen as Jesse says a few words. I hope she's more to the point, Morpheys, than you."

"It's been a pleasure," David smiled wryly.

"So Kady I think knows and David I don't think knows, but what does it matter anymore. I came through customs with a bunch of

Radcliff girls and a couple college guys, who cared. It was no big deal. I carried the dumb canvas bag, got it on a cart, and took it to a taxi waiting out front of Kennedy. It took off. I returned to my Boston friends and we planned a night on the town. The girls let the guys attend a bachelor's party. I think my brother Janson was already in town, already at the party, and that's about it. Nice girls, especially Dawn. She liked me and I liked her. She had these shaved eyebrows and sort of crossed eyes which made her look unsettling. David must remember her. Jude was a bitch, but Dawn was somebody to know."

David looked at Jesse Latimore. Of course, she was at his apartment, speaking with Jude and Dawn, and they were all off to ski the Black Mountains.

"I remember her. The eyes were unsettling, but she was likeable and Jude wasn't."

"You got in a fight with Jude's football guy, didn't you Morpheys?"

"I did. Knocked out in a beerhall putsch."

"Guy say something off color about Kady?"

"No, something about Arabs and oil and Nixon's draft, changed to a volunteer army. It was like the Sixties were over, or the Sixties had never been. I tossed a beer in the jock's face, and he punched my lights out."

"Well I didn't go skiing, we didn't. We went to Paris and saw the sights. Then we went to Orly and took a flight. Kallini had Kady's bag for me all filled to the brim. It got tossed in the trunk of a taxi, taken to Orly for the flight, and I took it off the turnstile at Kennedy. It was goddamn heavy, that I remember. But I got the jock to lift it on the cart, got it to the taxi, and had a drink with my fellow jetsetters, waiting for our limousine. That was that."

"That make sense to you, Morpheys?"

"No Jimmy, it doesn't."

"What do you mean?"

"What if I say, Jesse is only making up a story to suit you two? What if it was always me carrying the motherload of diamonds and dust through American customs for the Great Kallini, who mastered the known world, who works for the mafia, for the Brotherhood, for the

Movement, and maybe for the government too? What if Creep, you two, sweeps all this under the rug to make nice in the Middle East. I mean, big picture stuff. Why do you want to put this month of interrogation on a girl like Jesse Latimore, just because she's compliant and her brother's somebody big at Chase Bank, or CIA, or some new committee like yours to reelect the President."

"Morpheys, are you saying what I think you're saying?"

"I'm saying, don't blame Jesse Latimore and don't blame Kady Bontecott, blame somebody like me because with me you can make it stick. With me, you already got me. I'm sitting with you Jimmy Smith and with you Carol Hunter for over a month telling you some story of me and Kady taking the journey east and I'm writing every night I get home materials that sound interesting enough to actually happen, but never did."

"Is this true, Kady?" Carol turned on her because she distrusted David Morpheys from day one. Kady Bontecott wasn't like him. She had class and background, like Carol Hunter. They learned to tell the truth, when justice must be done.

Kady looked up, her gorgeous green eyes staring at David, she shook her head with wisps of hair and freckles on her disbelieving face. She wasn't sure what David told about their time together. She assumed the truth, colored as it was with literary pretension, but basically the truth. With Jesse Latimore, she was far less sure of the truth. Which was what David said. Okay she said to herself, this gets complicated.

"I don't know what David told you, or what he told Agent Smith, but when I knew him he was in the habit of telling me the truth, till the day the truth didn't matter anymore, because the truth was too hard to bear."

"Then we meet again."

20
After the Holidays

Come the dead time of January, no holidays liven up the snow and short days and cloudy skies. Just wait for the next white-out of all we know and believe in. David Morpheys waited in lock-up for a morning meeting with the team of Carol and Jimmy. They came riding in with Kady Bontecott, up the stairs, and into the interrogation room. They were all business. Kady asked if she could get them two cups of coffee. David said he'd lend her a hand. One cup fell into position and filled to the brim. Kady let the styrofoam stay behind the plastic glass.

"They're going to ask you to sign papers."

"And you Kady?"

"I'm asking you to sign the same papers I signed saying what we told Carol and Jimmy was the truth."

"Will my signature help you get on with your life?"

"Yes, it will help."

"Okay, give me some time. Not much. Just enough to exact some idea what happened. Nothing having to do with our time together on the journey east. That's done. That's put to paper for now. What we lived I'm happy to have on paper, or if paper doesn't keep, someplace back of my mind for later on."

"How much time?"

"Simply enough. No prodigal time. No time lapses. Enough, after having too much."

"Okay. I want to get back to classes and my life."

"As I do with mine. Is your life enough?"

"Don't ask those questions."

"Then it's day to day, okay."

Kady shook her drapery of hair, winked her green eyes, and sipped with both hands, the coffee David gave her. It was a meeting of the minds. It wasn't the mockery Carol Hunter used with him. It was the lithe figure of the girl in love with the little luxuries of her life and David had the pleasure of sharing some time with her. It was over, okay.

"Then you two must have had time to talk. Let's get started with what we came her to do."

Carol told Jimmy, as he pressed the recorder, they needed to be in New Hampshire that evening. They had plane times at the Dutchess Airport to land in Manchester at six that night. Jimmy said he'd be prompt.

"Any questions Morpheys, before we begin?"

"Should we expect, Carol, an arrival by Jesse Latimore?"

"No Morpheys. She returned to her math doctorate at Yale after what's termed a sabbatical to teach girls at Bennet."

"And arrive here to put an end to any doubts you had."

"Yes, she did, Morpheys. We know what we know, now. No more irrelevant information, interminable stories, and meditations on the meanings of life. We come to the conclusion, we can move on with our lives."

Jimmy broke in. "We hoped to share a meal at Joey Gallo's ristorante, all four of us, and leave on a high note."

"But time is of the essence, Jimmy. Show Morpheys the papers, let him read the statements, and sign them."

"Do the statements confirm Kady's and my innocence of all charges with regard to Kady's canvas bag used by Kurt Kallini to transport illegal drugs and diamonds into the United States?"

Jimmy nodded. "Yes, it confirms what you told us as the truth."

"Satisfied?" Carol inquired.

"Yes. After a few questions for you two."

"Don't waste our time?"

"I won't."

Carol looked over her half specs to Jimmy, who gave her an honest I don't know look. Agent Smith spoke into the audio recorder, saying at 9:07, they stopped for legal consultations. Click.

"Is Jesse Latimore cleared of all charges?"

"Her case is left pending for further review."

"For how long, Carol?"

"Indefinitely."

"Has a deal, or let's say with no legal precision, a modus operandi, been proposed to Kurt Kallini?"

"We reached Kallini at the Gobelin apartments in Paris, and yes a modus operandi has been proposed and accepted."

"Did it involve funds from his operations?"

"Yes, as originally, Kallini was tracked by Janson Latimore in the CIA, and his sister assisted in operations, more than half of Kallini's funds were used in the Middle East. Information was gotten on the Brotherhood's means of operations in many countries, and some co-operation obtained. Is that enough, Morpheys?"

"A few more questions, in exchange for the hundreds asked of Kady and me?"

"Has the new modus operandi included funds for your coming operations in New Hampshire's primary?"

"Yes, Kurt Kallini will indirectly be in support of President Nixon's committee for reelection. Kurt Kallini broke the laws of the United States and the fruits of his criminal activity will be put to good use."

"All?"

"By no means."

"Then some."

"Enough for him to live in his Gobelin sanctuary. Enough for others to turn a blind eye to his illegal actions and their effects on all concerned."

"The French are satisfied?"

"Yes, they have connections across North Africa."

"The Brotherhood are satisfied?"

"They are not involved, except as Kallini echoes their concerns."

"CIA, FBI, and Creep are satisfied?"

"With this part of the operation, yes. With these investigations which you took part, yes. With future operations time will tell."

"One last question."

"Please."

"Have Kady, her dad, and the Bontecott Stone family, have they been compensated for Kallini's action, which his relations were adversarial?"

Carol looked to Kady, and said, "I believe your dad's satisfied, justice has been done."

Kady nodded.

"Then show me the papers."

David read them, brief as they were, for flies in the ointment. For him and for her, they were interrogated, admonished of prima facie evidence as foundation for their investigation, what they did and didn't do with the bag in question, and cleared of any legal wrongdoing.

"Okay. No jovial dinner at Joey Gallo's place, but I thank you Carol Hunter for your patience and Jimmy Smith for you calm demeanor. Without further ado, let me sign the papers. There, done. Kiss the Sixties goodbye."

Kady reached her ringed hand to rest on his arm, gave him a green eyed stare, and nodded to him. Carol put the papers in her briefcase, Jimmy put away the recorder, and David helped Kady on with her coat. Three well-dressed professionals walked downstairs, past the check-out of Downstate Correctional Facility off Route 84, to their separate lives. David waited for security to buzz him through to the compound where he taught inmates with ten year sentences the rudiments of language and math for a GED diploma. Goodbye for good, Kady Bontecott.

CPSIA information can be obtained
at www.ICGtesting.com
Printed in the USA
LVOW12s2321241017
553666LV00001B/147/P